Frank Herbert

KU-132-905

The Dosadi Experiment

Futura
Macdonald & Co
London & Sydney

An Orbit Book

First published in Great Britain in 1978
by Victor Gollancz Limited

First Futura Publications edition 1978
Reprinted 1981

ISBN 0 7088 8035 5

Printed in Great Britain by
Hazell Watson & Viney Ltd
Aylesbury, Bucks

Futura Publications
A Division of
Macdonald & Co (Publishers) Ltd
Holywell House
Worship Street
London EC2A 2EN

Frank Herbert lives in Port Townsend, Washington. He is the author of the world-famous *Dune* trilogy, as well as a number of other popular works of science fiction.

In memory of Babe
because she knew
how to enjoy life.

When the Calebans first sent us one of their giant metal "beachballs," communicating through this device to offer the use of jumpdoors for interstellar travel, many in the Con Sentiency covertly began to exploit this gift of the stars for their own questionable purposes. Both the "Shadow Government" and some among the Gowachin people saw what is obvious today: that instantaneous travel across unlimited space involved powers which might isolate subject populations in gross numbers.

This observation at the beginning of the Dosadi Experiment came long before Saboteur Extraordinary Jorj X. McKie discovered that visible stars of our universe were either Calebans or the manifestations of Calebans in Con-Sentient space. (See *Whipping Star*, an account of McKie's discovery thinly disguised as fiction.)

What remains pertinent here is that McKie, acting for his Bureau of Sabotage, identified the Caleban called "Fannie Mae" as the visible star Thyone. This discovery of the Thyone-Fannie Mae identity ignited new interest in the Caleban Question and thus contributed to the exposure of the Dosadi Experiment—which many still believe was the most disgusting use of Sentients by Sentients in ConSentient history. Certainly, it remains the most gross psychological test of Sentient Beings ever performed, and the issue of informed consent has never been settled to everyone's satisfaction.

—From the first public account, *the Trial of Trials*

Justice belongs to those who claim it, but let the claimant beware lest he create new injustice by his claim and thus set the bloody pendulum of revenge into its inexorable motion.

—*Gowachin aphorism*

"Why are you so cold and mechanical in your Human relationships?"

Jorj X. McKie was to reflect on that Caleban question later. Had she been trying to alert him to the Dosadi Experiment and to what his investigation of that experiment might do to him? He hadn't even known about Dosadi at the time and the pressures of the Caleban communications trance, the accusatory tone she took, had precluded other considerations.

Still, it rankled. He didn't like the feeling that he might be a subject of her research into Humans. He'd always thought of that particular Caleban as his friend—if one could consider being friendly with a creature whose visible manifestation in this universe was a fourth-magnitude yellow sun visible from Central Central where the Bureau of Sabotage maintained its headquarters. And there was inevitable discomfort in Caleban communication. You sank into a trembling, jerking trance while they made their words appear in your consciousness.

But his uncertainty remained: had she tried to tell him something beyond the plain content of her words?

When the weather makers kept the evening rain period short, McKie liked to go outdoors immediately afterward and stroll in the park enclosure which BuSab provided for its employees on Central Central. As a Saboteur Extraordinary, McKie had free run of the enclosure and he liked the fresh smells of the place after a rain.

The park covered about thirty hectares, deep in a well of Bureau buildings. It was a scrambling hodgepodge of plantings cut by wide paths which circled and twisted through specimens from every inhabited planet of the known universe. No care had been taken to provide a particular area for any sentient species. If there was any plan to the park it was a maintenance plan with plants requiring similar conditions and care held in their own sectors. Giant Spear Pines from Sasak occupied a knoll near one corner surrounded by mounds of Flame Briar from Rudiria. There were bold stretches of lawn and hidden scraps of lawn, and some flat stretches of greenery which were not lawns at all but mobile sheets of predatory leaf imprisoned behind thin moats of caustic water.

Rain-jeweled flowers often held McKie's attention to the exclusion of all else. There was a single planting of Lilium Grossa, its red blossoms twice his height casting long shadows over a wriggling carpet of blue Syringa, each miniature bloom opening and closing at random like tiny mouths gasping for air.

Sometimes, floral perfumes stopped his progress and held him in a momentary olfactory thralldom while his eyes searched out the source. As often as not, the plant would be a dangerous one—a flesh eater or poison-sweat variety. Warning signs in flashing Galach guarded such plantings. Sona-barriers, moats, and force fields edged the winding paths in many areas.

McKie had a favorite spot in the park, a bench with its back to a fountain where he could sit and watch the shadows collect across fat yellow bushes from the floating islands of Tandaloor. The yellow bushes thrived because their roots were washed in running water hidden beneath the soil and renewed by the fountain. Beneath the yellow bushes there were faint gleams of phosphorescent silver enclosed by a force field and identified by a low sign:

"Sangeet Mobilus, a blood-sucking perennial from Bisaj. Extreme danger to all sentient species. Do not intrude any portion of your body beyond the force field."

As he sat on the bench, McKie thought about that sign. The universe often mixed the beautiful and the dangerous. This was a deliberate mixture in the park. The yellow bushes, the fragrant and benign Golden Iridens, had been mingled with Sangeet Mobilus. The two supported each other and both thrived. The ConSentient government which McKie served often made such mixtures . . . sometimes by accident.

Sometimes by design.

He listened to the plashing of the fountain while the shadows thickened and the tiny border lights came on along the paths. The tops of the buildings beyond the park became a palette where the sunset laid out its final display of the day.

In that instant, the Caleban contact caught him and he felt his body slip into the helpless communications trance. The mental tendrils were immediately identified—Fannie Mae. And he thought, as he often had, what an improbable name that was for a star entity. He heard no sounds, but his hearing centers responded as to spoken words, and the inward glow was unmistakable. It was Fannie Mae, her syntax far more sophisticated than during their earliest encounters.

"You admire one of us," she said, indicating his attention on the sun which had just set beyond the buildings.

"I try not to think of any star as a Caleban," he responded. "It interferes with my awareness of the natural beauty."

"Natural? McKie, you don't understand your own awareness, nor even how you employ it!"

That was her beginning—accusatory, attacking, unlike any

previous contact with this Caleban he'd thought of as friend. And she employed her verb forms with new deftness, almost as though showing off, parading her understanding of his language.

"What do you want, Fannie Mae?"

"I consider your relationships with females of your species. You have entered marriage relationships which number more than fifty. Not so?"

"That's right. Yes. Why do you . . ."

"I am your friend, McKie. What is your feeling toward me?"

He thought about that. There was a demanding intensity in her question. He owed his life to this Caleban with an improbable name. For that matter, she owed her life to him. Together, they'd resolved the Whipping Star threat. Now, many Calebans provided the jumpdoors by which other beings moved in a single step from planet to planet, but once Fannie Mae had held all of those jumpdoor threads, her life threatened through the odd honor code by which Calebans maintained their contractual obligations. And McKie had saved her life. He had but to think about their past interdependence and a warm sense of camaraderie suffused him.

Fannie Mae sensed this.

"Yes, McKie, that is friendship, is love. Do you possess this feeling toward Human female companions?"

Her question angered him. Why was she prying? His private sexual relationships were no concern of hers!

"Your love turns easily to anger," she chided.

"There are limits to how deeply a Saboteur Extraordinary can allow himself to be involved with anyone."

"Which came first, McKie—the Saboteur Extraordinary or these limits?"

Her response carried obvious derision. Had he chosen the Bureau because he was incapable of warm relationships? But he really cared for Fannie Mae! He admired her . . . and she could hurt him because he admired her and felt . . . felt *this way.*

He spoke out of his anger and hurt.

"Without the Bureau there'd be no ConSentiency and no need for Calebans."

"Yes, indeed. People have but to look at a dread agent from BuSab and know fear."

It was intolerable, but he couldn't escape the underlying warmth he felt toward this strange Caleban entity, this being who could creep unguarded into his mind and talk to him as no other being dared. If only he had found a woman to share that kind of intimacy . . .

And this was the part of their conversation which came back to haunt him. After months with no contact between them, why had she chosen that moment—just three days before the Dosadi crisis burst upon the Bureau? She'd pulled out his ego, his deepest sense of identity. She'd shaken that ego and then she'd skewered him with her barbed question:

"Why are you so cold and mechanical in your Human relationships?"

Her irony could not be evaded. She'd made him appear ridiculous in his own eyes. He could feel warmth, yes . . . even love, for a Caleban but not for a Human female. This unguarded feeling he held for Fannie Mae had never been directed at any of his marital companions. Fannie Mae had aroused his anger, then reduced his anger to verbal breast-beating, and finally to silent hurt. Still, the love remained.

Why?

Human females were bed partners. They were bodies which used him and which he used. That was out of the question with this Caleban. She was a star burning with atomic fires, her seat of consciousness unimaginable to other sentients. Yet, she could extract love from him. He gave this love freely and she knew it. There was no hiding an emotion from a Caleban when she sent her mental tendrils into your awareness.

She'd certainly known he would see the irony. That had to be part of her motive in such an attack. But Calebans seldom acted from a single motive—which was part of their charm and the essence of their most irritant exchanges with other sentient beings.

"McKie?" Softly in his mind.

"Yes." Angry.

"I show you now a fractional bit of my feeling toward your node."

Like a balloon being inflated by a swift surge of gas, he felt himself suffused by a projected sense of concern, of caring. He was drowning in it . . . wanted to drown in it. His entire body radiated this white-hot sense of protective attention. For a whole minute after it was withdrawn, he still glowed with it.

A fractional bit?

"McKie?" Concerned.

"Yes." Awed.

"Have I hurt you?"

He felt alone, emptied.

"No."

"The full extent of my nodal involvement would destroy you. Some Humans have suspected this about love."

Nodal involvement?

She was confusing him as she'd done in their first encounters. How could the Calebans describe love as . . . nodal involvement?

"Labels depend on viewpoint," she said. "You look at the universe through too narrow an opening. We despair of you sometimes."

There she was again, attacking.

He fell back on a childhood platitude.

"I am what I am and that's all I am."

"You may soon learn, friend McKie, that you're more than you thought."

With that, she'd broken the contact. He'd awakened in damp, chilly darkness, the sound of the fountain loud in his ears. Nothing he did would bring her back into communication, not even when he'd spent some of his own credits on a Taprisiot in a vain attempt to call her.

His Caleban friend had shut him out.

We have created a monster—enormously valuable and even useful yet extremely dangerous. Our monster is both beautiful and terrifying. We do not dare use this monster to its full potential, but we cannot release our grasp upon it.

> —Gowachin assessment of
> the Dosadi experiment

A bullet went *spang!* against the window behind Keila Jedrik's desk, richocheted and screamed off into the canyon street far below her office. Jedrik prided herself that she had not even flinched. The Elector's patrols would take care of the sniper. The patrols which swept the streets of Chu every morning would home on the sound of the shot. She held the casual hope that the sniper would escape back to the Rim Rabble, but she recognized this hope as a weakness and dismissed it. There were concerns this morning far more important than an infiltrator from the Rim.

Jedrik reached one hand into the corner of early sunlight which illuminated the contact plates of her terminal in the Master Accountancy computer. Those flying fingers—she could almost disassociate herself from them. They darted like insects at the waiting keys. The terminal was a functional instrument, symbol of her status as a Senior Liaitor. It sat all alone in its desk slot—grey, green, gold, black, white and deadly. Its grey screen was almost precisely the tone of her desk top.

With careful precision, her fingers played their rhythms

on the keys. The screen produced yellow numbers, all weighted and averaged at her command—a thin strip of destiny with violence hidden in its golden shapes.

Every angel carries a sword, she thought.

But she did not really consider herself an angel or her weapon a sword. Her real weapon was an intellect hardened and sharpened by the terrible decisions her planet required. Emotions were a force to be diverted within the self or to be used against anyone who had failed to learn what Dosadi taught. She knew her own weakness and hid it carefully: she'd been taught by loving parents (who'd concealed their love behind exquisite cruelty) that Dosadi's decisions were indeed terrible.

Jedrik studied the numbers on her computer display, cleared the screen and made a new entry. As she did this, she knew she took sustenance from fifty of her planet's Human inhabitants, Many of those fifty would not long survive this callous jape. In truth, her fingers were weapons of death for those who failed this test. She felt no guilt about those she slew. The imminent arrival of one Jorj X. McKie dictated her actions, precipitated them.

When she thought about McKie, her basic feeling was one of satisfaction. She'd waited for McKie like a predator beside a burrow in the earth. His name and identifying keys had been given to her by her chauffeur, Havvy, hoping to increase his value to her. She'd taken the information and made her usual investigation. Jedrik doubted that any other person on Dosadi could have come up with the result her sources produced: Jorj X. McKie was an adult human who could not possibly exist. No record of him could be found on all of Dosadi—not on the poisonous Rim, not in Chu's Warrens, not in any niche of the existing power structure. McKie did not exist, but he was due to arrive in Chu momentarily, smuggled into the city by a Gowachin temporarily under her control.

McKie was the precision element for which she had waited.

He wasn't merely a possible key to the God Wall (not a bent and damaged key like Havvy) but clean and certain. She'd never thought to attack this lock with poor instruments. There'd be one chance and only one; it required the best.

Thus fifty Dosadi Humans took their faceless places behind the numbers in her computer. Bait, expendable. Those who died by this act wouldn't die immediately. Forty-nine might never know they'd been deliberately submitted to early death by her deliberate choice. Some would be pushed back to the Rim's desperate and short existence. Some would die in the violent battles she was precipitating. Others would waste away in the Warrens. For most, the deadly process would extend across sufficient time to conceal her hand in it. But they'd been slain in her computer and she knew it. She cursed her parents (and the others before them) for this unwanted sensitivity to the blood and sinew behind these computer numbers. Those loving parents had taught her well. She might never see the slain bodies, need give not another thought to all but one of the fifty; still she sensed them behind her computer display . . . warm and pulsing.

Jedrik sighed. The fifty were bleating animals staked out to lure a special beast onto Dosadi's poisonous soil. Her fifty would create a fractional surplus which would vanish, swallowed before anyone realized their purpose.

Dosadi is sick, she thought. And not for the first time, she wondered: *Is this really Hell?*

Many believed it.

We're being punished.

But no one knew what they'd done to deserve punishment.

Jedrik leaned back, looked across her doorless office to the sound barrier and milky light of the hall. A strange Gowachin shambled past her doorway. He was a frog figure on some official errand, a packet of brown paper clutched in his knobby hands. His green skin shimmered as though he'd recently come from water.

The Gowachin reminded her of Bahrank, he who was bringing McKie into her net, Bahrank who did her bidding because she controlled the substance to which he was addicted. More fool he to let himself become an addict to anything, even to living. One day soon Bahrank would sell what he knew about her to the Elector's spies; by then it would be too late and the Elector would learn only what she wanted him to learn when she wanted him to learn it. She'd chosen Bahrank with the same care she'd used at her computer terminal, the same care which had made her wait for someone precisely like McKie. And Bahrank was Gowachin. Once committed to a project, the frog people were notorious for carrying out their orders in a precise way. They possessed an inbred sense of order but understood the limits of law.

As her gaze traversed the office, the sparse and functional efficiency of the space filled her with quiet amusement. This office presented an image of her which she had constructed with meticulous care. It pleased her that she would be leaving here soon never to return, like an insect shedding its skin. The office was four paces wide, eight long. Twelve black metal rotofiles lined the wall on her left, dark sentinels of her methodical ways. She had reset their locking codes and armed them to destroy their contents when the Elector's toads pried into them. The Elector's people would attribute this to outrage, a last angry sabotage. It would be some time before accumulating doubts would lead them to reassessment and to frustrated questions. Even then they might not suspect her hand in the elimination of fifty Humans. She, after all, was one of the fifty.

This thought inflicted her with a momentary sense of unfocused loss. How pervasive were the seductions of Dosadi's power structure! How subtle! What she'd just done here introduced a flaw into the computer system which ruled the distribution of non-poisonous food in Dosadi's only city. Food—here was the real base of Dosadi's social pyramid, solid and ugly. The flaw removed her from a puissant niche in that pyramid. She had worn the persona of Keila Jedrik-Liaitor for many years, long enough to learn enjoyment of the power system. Losing one valuable counter in Dosadi's endless survival game, she must now live and act only with the persona of Keila Jedrik-Warlord. This was an all-or-nothing move, a gambler's plunge. She felt the nakedness of it. But this gamble had begun long ago, far back in Dosadi's contrived history, when her ancestors had recognized the nature of this planet and had begun breeding and training for the individual who would take this plunge.

I am that individual, she told herself. *This is our moment.*

But had they truly assessed the problem correctly?

Jedrik's glance fell on the single window which looked out into the canyon street. Her own reflection stared back: a face too narrow, thin nose, eyes and mouth too large. Her hair could be an interesting black velvet helmet if she let it grow, but she kept it cropped short as a reminder that she was not a magnetic sex partner, that she must rely on her wits. That was the way she'd been bred and trained. Dosadi had taught her its cruelest lessons early. She'd grown tall while still in her teens, carrying more height in her body than in her legs so that she appeared even taller when seated. She looked down on most Gowachin and Human males in more ways than one. That was another gift (and lesson) from her *loving* parents and from their ancestors. There was no escaping this Dosadi lesson.

What you love or value will be used against you.

She leaned forward to hide her disquieting reflection, peered far down into the street. There, that was better. Her fellow Dosadis no longer were warm and pulsing people. They were reduced to distant movements, as impersonal as the dancing figures in her computer.

Traffic was light, she noted. Very few armored vehicles moved, no pedestrians. There'd been only that one shot at her window. She still entertained a faint hope that the sniper had escaped. More likely a patrol had caught the fool. The Rim Rabble persisted in testing Chu's defenses despite the boringly repetitive results. It was desperation. Snipers seldom waited until the day was deep and still and the patrols were scattered, those hours when even some among the most powerful ventured out.

Symptoms, all symptoms.

Rim sorties represented only one among many Dosadi symptoms which she'd taught herself to read in that precarious climb whose early stage came to climax in this room. It was not just a thought, but more a sense of familiar awareness to which she returned at oddly reflexive moments in her life.

We have a disturbed relationship with our past which religion cannot explain. We are primitive in unexplainable ways, our lives woven of the familiar and the strange, the reasonable and the insane.

It made some insane choices magnificently attractive.

Have I made an insane choice?

No!

The data lay clearly in her mind, facts which she could not obliterate by turning away from them. Dosadi had been designed from a cosmic grab bag: "Give them one of these and one of these and one of these . . ."

It made for incompatible pairings.

The DemoPol with which Dosadi juggled its computer-monitored society didn't fit a world which used energy transmitted from a satellite in geosynchronous orbit. The DemoPol reeked of primitive ignorance, something from a society which had wandered too far down the path of legalisms—a law for everything and everything managed by law. The dogma that a God-inspired few had chosen Chu's river canyon in which to build a city insulated from this poisonous planet, and that only some twenty or so generations earlier, remained indigestible. And that energy satellite which hovered beneath the God Wall's barrier—that stank of a long and sophisticated evolution during which something as obviously flawed as the DemoPol would have been discarded.

It was a cosmic grab bag designed for a specific purpose which her ancestors had recognized.

We did not evolve on this planet.

The place was out of phase with both Gowachin and Human. Dosadi employed computer memories and physical files side by side for identical purposes. And the number of addictive substances to be found on Dosadi was outrageous. Yet this was played off against a religion so contrived, so gross in its demands for "simple faith" that the two conditions remained at constant war. The mystics died for their "new insights" while the holders of "simple faith" used control of the addictive substances to gain more and more power. The only real faith on Dosadi was that you survived by power and that you gained power by controlling what others required for survival. Their society understood the medicine of bacteria, virus and brain control, but these could not stamp out the Rim and Warren Underground where *jabua* faith healers cured their patients with the smoke of burning weeds.

And they could not stamp out (not yet) Keila Jedrik because she had seen what she had seen. Two by two the incompatible things ebbed and flowed around her, in the city of Chu and the surrounding Rim. It was the same in every case: a society which made use of one of these things could not naturally be a society which used the other.

Not naturally.

All around her, Jedrik sensed Chu with its indigestible polarities. They had only two species: Human and Gowachin. Why two? Were there no other species in this universe? Subtle hints in some of Dosadi's artifacts suggested an evolution for appendages other than the flexible fingers of Gowachin and Human.

Why only one city on all of Dosadi?

Dogma failed to answer.

The Rim hordes huddled close, always seeking a way into Chu's insulated purity. But they had a whole planet behind them. Granted it was a poisonous planet, but it had other rivers, other places of potential sanctuary. The survival of both species argued for the building of more sanctuaries, many more than that pitiful hole which Gar and Tria thought they masterminded. No . . . Chu stood alone—almost twenty kilometers wide and forty long, built on hills and silted islands where the river slowed in its deep canyon. At last count, some eighty-nine million people lived here and three times that number eked a short life on the Rim—pressing, always pressing for a place in the poison-free city.

Give us your precious bodies, you stupid Rimmers!

They heard the message, knew its import and defied it. What had the people of Dosadi done to be imprisoned here? What had their ancestors done? It was right to build a religion upon hate for such ancestors . . . provided such ancestors were guilty.

Jedrik leaned toward the window, peered upward at the God Wall, that milky translucence which imprisoned Dosadi, yet through which those such as this Jorj X. McKie could come at will. She hungered to see McKie in person, to confirm that he had not been contaminated as Havvy had been contaminated.

It was a McKie she required now. The transparently contrived nature of Dosadi told her that there must be a McKie. She saw herself as the huntress, McKie her natural prey. The false identity she'd built in this room was part of her bait. Now, in the season of McKie, the underlying religious cant by which Dosadi's powerful maintained their private illusions would crumble. She could already see the beginnings of that dissolution; soon, everyone would see it.

She took a deep breath. There was a purity in what was about to happen, a simplification. She was about to divest herself of one of her two lives, taking all of her awareness into the persona of that other Keila Jedrik which all of Dosadi would soon know. Her people had kept her secret well, hiding a fat and sleazy blonde person from their fellow Dosadis, exposing just enough of that one to "X" that the powers beyond the God Wall might react in the proper design. She felt cleansed by the fact that the disguise of that other life had begun to lose its importance. The whole of her could begin to surface in that other place. And McKie had precipitated this metamorphosis. Jedrik's thoughts were clear and direct now:

Come into my trap, McKie. You will take me higher than the palace apartments of the Council Hills.

Or into a deeper hell than any nightmare has imagined.

How to start a war? Nurture your own latent hungers for power. Forget that only madmen pursue power for its own sake. Let such madmen gain power—even you. Let such madmen act behind their conventional masks of sanity. Whether their masks be fashioned from the delusions of defense or the theological aura of law, war will come.

—Gowachin aphorism

The odalarm awoke Jorj X. McKie with a whiff of lemon. For just an instant his mind played tricks on him. He thought he was on Tutalsee's gentle planetary ocean floating softly on his garlanded island. There were lemons on his floating island, banks of Hibiscus and carpets of spicy Alyssum. His bowered cottage lay in the path of perfumed breezes and the lemon . . .

Awareness came. He was not on Tutalsee with a loving companion; he was on a trained bedog in the armored efficiency of his Central Central apartment; he was back in the heart of the Bureau of Sabotage; he was back at work.

McKie shuddered.

A planet full of people could die today . . . or tomorrow.

It would happen unless someone solved this Dosadi mystery. Knowing the Gowachin as he did, McKie was convinced of it. The Gowachin were capable of cruel decisions, especially where their species pride was at stake, or for reasons which other species might not understand. Bildoon, his Bureau chief, assessed this crisis the same way. Not since the Caleban

25

problem had such enormity crossed the ConSentient horizon.

But where was this endangered planet, this Dosadi?

After a night of sleep suppression, the briefings about Dosadi came back vividly as though part of his mind had remained at work sharpening the images. Two operatives, one Wreave and one Laclac, had made the report. The two were reliable and resourceful. Their sources were excellent, although the information was sparse. The two also were bucking for promotion at a time when Wreaves and Laclacs were hinting at discrimination against their species. The report required special scrutiny. No BuSab agent, regardless of species, was above some internal testing, a deception designed to weaken the Bureau and gain coup merits upon which to ride into the director's office.

However, BuSab was still directed by Bildoon, a PanSpechi in Human form, the fourth member of his creche to carry that name. It had been obvious from Bildoon's first words that he believed the report.

"McKie, this thing could set Human and Gowachin at each others' throats."

It was an understandable idiom, although in point of fact you would go for the Gowachin abdomen to carry out the same threat. McKie already had acquainted himself with the report and, from internal evidence to which his long association with the Gowachin made him sensitive, he shared Bildoon's assessment. Seating himself in a grey chairdog across the desk from the director in the rather small, windowless office Bildoon had lately preferred, McKie shifted the report from one hand to the other. Presently, recognizing his own nervous mannerism, he put the report on the desk. It was on coded memowire which played to trained senses when passed through the fingers or across other sensitive appendages.

"Why couldn't they pinpoint this Dosadi's location?" McKie asked.

"It's known only to a Caleban."

"Well, they'll . . ."

"The Calebans refuse to respond."

McKie stared across the desk at Bildoon. The polished surface reflected a second image of the BuSab director, an inverted image to match the upright one. McKie studied the reflection. Until you focused on Bildoon's faceted eyes (how like an insect's eyes they were), this PanSpechi appeared much like a Human male with dark hair and pleasant round face. Perhaps he'd put on more than the form when his flesh had been molded to Human shape. Bildoon's face displayed emotions which McKie read in Human terms. The director appeared angry.

McKie was troubled.

"Refused?"

"The Calebans don't deny that Dosadi exists or that it's threatened. They refuse to discuss it."

"Then we're dealing with a Caleban contract and they're obeying the terms of that contract."

Recalling that conversation with Bildoon as he awakened in his apartment, McKie lay quietly thinking. Was Dosadi some new extension of the Caleban Question?

It's right to fear what we don't understand.

The Caleban mystery had eluded ConSentient investigators for too long. He thought of his recent conversation with Fannie Mae. When you thought you had something pinned down, it slipped out of your grasp. Before the Calebans gift of jumpdoors, the ConSentiency had been a relatively slow and understandable federation of the known sentient species. The universe had contained itself in a shared space of recognizable dimensions. The ConSentiency of those days had grown in a way likened to expanding bubbles. It had been linear.

Caleban jumpdoors had changed that with an explosive acceleration of every aspect of life. Jumpdoors had been an immediately disruptive tool of power. They implied infinite usable dimensions. They implied many other things only faintly understood. Through a jumpdoor you stepped from a room on Tutalsee into a hallway here on Central Central. You walked through a jumpdoor here and found yourself in a garden on Paginui. The intervening "normal space" might be measured in light years or parsecs, but the passage from one place to the other ignored such old concepts. And to this day, ConSentient investigators did not understand how the jumpdoors worked. Concepts such as "relative space" didn't explain the phenomenon; they only added to the mystery.

McKie ground his teeth in frustration. Calebans inevitably did that to him. What good did it do to think of the Calebans as visible stars in the space his body occupied? He could look up from any planet where a jumpdoor deposited him and examine the night sky. Visible stars: ah, yes. Those are Calebans. What did that tell him?

There was a strongly defended theory that Calebans were but a more sophisticated aspect of the equally mysterious Taprisiots. The ConSentiency had accepted and employed Taprisiots for thousands of standard years. A Taprisiot presented sentient form and size. They appeared to be short lengths of tree trunk cut off at top and bottom and with oddly protruding stub limbs. When you touched them they were warm and resilient. They were fellow beings of the ConSentiency. But just as the Calebans took your flesh across the parsecs, Taprisiots took your awareness across those same parsecs to merge you with another mind.

Taprisiots were a communications device.

But current theory said Taprisiots had been introduced to prepare the ConSentiency for Calebans.

It was dangerous to think of Taprisiots as merely a convenient means of communication. Equally dangerous to think of Calebans as "transportation facilitators." Look at the socially disruptive effect of jumpdoors! And when you employed a Taprisiot, you had a constant reminder of danger: the communications trance which reduced you to a twitching zombie while you made your call. No . . . neither Calebans nor Taprisiots should be accepted without question.

With the possible exception of the PanSpechi, no other species knew the first thing about Caleban and Taprisiot phenomena beyond their economic and personal value. They were, indeed, valuable, a fact reflected in the prices often paid for jumpdoor and long-call services. The PanSpechi denied that they could explain these things, but the PanSpechi were notoriously secretive. They were a species where each *individual* consisted of five bodies and only one dominant ego. The four reserves lay somewhere in a hidden creche. Bildoon had come from such a creche, accepting the communal ego from a creche-mate whose subsequent fate could only be imagined. PanSpechi refused to discuss internal creche matters except to admit what was obvious on the surface: that they could grow a simulacrum body to mimic most of the known species in the ConSentiency.

McKie felt himself overcome by a momentary pang of xenophobia.

We accept too damned many things on the explanations of people who could have good reasons for lying.

Keeping his eyes closed, McKie sat up. His bedog rippled gently against his buttocks.

Blast and damn the Calebans! Damn Fannie Mae!

He'd already called Fannie Mae, asking about Dosadi. The result had left him wondering if he really knew what Calebans meant by friendship.

"Information not permitted."

What kind of an answer was that? Especially when it was the only response he could get.

Not permitted?

The basic irritant was an old one: BuSab had no real way of applying its "gentle ministrations" to the Calebans.

But Calebans had never been known to lie. They appeared

painfully, explicitly honest . . . as far as they could be understood. But they obviously withheld information. Not permitted! Was it possible they'd let themselves be accessories to the destruction of a planet and that planet's entire population?

McKie had to admit it was possible.

They might do it out of ignorance or from some stricture of Caleban morality which the rest of the ConSentiency did not share or understand. Or for some other reason which defied translation. They said they looked upon all life as "precious nodes of existence." But hints at peculiar exceptions remained. What was it Fannie Mae had once said?

"Dissolved well this node."

How could you look at an individual life as a "node"?

If association with Calebans had taught him anything, it was that understanding between species was tenuous at best and trying to understand a Caleban could drive you insane. In what medium did a node dissolve?

McKie sighed.

For now, this Dosadi report from the Wreave and Laclac agents had to be accepted on its own limited terms. Powerful people in the Gowachin Confederacy had sequestered Humans and Gowachin on an unlisted planet. Dosadi—location unknown, but the scene of unspecified experiments and tests on an imprisoned population. This much the agents insisted was true. If confirmed, it was a shameful act. The frog people would know that, surely. Rather than let their shame be exposed, they could carry out the threat which the two agents reported: blast the captive planet out of existence, the population and all of the incriminating evidence with it.

McKie shuddered.

Dosadi, a planet of thinking creatures—*sentients.* If the Gowachin carried out their violent threat, a living world would be reduced to blazing gases and the hot plasma of atomic particles. Somewhere, perhaps beyond the reach of other eyes, something would strike fire against the void. The tragedy would require less than a standard second. The most concise thought about such a catastrophe would require a longer time than the actual event.

But if it happened and the other ConSentient species received absolute proof that it had happened . . . ahhh, then the ConSentiency might well be shattered. Who would use a jumpdoor, suspecting that he might be shunted into some hideous experiment? Who would trust a neighbor, if that neighbor's habits, language, and body were different from his own? Yes . . . there would be more than Humans and Gowachin *at each others' throats.* These were things all the species feared. Bildoon realized this. The threat to this mysterious Dosadi was a threat to all.

McKie could not shake the terrible image from his mind: an explosion, a bright blink stretching toward its own darkness. And if the ConSentiency learned of it . . . in that instant before their universe crumbled like a cliff dislodged in a lightning bolt, what excuses would be offered for the failure of reason to prevent such a thing?

Reason?

McKie shook his head, opened his eyes. It was useless to dwell on the worst prospects. He allowed the apartment's sleep gloom to invade his senses, absorbed the familiar presence of his surroundings.

I'm a Saboteur Extraordinary and I've a job to do.

It helped to think of Dosadi that way. Solutions to problems often depended upon the will to succeed, upon sharpened skills and multiple resources. BuSab owned those resources and those skills.

McKie stretched his arms high over his head, twisted his blocky torso. The bedog rippled with pleasure at his movements. He whistled softly and suffered the kindling of morning light as the apartment's window controls responded. A yawn stretched his mouth. He slid from the bedog and padded across to the window. The view stretched away beneath a sky like stained blue paper. He stared out across the spires and rooftops of Central Central. Here lay the heart of the domine planet from which the Bureau of Sabotage spread its multifarious tentacles.

He blinked at the brightness, took a deep breath.

The Bureau. The omnipresent, omniscient, omnivorous Bureau. The one source of unmonitored governmental violence remaining in the ConSentiency. Here lay the norm against which sanity measured itself. Each choice made here demanded utmost delicacy. Their common enemy was that never-ending sentient yearning for absolutes. And each hour of every waking workday, BuSab in all of its parts asked itself:

"What are we if we succumb to unbridled violence?"

The answer was there in deepest awareness:

"Then we are useless."

ConSentient government worked because, no matter how they defined it, the participants believed in a common justice personally achievable. The *Government* worked because BuSab sat at its core like a terrible watchdog able to attack itself or any seat of power with a delicately balanced immunity. Government worked because there were places where it could not act without being chopped off. An appeal to BuSab made the individual as powerful as the ConSentiency. It all came down to the cynical, self-effacing behavior of the carefully chosen BuSab tentacles.

I don't feel much like a BuSab tentacle this morning, McKie thought.

In his advancing years, he'd often experienced such mornings. He had a personal way of dealing with this mood: he buried himself in work.

McKie turned, crossed to the baffle into his bath where he turned his body over to the programmed ministrations of his morning toilet. The psyche-mirror on the bath's far wall reflected his body while it examined and adjusted to his internal conditions. His eyes told him he was still a squat, dark-skinned gnome of a Human with red hair, features so large they suggested an impossible kinship with the frog people of the Gowachin. The mirror did not reflect his mind, considered by many to be the sharpest legal device in the ConSentiency.

The Daily Schedule began playing to McKie as he emerged from the bath. The DS suited its tone to his movements and the combined analysis of his psychophysical condition.

"Good morning, ser," it fluted.

McKie, who could interpret the analysis of his mood from the DS tone, put down a flash of resentment. Of course he felt angry and concerned. Who wouldn't under these circumstances?

"Good morning, you dumb inanimate object," he growled. He slipped into a supple armored pullover, dull green and with the outward appearance of cloth.

The DS waited for his head to emerge.

"You wanted to be reminded, ser, that there is a full conference of the Bureau Directorate at nine local this morning, but the . . ."

"Of all the stupid . . ." McKie's interruption stopped the DS. He'd been meaning for some time to reprogram the damned thing. No matter how carefully you set them, they always got out of phase. He didn't bother to bridle his mood, merely spoke the key words in full emotional spate: "Now you hear me, machine: don't you ever again choose that buddy-buddy conversational pattern when I'm in this mood! I want nothing *less* than a reminder of that conference. When you list such a reminder, don't even suggest remotely that it's my wish. Understood?"

"Your admonition recorded and new program instituted, ser." The DS adopted a brisk, matter of fact tone as it continued: "There is a new reason for alluding to the conference."

"Well, get on with it."

McKie pulled on a pair of green shorts and matching kilt of armored material identical to that of the pullover.

The DS continued:

"The conference was alluded to, ser, as introduction to a new datum: you have been asked not to attend."

McKie, bending to fit his feet into self-powered racing boots, hesitated, then:

"But they're still going to have a showdown meeting with all the Gowachin in the Bureau?"

"No mention of that, ser. The message was that you are to depart immediately this morning on the field assignment which was discussed with you. Code Geevee was invoked. An unspecified Gowachin Phylum has asked that you proceed at once to their home planet. That would be Tandaloor. You are to consult there on a problem of a legal nature."

McKie finished fitting the boots, straightened. He could feel all of his accumulated years as though there'd been no geriatric intervention. Geevee invoked a billion kinds of hell. It put him on his own with but one shopside backup facility: a Taprisiot monitor. He'd have his own Taprisiot link sitting safely here on CC while he went out and risked his vulnerable flesh. The Taprisiot served only one function: to note his death and record every aspect of his final moments—every thought, every memory. This would be part of the next agent's briefing. And the next agent would get his own Taprisiot monitor etcetera, etcetera, etcetera . . . BuSab was notorious for gnawing away at its problems. The Bureau never gave up. But the astronomical cost of such a Taprisiot monitor left the operative so gifted with only one conclusion: odds were not in his favor. There'd be no accolades, no cemetery rites for a dead hero . . . probably not even the physical substance of a hero for private grieving.

McKie felt less and less heroic by the minute.

Heroism was for fools and BuSab agents were not employed for their foolishness. He saw the reasoning, though.

He was the best qualified non-Gowachin for dealing with the Gowachin. He looked at the nearest DS voder.

"Was it suggested that someone doesn't want me at that conference?"

"There was no such speculation."

"Who gave you this message?"

"Bildoon. Verified voiceprint. He asked that your sleep not be interrupted, that the message be given to you on awakening."

"Did he say he'd call back or ask me to call him?"

"No."

"Did Bildoon mention Dosadi?"

"He said the Dosadi problem is unchanged. Dosadi is not in my banks, ser. Did you wish me to seek more info . . ."

"No! I'm to leave immediately?"

"Bildoon said your orders have been cut. In relationship to Dosadi, he said, and these are his exact words: 'The worst is probable. They have all the motivation required.' "

McKie ruminated aloud: "All the motivation . . . selfish interest or fear . . ."

"Ser, are you inquiring of . . ."

"No, you stupid machine! I'm thinking out loud. People do that. We have to sort things out in our heads, put a proper evaluation on available data."

"You do it with extreme inefficiency."

This startled McKie into a flash of anger. "But this job takes a sentient, a *person*, not a machine! Only a person can make the responsible decision. And I'm the only agent who understands them sufficiently."

"Why not set a Gowachin agent to ferret out their . . ."

"So you've worked it out?"

"It was not difficult, even for a machine. Sufficient clues were provided. And since you'll get a Taprisiot monitor, the project involves danger to your person. While I do not have specifics about Dosadi, the clear inference is that the Gowachin have engaged in questionable activity. Let me remind McKie that the Gowachin do not admit guilt easily. Very few non-Gowachin are considered by them to be worthy of their company and confidence. They do not like to feel dependent upon non-Gowachin. In fact, no Gowachin enjoys any dependent condition, not even when dependent upon another Gowachin. This is at the root of their law."

This was a more emotionally loaded conversation than McKie had ever before heard from his DS. Perhaps his constant refusal to accept the thing on a personal anthropomorphic basis had forced it into this adaptation. He suddenly felt almost shy with the DS. What it had said was pertinent, and more than that, vitally important in a particular way: chosen to help him to the extent the DS was capable. In McKie's thoughts, the DS was suddenly transformed into a valued confidante.

As though it knew his thoughts, the DS said:

"I'm still a machine. You are inefficient, but as you have correctly stated you have ways of arriving at accuracy which machines do not understand. We can only . . . guess, and we are not really programmed to guess unless specifically ordered to do so on a given occasion. Trust yourself."

"But you'd rather I were not killed?"

"That is my program."

"Do you have any more helpful suggestions?"

"You would be advised to waste as little time as possible here. There was a tone of urgency in Bildoon's voice."

McKie stared at the nearest voder. Urgency in Bildoon's voice? Even under the most urgent necessity, Bildoon had never sounded urgent to McKie. Certainly, Dosadi could be an urgent matter, but . . . Why should that sound a sour note?

"Are you sure he sounded urgent?"

"He spoke rapidly and with obvious tensions."

"Truthful?"

"The tone-spikes lead to that conclusion."

McKie shook his head. Something about Bildoon's behavior in this matter didn't ring true, but whatever it was it escaped the sophisticated reading circuits of the DS.

And my circuits, too.

Still troubled, McKie ordered the DS to assemble a full travel kit and to read out the rest of the schedule. He moved to the tool cupboard beside his bath baffle as the DS began reeling off the schedule.

His day was to start with the Taprisiot appointment. He listened with only part of his attention, taking care to check the toolkit as the DS assembled it. There were plastipiks. He handled them gently as they deserved. A selection of stims followed. He rejected these, counting on the implanted sense/muscle amplifiers which increased the capabilities of senior BuSab agents. Explosives in various denominations went into the kit—raygens, pentrates. Very careful with these dangerous items. He accepted multilenses, a wad of uniflesh with matching mediskin, solvos, miniputer. The DS extruded a life-monitor bead for the Taprisiot linkage. He swallowed it to give the bead time to anchor in his stomach before the Taprisiot appointment. A holoscan and matching blanks were accepted, as were ruptors and comparators. He rejected the adapter for simulation of target identities. It was doubtful he'd have time or facilities for such sophisticated refinements. Better to trust his own instincts.

Presently, he sealed the kit in its wallet, concealed the wallet in a pocket. The DS had gone rambling on:

". . . and you'll arrive on Tandaloor at a place called Holy Running. The time there will be early afternoon."

Holy Running!

McKie riveted his attention to this datum. A Gowachin saying skittered through his mind: *The Law is a blind guide, a pot of bitter water. The Law is a deadly contest which can change as waves change.*

No doubt of what had led his thoughts into that path. Holy Running was the place of Gowachin myth. Here, so their stories said, lived Mrreg, the monster who had set the immutable pattern of Gowachin character.

And now, McKie suspected he knew which Gowachin Phylum had summoned him. It could be any one of five Phyla at Holy Running, but he felt certain it'd be the worst of those five—the most unpredictable, the most powerful, the most feared. Where else could a thing such as Dosadi originate?

McKie addressed his DS:

"Send in my breakfast. Please record that the condemned person ate a hearty breakfast."

The DS, programmed to recognize rhetoric for which there was no competent response, remained silent while complying.

*All sentient beings are created unequal. The best society pro-
vides each with equal opportunity to float at his own level.*

—*The Gowachin Primary*

By mid-afternoon, Jedrik saw that her gambit had been accepted. A surplus of fifty Humans was just the right size to be
taken by a greedy underling. Whoever it was would see the
possibilities of continuing—ten here, thirty there—and because of the way she'd introduced this *flaw,* the next people
discarded would be mostly Humans, but with just enough
Gowachin to smack of retaliation.

It'd been difficult carrying out her daily routine knowing
what she'd set in motion. It was all very well to accept the fact
that you were *going* into danger. When the actual moment
arrived, it always had a different character. As the subtle and
not so subtle evidence of success accumulated, she felt the
crazy force of it rolling over her. Now was the time to think
about her true power base, the troops who would obey her
slightest hint, the tight communictions linkage with the Rim,
the carefully selected and trained lieutenants. Now was the
time to think about McKie slipping so smoothly into her trap.
She concealed elation behind a facade of anger. They'd expect her to be angry.

The evidence began with a slowed response at her computer terminal. Someone was monitoring. Whoever had taken her bait wanted to be certain she was expandable. Wouldn't want to eliminate someone and then discover that the eliminated someone was essential to the power structure. She'd made damned sure to cut a wide swath into a region which could be made non-essential.

The microsecond delay from the monitoring triggered a disconnect on her telltale circuit, removing the evidence of her preparations before anyone could find it. She didn't think there'd be that much caution in anyone who'd accept this gambit, but unnecessary chances weren't part of her plan. She removed the telltale timer and locked it away in one of the filing cabinets, there to be destroyed with the other evidence when the Elector's toads came prying. The lonely blue flash would be confined by metal walls which would heat to a nice blood red before lapsing into slag and ashes.

In the next stage, people averted their faces as they walked past her office doorway.

Ahhh, the accuracy of the rumor-trail.

The avoidance came so naturally: a glance at a companion on the other side, concentration on material in one's hands, a brisk stride with gaze fixed on the corridor's ends. Important business up there. No time to stop and chat with Keila Jedrik today.

By the Veil of Heaven! They were so transparent!

A Gowachin walked by examining the corridor's blank opposite wall. She knew that Gowachin: one of the Elector's spies. What would he tell Elector Broey today? Jedrik glared at the Gowachin in secret glee. By nightfall, Broey would know who'd picked up her gambit, but it was too small a bite to arouse his avarice. He'd merely log the information for possible future use. It was too early for him to suspect a sacrifice move.

A Human male followed the Gowachin. He was intent on

the adjustment of his neckline and that, of course, precluded a glance at a Senior Liaitor in her office. His name was Drayjo. Only yesterday, Drayjo had made courting gestures, bending toward her over this very desk to reveal the muscles under his light grey coveralls. What did it matter that Drayjo no longer saw her as a useful conquest. His face was a wooden door, closed, locked, hiding nothing.

Avert your face, you clog!

When the red light glowed on her terminal screen, it came as anticlimax. Confirmation that her gambit had been accepted by someone who would shortly regret it. Communication flowed across the screen:

"Opp SD22240268523ZX."

Good old ZX!

Bad news always developed its own coded idiom. She read what followed, anticipating every nuance:

"The Mandate of God having been consulted, the following supernumerary functions are hereby reduced. If your position screen carries your job title with an underline, you are included in the reduction.

"Senior Liaitor."

Jedrik clenched her fists in simulated anger while she glared at the underlined words. It was done. Opp-Out, the good old Double-O. Through its pliable arm, the DemoPol, the Sacred Congregation of the Heavenly Veil had struck again.

None of her eleation showed through her Dosadi controls. Someone able to see beyond immediate gain would note presently that only Humans had received this particular good old Double-O. Not one Gowachin there. Whoever made that observation would come sniffing down the trail she'd deliberately left. Evidence would accumulate. She thought she knew who would read that accumulated evidence for Broey. It would be Tria. It was not yet time for Tria to entertain doubts. Broey would hear what Jedrik wanted him to hear. The Dosadi power game would be played by Jedrik's rules then, and by the time others learned the rules it'd be too late.

She counted on the factor which Broey labeled "instability of the masses." Religious twaddle! Dosadi's masses were unstable only in particular ways. Fit a conscious justification to their innermost unconscious demands and they became a predictable system which would leap into predictable actions—especially with a psychotic populace whose innermost demands could never be faced consciously by the individuals. Such a populace remained highly useful to the initiates. That was why they maintained the DemoPol with its mandate-of-God sample. The tools of government were not difficult to understand. All you needed was a pathway into the system, a place where what *you* did touched a new reality.

Broey would think himself the target of her action. More fool he.

Jedrik pushed back her chair, stood and strode to the window hardly daring to think about where her actions would truly be felt. She saw that the sniper's bullet hadn't even left a mark on the glass. These new windows were far superior to the old ones which had taken on dull streaks and scratches after only a few years.

She stared down at the light on the river, carefully preserving this moment, prolonging it.

I won't look up yet, not yet.

Whoever had accepted her gambit would be watching her now. Too late! Too late!

A streak of orange-yellow meandered in the river current: contaminants from the Warren factories . . . poisons. Presently, not looking too high yet, she lifted her gaze to the silvered layers of the Council Hills, to the fluting inverted-stalagmites of the high apartments to which the denizens of Chu aspired in their futile dreams. Sunlight gleamed from the power bulbs which adorned the apartments on the hills.

The great crushing wheel of government had its hub on those hills, but the impetus for that wheel had originated elsewhere.

Now, having prolonged the moment while anticipation enriched it, Jedrik lifted her gaze to that region above the Council Hills, to the sparkling streamers and grey glowing of the barrier veil, to the God Wall which englobed her planet in its impenetrable shell. The Veil of Heaven looked the way it always looked in this light. There was no apparent change. But she *knew* what she had done.

Jedrik was aware of subtle instruments which revealed other suns and galaxies beyond the God Wall, places where other planets must exist, but her people had only this one planet. That barrier up there and whoever had created it insured this isolation. Her eyes blurred with quick tears which she wiped away with real anger at herself. Let Broey and his toads believe themselves the only objects of her anger. She would carve a way beyond them through that deadly veil. No one on Dosadi would ever again cower beneath the hidden powers who lived in the sky!

She lowered her gaze to the carpet of factories and Warrens. Some of the defensive walls were faintly visible in the layers of smoke which blanketed the teeming scramble of life upon which the city fed. The smoke erased fine details to separate the apartment hills from the earth. Above the smoke, the fluted buildings became more a part of sky than of ground. Even the ledged, set-back walls of the canyon within which Chu created its sanctuary were no longer attached to the ground, but floated separate from this place where people could survive to a riper maturity on Dosadi. The smoke dulled the greens of ledges and Rim where the Rabble waged a losing battle for survival. Twenty years was old out there. In that pressure, they fought for a chance to enter Chu's protective confines by any means available, even welcoming the opportunity to eat garbage from which the poisons of this planet had been removed. The worst of Chu was better than their best, which only proved that the conditions of hell were relative.

I seek escape through the God Wall for the same reasons the Rabble seeks entrance to Chu.

In Jedrik's mind lay a graph with an undulant line. It combined many influences: Chu's precious food cycle and economics, Rim incursions, spots which flowed across their veiled sun, subtle planetary movements, atmospheric electricity, gravitational flows, magnetronic fluctuations, the dance of numbers in the Liaitor banks, the seemingly random play of cosmic rays, the shifting colors in the God Wall . . . and mysterious jolts to the entire system which commanded her most concentrated attention. There could be only one source for such jolts: a manipulative intelligence outside the planetary influence of Dosadi. She called that force "X," but she had broken "X" into components. One component was a simulation model of Elector Broey which she carried firmly in her head, not needing any of the mechanical devices for reading such things. "X" and all of its components were as real as anything else on the chart in her mind. By their interplay she read them.

Jedrik addressed herself silently to "X":

By your actions I know you and you are vulnerable.

Despite all of the Sacred Congregation's prattle, Jedrik and her people knew the God Wall had been put there for a specific purpose. It was the purpose which pressed living flesh into Chu from the Rim. It was the purpose which jammed too many people into too little space while it frustrated all attempts to spread into any other potential sanctuary. It was the purpose which created people who possessed that terrifying mental template which could trade flesh for flesh . . . Gowachin or Human. Many clues revealed themselves around her and came through that radiance in the sky, but she refused as yet to make a coherent whole out of that purpose. Not yet.

I need this McKie!

With a Jedrik-maintained tenacity, her people knew that the regions beyond the barrier veil were not heaven or hell. Dosadi was hell, but it was a *created* hell. *We will know soon . . . soon.*

This moment had been almost nine Dosadi generations in preparation: the careful breeding of a specific individual who carried in one body the talents required for this assault on "X," the exquisitely detailed education of that weapon-in-fleshly-form . . . and there'd been all the rest of it—whispers, unremarked observations in clandestine leaflets, help for people who held particular ideas and elimination of others whose concepts obstructed, the building of a Rim-Warren communications network, the slow and secret assembly of a military force to match the others which balanced themselves at the peaks of Dosadi power . . . All of these things and much more had prepared the way for those numbers introduced into her computer terminal. The ones who appeared to rule Dosadi like puppets—those ones could be read in many ways and this time the rulers, both visible and hidden, had made one calculation while Jedrik had made another calculation.

Again, she looked up at the God Wall.

You out there! Keila Jedrik knows you're there. And you can be baited, you can be trapped. You are slow and stupid. And you think I don't know how to use your McKie. Ahhh, sky demons, McKie will open your veil for me. My life's a wrath and you're the objects of my wrath. I dare what you would not.

Nothing of this revealed itself on her face nor in any movement of her body.

Arm yourself when the Frog God smiles.

—Gowachin admonition

McKie began speaking as he entered the Phylum sanctus: "I'm Jorj X. McKie of the Bureau of Sabotage."

Name and primary allegiance, that was the drill. If he'd been a Gowachin, he'd have named his Phylum or would've favored the room with a long blink to reveal the identifying Phylum tatoo on his eyelids. As a non-Gowachin, he didn't need a tatoo.

He held his right hand extended in the Gowachin peace sign, palm down and fingers wide to show that he held no weapon there and had not extended his claws. Even as he entered, he smiled, knowing the effect this would have on any Gowachin here. In a rare mood of candor, one of his old Gowachin teachers had once explained the effect of a smiling McKie.

"We feel our bones age. It is a very uncomfortable experience."

McKie understood the reason for this. He possessed a thick, muscular body—a swimmer's body with light mahogany skin. He walked with a swimmer's rolling gait. There

46

were Polynesians in his Old Terran ancestry, this much was known in the Family Annals. Wide lips and a flat nose dominated his face; the eyes were large and placidly brown. There was a final genetic ornamentation to confound the Gowachin: red hair. He was the Human equivalent of the greenstone sculpture found in every Phylum house here on Tandaloor. McKie possessed the face and body of the Frog God, the Giver of Law.

As his old teacher had explained, no Gowachin ever fully escaped feelings of awe in McKie's presence, especially when McKie smiled. They were forced to hide a response which went back to the admonition which every Gowachin learned while still clinging to his mother's back.

Arm yourselves! McKie thought.

Still smiling, he stopped after the prescribed eight paces, glanced once around the room, then narrowed his attention. Green crystal walls confined the sanctus. It was not a large space, a gentle oval of perhaps twenty meters in its longest dimension. A single oval window admitted warm afternoon light from Tandaloor's golden sun. The glowing yellow created a contrived *spiritual ring* directly ahead of McKie. The light focused on an aged Gowachin seated in a brown chairdog which had spread itself wide to support his elbows and webbed fingers. At the Gowachin's right hand stood an exquisitely wrought wooden swingdesk on a scrollwork stand. The desk held one object: a metal box of dull blue about fifteen centimeters long, ten wide, and six deep. Standing behind the blue box in the servant-guard position was a red-robed Wreave, her fighting mandibles tucked neatly into the lower folds of her facial slit.

This Phylum was initiating a Wreave!

The realization filled McKie with disquiet. Bildoon had not warned him about Wreaves on Tandaloor. The Wreave indicated a sad shift among the Gowachin toward a particular kind of violence. Wreaves never danced for joy, only for death. And this was the most dangerous of Wreaves, a *female*, recognizable as such by the jaw pouches behind her mandibles. There'd be two males somewhere nearby to form the breeding triad. Wreaves never ventured from their home soil otherwise.

McKie realized he no longer was smiling. These damnable Gowachin! They'd known the effect a Wreave female would have on him. Except in the Bureau, where a special dispensation prevailed, dealing with Wreaves required the most delicate care to avoid giving offence. And because they periodically exchanged triad members, they developed extended families of gigantic proportions wherein offending one member was to offend them all.

These reflections did not sit well with the chill he'd experienced at sight of the blue box on the swingdesk. He still did not know the identity of this Phylum, but he knew what that blue box had to be. He could smell the peculiar scent of antiquity about it. His choices had been narrowed.

"I know you, McKie," the ancient Gowachin said.

He spoke the ritual in standard Galach with a pronounced burr, a fact which revealed he'd seldom been off this planet. His left hand moved to indicate a white chairdog positioned at an angle to his right beyond the swingdesk, yet well within striking range of the silent Wreave.

"Please seat yourself, McKie."

The Gowachin glanced at the Wreave, at the blue box, returned his attention to McKie. It was a deliberate movement of the pale yellow eyes which were moist with age beneath bleached green brows. He wore only a green apron with white shoulder straps which outlined crusted white chest ventricles. The face was flat and sloping with pale, puckered nostrils below a faint nose crest. He blinked and revealed the tatoos on his eyelids. McKie saw there the dark, swimming circle of the Running Phylum, that which legend said had been the first to accept Gowachin Law from the Frog God.

His worst fears confirmed, McKie seated himself and felt the white chairdog adjust to his body. He cast an uneasy glance at the Wreave, who towered behind the swingdesk like a red-robed executioner. The flexing bifurcation which served as Wreave legs moved in the folds of the robe, but without tension. This Wreave was not yet ready to dance. McKie reminded himself that Wreaves were careful in all matters. This had prompted the ConSentient expression, "a Wreave bet." Wreaves were noted for waiting for the sure thing.

"You see the blue box," the old Gowachin said.

It was a statement of mutual understanding, no answer required, but McKie took advantage of the opening.

"However, I do not know your companion."

"This is Ceylang, Servant of the Box."

Ceylang nodded acknowledgment.

A fellow BuSab agent had once told McKie how to count the number of triad exchanges in which a Wreave female had participated.

"A tiny bit of skin is nipped from one of her jaw pouches by the departing companion. It looks like a little pockmark."

Both of Ceylang's pouches were peppered with exchange pocks. McKie nodded to her, formal and correct, no offense intended, none given. He glanced at the box which she served.

McKie had been a Servant of the Box once. This was where you began to learn the limits of legal ritual. The Gowachin words for this novitiate translated as "The Heart of Disrespect." It was the first stage on the road to Legum. The old Gowachin here was not mistaken: McKie as one of the few non-Gowachin ever admitted to Legum status, to the practice of law in this planetary federation, would *see* that blue box and know what it contained. There would be a small brown book printed on pages of ageless metal, a knife with the blood of many sentient beings dried on its black surface, and lastly a grey rock, chipped and scratched over the millennia in which it'd been used to pound on wood and call Gowachin courts into session. The box and its contents symbolized all that was mysterious and yet practical about Gowachin Law. The book was ageless, yet not to be read and reread; it was sealed in a box where it could be thought upon as a thing which marked a beginning. The knife carried the bloody residue of many endings. And the rock—that came from the natural earth where things only changed, never beginning or ending. The entire assemblage, box and contents, represented a window into the soul of the Frog God's minions. And now they were educating a Wreave as Servant of the Box.

McKie wondered why the Gowachin had chosen a deadly Wreave, but dared not enquire. The blue box, however, was another matter. It said with certainty that a planet called Dosadi would be named openly here. The thing which BuSab had uncovered was about to become an issue in Gowachin Law. That the Gowachin had anticipated Bureau action spoke well of their information sources. A sense of careful choosing radiated from this room. McKie assumed a mask of relaxation and remained silent.

The old Gowachin did not appear pleased by this. He said: "You once afforded me much amusement, McKie."

That might be a compliment, probably not. Hard to tell. Even if it were a compliment, coming from a Gowachin it would contain signal reservations, especially in legal matters. McKie held his silence. This Gowachin was big power and no mistake. Whoever misjudged him would hear the Courtarena's final trumpet.

"I watched you argue your first case in our courts," the Gowachin said. "Betting was nine-point-three to three-point-eight that we'd see your blood. But when you concluded by demonstrating that eternal sloppiness was the price of liberty . . . ahhh, that was a master stroke. It filled many a Legum with envy. Your words clawed through the skin of Gowachin Law to get at the meat. And at the same time you amused us. That was the supreme touch."

Until this moment, McKie had not even suspected that there'd been amusement for anyone in that first case. Present circumstances argued for truthfulness from the old Gowachin, however. Recalling that first case, McKie tried to reassess it in the light of this revelation. He remembered the case well. The Gowachin had charged a Low Magister named Klodik with breaking his most sacred vows in an issue of justice. Klodik's crime was the release of thirty-one fellow Gowachin from their primary allegiance to Gowachin Law and the purpose of that was to qualify the thirty-one for service in BuSab. The hapless prosecutor, a much-admired Legum named Pirgutud, had aspired to Klodik's position and had made the mistake of trying for a direct conviction. McKie had thought at the time that the wiser choice would've been to attempt discrediting the legal structure under which Klodik had been arraigned. This would have thrown judgment into the area of popular choice, and there'd been no doubt that Klodik's early demise would've been popular. Seeing this opening, McKie had attacked the prosecutor as a legalist, a stickler, one who preferred Old Law. Victory had been relatively easy.

When it had come to the knife, however, McKie had found himself profoundly reluctant. There'd been no question of selling Pirgutud back to his own Phylum. BuSab had needed a non-Gowachin Legum . . . the whole non-Gowachin universe had needed this. The few other non-Gowachin who'd attained Legum status were all dead, every last one of them in the Courtarena. A current of animosity toward the Gowachin worlds had been growing. Suspicion fed on suspicion.

Pirgutud had to die in the traditional, the formal, way. He'd known it perhaps better than McKie. Pirgutud, as required, had bared the heart area beside his stomach and clasped his hands behind his head. This extruded the stomach circle, providing a point of reference.

The purely academic anatomy lessons and the practice sessions on lifelike dummies had come to deadly focus.

"Just to the left of the stomach circle imagine a small triangle with an apex at the center of the stomach circle extended horizontally and the base even with the bottom of the stomach circle. Strike into the lower outside corner of this triangle and slightly upward toward the midline."

About the only satisfaction McKie had found in the event was that Pirgutud had died cleanly and quickly with one stroke. McKie had not entered Gowachin Law as a "hacker."

What had there been in that case and its bloody ending to amuse the Gowachin? The answer filled McKie with a profound sense of peril.

The Gowachin were amused at themselves because they had so misjudged me! But I'd planned all along for them to misjudge me. That was what amused them!

Having provided McKie with a polite period for reflection, the old Gowachin continued:

"I'd bet against you, McKie. The odds, you understand? You delighted me nonetheless. You instructed us while winning your case in a classic manner which would've done credit to the best of us. That is one of the Law's purposes, of course: to test the qualities of those who choose to employ it. Now what did you expect to find when you answered our latest summons to Tandaloor?"

The question's abrupt shift almost caught McKie by surprise.

I've been too long away from the Gowachin, he thought. *I can't relax even for an instant.*

It was almost a palpable thing: if he missed a single beat of the rhythms in this room, he and an entire planet could fall before Gowachin judgment. For a civilization which based its law on the Courtarena where any participant could be sacrificed, anything was possible. McKie chose his next words with life-and-death care.

"You summoned me, that is true, but I came on official business of my Bureau. It's the Bureau's expectations which concern me."

"Then you are in a difficult position because you're also a Legum of the Gowachin Bar subject to our demands. Do you know me?"

This was a Magister, a *Foremost-Speaker* from the "Phylum of Phylums," no doubt of it. He was a survivor in one of the most cruel traditions known to the sentient universe. His abilities and resources were formidable and he was on his home ground. McKie chose the cautious response.

"On my arrival I was told to come to this place at this time. That is what I know."

The least thing that is known shall govern your acts. This was the course of evidence for the Gowachin. McKie's response put a legal burden on his questioner.

The old Gowachin's hands clutched with pleasure at the level of artistry to which this contest had risen. There was a momentary silence during which Ceylang gathered her robe tightly and moved even closer to the swingdesk. Now, there was tension in her movements. The Magister stirred, said:

"I have the disgusting honor to be High Magister of the Running Phylum, Aritch by name."

As he spoke, his right hand thrust out, took the blue box, and dropped it into McKie's lap. "I place the binding oath upon you in the name of the book!"

As McKie had expected, it was done swiftly. He had the box in his hands while the final words of the ancient legal challenge were ringing in his ears. No matter the ConSentient modifications of Gowachin Law which might apply in this situation, he was caught in a convoluted legal maneuvering. The metal of the box felt cold against his fingers. They'd confronted him with *the* High Magister. The Gowachin were dispensing with many preliminaries. This spoke of time pressures and a particular assessment of their own predicament. McKie reminded himself that he was dealing with people who found pleasure in their own failures, could be amused by death in the Courtarena, whose most consummate pleasure came when the currents of their own Law were changed artistically.

McKie spoke with the careful formality which ritual required if he were to emerge alive from this room.

"Two wrongs may cancel each other. Therefore, let those who do wrong do it together. That is the true purpose of Law."

Gently, McKie released the simple swing catch on the box, lifted the lid to verify the contents. This must be done with precise attention to formal details. A bitter, musty odor touched his nostrils as the lid lifted. The box held what he'd expected: the book, the knife, the rock. It occurred to McKie then that he was holding the original of all such boxes. It was a thing of enormous antiquity—thousands upon thousands of standard years. Gowachin professed the belief that the Frog God had created this box, this *very* box, and its contents as a model, the symbol of "the only workable Law."

Careful to do it with his right hand, McKie touched each item of the box in its turn, closed the lid and latched it. As he did this, he felt that he stepped into a ghostly parade of Legums, names imbedded in the minstrel chronology of Gowachin history.

Bishkar who concealed her eggs . . .

Kondush the Diver . . .

Dritaik who sprang from the marsh and laughed at Mrreg . . .

Tonkeel of the hidden knife . . .

McKie wondered then how they would sing about him. Would it be *McKie the blunderer?* His thoughts raced through review of the necessities. The primary necessity was Aritch. Little was known about this High Magister outside the Gowachin Federation, but it was said that he'd once won a case by finding a popular bias which allowed him to kill a judge. The commentary on this coup said Aritch "embraced the Law in the same way that salt dissolves in water." To the initiates, this meant Aritch personified the basic Gowachin attitude toward their Law: "respectful disrespect." It was a peculiar form of sanctity. Every movement of your body was as important as your words. The Gowachin made it an aphorism.

"You hold your life in your mouth when you enter the Courtarena."

They provided legal ways to kill any participant—judges, Legums, clients . . . But it must be done with exquisite legal finesse, with its justifications apparent to all observers, and with the most delicate timing. Above all, one could kill in the arena only when no other choice offered the same worshipful disrespect for Gowachin Law. Even while changing the Law, you were required to revere its sanctity.

When you entered the Courtarena, you had to feel that peculiar sanctity in every fiber. The forms . . . the forms . . . the forms . . . With that blue box in his hands, the deadly forms of Gowachin Law dominated every movement, every word. Knowing McKie was not Gowachin-born, Aritch was putting time pressures on him, hoping for an immediate flaw. They didn't want this Dosadi matter in the arena. That was the immediate contest. And if it did get to the arena . . . well, the crucial matter would be selection of the judges. Judges were chosen with great care. Both sides maneuvered in this, being cautious not to intrude a professional legalist onto the bench. Judges could represent those whom the Law had offended. They could be private citizens in any number satisfactory to the opposing forces. Judges could be (and often were) chosen for their special knowledge of a case at hand. But here you were forced to weigh the subtleties of prejudgment. Gowachin Law made a special distinction between prejudgment and bias.

McKie considered this.

The interpretation of bias was: "If I can rule for a particular side I will do so."

For prejudgment: "No matter what happens in the arena I will rule for a particular side."

Bias was permitted, but not prejudgment.

Aritch was the first problem, his possible prejudgments, his bias, his inborn and most deeply conditioned attitudes. In his deepest feelings, he would look down on all non-Gowachin legal systems as "devices to weaken personal character through appeals to illogic, irrationality, and to ego-centered selfishness in the name of high purpose."

If Dosadi came to the arena, it would be tried under modified Gowachin Law. The modifications were a thorn in the Gowachin skin. They represented concessions made for entrance into the ConSentiency. Periodically, the Gowachin tried to make their Law the basis for all ConSentient Law.

McKie recalled that a Gowachin had once said of ConSentient Law:

"It fosters greed, discontent, and competitiveness not based on excellence but on appeals to prejudice and materialism."

Abruptly, McKie remembered that this was a quotation attributed to Aritch, High Magister of the Running Phylum. Were there even more deeply hidden motives in what the Gowachin did here?

Showing signs of impatience, Aritch inhaled deeply through his chest ventricles, said:

"You are now my Legum. To be convicted is to go free because this marks you as enemy of all government. I know you to be such an enemy, McKie."

"You know me," McKie agreed.

It was more than ritual response and obedience to forms, it was truth. But it required great effort for McKie to speak it calmly. In the almost fifty years since he'd been admitted to the Gowachin Bar, he'd served that ancient legal structure four times in the Courtarena, a minor record among the ordinary Legums. Each time, his personal survival had been in the balance. In all of its stages, this contest was a deadly battle. The loser's life belonged to the winner and could be taken at the winner's discretion. On rare occasions, the loser might be sold back to his own Phylum as a menial. Even the losers disliked this choice.

Better clean death than dirty life.

The blood-encrusted knife in the blue box testified to the more popular outcome. It was a practice which made for rare litigation and memorable court performances.

Aritch, speaking with eyes closed and the Running Phylum tatoos formally displayed, brought their encounter to its testing point.

"Now McKie, you will tell me what official matters of the Bureau of Sabotage bring you to the Gowachin Federation."

Law must retain useful ways to break with traditional forms because nothing is more certain than that the forms of Law remain when all justice is gone.

—*Gowachin aphorism*

He was tall for a Dosadi Gowachin, but fat and ungroomed. His feet shuffled when he walked and there was a permanent stoop to his shoulders. A flexing wheezing overcame his chest ventricles when he became excited. He knew this and was aware that those around him knew it. He often used this characteristic as a warning, reminding people that no Dosadi held more power than he, and that power was deadly. All Dosadi knew his name: Broey. And very few misinterpreted the fact that he'd come up through the Sacred Congregation of the Heavenly Veil to his post as chief steward of Control: The Elector. His private army was Dosadi's largest, most efficient, and best armed. Broey's intelligence corps was a thing to invoke fear and admiration. He maintained a fortified suite atop his headquarters building, a structure of stone and plasteel which fronted the main arm of the river in the heart of Chu. Around this core, the twisting walled fortifications of the city stepped outward in concentric rings. The only entrance to Broey's citadel was through a guarded Tube Gate in a subbasement, designated

TG One. TG One admitted the select of the select and no others.

In the forenoon, the ledges outside Broey's windows were a roosting place for carrion birds, who occupied a special niche on Dosadi. Since the Lords of the Veil forbade the eating of sentient flesh by sentient, this task devolved upon the birds. Flesh from the people of Chu and even from the Rim carried fewer of the planet's heavy metals. The carrion birds prospered. A flock of them strutted along Broey's ledge, coughing, squawking, defecating, brushing against each other with avian insolence while they watched the outlying streets for signs of food. They also watched the Rim, but it had been temporarily denied to them by a sonabarrier. Bird sounds came through a voder into one of the suite's eight rooms. This was a yellow-green space about ten meters long and six wide occupied by Broey and two Humans.

Broey uttered a mild expletive at the bird noise. The confounded creatures interfered with clear thinking. He shuffled to the window and silenced the voder. In the sudden quiet he looked out at the city's perimeter and the lower ledges of the enclosing cliffs. Another Rim foray had been repulsed out there in the night. Broey had made a personal inspection in a convoy of armored vehicles earlier. The troops liked it that he occasionally shared their dangers. The carrion birds already had cleaned up most of the mess by the time the armored column swept through. The flat back structure of Gowachin, who had no front rib cage, had been easily distinguishable from the white framework which had housed Human organs. Only a few rags of red and green flesh had marked where the birds had abandoned their feast when the sonabarriers herded them away.

When he considered the sonabarriers, Broey's thoughts grew hard and clear. The sonabarriers were one of Gar's damned affectations! *Let the birds finish it.*

But Gar insisted a few bodies be left around to make the

point for the Rim survivors that their attacks were hopeless.
The bones by themselves would be just as effective.
Gar was bloody minded.

Broey turned and glanced across the room past his two
Human companions. Two of the walls were taken up by
charts bearing undulant squiggles in many colors. On a table
at the room's center lay another chart with a single red line.
The line curved and dipped, ending almost in the middle of
the chart. Near this terminus lay a white card and beside it
stood a Human male statuette with an enormous erection
which was labeled "Rabble." It was a subversive, forbidden
artifact of Rim origin. The people of the Rim knew where
their main strength lay: breed, breed, breed . . .

The Humans sat facing each other across the chart. They
fitted into the space around them through a special absorp-
tion. It was as though they'd been initiated into the secrets of
Broey's citadel through an esoteric ritual both forbidding
and dangerous.

Broey returned to his chair at the head of the table, sat
down, and quietly continued to study his companions. He experienced amusement to feel his fighting claws twitch beneath their finger shields as he looked at the two. Yes—trust
them no more than they trusted him. They had their own
troops, their own spies—they posed real threat to Broey but
often their help was useful. Just as often they were a nui-
sance.

Quilliam Gar, the Human male who sat with his back to the
windows, looked up as Broey resumed his seat. Gar snorted,
somehow conveying that he'd been about to silence the voder
himself.

Damned carrion birds! But they were useful . . . useful.
The Rim-born were always ambivalent about the birds.

Gar rode his chair as though talking down to ranks of the
uninformed. He'd come up through the educational services
in the Convocation before joining Broey. Gar was thin with

an inner emaciation so common that few on Dosadi gave it any special notice. He had the hunter's face and eyes, carried his eighty-eight years as though they were twice that. Hairline wrinkles crawled down his cheeks. The bas-relief of veins along the backs of his hands and the grey hair betrayed his Rim origins, as did a tendency to short temper. The Labor Pool green of his clothing fooled very few, his face was that well known.

Across from Gar sat his eldest daughter and chief lieutenant, Tria. She'd placed herself there to watch the windows and the cliffs. She'd also been observing the carrion birds, rather enjoying their sounds. It was well to be reminded here of what lay beyond the city's outer gates.

Tria's face held too much brittle sharpness to be considered beautiful by any except an occasional Gowachin looking for an exotic experience or a Warren laborer hoping to use her as a step out of peonage. She often disconcerted her companions by a wide-eyed, cynical stare. She did this with an aristocratic sureness which commanded attention. Tria had developed the gesture for just this purpose. Today, she wore the orange with black trim of Special Services, but without a brassard to indicate the branch. She knew that this led many to believe her Broey's personal toy, which was true but not in the way the cynical supposed. Tria understood her special value: she possessed a remarkable ability to interpret the vagaries of the DemoPol.

Indicating the red line on the chart in front of her, Tria said, "She has to be the one. How can you doubt it?" And she wondered why Broey continued to worry at the obvious.

"Keila Jedrik," Broey said. And again: "Keila Jedrik."

Gar squinted at his daughter.

"Why would she include herself among the fifty who . . ."

"She sends us a message," Broey said. "I hear it clearly now." He seemed pleased by his own thoughts.

Gar read something else in the Gowachin's manner.

"I hope you're not having her killed."

"I'm not as quick to anger as are you Humans," Broey said.

"The usual surveillance?" Gar asked.

"I haven't decided. You know, don't you, that she lives a rather celibate life? Is it that she doesn't enjoy the males of your species?"

"More likely they don't enjoy her," Tria said.

"Interesting. Your breeding habits are so peculiar."

Tria shot a measuring stare at Broey. She wondered why the Gowachin had chosen to wear black today. It was a robe-like garment cut at a sharp angle from shoulders to waist, clearing his ventricles. The ventricles revolted her and Broey knew this. The very thought of them pressing against her . . . She cleared her throat. Broey seldom wore black; it was the happy color of priestly celebrants. He wore it, though, with a remoteness which suggested that thoughts passed through his mind which no other person could experience.

The exchange between Broey and his daughter worried Gar. He could not help but feel the oddity that each of them tried to present a threatening view of events by withholding some data and coloring other data.

"What if she runs out to the Rim?" Gar asked.

Broey shook his head.

"Let her go. She's not one to stay on the Rim."

"Perhaps we should have her picked up," Gar said.

Broey stared at him, then:

"I've gained the distinct impression that you've some private plan in mind. Are you prepared to share it?"

"I've no idea what you . . ."

"Enough!" Broey shouted. His ventricles wheezed as he inhaled.

Gar held himself very quiet.

Broey leaned toward him, noting that this exchange amused Tria.

"It's too soon to make decisions we cannot change! This is a time for ambiguity."

Irritated by his own display of anger, Broey arose and hurried into his adjoining office, where he locked the door. It was obvious that those two had no more idea than he where Jedrik had gone to ground. But it was still his game. She couldn't hide forever. Seated once more in his office, he called Security.

"Has Bahrank returned?"

A senior Gowachin officer hurried into the screen's view, looked up.

"Not yet."

"What precautions to learn where he delivers his cargo?"

"We know his entry gate. It'll be simple to track him."

"I don't want Gar's people to know what you're doing."

"Understood."

"That other matter?"

"Pcharky may have been the last one. He could be dead, too. The killers were thorough."

"Keep searching."

Broey put down a sense of disquiet. Some very un-Dosadi things were happening in Chu . . . and on the Rim. He felt that things occurred which his spies could not uncover. Presently, he returned to the more pressing matter.

"Bahrank is not to be interfered with until afterward."

"Understood."

"Pick him up well clear of his delivery point and bring him to your section. I will interview him personally."

"Sir, his addiction to . . ."

"I know the hold she has on him. I'm counting on it."

"We've not yet secured any of that substance, sir, although we're still trying."

"I want success, not excuses. Who's in charge of that?"

"Kidge, sir. He's very efficient in this . . ."

"Is Kidge available?"

"One moment, sir. I'll put him on."

Kidge had a phlegmatic Gowachin face and rumbling voice.

"Do you want a status report, sir?"

"Yes."

"My Rim contacts believe the addictive substance is derived from a plant called 'tibac.' We have no prior record of such a plant, but the outer Rabble has been cultivating it lately. According to my contacts, it's extremely addictive to Humans, even more so to us."

"No record? What's its origin? Do they say?"

"I talked personally to a Human who'd recently returned from upriver where the outer Rabble reportedly has extensive plantations of this 'tibac.' I promised my informant a place in the Warrens if he provides me with a complete report on the stuff and a kilo packet of it. This informant says the cultivators believe tibac has religious significance. I didn't see any point in exploring that."

"When do you expect him to deliver?"

"By nightfall at the latest."

Broey held his silence for a moment. *Religious significance.* More than likely the plant came from beyond the God Wall then, as Kidge implied. But why? What were *they* doing?

"Do you have new instructions?" Kidge asked.

"Get that substance up to me as soon as you can."

Kidge fidgeted. He obviously had another question, but was unwilling to ask it. Broey glared at him.

"Yes? What is it?"

"Don't you want the substance tested first?"

It was a baffling question. Had Kidge withheld vital information about the dangers of this tibac? One never knew from what quarter an attack might come. But Kidge was held in his own special bondage. He knew what could happen to him if he failed Broey. And Jedrik had handled this stuff. But why had Kidge asked this question? Faced with such unknowns, Broey tended to withdraw into himself, eyes veiled by the nictating membrane while he weighed the possibilities. Presently, he stirred, looked at Kidge in the screen.

"If there's enough of it, feed some to volunteers—both Human and Gowachin. Get the rest of it up to me immediately, even while you're testing, but in a sealed container."

"Sir, there are rumors about this stuff. It'll be difficult getting real volunteers."

"You'll think of something."

Broey broke the connection, returned to the outer room to make his political peace with Gar and Tria. He was not ready to blunt that pair . . . not yet.

They were sitting just as he'd left them. Tria was speaking:

" . . . the highest probability and I have to go on that."

Gar merely nodded.

Broey seated himself, nodded to Tria, who continued as though there'd been no hiatus.

"Clearly, Jedrik's a genuis. And her Loyalty Index! That has to be false, contrived. And look at her decisions: one questionable decision in four years. One!"

Gar moved a finger along the red line on the chart. It was a curiously sensuous gesture, as though he were stroking flesh.

Broey gave him a verbal prod.

"Yes, Gar, what is it?"

"I was just wondering if Jedrik could be another . . ."

His glance darted ceilingward, back to the chart. They all understood his allusion to intruders from beyond the God Wall.

Broey looked at Gar as though awakening from an interrupted thought. What'd that fool Gar mean by raising such a question at this juncture? The required responses were so obvious.

"I agree with Tria's analysis," Broey said. "As to your question . . ." He gave a Human shrug. "Jedrik reveals some of the classic requirements, but . . ." Again, that shrug. "This is still the world God gave us."

Colored as they were by his years in the Sacred Congregation, Broey's words took on an unctuous overtone, but in this room the message was strictly secular.

"The others have been such disappointments," Gar said. "Especially Havvy." He moved the statuette to a more central position on the chart.

"We failed because we were too eager," Tria said, her voice snappish. "Poor timing."

Gar scratched his chin with his thumb. Tria sometimes disturbed him by that accusatory tone she took toward their failures. He said:

"But . . . if she turns out to be one of *them* and we haven't allowed for it . . ."

"We'll look through that gate when we come to it," Broey said. " *If* we come to it. Even another failure could have its uses. The food factories will give us a substantial increase at the next harvest. That means we can postpone the more troublesome political decisions which have been bothering us."

Broey let this thought hang between them while he set himself to identifying the lines of activity revealed by what had happened in this room today. Yes, the Humans betrayed unmistakable signs that they behaved according to a secret plan. Things were going well, then: they'd attempt to supersede him soon . . . and fail.

A door behind Tria opened. A fat Human female entered. Her body bulbed in green coveralls and her round face appeared to float in a halo of yellow hair. Her cheeks betrayed the telltale lividity of *dacon* addiction. She spoke subserviently to Gar.

"You told me to interrupt if . . ."

"Yes, yes."

Gar waved to indicate she could speak freely. The gesture's significance did not escape Broey. Another part of their set piece.

"We've located Havvy but Jedrik's not with him."

Gar nodded, addressed Broey:

"Whether Jedrik's an agent or another puppet, this whole thing smells of something *they* have set in motion."

Once more, his gaze darted ceilingward.

"I will act on that assumption," Tria said. She pushed her chair back, arose. "I'm going into the Warrens."

Broey looked up at her. Again, he felt his talons twitch beneath their sheaths. He said:

"Don't interfere with them."

Gar forced his gaze away from the Gowachin while his mind raced. Often, the Gowachin were difficult to read, but Broey had been obvious just then: he was confident that he could locate Jedrik and he didn't care who knew it. That could be very dangerous.

Tria had seen it, too, of course, but she made no comment, merely turned and followed the fat woman out of the room.

Gar arose like a folding ruler being opened to its limit. "I'd best be getting along. There are many matters requiring my personal attention."

"We depend on you for a great deal," Broey said.

He was not yet ready to release Gar, however. Let Tria get well on her way. Best to keep those two apart for a spell. He said:

"Before you go, Gar. Several things still bother me. Why was Jedrik so precipitate? And why destroy her records? What was it that we were not supposed to see?"

"Perhaps it was an attempt to confuse us," Gar said, quoting Tria. "One thing's sure: it wasn't just an angry gesture."

"There must be a clue somewhere," Broey said.

"Would you have us risk an interrogation of Havvy?"

"Of course not!"

Gar showed no sign that he recognized Broey's anger. He said:

"Despite what you and Tria say, I don't think we can afford

another mistake at this time. Havvy was . . . well . . ."

"If you recall," Broey said, "Havvy was not one of Tria's mistakes. She went along with us under protest. I wish now we'd listened to her." He waved a hand idly in dismissal. "Go see to your important affairs." He watched Gar leave.

Yes, on the basis of the Human's behavior it was reasonable to assume he knew nothing as yet about this *infiltrator* Bahrank was bringing through the gates. Gar would've concealed such valuable information, would not have dared raise the issue of a God Wall intrusion . . . Or would he? Broey nodded to himself. This must be handled with great delicacy.

We will now explore the particular imprint which various governments make upon the individual. First, be sure you recognize the primary governing force. For example, take a careful look at Human history. Humans have been known to submit to many constraints: to rule by Autarchs, by Plutarchs, by the power seekers of the many Republics, by Oligarchs, by tyrant Majorities and Minorities, by the hidden suasions of Polls, by profound instincts and shallow juvenilities. And always, the governing force as we wish you now to understand this concept was whatever the individual believed had control over his immediate survival. Survival sets the pattern of imprint. During much of Human history (and the pattern is similar with most sentient species) Corporation presidents held more survival in their casual remarks than did the figurehead officials. We of the ConSentiency cannot forget this as we keep watch on the Multiworld Corporations. We dare not even forget it of ourselves. Where you work for your own survival, this dominates your imprint, this dominates what you believe.

—Instruction Manual
Bureau of Sabotage

Never do what your enemy wants you to do, McKie reminded himself.

In this moment, Aritch was the enemy, having placed the binding oath of Legum upon an agent of BuSab, having demanded information to which he had no right. The old Gowachin's behavior was consistent with the demands of his own legal system, but it immediately magnified the area of conflict by an enormous factor. McKie chose a minimal response.

69

"I'm here because Tandaloor is the heart of the Gowachin Federation."

Aritch, who'd been sitting with his eyes closed to emphasize the formal client-Legum relationship, opened his eyes to glare at McKie.

"I remind you *once* that I am your client."

Signs indicating a dangerous new tension in the Wreave servant were increasing, but McKie was forced to concentrate his attention on Aritch.

"You name your *self* client. Very well. The client must answer truthfully such questions as the Legum asks when the legal issues demand it."

Aritch continued to glare at McKie, latent fire in the yellow eyes. Now, the battle was truly joined.

McKie sensed how fragile was the relationship upon which his survival depended. The Gowachin, signatories to the great ConSentiency Pact binding the species of the known universe, were legally subject to certain BuSab intrusions. But Aritch had placed them on another footing. If the Gowachin Federation disagreed with McKie/Agent, they could take him into the Courtarena as a Legum who had wronged a client. With the entire Gowachin Bar arrayed against him, McKie did not doubt which Legum would *taste the knife.* His one hope lay in avoiding immediate litigation. That was, after all, the real basis of Gowachin Law.

Moving a step closer to specifics, McKie said:

"My Bureau has uncovered a matter of embarrassment to the Gowachin Federation."

Aritch blinked twice.

"As we suspected."

McKie shook his head. They didn't *suspect,* they knew. He counted on this: that the Gowachin understood why he'd answered their summons. If any Sentiency under the Pact could understand his position, it had to be the Gowachin. BuSab reflected Gowachin philosophy. Centuries had passed since the great convulsion out of which BuSab had originated, but the ConSentiency had never been allowed to forget that birth. It was taught to the young of every species.

"Once, long ago, a tyrannical majority captured the government. They said they would make all individuals equal. They meant they would not let any individual be better than another at doing anything. Excellence was to be suppressed or concealed. The tyrants made their government act with great speed 'in the name of the people.' They removed delays and red tape wherever found. There was little deliberation. Unaware that they acted out of an unconscious compulsion to prevent all change, the tryants tried to enforce a grey sameness upon every population.

"Thus the powerful governmental machine blundered along at increasingly reckless speed. It took commerce and all the important elements of society with it. Laws were thought of and passed within hours. Every society came to be twisted into a suicidal pattern. People became unprepared for those changes which the universe demands. They were unable to change.

"It was the time of *brittle money,* 'appropriated in the morning and gone by nightfall,' as you learned earlier. In their passion for sameness, the tyrants made themselves more and more powerful. All others grew correspondingly weaker and weaker. New bureaus and directorates, odd ministries, leaped into existence for the most improbable purposes. These became the citadels of a new aristocracy, rulers who kept the giant wheel of government careening along, spreading destruction, violence, and chaos wherever they touched.

"In those desperate times, a handful of people (the Five Ears, their makeup and species never revealed) created the Sabotage Corps to slow that runaway wheel of government. The original corps was bloody, violent, and cruel. Gradually, the original efforts were replaced by more subtle methods. The governmental wheel slowed, became more manageable. Deliberation returned.

"Over the generations, that original Corps became a Bureau, the Bureau of Sabotage, with its present Ministerial powers, preferring diversion to violence, but ready for violence when the need arises."

They were words from McKie's own teens, generators of a concept modified by his experiences in the Bureau. Now, he was aware that this directorate composed of all the known sentient species was headed into its own entropic corridors. Someday, the Bureau would dissolve or be dissolved, but the universe still needed them. The old imprints remained, the old futile seeking after absolutes of sameness. It was the ancient conflict between what the individual saw as personal needs for immediate survival and what the totality required if *any* were to survive. And now it was the Gowachin versus the ConSentiency, and Aritch was the champion of his people.

McKie studied the High Magister carefully, sensitive to the unrelieved tensions in the Wreave attendant. Would there be violence in this room? It was a question which remained unanswered as McKie spoke.

"You have observed that I am in a difficult position. I do not enjoy the embarrassment of revered teachers and friends, nor of their compatriots. Yet, evidence has been seen . . ."

He let his voice trail off. Gowachin disliked dangling implications.

Aritch's claws slid from the sheaths of his webbed fingers.

"Your client wishes to hear of this evidence."

Before speaking, McKie rested his hand on the latch of the box in his lap.

"Many people from two species have disappeared. Two species: Gowachin and Human. Singly, these were small matters, but these disappearances have been going on for a long time—perhaps twelve or fifteen generations by the old Human reckoning. Taken together, these disappearances are massive. We've learned that there's a planet called Dosadi where these people were taken. Such evidence as we have has been examined carefully. It all leads to the Gowachin Federation."

Aritch's fingers splayed, a sign of acute embarrassment. Whether assumed or real, McKie could not tell.

"Does your Bureau accuse the Gowachin?"

"You know the function of my Bureau. We do not yet know the location of Dosadi, but we'll find it."

Aritch remained silent. He knew BuSab had never given up on a problem.

McKie raised the blue box.

"Having thrust this upon me, you've made me guardian of your fate, client. You've no rights to inquire as to my methods. I will not follow *old* law."

Aritch nodded.

"It was my argument that you'd react thus."

He raised his right hand.

The rhythmic "death flexion" swept over the Wreave and her fighting mandibles darted from her facial slit.

At the first movement from her, McKie whipped open the blue box, snatched out book and knife. He spoke with a firmness his body did not feel:

"If she makes the slightest move toward me, my blood will defile this book." He placed the knife against his own wrist. "Does your Servant of the Box know the consequences? The history of the Running Phylum would end. Another Phylum would be presumed to've accepted the Law from its Giver. The name of this Phylum's *last* High Magister would be erased from living thought. Gowachin would eat their own eggs at the merest hint that they had Running Phylum blood in their veins."

Aritch remained frozen, right hand raised. Then:

"McKie, you are revealed as a sneak. Only by spying on our most sacred rituals could you know this."

"Did you think me some fearful, pliable dolt, client? I am a true Legum. A Legum does not have to sneak to learn the Law. When you admitted me to your Bar you opened every door."

Slowly, muscles quivering, Aritch turned and spoke to the Wreave:

"Ceylang?"

She had difficulty speaking while her poison-tipped fighting mandibles remained extruded.

"Your command?"

"Observe this Human well. Study him. You will meet again."

"I obey."

"You may go, but remember my words."

"I remember."

McKie, knowing the death dance could not remain uncompleted, stopped her.

"Ceylang!"

Slowly, reluctantly, she looked at him.

" *Do* observe me well, Ceylang. I am what you hope to be. And I warn you: unless you shed your Wreave skin you will never be a Legum." He nodded in dismissal. "Now, you may go."

In a fluid swish of robes she obeyed, but her fighting mandibles remained out, their poison tips glittering. Somewhere in her triad's quarters, McKie knew, there'd be a small feathered pet which would die presently with poison from its mistress burning through its veins. Then the death dance would be ended and she could retract her mandibles. But the hate would remain.

When the door had closed behind the red robe, McKie restored book and knife to the box, returned his attention to Aritch. Now, when McKie spoke, it was really Legum to client without any sophistry, and they both knew it.

"What would tempt the High Magister of the renowned Running Phylum to bring down the Arch of Civilization?"

McKie's tone was conversational, between equals.

Aritch had trouble adjusting to the new status. His thoughts were obvious. If McKie had witnessed a Cleansing Ritual, McKie had to be accepted as a Gowachin. But McKie was *not* Gowachin. Yet he'd been accepted before the Gowachin Bar . . . and if he'd seen that most sacred ritual . . .

Presently, Aritch spoke.

"Where did you see the ritual?"

"It was performed by the Phylum which sheltered me on Tandaloor."

"The Dry Heads?"

"Yes."

"Did they know you witnessed?"

"They invited me."

"How did you shed your skin?"

"They scraped me raw and preserved the scrapings."

Aritch took some time digesting this. The Dry Heads had played their own secret game of Gowachin politics and now the secret was out. He had to consider the implications. What had they hoped to gain? He said:

"You wear no tatoo."

"I've never made formal application for Dry Heads membership."

"Why?"

"My primary allegiance is to BuSab."

"The Dry Heads know this?"

"They encourage it."

"But what motivated them to . . ."

McKie smiled.

Aritch glanced at a veiled alcove at the far end of the sanctum, back to McKie. A likeness to the Frog God?

"It'd take more than that."

McKie shrugged.

Aritch mused aloud:

"The Dry Heads supported Klodik in his crime when you . . ."

"Not crime."

"I stand corrected. You won Klodik's freedom. And after your victory the Dry Heads invited you to the Cleansing Ritual."

"A Gowachin in BuSab cannot have divided allegiance."

"But a Legum serves only the Law!"

"BuSab and Gowachin Law are not in conflict."

"So the Dry Heads would have us believe."

"Many Gowachin believe it."

"But Klodik's case was not a true test."

Realization swept through McKie: Aritch regretted more than a lost bet. He'd put his money with his hopes. It was time then to redirect this conversation.

"I am your Legum."

Aritch spoke with resignation.

"You are."

"Your Legum wishes to hear of the Dosadi problem."

"A thing is not a problem until it arouses sufficient concern." Aritch glanced at the box in McKie's lap. "We're dealing with differences in values, changes in values."

McKie did not believe for an instant this was the tenor of Gowachin defense, but Aritch's words gave him pause. The Gowachin combined such an odd mixture of respect and disrepect for their Law and all government. At the root lay their unchanging rituals, but above that everything remained as fluid as the seas in which they'd evolved. Constant fluidity was the purpose behind their rituals. You never entered any exchange with Gowachin on a sure-footed basis. They did something different every time . . . religiously. It was their nature. *All ground is temporary. Law is made to be changed.* That was their catechism. *To be a Legum is to learn where to place your feet.*

"The Dry Heads did something different," McKie said.

This plunged Aritch into gloom. His chest ventricles wheezed, indicating he'd speak *from the stomach.*

"The people of the ConSentiency come in so many different forms: Wreaves (a flickering glance doorward), Sobarips, Laclacs, Calebans, PanSpechi, Palenki, Chithers, Taprisiots, Humans, we of the Gowachin . . . so many. The unknowns between us defy counting."

"As well count the drops of water in a sea."

Aritch grunted, then:

"Some diseases cross the barriers between species."

McKie stared at him. Was Dosadi a medical experiment station? Impossible! There would be no reason for secrecy then. Secrecy defeated the efforts to study a common problem and the Gowachin knew it.

"You are not studying Gowachin-Human diseases."

"Some diseases attack the psyche and cannot be traced to any physical agent."

McKie absorbed this. Although Gowachin definitions were difficult to understand, they permitted no aberrant behavior. Different behavior, yes; aberrant behavior, no. You could challenge the Law, not the ritual. They were compulsive in this regard. They slew the ritual deviant out of hand. It required enormous restraint on their part to deal with another species.

Aritch continued:

"Terrifying psychological abrasions occur when divergent species confront each other and are forced to adapt to new ways. We seek new knowledge in this arena of behavior."

McKie nodded.

One of his Dry Head teachers had said it: "No matter how painful, life must adapt or die."

It was a profound revelation about how Gowachin applied their insight to themselves. Law changed, but it changed on a foundation which could not be permitted the slighest change. "Else, how do we know where we are or where we have been?" But encounters with other species changed the foundation. Life adapted . . . willingly or by force.

McKie spoke with care.

"Psychological experiments with people who've not given their informed consent are still illegal . . . even among the Gowachin."

Aritch would not accept this argument.

"The ConSentiency in all of its parts has accumulated a long history of scientific studies into behavioral and biomedical questions where people are the final test site."

McKie said:

"And the first issue when you propose such an experiment is 'How great is the known risk to the subjects?'"

"But, my dear Legum, *informed consent* implies that the experimenter knows all the risks and can describe them to his test subjects. I ask you: how can that be when the experiment goes beyond what you already know? How can you describe risks which you cannot anticipate?"

"You submit a proposal to many recognized experts in the field," McKie said. "They weigh the proposed experiment against whatever value the new knowledge is expected to uncover."

"Ahh, yes. We submit our proposal to fellow researchers, to people whose *mission*, whose very view of their own personal identity is controlled by the belief that they can improve the lot of all sentient beings. Tell me, Legum: do review boards composed of such people reject many experimental proposals?"

McKie saw the direction of the argument. He spoke with care.

"They don't reject many proposals, that's true. Still, you didn't submit your Dosadi protocol to any outside review. Was that to keep it secret from your own people or from others?"

"We feared the fate of our proposal should it run the gantlet of other species."

"Did a Gowachin majority approve your project?"

"No. But we both know that having a majority set the experimental guidelines gives no guarantee against dangerous projects."

"Dosadi has proved dangerous?"

Aritch remained silent for several deep breaths, then:

"It has proved dangerous."

"To whom?"

"Everyone."

It was an unexpected answer, adding a new dimension to Aritch's behavior. McKie decided to back up and test the revelation. "This Dosadi project was approved by a minority among the Gowachin, a minority willing to accept a dangerous risk-benefit ratio."

"You have a way of putting these matters, McKie, which presupposes a particular kind of guilt."

"But a majority in the ConSentiency might agree with my description?"

"Should they ever learn of it."

"I see. Then, in accepting a dangerous risk, what were the future benefits you expected?"

Aritch emitted a deep grunt.

"Legum, I assure you that we worked only with volunteers and they were limited to Humans and Gowachin."

"You evade my question."

"I merely defer an answer."

"Then tell me, did you explain to your volunteers that they had a choice, that they could say 'no'? Did you tell them they might be in danger?"

"We did not try to frighten them . . . no."

"Was any one of you concerned about the free destiny of your *volunteers*?"

"Be careful how you judge us, McKie. There is a fundamental tension between science and freedom—no matter how science is viewed by its practitioners nor how freedom is sensed by those who believe they have it."

McKie was reminded of a cynical Gowachin aphorism: *To*

believe that you are free is more important than being free. He said:

"Your volunteers were lured into this project."

"Some would see it that way."

McKie reflected on this. He still did not know precisely what the Gowachin had done on Dosadi, but he was beginning to suspect it'd be something repulsive. He could not keep this fear from his voice.

"We return to the question of expected benefits."

"Legum, we have long admired your species. You gave us one of our most trusted maxims: *No species is to be trusted farther than it is bound by its own interests.*"

"That's no longer sufficient justification for. . ."

"We derive another rule from your maxim: *It is wise to guide your actions in such a way that the interests of other species coincide with the interests of your species.*"

McKie stared at the High Magister. Did this crafty old Gowachin seek a Human-Gowachin conspiracy to suppress evidence of what had been done on Dosadi? Would he dare such a gambit? Just how bad was this Dosadi fiasco?

To test the issue, McKie asked:

"What benefits did you expect? I insist."

Aritch slumped. His chairdog accommodated to the new position. The High Magister favored McKie with a heavy-lidded stare for a long interval, then:

"You play this game better than we'd ever hoped."

"With you, Law and Government are always a game. I come from another arena."

"Your Bureau."

"And I was trained as a Legum."

"Are you *my* Legum?"

"The binding oath is binding on me. Have you no faith in. . ."

McKie broke off, overwhelmed by a sudden insight. Of course! The Gowachin had known for a long time that Dosadi would become a legal issue.

"Faith in what?" Aritch asked.

"Enough of these evasions!" McKie said. "You had your Dosadi problem in mind when you trained me. Now, you act as though you distrust your own plan."

Aritch's lips rippled.

"How strange. You're more Gowachin than a Gowachin."

"What benefits did you expect when you took this risk?"

Aritch's fingers splayed, stretching the webs.

"We hoped for a quick conclusion and benefits to offset the natural animosities we knew would arise. But it's now more than twenty of your generations, not twelve or fifteen, that we've grasped the firebrand. Benefits? Yes, there are some, but we dare not use them or free Dosadi from bondage lest we raise questions which we cannot answer without revealing our. . .source."

"The benefits!" McKie said. "Your *Legum* insists."

Aritch exhaled a shuddering breath through his ventricles.

"Only the Caleban who guards Dosadi knows its location and she is charged to give access without revealing that place. Dosadi is peopled by Humans and Gowachin. They live in a single city they call Chu. Some ninety million people live there, almost equally divided between the two species. Perhaps three times that number live outside Chu, on the Rim, but they're outside the experiment. Chu is approximately eight hundred square kilometers."

The population density shocked McKie. Millions per kilometer. He had difficulty visualizing it. Even allowing for a city's vertical dimension . . . and burrowing . . . There'd be some, of course, whose power bought them space, but the others . . . Gods! Such a city would be crawling with people, no escaping the pressure of your fellows anywhere except on that unexplained Rim. McKie said as much to Aritch.

The High Magister confirmed this.

"The population density is very great in some areas. The people of Dosadi call these areas 'Warrens' for good reason."

"But why? With an entire planet to live on . . ."

"Dosadi is poisonous to our forms of life. All of their food comes from carefully managed hydroponics factories in the heart of Chu. Food factories and the distribution are managed by warlords. Everything is under a quasi-military form of management. But life expectancy in the city is four times that outside."

"You said the population outside the city was much larger than. . ."

"They breed like mad animals."

"What possible benefits could you have expected from . . ."

"Under pressure, life reveals its basic elements."

McKie considered what the High Magister had revealed. The picture of Dosadi was that of a seething mass. Warlords . . . He visualized walls, some people living and working in comparative richness of space while others . . . Gods! It was madness in a universe where some highly habitable planets held no more than a few thousand people. His voice brittle, McKie addressed himself to the High Magister.

"These basic elements, the *benefits* you sought . . . I wish to hear about them."

Aritch hitched himself forward.

"We have discovered new ways of association, new devices of motivation, unsuspected drives which can impose themselves upon an entire population."

"I require specific and explicit enumeration of these discoveries."

"Presently, Legum . . . presently."

Why did Aritch delay? Were the so-called benefits insignificant beside the repulsive horror of such an experiment? McKie ventured another tack.

"You say this planet is poisonous. Why not remove the inhabitants a few at a time, subject them to memory erasure if you must, and feed them out into the ConSentiency as new . . ."

"We dare not! First, the inhabitants have developed an immunity to erasure, a by-product of those poisons which do get into their diet. Second, given what they have become on Dosadi . . . How can I explain this to you?"

"Why don't the people just leave Dosadi? I presume you deny them jumpdoors, but rockets and other mechanical . . ."

"We will not permit them to leave. Our Caleban encloses Dosadi in what she calls a 'tempokinetic barrier' which our test subjects cannot penetrate."

"Why?"

"We will destroy the entire planet and everything on it rather than loose this population upon the ConSentiency."

"What are the people of Dosadi that you'd even contemplate such a thing?"

Aritch shuddered.

"We have created a monster."

Every government is run by liars and nothing they say should be believed.

> —*Attributed to an ancient Human journalist*

As she hurried across the roof of the adjoining parking spire at midafternoon of her final day as a Liaitor, Jedrik couldn't clear her mind of the awareness that she was about to shed another mark of rank. Stacked in the building beneath her, each one suspended by its roof grapples on the conveyor track, were the vehicles of the power merchants and their minions. The machines varied from the giant *jaigers* heavy with armor and weapons and redundant engine systems, of the ruling few, down to the tiny black skitters assigned to such as herself. Ex-minion Jedrik knew she was about to take a final ride in the machine which had released her from the morning and evening crush on the underground walkways.

She had timed her departure with care. The ones who rode in the *jaigers* would not have reassigned her *skitter* and its driver. That driver, Havvy, required her special attentions in this last ride, this narrow time slot which she had set aside for dealing with him.

Jedrik sensed events rushing at their own terrible pace

now. Just that morning she had loosed death against fifty Humans. Now, the avalanche gathered power.

The parking spire's roof pavement had been poorly repaired after the recent explosive destruction of three Rim guerrillas. Her feet adjusted to the rough paving as she hurried across the open area to the drop chute. At the chute, she paused and glanced westward through Chu's enclosing cliffs. The sun, already nearing its late afternoon line on the cliffs, was a golden glow beyond the God Wall's milky barrier. To her newly sensitized fears, that was not a sun but a malignant eye which peered down at her.

By now, the rotofiles in her office would've been ignited by the clumsy intrusion of the LP toads. There'd be a delay while they reported this, while it was bucked up through the hierarchy to a level where somebody dared make an important decision.

Jedrik fought against letting her thoughts fall into trembling shadows. After the rotofiles, other data would accumulate. The Elector's people would grow increasingly suspicious. But that was part of her plan, a layer with many layers.

Abruptly, she stepped into the chute, dropped to her parking level, stared across the catwalks at her *skitter* dangling among the others. Havvy sat on the sloping hood, his shoulders in their characteristic slouch. Good. He behaved as expected. A certain finesse was called for now, but she expected no real trouble from anyone as shallow and transparent as Havvy. Still, she kept her right hand in the pocket where she'd secreted a small but adequate weapon. Nothing could be allowed to stop her now. She had selected and trained lieutenants, but none of them quite matched her capabilities. The military force which had been prepared for this moment needed Jedrik for that extra edge which could pluck victory from the days ahead of them.

For now, I must float like a leaf above the hurricane.

Havvy was reading a book, one of those pseudodeep

things he regularly affected, a book which she knew he would not understand. As he read, he pulled at his lower lip with thumb and forefinger, the very picture of a deep intellectual involvement with important ideas. But it was only a picture. He gave no sign that he heard Jedrik hurrying toward him. A light breeze flicked the pages and he held them with one finger. She could not yet see the title, but assumed this book would be on the contraband list as was much of his reading. That was about the peak of Havvy's risk taking, not great but imbued with a certain false glamor. Another picture.

She could see him quite distinctly now in readable detail. He should have looked up by now but still sat absorbed in his book. Havvy possessed large brown eyes which he obviously believed he employed with deceptive innocence. The real innocence went far beyond his shallow attempts at deception. Jedrik's imagination easily played the scene should one of Broey's people confront Havvy in this pose.

"*A contraband book?*" Havvy would ask, playing his brown eyes for all their worthless innocence. "*I didn't think there were any more of those around. Thought you'd burned them all. Fellow handed it to me on the street when I asked what he was reading.*"

And the Elector's spy would conceal a sneer while asking, "*Didn't you question such a gift?*"

Should it come to that, things would grow progressively stickier for Havvy along the paths he could not anticipate. His *innocent* brown eyes would deceive one of the Elector's people no more than they deceived her. In view of this, she read other messages in the fact that Havvy had produced her key to the god Wall—this Jorj X. McKie. Havvy had come to her with his heavy-handed conspiratorial manner:

"The Rim wants to send in a new agent. We thought you might. . ."

And every datum he'd divulged about this oddity, every question he'd answered with his transparent candor, had increased her tension, surprise, and elation.

Jedrik thought upon these matters as she approached Havvy.

He sensed her presence, looked up. Recognition and something unexpected—a watchfulness half-shielded—came over him. He closed his book.

"You're early."

"As I said I'd be."

This new manner in Havvy set her nerves on edge, raised old doubts. No course remained for her except attack.

"Only toads don't break routine," she said.

Havvy's gaze darted left, right, returned to her face. He hadn't expected this. It was a bit more open risk than Havvy relished. The Elector had spy devices everywhere. Havvy's reaction told her what she wanted to know, however. She gestured to the *skitter*.

"Let's go."

He pocketed his book, slid down, and opened her door. His actions were a bit too brisk. The button tab on one of his green-striped sleeves caught a door handle. He freed himself with an embarrassed flurry.

Jedrik slipped into the passenger harness. Havvy slammed the door a touch too hard. Nervous. Good. He took his place at the power bar to her left, kept his profile to her when he spoke.

"Where?"

"Head for the apartment."

A slight hesitation, then he activated the grapple tracks. The skitter jerked into motion, danced sideways, and slid smoothly down the diveway to the street.

As they emerged from the parking spire's enclosing shadows, even before the grapple released and Havvy activated the skitter's own power, Jedrik firmed her decision not to look back. The Liaitor building had become part of her past, a pile of grey-green stones hemmed by other tall structures with, here and there, gaps to the cliffs and the river's arms.

That part of her life she now excised. Best it were done cleanly. Her mind must be clear for what came next. What came next was war.

It wasn't often that a warrior force lifted itself out of Dosadi's masses to seek its place in the power structure. And the force she had groomed would strike fear into millions. It was the fears of only a few people that concerned her now, though, and the first of these was Havvy.

He drove with his usual competence, not overly proficient but adequate. His knuckles were white on the steering arms, however. It was still the Havvy she knew moving those muscles, not one of the evil identities who could play their tricks in Dosadi flesh. That was Havvy's usefulness to her and his failure. He was Dosadi-flawed, corrupted. That could not be permitted with McKie.

Havvy appeared to have enough good sense to fear her. Jedrik allowed this emotion to ferment in him while she studied the passing scene. There was little traffic and all of that was armored. The occasional tube access with its sense of weapons in the shadows and eyes behind the guard slits—all seemed normal. It was too soon for the hue and cry after an errant Senior Liaitor.

They went through the first walled checkpoint without delay. The guards were efficiently casual, a glance at the skitter and the identification brassards of the occupants. It was all routine.

The danger with routines, she told herself, was that they very soon became boring. Boredom dulled the senses. That was a boredom which she and her aides constantly guarded against among their warriors. This new force on Dosadi would create many shocks.

As Havvy took them up the normal ring route through the walls, the streets became wide, more open. There were garden plantings in the open here, poisonous but beautiful. Leaves were purple in the shadows. Barren dirt beneath the bushes glittered with corrosive droplets, one of Dosadi's little ways of protecting territory. Dosadi taught many things to those willing to learn.

Jedrik turned, studied Havvy, the way he appeared to concentrate on his driving with an air of stored-up energy. That was about as far as Havvy's learning went. He seemed to know some of his own deficiencies, must realize that many wondered how he held a driver's job, even for the middle echelons, when the Warrens were jammed with people violently avaricious for any step upward. Obviously, Havvy carried valuable secrets which he sold on a hidden market. She had to nudge that hidden market now. Her act must appear faintly clumsy, as though events of this day had confused her.

"Can we be overheard?" she asked.

That made no difference to her plans, but it was the kind of clumsiness which Havvy would misinterpret in precisely the way she now required.

"I've disarmed the transceiver the way I did before," he said. "It'll look like a simple breakdown if anyone checks."

To no one but you, she thought.

But it was the level of infantile response she'd come to expect from Havvy. She picked up his gambit, probing with real curiosity.

"You expected that we'd require privacy today?"

He almost shot a startled look at her, caught himself, then:

"Oh, no! It was a precaution. I have more information to sell you."

"But you *gave* me the information about McKie."

"That was to demonstrate my value."

Oh, Havvy! Why do you try?

"You have unexpected qualities," she said, and marked that he did not even detect the first level of her irony. "What's this information you wish to sell?"

"It concerns this McKie."

"Indeed?"

"What's it worth to you?"

"Am I your only market, Havvy?"

His shoulder muscles bunched as his grip grew even tighter on the steering arms. The tensions in his voice were remarkably easy to read.

"Sold in the right place my information could guarantee maybe five years of easy living—no worries about food or good housing or anything."

"Why aren't you selling it in such a place?"

"I didn't say I *could* sell it. There are buyers and then there are buyers."

"And then there are the ones who just take?"

There was no need for him to answer and it was just as well. A barrier dropped in front of the skitter, forcing Havvy to a quick stop. For just an instant, fear gripped her and she felt her reflexes prevent any bodily betrayal of the emotion. Then she saw that it was a routine stop while repair supplies were trundled across the roadway ahead of them.

Jedrik peered out the window on her right. The interminable repair and strengthening of the city's fortifications was going on at the next lower level. Memory told her this was the eighth layer of city protection on the southwest. The noise of pounding rock hammers filled the street. Grey dust lay everywhere, clouds of it drifting. She smelled burnt flint and that bitter metallic undertone which you never quite escaped anywhere in Chu, the smell of the poison death which Dosadi ladled out to its inhabitants. She closed her mouth and took shallow breaths, noted absently that the labor crew was all Warren, all Human, and about a third of them women. None of the women appeared older than fifteen. They already had that hard alertness about the eyes which the Warren-born never lost.

A young male strawboss went by trailing a male assistant, an older man with bent shoulders and straggly grey hair. The older man walked with slow deliberation and the young strawboss seemed impatient with him, waving the assistant to keep up. The important subtleties of the relationship thus

revealed were entirely lost on Havvy, she noted. The strawboss, as he passed one of the female laborers, looked her up
and down with interest. The worker noted his attention and
exerted herself with the hammer. The strawboss said something to his assistant, who went over and spoke to the young
female. She smiled and glanced at the strawboss, nodded.
The strawboss and assistant walked on without looking back.
The obvious arrangement for later assignation would have
gone without Jedrik's conscious notice except that the young
female strongly resembled a woman she'd once known . . .
dead now as were so many of her early companions.

A bell began to ring and the barrier lifted.

Havvy drove on, glancing once at the strawboss as they
passed him. The glance was not returned, telling Jedrik that
the strawboss had assessed the skitter's occupants much earlier.

Jedrik picked up the conversation with Havvy where
they'd left it.

"What makes you think you could get more from me than
from someone else?"

"Not more . . . It's just that there's less risk with you."

The truth was in his voice, that innocent instrument which
told so much about Havvy. She shook her head.

"You want me to take the risk of selling higher up?"

After a long pause, Havvy said:

"You know a safer way for me to operate?"

"I'd have to use you somewhere along the line for verifica-
tion."

"But I'd be under your protection then."

"Why should I protect you when you're no longer of value?"

"What makes you think this is all the information I can
get?"

Jedrik allowed herself a sigh, wondered why she continued
this empty game.

"We might both run into a taker, Havvy."

Havvy didn't respond. Surely, he'd considered this in his foolish game plan.

They passed a squat brown building on the left. Their street curved upward around the building and passed through a teeming square at the next higher level. Between two taller buildings on the right, she glimpsed a stretch of a river channel, then it was more buildings which enclosed them like the cliffs of Chu, growing taller as the skitter climbed.

As she'd known, Havvy couldn't endure her silence.

"What're you going to do?" he asked.

"I'll pay one year of such protection as I can offer."

"But this is . . ."

"Take it or leave it."

He heard the finality but, being Havvy, couldn't give up. It was his one redeeming feature.

"Couldn't we even discuss a . . ."

"We won't discuss anything! If you won't sell at my price, then perhaps I should become a taker."

"That's not like you!"

"How little you know. I can buy informants of your caliber far cheaper."

"You're a hard person."

Out of compassion, she ventured a tiny lesson. "That's how to survive. But I think we should forget this now. Your information is probably something I already know, or something useless."

"It's worth a lot more than you offered."

"So you say, but I know you, Havvy. You're not one to take big risks. Little risks sometimes, big risks never. Your information couldn't be of any great value to me."

"If you only knew."

"I'm no longer interested, Havvy."

"Oh, that's great! You bargain with me and then pull out after I've. . ."

"I was *not* bargaining!" Wasn't the fool capable of anything?

"But you . . ."

"Havvy! Hear me with care. You're a little tad who's stumbled onto something you believe is important. It's actually nothing of great importance, but it's big enough to frighten you. You can't think of a way to sell this information without putting your neck in peril. That's why you came to me. You presume to have me act as your agent. You presume too much."

Anger closed his mind to any value in her words.

"I take risks!"

She didn't even try to keep amusement from her voice. "Yes, Havvy, but never where you think. So here's a risk for you right out in the open. Tell me your valuable information. No strings. Let me judge. If I think it's worth more than I've already offered I'll pay more. If I already have this information or it's otherwise useless, you get nothing."

"The advantage is all on your side!"

"Where it belongs."

Jedrik studied Havvy's shoulders, the set of his head, the rippling of muscles under stretched fabric as he drove. He was supposed to be pure Labor Pool and didn't even know that silence was the guardian of the LP: *Learning silence, you learn what to hear.* The LP seldom volunteered anything. And here was Havvy, so far from that and other LP traditions that he might never have experienced the Warren. *Had* never experienced it until he was too old to learn. Yet he talked of friends on the Rim, acted as though he had his own conspiratorial cell. He held a job for which he was barely competent. And everything he did revealed his belief that all of these things would not tell someone of Jedrik's caliber the essential facts about him.

Unless his were a marvelously practiced act.

She did not believe such a marvel, but there was a cautionary element in recognizing the remote possibility. This and the obvious flaws in Havvy had kept her from using him as a key to the God Wall.

They were passing the Elector's headquarters now. She turned and glanced at the stone escarpment. Her thoughts were a thorn thicket. Every assumption she made about Havvy required a peculiar protective reflex. A non-Dosadi reflex. She noted workers streaming down the steps toward the tube entrance of the Elector's building. Her problem with Havvy carried an odd similarity to the problem she knew Broey would encounter when it came to deciding about an ex-Liaitor named Keila Jedrik. She had studied Broey's decisions with a concentrated precision which had tested the limits of her abilities. Doing this, she had changed basic things about herself, had become oddly non-Dosadi. They would no longer find Keila Jedrik in the DemoPol. No more than they'd find Havvy or this McKie there. But if she could do this . . .

Pedestrian traffic in this region of extreme caution had slowed Havvy to a crawl. More of the Elector's workers were coming up from the Tube Gate One exit, a throng of them as though released on urgent business. She wondered if any of her fifty flowed in that throng.

I must not allow my thoughts to wander.

To float like an *aware* leaf was one thing, but she dared not let herself enter the hurricane. . .not yet. She focused once more on the silent, angry Havvy.

"Tell me, Havvy, did you ever kill a person?"

His shoulders stiffened.

"Why do you ask such a question?"

She stared at his profile for an adequate time, obviously reflecting on this same question.

"I presumed you'd answer. I understand now that you will not answer. This is not the first time I've made that mistake."

Again, Havvy missed the lesson.

"Do you ask many people that question?"

"That doesn't concern you now."

She concealed a profound sadness.

Havvy hadn't the wit to read even the most blatant of the surface indicators. He compounded the useless.

"You can't justify such an intrusion into my . . ."

"Be still, little man! Have you learned nothing? Death is often the only means of evoking an appropriate answer."

Havvy saw this only as an utterly unscrupulous response as she'd known he would. When he shot a probing stare at her, she lifted an eyebrow in a cynical shrug. Havvy continued to divide his attention between the street and her face, apprehensive, fearful. His driving degenerated, became actively dangerous.

"Watch what you're doing, you fool!"

He turned more of his attention to the street, presuming this the greater danger.

The next time he glanced at her, she smiled, knowing Havvy would be unable to detect any lethal change in this gesture. He already wondered if she would attack, but guessed she wouldn't do it while he was driving. He doubted, though, and his doubts made him even more transparent. Havvy was no marvel. One thing certain about him: he came from beyond the God Wall, from the lands of "X," from the place of McKie. Whether he worked for the Elector was immaterial. In fact, it grew increasingly doubtful that Broey would employ such a dangerous, a *flawed* tool. No pretense at foolhardy ignorance of Dosadi's basic survival lessons could be this perfect. The pretender would not survive. Only the truly ignorant could have survived to Havvy's age, allowed to go on living as a curiosity, a possible source of interesting data . . . *interesting* data, not necessarily useful.

Having left resolution of the Havvy Problem to the ultimate moment, wringing every last bit of usefulness from him, she knew her course clearly. Whoever protected Havvy, her questions placed the precisely modulated pressure upon them and left her options open.

"What is your valued information?" she asked.

Sensing now that he bought life with every response, Havvy pulled the skitter to the curb at a windowless building wall, stopped, and stared at her.

She waited.

"McKie . . ." He swallowed. "McKie comes from beyond the God Wall."

She allowed laughter to convulse her and it went deeper than she'd anticipated. For an instant, she was helpless with it and this sobered her. Not even Havvy could be permitted such an advantage.

Havvy was angry.

"What's funny?"

"You are. Did you imagine for even a second that I wouldn't recognize someone alien to Dosadi? Little man, how *have* you survived?"

This time, he read her correctly. It threw him back on his only remaining resource and it even answered her question.

"Don't underestimate my value."

Yes, of course: the unknown value of "X." And there was a latent threat in his tone which she'd never heard there before. Could Havvy call on protectors from beyond the God Wall? That didn't seem possible, given his circumstances, but it had to be considered. It wouldn't do to approach her larger problem from a narrow viewpoint. People who could enclose an entire planet in an impenetrable barrier would have other capabilities she had not even imagined. Some of these creatures came and went at will, as though Dosadi were merely a casual stopping point. And the travelers from "X" could change their bodies; that was the single terrible fact which must never be forgotten; that was what had led her ancestors to breed for a Keila Jedrik.

Such considerations always left her feeling almost helpless, shaken by the ultimate unknowns which lay in her path. Was Havvy still Havvy? Her trusted senses answered: yes. Havvy was a spy, a diversion, an amusement. And he was something else which she could not fathom. It was maddening. She could read every nuance of his reactions, yet questions remained. How could you ever understand these creatures from beyond the Veil of Heaven? They were transparent to Dosadi eyes, but that transparency itself confused one.

On the other hand, how could the people of "X" hope to understand (and thus anticipate) a Keila Jedrik? Every evidence of her senses told her that Havvy saw only a surface Jedrik which she wanted him to see. His spying eyes reported what she wanted them to report. But the enormous interests at stake here dictated a brand of caution beyond anything she'd ever before attempted. The fact that she saw this arena of explosive repercussions, however, armed her with grim satisfaction. The idea that a Dosadi *puppet* might rebel against "X" and fully understand the nature of such rebellion, surely that idea lay beyond their capabilities. They were overconfident while she was filled with wariness. She saw no way of hiding her movements from the people beyond the God Wall as she hid from her fellow Dosadis. "X" had ways of spying that no one completely evaded. They would know about the two Keila Jedriks. She counted on only one thing: that they could not see her deepest thoughts, that they'd read only that surface which she revealed to them.

Jedrik maintained a steady gaze at Havvy while these considerations flowed through her mind. Not by the slightest act did she betray what went on in her mind. That, after all, was Dosadi's greatest gift to its survivors.

"Your information is valueless," she said.

He was accusatory. "You already knew!"

What did he hope to catch with such a gambit? Not for the first time, she asked herself whether Havvy might represent the best that "X" could produce? Would they knowingly send their dolts here? It hardly seemed possible. But how could Havvy's childish incompetence command such tools of power as the God Wall implied? Were the people of "X" the decadent descendants of greater beings?

Even though his own survival demanded it, Havvy would not remain silent.

"If you didn't already know about McKie . . . then you . . . you don't believe me!"

This was too much. Even for Havvy it was too much and she told herself: *despite the unknown powers of "X," he will have to die. He muddies the water. Such incompetence cannot be permitted to breed.*

It would have to be done without passion, not like a Gowachin male weeding his own tads, but with a kind of clinical decisiveness which "X" could not misunderstand.

For now, she had arranged that Havvy take her to a particular place. He still had a role to perform. Later, with discreet attention to the necessary misdirections, she would do what had to be done. Then the next part of her plan could be assayed.

All persons act from beliefs they are conditioned not to question, from a set of deeply seated prejudices. Therefore, whoever presumes to judge must be asked: "How are you affronted?" And this judge must begin there to question inwardly as well as outwardly.

> —*"The Question"*
> *from Ritual of the Courtarena*
> *Guide to Servants of the Box*

"One might suspect you of trying to speak under water," McKie accused.

He still sat opposite Aritch in the High Magister's sanctus, and this near-insult was only one indicator marking the changed atmosphere between them. The sun had dropped closer to the horizon and its *spiritual ring* no longer outlined Aritch's head. The two of them were being more direct now, if not more candid, having explored individual capacities and found where profitable discourse might be directed.

The High Magister flexed his thigh tendons.

Knowing these people from long and close observation, McKie realized the old Gowachin was in pain from prolonged inactivity. That was an advantage to be exploited. McKie held up his left hand, enumerated on his fingers:

"You say the original volunteers on Dosadi submitted to memory erasure, but many of their descendants are immune to such erasure. The present population knows nothing about our ConSentient Universe."

"As far as the present Dosadi population comprehends,

99

they are the only people on the only inhabited planet in existence."

McKie found this hard to believe. He held up a third finger.

Aritch stared with distaste at the displayed hand. *There were no webs between the alien fingers!*

McKie said, "And you tell me that a DemoPol backed up by certain religious injunctions is the primary tool of government there?"

"An original condition of our experiment," Aritch said.

It was not a comprehensive answer, McKie observed. Original conditions invariably changed. McKie decided to come back to this after the High Magister had submitted to more muscle pain.

"Do the Dosadi know the nature of the Caleban barrier which encloses them?"

"They've tried rocket probes, primitive electromagnetic projections. They understand that those energies they can produce will not penetrate their 'God Wall.'"

"Is that what they call the barrier?"

"That or 'The Heavenly Veil.' To some degree, these labels measure their attitude toward the barrier."

"The DemoPol can serve many governmental forms," McKie said. "What's the basic form of their government?"

Aritch considered this, then:

"The form varies. They've employed some eighty different governmental forms."

Another nonresponsive answer. Aritch did not like to face the fact that their experiment had assumed warlord trappings. McKie thought about the DemoPol. In the hands of adepts and with a population responsive to the software probes by which the computer data was assembled, the DemoPol represented an ultimate tool for manipulation of a populace. The ConSentiency outlawed its use as an assault on individual rights and freedoms. The Gowachin had broken this prohibition, yes, but a more interesting datum was surfacing: Dosadi had employed some eighty different governmental forms without rejecting the DemoPol. That implied frequent changes.

"How often have they changed their form of government?"

"You can divide the numbers as easily as I," Aritch said. His tone was petulant.

McKie nodded. One thing had become quite clear.

"Dosadi's masses know about the DemoPol, but you won't let them remove it!"

Aritch had not expected this insight. He responded with revealing sharpness which was amplified by his muscle pains.

"How did you learn that?"

"You told me."

"I?"

"Quite plainly. Such frequent change is responsive to an irritant—the DemoPol. They change the forms of government, but leave the irritant. Obviously, they cannot remove the irritant. That was clearly part of your experiment—to raise a population resistant to the DemoPol."

"A resistant population, yes," Aritch said. He shuddered.

"You've fractured ConSentient Law in many places," McKie said.

"Does my Legum presume to judge me?"

"No. But if I speak with a certain bitterness, please recall that I am a Human. I embrace a profound sympathy for the Gowachin, but I remain Human."

"Ahhhh, yes. We must not forget the long Human association with DemoPols."

"We survive by selecting the best decision makers," McKie said.

"And a DemoPol elevates mediocrity."

"Has that happened on Dosadi?"

"No."

"But you wanted them to try many different governmental forms?"

The High Magister shrugged, remained silent.

"We Humans found that the DemoPol does profound damage to social relationships. It destroys preselected portions of a society."

"And what could we hope to learn by *damaging* our Dosadi society?"

"Have we arrived back at the question of expected benefits?"

Aritch stretched his aching muscles.

"You are persistent, McKie. I will say that."

McKie shook his head sadly.

"The DemoPol was always held up to us as the ultimate equalizer, a source of decision-making miracles. It was supposed to produce a growing body of knowledge about what a society really needed. It was thought to produce justice in all cases despite any odds."

Aritch was irritated. He leaned forward, wincing at the pain of his old muscles.

"One might make the same accusations about the *Law* as practiced everywhere except on Gowachin worlds!"

McKie suppressed a sharp response. Gowachin training had forced him to question assumptions about the uses of law in the ConSentiency, about the inherent rightness of any aristocracy, any power bloc whether majority or minority. It was a BuSab axiom that all power blocs tended toward aristocratic forms, that the descendants of decision makers dominated the power niches. BuSab never employed offspring of their agents.

Aritch repeated himself, a thing Gowachin seldom did.

"Law is delusion and fakery, McKie, everywhere except on the Gowachin worlds! You give your law a theological aura. You ignore the ways it injures your societies. Just as with the

DemoPol, you hold up your law as the unvarying source of justice. When you . . . "

"BuSab has . . . "

"No! If something's wrong in your societies, what do you do? You create new law. You never think to remove law or disarm the law. You make more law! You create more legal professionals. We Gowachin sneer at you! We always strive to reduce the number of laws, the number of Legums. A Legum's first duty is to avoid litigation. When we create new Legums, we always have specific problems in mind. We anticipate the ways that laws damage our society."

It was the opening McKie wanted.

"Why are you training a Wreave?"

Belatedly, Aritch realized he had been goaded into revealing more than he had wanted.

"You are good, McKie. Very good."

"Why?" McKie persisted. "Why a Wreave?"

"You will learn why in time."

McKie saw that Aritch would not expand on this answer, but there were other matters to consider now. It was clear that the Gowachin had trained him for a specific problem: Dosadi. To train a Wreave as Legum, they'd have an equally important problem in mind . . . perhaps the same problem. A basic difference in the approach to law, species differentiated, had surfaced, however, and this could not be ignored. McKie well understood the Gowachin disdain for all legal systems, including their own. They were educated from infancy to distrust any community of professionals, especially legal professionals. A Legum could only tread their religious path when he completely shared that distrust.

Do I share that distrust?

He thought he did. It came naturally to a BuSab agent. But most of the ConSentiency still held its professional communities in high esteem, ignoring the nature of the intense competition for new achievements which invariably overcame such communities: *new* achievements, *new* recognition. But the *new* could be illusion in such communities because they always maintained a peer review system nicely balanced with peer pressures for ego rewards.

"Professional always means power," the Gowachin said.

The Gowachin distrusted power in all of its forms. They gave with one hand and took with the other. Legums faced death whenever they used the Law. To make *new* law in the Gowachin Courtarena was to bring about the elegant dissolution of old law with a concomitant application of justice.

Not for the first time, McKie wondered about the unknown problems a High Magister must face. It would have to be a delicate existence indeed. McKie almost formed a question about this, thought better of it. He shifted instead to the unknowns about Dosadi. *God Wall? Heavenly Veil?*

"Does Dosadi often accept a religious oligarchy?"

"As an outward form, yes. They currently are presided over by a supreme Elector, a Gowachin by the name of Broey."

"Have Humans ever held power equal to Broey's?"

"Frequently."

It was one of the most responsive exchanges that McKie had achieved with Aritch. Although he knew he was following the High Magister's purpose, McKie decided to explore this.

"Tell me about Dosadi's *social* forms."

"They are the forms of a military organization under constant attack or threat of attack. They form certain cabals, certain power enclaves whose influences shift."

"Is there much violence?"

"It is a world of constant violence."

McKie absorbed this. Warlords. Military society. He knew he had just lifted a corner of the real issue which had brought the Gowachin to the point of obliterating Dosadi. It was an area to be approached with extreme caution. McKie chose a flanking approach.

"Aside from the military forms, what are the dominant occupations? How do they perceive guilt and innocence? What are their forms of punishment, of absolution? How do they . . . "

"You do not confuse me, McKie. Consider, Legum: there are better ways to answer such questions."

Brought up short by the Magister's chiding tone, McKie fell into silence. He glanced out the oval window, realizing he'd been thrown onto the defensive with exquisite ease. McKie felt the nerves tingling along his spine. Danger! Tandaloor's golden sun had moved perceptibly closer to the horizon. That horizon was a blue-green line made hazy by kilometer after kilometer of hair trees whose slender female fronds waved and hunted in the air. Presently, McKie turned back to Aritch.

Better ways to answer such questions.

It was obvious where the High Magister's thoughts trended. The experimenters would, of course, have ways of watching their experiment. They could also influence their experiment, but it was obvious there were limits to this influence. A population resistant to outside influences? The implied complications of this Dosadi problem daunted McKie. Oh, the circular dance the Gowachin always performed!

Better ways.

Aritch cleared his ventricle passages with a harsh exhalation, then:

"Anticipating the possibility that others would censure us, we gave our test subjects the Primary."

Devils incarnate! The Gowachin set such store on their damned Primary! Of course all people were created unequal and had to find their own level!

McKie knew he had no choice but to plunge into the maelstrom.

"Did you also anticipate that you'd be charged with violating sentient rights on a massive scale?"

Aritch shocked him by a brief puffing of jowls, the Gowachin shrug.

McKie allowed himself a warning smile.

"I remind the High Magister that *he* raised the issue of the Primary."

"Truth is truth."

McKie shook his head sharply, not caring what this revealed. The High Magister couldn't possibly have that low an estimation of his Legum's reasoning abilities. *Truth indeed!*

"I'll give you truth: the ConSentiency has laws on this subject to which the Gowachin are signatories!"

Even as the words fell from his lips, McKie realized this was precisely where Aritch had wanted him to go. *They've learned something from Dosadi! Something crucial!*

Aritch massaged the painful muscles of his thighs, said, "I remind *you*, Legum, that we peopled Dosadi with volunteers."

"Their descendants volunteered for nothing!"

"Ancestors always volunteer their descendants—for better or for worse. Sentient rights? Informed consent? The ConSentiency has been so busy building law upon law, creating its great illusion of rights, that you've almost lost sight of the Primary's guiding principle: to develop our capacities. People who are never challenged never develop *survival* strengths!"

Despite the perils, McKie knew he had to press for the answer to his original question: *benefits.*

"What've you learned from your monster?"

"You'll soon have a complete answer to that question."

Again, the implication that he could actually watch Dosadi. But first it'd be well to disabuse Aritch of any suspicion that McKie was unaware of the root implications. The issue had to be met head on

"You're not going to implicate me."

"Implicate you?" There was no mistaking Aritch's surprise.

"No matter how you use what you've learned from Dosadi, you'll be suspected of evil intent. Whatever anyone learns from . . . "

"Oh, that. New data gives one power."

"And *you* do not confuse *me*, Aritch. In the history of every species there are many examples of places where new data has been gravely abused."

Aritch accepted this without question. They both knew the background. The Gowachin distrusted power in all of its forms, yet they used power with consummate skill. The trend of McKie's thoughts lay heavily in this room now. To destroy Dosadi would be to hide whatever the Gowachin had learned there. McKie, a non-Gowachin, therefore, would learn these things, would share the mantle of suspicion should it be cast. The historical abuses of new data occurred between the time that a few people learned the important thing and the time when that important thing became general knowledge. To the Gowachin and to BuSab it was the "Data Gap," a source of constant danger.

"We would not try to hide *what* we've learned," Aritch said, "only how we learned it."

"And it's just an academic question whether you destroy an entire planet and every person on it!"

"Ahh, yes: academic. What you don't know, McKie, is that one of our test subjects on Dosadi has initiated, all on her own, a course of events which will destroy Dosadi very quickly whether we act or not. You'll learn all about this very soon when, like the good Legum we know you to be, you go there to experience this monster with your own flesh."

In the name of all that we together hold holy I promise three things to the sacred congregation of people who are subject to my rule. In the first place, that the holy religion which we mutually espouse shall always preserve their freedom under my auspices; secondly, that I will temper every form of rapacity and inequity which may inflict itself upon us all; and thirdly, that I will command swift mercy in all judgments, that to me and to you the gracious Lord may extend His Recognition.

> —The Oath of Power,
> Dosadi Sacred Congregation papers

Broey arose from prayer, groped behind him for the chair, and sank into it. Enclosed darkness surrounded him. The room was a shielded bubble attached to the bottom of his Graluz. Around the room's thick walls was the warm water which protected his females and their eggs. Access to the bubble was through a floor hatch and a twisting flooded passage from the Graluz. Pressure in the bubble excluded the water, but the space around Broey smelled reassuringly of the Graluz. This helped reinforce the mood he now required.

Presently, the God spoke to him. Elation filled Broey. God spoke to him, only to him. Words hissed within his head. Scenes impinged themselves upon his vision centers.

Yes! Yes! I keep the DemoPol!

God was reassured and reflected that reassurance.

Today, God showed him a ritual Broey had never seen before. The ritual was only for Gowachin. The ritual was called Laupuk. Broey saw the ritual in all of its gory details, felt the *rightness* of it as though his very cells accepted it.

Responsibility, expiation—these were the lessons of Laupuk. God approved when Broey expressed understanding.

They communicated by words which Broey expressed silently in his thoughts, but there were other thoughts which God could not perceive. Just as God no doubt held thoughts which were not communicated to Broey. God used people, people used God. Divine intervention with cynical overtones. Broey had learned the Elector's role through a long and painful apprenticeship.

I am your servant, God.

As God admonished, Broey kept the secret of his private communion. It suited his purpose to obey, as it obviously suited God's purpose. There were times, though, when Broey wanted to shout it:

"You fools! I speak with the voice of God!"

Other Electors had made that mistake. They'd soon fallen from the seat of power. Broey, drawing on several lifetimes of assembled experiences, knew he must keep this power if he ever were to escape from Dosadi.

Anyway, the fools did his bidding (and therefore God's) without divine admonition. All was well. One presented a selection of thoughts to God . . . being careful always where and when one reviewed private thoughts. There were times when Broey felt God within him when there'd been no prayer, no preparations here in the blackness of this bubble room. God might peer out of Broey's eyes at any time—softly, quietly—examining His world and its works through mortal senses.

"I guard My servant well."

The warmth of reassurance which flowed through Broey then was like the warmth of the Graluz when he'd still been a tad clinging to his mother's back. It was a warmth and sense of safety which Broey tempered with a deep awareness of that other Graluz time: a giant grey-green adult male Gowachin ravening through the water, devouring those tads not swift enough, alert enough to escape.

I was one of the swift.

Memory of that plunging, frantic flight in the Graluz had taught Broey how to behave with God.

In his bubble room's darkness, Broey shuddered. Yes, the ways of God were cruel. Thus armed, a servant of God could be equally cruel, could surmount the fact that he knew what it was to be both Human and Gowachin. He need only be the pure servant of God. This thought he shared.

Beware, McKie. God has told me whence you come. I know your intentions. Hold fast to the narrow path, McKie. You risk my displeasure.

Behavioral engineering in all of its manifestations always degenerates into merciless manipulation. It reduces all (manipulators and manipulated alike) to a deadly "mass effect." The central assumption, that manipulation of individual personalities can achieve uniform behavioral responses, has been exposed as a lie by many species but never with more telling effect than by the Gowachin on Dosadi. Here, they showed us the "Walden Fallacy" in ultimate foolishness, explaining: "Given any species which reproduces by genetic mingling such that every individual is a unique specimen, all attempts to impose a decision matrix based on assumed uniform behavior will prove lethal."

—*The Dosadi Papers,
BuSab reference*

McKie walked through the jumpdoor and, as Aritch's aides had said, found himself on sand at just past Dosadi's midmorning. He looked up, seeking his first real-time view of the God Wall, wanting to share the Dosadi feeling of that enclosure. All he saw was a thin haze, faintly silver, disappointing. The sun circle was more defined than he'd expected and he knew from the holographic reproductions he'd seen that a few of the third-magnitude stars would be filtered out at night. What else he'd expected, McKie could not say, but somehow this milky veil was not it. Too thin, perhaps. It appeared insubstantial, too weak for the power it represented.

The visible sun disk reminded him of another urgent necessity, but he postponed that necessity while he examined his surroundings.

A tall white rock? Yes, there it was on his left.

They'd warned him to wait beside that rock, that he'd be relatively safe there. Under no circumstances was he to wander from this contact point.

"We can tell you about the dangers of Dosadi, but words are not enough. Besides, the place is always developing new threats."

Things he'd learned in the briefing sessions over the past weeks reinforced the warning. The rock, twice as tall as a Human, stood only a few paces away, massive and forbidding. He went over and leaned against it. Sand grated beneath his feet He smelled unfamiliar perfumes and acridities. The sun-warmed surface of the rock gave its energy to his flesh through the thin green coveralls they'd insisted he wear.

McKie longed for his armored clothing and its devices to amplify muscles, but such things were not permitted. Only a reduced version of his toolkit had been allowed and that reluctantly, a compromise. McKie had explained that the contents would be destroyed if anyone other than himself tried to pry into the kit's secrets. Still, they'd warned him never to open the kit in the presence of a Dosadi native.

"The most dangerous thing you can do is to underestimate any of the Dosadi."

McKie, staring around him, saw no Dosadi.

Far off across a dusty landscape dotted with yellow bushes and brown rocks, he identified the hazy spires of Chu rising out of its river canyon. Heat waves dizzied the air above the low scrub, giving the city a magical appearance.

McKie found it difficult to think about Chu in the context of what he'd learned during the crash course the Gowachin had given him. Those magical fluting spires reached heavenward from a muck where "you can buy anything . . . anything at all."

Aritch's aides had sewn a large sum in Dosadi currency into the seams of his clothing but, at the same time, had forced him to digest hair-raising admonitions about "any show of unprotected wealth."

The jumpdoor attendants had recapitulated many of the most urgent warnings, adding:

"You may have a wait of several hours. We're not sure. Just stay close to that rock where you'll be relatively safe. We've made protective arrangements which should work. Don't eat or drink anything until you get into the city. You'll be faintly sick with the diet change for a few days, but your body should adjust."

"*Should* adjust?"

"Give it time."

He'd asked about specific dangers to which he should be most alert.

"Stay clear of any Dosadi natives except your contacts. Above all, don't even appear to threaten anyone."

"What if I get drowsy and take a nap?

They'd considered this, then:

"You know, that might be the safest thing to do. Anyone who'd dare to nap out there would have to be damned well protected. There'd be some risk, of course, but there always is on Dosadi. But they'd be awfully leery of anyone casual enough to nap out there."

Again, McKie glanced around.

Sharp whistlings and a low rasp like sand across wood came from behind the tall rock. Quietly, McKie worked his way around to where he could see the sources of these noises. The whistling was a yellow lizard almost the color of the bushes beaneath which it crouched. The rasp came from a direction which commanded the lizard's attention. Its source appeared to be a small hole beneath another bush. McKie thought he detected in the lizard only a faint curiosity about himself. Something about that hole and the noise issuing from it demanded a great deal of concentrated attention.

Something stirred in the hole's blackness.

The lizard crouched, continued to whistle.

An ebony creature about the size of McKie's fist emerged from the hole, darted forward, saw the lizard. Wings shot from the newcomer's sides and it leaped upward, but it was too late. With a swiftness which astonished McKie, the lizard

shot forward, balled itself around its prey. A slit opened in
the lizard's stomach, surrounded the ebony creature. With a
final rasping, the black thing vanished into the lizard.

All this time, the lizard continued to whistle. Still whistling
it crawled into the hole from which its prey had come.

"Things are seldom what they seem to be on Dosadi,"
McKie's teachers had said.

He wondered now what he had just seen.

The whistling had stopped.

The lizard and its prey reminded McKie that, as he'd been
warned, there had not been time to prepare him for every
new detail on Dosadi. He crouched now and, once more,
studied his immediate surroundings.

Tiny jumping things like insects inhabited the narrow line
of shade at the base of the white rock. Green (blossoms?)
opened and closed on the stems of the yellow bushes. The
ground all around appeared to be a basic sand and clay, but
when he peered at it closely he saw veins of blue and red
discoloration. He turned his back on the distant city, saw far
away mountains: a purple graph line against silver sky. Rain
had cut an arroyo in that direction. He saw touches of darker
green reaching from the depths. The air tasted bitter.

Once again, McKie made a sweeping study of his surroundings, seeking any sign of threat. Nothing he could
identify. He palmed an instrument from his toolkit, stood
casually and stretched while he turned toward Chu. When he
stole a glance at the instrument, it revealed a sonabarrier at
the city. Absently scratching himself to conceal the motion,
he returned the instrument to his kit. Birds floated in the silver sky above the sonabarrier.

Why a sonabarrier? he wondered.

It would stop wild creatures, but not people. His teachers
had said the sonabarrier excluded pests, vermin. The explanation did not satisfy McKie.

Things are seldom what they seem.

Despite the God Wall, that sun was hot. McKie sought the

shady side of the rock. Seated there, he glanced at the small white disk affixed to the green lapel at his left breast: OP40331-D404. It was standard Galach script, the lingua franca of the ConSentiency.

"They speak only Galach on Dosadi. They may detect an accent in your speech, but they won't question it."

Aritch's people had explained that this badge identified McKie as an open-contract worker, one with slightly above average skills in a particular field, but still part of the Labor Pool and subject to assignment outside his skill.

"This puts you three hierarchical steps from the Rim," they'd said.

It'd been his own choice. The bottom of the social system always had its own communications channels flowing with information based on accurate data, instinct, dream stuff, and what was fed from the top with deliberate intent. Whatever happened here on Dosadi, its nature would be revealed in the unconscious processes of the Labor Pool. In the Labor Pool, he could tap that revealing flow.

"I'll be a weaver," he'd said, explaining that it was a hobby he'd enjoyed for many years.

The choice had amused his teachers. McKie had been unable to penetrate the reason for their amusement.

"It is of no importance right now. One choice is as good as another."

They'd insisted he concentrate on what he'd been doing at the time, learning the signal mannerisms of Dosadi. Indeed, it'd been a hectic period on Tandaloor after Aritch's insistence (with the most reasonable of arguments) that the best way for his Legum to proceed was to go personally to Dosadi. In retrospect, the arguments remained persuasive, but McKie had been surprised. For some reason which he could not now identify, he had expected a less involved *overview* of the experiment, watching through instruments and the spying abilities of the Caleban who guarded the place.

McKie was still not certain how they expected him to pull

this hot palip from the cooker, but it was clear they expected it. Aritch had been mysteriously explicit:

"You are Dosadi's best chance for survival and our own best chance for . . . understanding."

They expected their Legum to save Dosadi while exonerating the Gowachin. It was a Legum's task to win for his client, but these had to be the strangest circumstances, with the client retaining the absolute power of destruction over the threatened planet.

On Tandaloor, McKie had been allowed just time for short naps. Even then, his sleep had been restless, part of his mind infernally aware of where he lay: the bedog strange and not quite attuned to his needs, the odd noises beyond the walls—water gurgling somewhere, always water.

When he'd trained there as a Legum, that had been one of his first adjustments: the uncertain rhythms of disturbed water. Gowachin never strayed far from water. The Graluz—that central pool and sanctuary for females, the place where Gowachin raised those tads which survived the ravenous *weeding* by the male parent—the Graluz always remained a central fixation for the Gowachin. As the saying put it:

"If you do not understand the Graluz, you do not understand the Gowachin."

As such sayings went, it was accurate only up to a point.

But there was always the water, contained water, the nervous slapping of wavelets against walls. The sound conveyed no fixed rhythms, but it was a profound clue to the Gowachin: contained, yet always different.

For all short distances, swimming tubes connected Gowachin facilities. They traversed long distances by jumpdoor or in hissing jetcars which moved on magnetic cushions. The comings and goings of such cars had disturbed McKie's sleep during the period of the crash course on Dosadi. Sometimes, desperately tired, his body demanding rest, he would find himself awakened by voices. And the subtle interference of the other sounds—the cars, the waves—made eavesdropping difficult. Awake in the night, McKie would strain for meaning. He felt like a spy listening for vital clues, seeking every nuance in the casual conversations of people beyond his walls. Frustrated, always frustrated, he had retreated into sleep. And when, as happened occasionally, all sound ceased, this brought him to full alert, heart pounding, wondering what had gone wrong.

And the odors! What memories they brought back to him. Graluz musk, the bitter pressing of exotic seeds, permeated every breath. Fern tree pollen intruded with its undertones of citrus. And the caraeli, tiny, froglike pets, invaded your sleep at every dawning with their exquisite belling arias.

During those earlier days of training on Tandaloor, McKie had felt more than a little lost, hemmed in by threatening strangers, constantly aware of the important matters which rode on his success. But things were different after the interview with Aritch. McKie was now a trained, tested, and proven Legum, not to mention a renowned agent of BuSab. Yet there were times when the mood of those earlier days intruded. Such intrusions annoyed him with their implication that he was being maneuvered into peril against his will, that the Gowachin secretly laughed as they prepared him for some ultimate humiliation. They were not above such a jest. Common assessment of Gowachin by non-Gowachin said the Frog God's people were so ultimately civilized they had come full circle into a form of primitive savagery. Look at the way Gowachin males slaughtered their own newborn tads!

Once, during one of the rare naps Aritch's people permitted him, McKie had awakened to sit up and try to shake off that depressing mood of doom. He told himself true things: that the Gowachin flattered him now, deferred to him, treated him with that quasireligious respect which they paid to all Legums. But there was no evading another truth: the Gowachin had groomed him for their Dosadi problem over a long period of time, and they were being less than candid with him about that long process and its intentions.

There were always unfathomed mysteries when dealing with Gowachin.

When he'd tried returning to sleep that time, it was to encounter disturbing dreams of massed sentient flesh (both pink and green) all naked and quite defenseless before the onslaughts of gigantic Gowachin males.

The dream's message was clear. The Gowachin might very well destroy Dosadi in the way (and for similar reasons) that they winnowed their own tads—searching, endlessly searching, for the strongest and most resilient survivors.

The problem they'd dumped in his lap daunted McKie. If the slightest inkling of Dosadi leaked into common awareness without a concurrent justification, the Gowachin Federation would be hounded unmercifully. The Gowachin had clear and sufficient reason to destroy the evidence—or to let the evidence destroy itself.

Justification.

Where was that to be found? In the elusive benefits which had moved the Gowachin to mount this experiment?

Even if he found that justification, Dosadi would be an upheaval in the ConSentiency. It'd be the subject of high drama. More than twenty generations of Humans and Gowachin surfacing without warning! Their lonely history would titillate countless beings. The limits of language would be explored to wring the last drop of emotive essence from this revelation.

No matter how explained, Gowachin motives would come in for uncounted explorations and suspicions.

Why did they *really* do it? What happened to their original volunteers?

People would look backward into their own ancestry— Human and Gowachin alike. "Is that what happened to Un-

cle Elfred?" Gowachin phylum records would be explored.
"Yes! Here are two—gone without record!"

Aritch's people admitted that "a very small minority" had
mounted this project and kept the lid on it. Were they completely sane, this Gowachin cabal?

McKie's short naps were always disturbed by an obsequi-
ous Gowachin bowing over his bedog, begging him to return
at once to the briefing sessions which prepared him for survival on Dosadi.

Those briefing sessions! The implied prejudices hidden in
every one raised more questions than were answered. McKie
tried to retain a reasoned attitude, but irritants constantly as-
sailed him.

Why had the Gowachin of Dosadi taken on Human emotional characteristics? Why were Dosadi's Humans aping Gowachin social compacts? Were the Dosadi truly aware of why
they changed governmental forms so often?

The bland answer to this frequent questions enraged
McKie.

"All will be made clear when you experience Dosadi for
yourself."

He'd finally fallen into a counterirritant patter:

"You don't really know the answer, do you? You're hoping
I'll find out for you!"

Some of the data recitals bored McKie. While listening to a
Gowachin explain what was known about Rim relationships,
he would find himself distracted by people passing in the
multisentient access way outside the briefing area.

Once, Ceylang entered and sat at the side of the room,
watching him with a hungry silence which rubbed McKie's
sensibilities to angry rawness. He'd longed for the blue metal
box then, but once the solemn investment had pulled the
mantle of Legumic protection around him, the box had been
removed to its sacred niche. He'd not see it again unless this

issue entered the Courtarena. Ceylang remained an unanswered question among many. Why did that dangerous Wreave female haunt this room without contributing one thing? He suspected they allowed Ceylang to watch him through remote spy devices. Why did she choose that once to come in person? To let him know he was being observed? It had something to do with whatever had prompted the Gowachin to train a Wreave. They had some future problem which only a Wreave could solve. They were grooming this Wreave as they'd groomed him. Why? What Wreave capabilities attracted the Gowachin? How did this Wreave female differ from other Wreaves? Where were her loyalties? What was the 'Wreave Bet'?

This led McKie into another avenue never sufficiently explored: what Human capabilities had led the Gowachin to him? Dogged persistence? A background in Human law? The essential individualism of the Human?

There were no sure answers to these questions, no more than there were about the Wreave. Her presence continued to fascinate him, however. McKie knew many things about Wreave society not in common awareness outside the Wreave worlds. They were, after all, integral and valued partners in BuSab. In shared tasks, a camaraderie developed which often prompted intimate exchanges of information. Beyond the fact that Wreaves required a breeding triad for reproduction, he knew that Wreaves had never discovered a way to determine in advance which of the Triad would be capable of nursing the offspring. This formed an essential building stone in Wreave society. Periodically, this person from the triad would be exchanged for a like person from another triad. This insured their form of genetic dispersion and, of equal importance, built countless linkages throughout their civilization. With each such linkage went requirements for unquestioning support in times of trouble.

A Wreave in the Bureau had tried to explain this:

"Take, for example, the situation where a Wreave is murdered or, even worse, deprived of essential vanity. The guilty party would be answerable *personally* to millions upon millions of us. Wherever the triad exchange has linked us, we are required to respond intimately to the insult. The closest thing you have to this, as I understand it, is familial responsibility. We have this familial responsibility for vendetta where such affronts occur. You have no idea how difficult it was to release those of us in BuSab from this . . . this bondage, this network of responsibility."

The Gowachin would know this about the Wreaves, McKie thought. Had this characteristic attracted the Gowachin or had they chosen in spite of it, making their decision because of some other Wreave aspect? Would a Wreave Legum continue to share that network of familial responsibility? How could that be? Wreave society could only offend a basic sensibility of the Gowachin. The Frog God's people were even more . . . more *exclusive* and individual than Humans. To the Gowachin, family remained a private thing, walled off from strangers in an isolation which was abandoned only when you entered your chosen phylum.

As he waited beside the white rock on Dosadi, McKie reflected on these matters, biding his time, listening. The alien heat, the smells and unfamiliar noises, disturbed him. He'd been told to listen for the sound of an internal combustion engine. Internal combustion! But the Dosadi used such devices outside the city because they were more powerful (although much larger) than the beamed impulse drivers which they used within Chu's walls.

"The fuel is alcohol. Most of the raw materials come from the Rim. It doesn't matter how much poison there is in such fuel. They ferment bushes, trees, ferns . . . anything the Rim supplies."

A sleepy quiet surrounded McKie now. For a long time he'd been girding himself to risk the thing he knew he would have to do once he were alone on Dosadi. He might never again be this alone here, probably not once he was into Chu's Warrens. He knew the futility of trying to contact his Taprisiot monitor. Aritch, telling him the Gowachin knew Bu-Sab had bought "Taprisiot insurance," had said:

"Not even a Taprisiot call can penetrate the God Wall."

In the event of Dosadi's destruction, the Caleban contract ended. McKie's Taprisiot might even have an instant to complete the death record of McKie's memories. Might. That was academic to McKie in his present circumstances. The Calebans owed him a debt. The Whipping Star threat had been as deadly to Calebans as to any other species which had ever used jumpdoors. The threat had been real and specific. Users of jumpdoors and the Caleban who controlled those jumpdoors had been doomed. "Fannie Mae" had expressed the debt to McKie in her own peculiar way:

"The owing of me to thee connects to no ending."

Aritch could have alerted his Dosadi guardian against any attempt by McKie to contact another Caleban. McKie doubted this. Aritch had specified a ban against Taprisiot calls. But all Calebans shared an awareness at some level. If Aritch and company had been lulled into a mistaken assumption about the security of their barrier around Dosadi . . .

Carefully, McKie cleared his mind of any thoughts about Taprisiots. This wasn't easy. It required a Sufi concentration upon a particular *void*. There could be no accidental thrust of his mind at the Taprisiot waiting in the safety of Central Central with its endless patience. Everything must be blanked from awareness except a clear projection toward Fannie Mae.

McKie visualized her: the star Thyone. He recalled their long hours of mental give and take. He projected the warmth of emotional attachment, recalling her recent demonstration of "nodal involvement."

Presently, he closed his eyes, amplified that internal image which now suffused his mind. He felt his muscles relax. The warm rock against his back, the sand beneath him, faded from awareness. Only the glowing presence of a Caleban remained in his mind.

"Who calls?"

The words touched his auditory centers, but not his ears.

"It's McKie, friend of Fannie Mae. Are you the Caleban of the God Wall?"

"I am the God Wall. Have you come to worship?"

McKie felt his thoughts stumble. Worship? The projection from this Caleban was echoing and portentous, not at all like the probing curiosity he always sensed in Fannie Mae. He fought to regain that first clear image. The inner glow of a Caleban contact returned. He supposed there might be something worshipful in this experience. You were never absolutely certain of a Caleban's meaning.

"It's McKie, friend of Fannie Mae," he repeated.

The glow within McKie dimmed, then: "But you occupy a point upon Dosadi's wave."

That was a familiar kind of communication, one to which McKie could apply previous experience in the hope of a small understanding, an approximation.

"Does the God Wall permit me to contact Fannie Mae?"

Words echoed in his head:

"One Caleban, all Caleban."

"I wish converse with Fannie Mae."

"You are not satisfied with your present body?"

McKie felt his body then, the trembling flesh, the zombie-like trance state which went with Caleban or Taprisiot contact. The question had no meaning to him, but the body contact was real and it threatened to break off communication. Slowly, McKie fought back to that tenuous mind-presence.

"I am Jorj X. McKie. Calebans are in my debt."

"All Calebans know this debt."

"Then honor your debt."

He waited, trying not to grow tense.

The glow within his head was replaced by a new presence. It insinuated itself into McKie's awareness with penetrating familiarity—not full mental contact, but rather a playing upon those regions of his brain where sight and sound were interpreted. McKie recognized this new presence.

"Fannie Mae!"

"What does McKie require?"

For a Caleban, it was quite a direct communication. McKie, noting this, responded more directly:

"I require your help."

"Explain."

"I may be killed here . . . ahh, have an end to my node here on Dosadi."

"Dosadi's wave," she corrected him.

"Yes. And if that happens, if I die here, . have friends on Central Central . . . on Central Central's wave . . . friends there who must learn everything that's in my mind when I die."

"Only Taprisiot can do this. Dosadi contract forbids Taprisiots."

"But if Dosadi is destroyed . . ."

"Contract promise passes no ending, McKie."

"You cannot help me?"

"You wish advice from Fannie Mae?"

"Yes."

"Fannie Mae able to maintain contact with McKie while he occupies Dosadi's wave."

Constant trance? McKie was shocked.

She caught this.

"No trance. McKie's nexus known to Fannie Mae."

"I think not. I can't have any distractions here."

"Bad choice."

She was petulant.

"Could you provide me with a personal jumpdoor to . . . "

"Not with node ending close to ending for Dosadi wave."

"Fannie Mae, do you know what the Gowachin are doing here on Dosadi? This . . ."

"Caleban contract, McKie."

Her displeasure was clear. You didn't question the honor of a Caleban's word-writ. The Dosadi contract undoubtedly contained specific prohibitions against any revelations of what went on here. McKie was dismayed. He was tempted to leave Dosadi immediately.

Fannie Mae got this message, too.

"McKie can leave now. Soon, McKie cannot leave in his own body/node."

"Body/node?"

"Answer not permitted."

Not permitted!

"I thought you were my friend, Fannie Mae!"

Warmth suffused him.

"Fannie Mae possesses friendship for McKie."

"Then why won't you help me?"

"You wish to leave Dosadi's wave in this instant?"

"No!"

"Then Fannie Mae cannot help."

Angry, McKie began to break the contact.

Fannie Mae projected sensations of frustration and hurt. "Why does McKie refuse advice? Fannie Mae wishes . . ."

"I must go. You know I'm in a trance while we're in contact. That's dangerous here. We'll speak another time. I appreciate your wish to help and your new clarity, but . . ."

"Not clarity! Very small hole in understanding but Human keeps no more dimension!"

Obvious unhappiness accompanied this response, but she

broke the contact. McKie felt himself awakening, his fingers and toes trembling with cold. Caleban contact had slowed his metabolism to a dangerous low. He opened his eyes.

A strange Gowachin clad in the yellow of an armored vehicle driver stood over him. A tracked machine rumbled and puffed in the background. Blue smoke enveloped it. McKie stared upward in shock.

The Gowachin nodded companionably.

"You are ill?"

We of the Sabotage Bureau remain legalists of a special category. We know that too much law injures a society; it is the same with too little law. One seeks a balance. We are like the balancing force among the Gowachin: without hope of achieving heaven in the society of mortals, we seek the unattainable. Each agent knows his own conscience and why he serves such a master. That is the key to us. We serve a mortal conscience for immortal reasons. We do it without hope of praise or the sureness of success.

—*The early writings of Bildoon, PanSpechi Chief of BuSab*

They moved out onto the streets as soon as the afternoon shadows gloomed the depths of the city, Tria and six carefully chosen companions, all of them young Human males. She'd musked herself to key them up and she led them down dim byways where Broey's spies had been eliminated. All of her troop was armored and armed in the fashion of an ordinary sortie team.

There'd been rioting nearby an hour earlier, not sufficiently disruptive to attract large military attention, but a small Gowachin salient had been eliminated from a Human enclave. A sortie team was the kind of thing this Warren could expect after such a specific species adjustment. Tria and her six companions were not likely to suffer attack. None of the rioters wanted a large-scale mopping up in the area.

A kind of hushed, suspenseful waiting pervaded the streets.

They crossed a wet intersection, green and red ichor in the gutters. The smell of the dampness told her that a Graluz had been broached and its waters freed to wash through the streets.

127

That would attract retaliation. Some Human children were certain to be killed in the days ahead. An old pattern.

The troop crossed the riot area presently, noting the places where bodies had fallen, estimating casualties. All bodies had been removed. Not a scrap remained for the birds.

They emerged from the Warrens soon afterward, passing through a Gowachin-guarded gate, Broey's people. A few blocks along they went through another gate, Human guards, all in Gar's pay. Broey would learn of her presence here soon, Tria knew, but she'd said she was going into the Warrens. She came presently to an alleyway across from a Second Rank building. The windowless grey of the building's lower floors presented a blank face broken only by the lattice armor of the entrance gate. Behind the gate lay a dimly lighted passage. Its deceptively plain walls concealed spy devices and automatic weapons.

Holding back her companions with a hand motion, Tria waited in the dark while she studied the building entrance across from her. The gate was on a simple latch. There was one doorguard in an alcove on the left near the door which was dimly visible beyond the armorwork of the gate. A building defense force stood ready to come at the doorguard's summons or at the summons of those who watched through the spy devices.

Tria's informants said this was Jedrik's bolt hole. Not in the deep Warrens at all. Clever. But Tria had maintained an agent in this building for years, as she kept agents in many buildings. A conventional precaution. Everything depended on timing now. Her agent in the building was poised to eliminate the inner guards at the spy device station. Only the doorguard would remain. Tria waited for the agreed upon moment.

The street around her smelled of sewage: an open reclamation line. Accident? Riot damage? Tria didn't like the feeling of this place. What was Jedrik's game? Were there unknown surprises built into this guarded building? Jedrik must know by now that she was suspected of inciting the riot—and of other matters. But would she feel safe there in her own enclave? People tended to feel safe among their own people. She couldn't have a very large force around her, though. Still, some private plot worked itself through the devious pathways of Jedrik's mind, and Tria had not yet fathomed all of that plot. There were surface indicators enough to risk a confrontation, a parley. It was possible that Jedrik flaunted herself here to attract Tria. The potential in that possibility filled Tria with excitement.

Together, we'd be unbeatable!

Yes, Jedrik fitted the image of a superb agent. With the proper organization around her . . .

Once more, Tria glanced left and right. The streets were appropriately empty. She checked the time. Her moment had come. With hand motions, she sent flankers out left and right and another young male probing straight across the street to the gate. When they were in place, she slipped across with her three remaining companions in a triangular shield ahead.

The doorguard was a Human with grey hair and a pale face which glistened yellow in the dim light of the passage. His lids were heavy with a recent dose of his personal drug, which Tria's agent had supplied.

Tria opened the gate, saw that the guard carried a round dead-man switch in his right hand as expected. His grin was gap toothed as he held the switch toward her. She knew he'd recognized her. Much depended now on her agent's accuracy.

"Do you want to die for the frogs?" Tria asked.

He knew about the rioting, the trouble in the streets. And he was Human, with Human loyalties, but he knew she worked for Broey, a Gowachin. The question was precisely calculated to fill him with indecision. Was she a turncoat? He had his Human loyalties and a fanatic's dependence upon this guard post which kept him out of the depths. And there was his personal addiction. All doorguards were addicted to something, but this one took a drug which dulled his senses and made it difficult for him to correlate several lines of thought. He wasn't supposed to use his drug on duty and this troubled him now. There were so many matters to be judged, and Tria had asked the right question. He didn't want to die for the frogs.

She pointed to the dead-man switch, a question.

"It's only a signal relay," he said. "No bomb in this one."

She remained silent, forcing him to focus on his doubts.

The guard swallowed. "What do you . . ."

"Join us or die."

He peered past her at the others. Things such as this happened frequently in the Warrens, not very often here on the slopes which led up to the heights. The guard was not a one trusted with full knowledge of whom he guarded. He had explicit instructions and a dead-man relay to warn of intruders. Others were charged with making the more subtle distinctions, the real decisions. That was this building's weak point.

"Join who?" he asked.

There was false belligerency in his voice, and she knew she had him then.

"Your own kind."

This locked his drug-dulled mind onto its primary fears. He knew what he was supposed to do: open his hand. That released the alarm device in the dead-man switch. He could do this of his own volition and it was supposed to deter attackers from killing him. A dead man's hand opened anyway. But he'd been fed with suspicions to increase his doubts. The device in his hand might not be a simple signal transmitter. What if it actually were a bomb? He'd had many long hours to wonder about that.

"We'll treat you well," Jedrik said.

She put a companionable arm around his shoulder, letting him get the full effect of her musk while she held out her other hand to show that it carried no weapon. "Demonstrate to my companion here how you pass that to your relief."

One of the young males stepped forward.

The guard showed how it was done, explaining slowly as he passed the device. "It's easy once you get the trick of it."

When her companion had the thing firmly in hand, she raised her arm from the guard's shoulder, touched his carotid artery with a poisoned needle concealed in a fingernail. The guard had only time to draw one gasping breath, his eyes gaping, before he sank from her embrace.

"I treated him well," she said.

Her companions grinned. It was the kind of thing you learned to expect from Tria. They dragged the body out of sight into the guard alcove, and the young male with the signal device took his place at the door. The others protected Tria with their bodies as they swept into the building. The whole operation had taken less than two minutes. Everything was working smoothly, as Tria's operations were expected to work.

The lobby and its radiating hallways were empty.

Good.

Her agent in this building deserved a promotion.

They took a stairway rather than trust an elevator. It was only three short flights. The upper hallway also was empty. Tria led the way to the designated door, used the key her agent had supplied. The door opened without a sound and they surged into the room.

Inside, the shades had been pulled, and there was no artificial illumination. Her companions took up their places at the closed door and along both flanking walls. This was the most dangerous moment, something only Tria could handle.

Light came from thin strips where shades did not quite

seal a south window. Tria discerned dim shapes of furniture, a bed with an indeterminate blob of darkness on it.

"Jedrik?" A whisper.

Tria's feet touched soft fabric, a sandal.

"Jedrik?"

Her shin touched the bed. She held a weapon ready while she felt for the dark blob. It was only a mound of bedding. She turned.

The bathroom door was closed, but she could make out a thin slot of light at the bottom of the door. She skirted the clothing and sandal on the floor, stood at one side, and motioned a companion to the other side. Thus far they had operated with a minimum of sound.

Gently, she turned the knob, thrust open the door. There was water in a tub and a body face down, one arm hanging flaccidly over the edge, fingers dangling. A dark purple welt was visible behind and beneath the left ear. Tria lifted the head by the hair, stared at the face, lowered it gently to avoid splashing. It was her agent, the one she'd trusted for the intelligence to set up this operation. And the death was characteristic of a Gowachin ritual slaying: that welt under the ear. A Gowachin talon driven in there to silence the victim before drowning? Or had it just been made to appear like a Gowachin slaying?

Tria felt the whole operation falling apart around her, sensed the uneasiness of her companions. She considered calling Gar from where she stood, but a feeling of fear and revulsion came over her. She stepped out into the bedroom before opening her communicator and thumbing the emergency signal.

"Central." The voice was tense in her ear.

She kept her own voice flat. "Our agent's dead."

Silence. She could imagine them centering the locator on her transmission, then: "There?"

"Yes. She's been murdered."

Gar's voice came on: "That can't be. I talked to her less than an hour ago. She. . ."

"Drowned in a tub of water," Tria said. "She was knocked out first—something sharp driven in under an ear."

There was silence again while Gar absorbed this data. He would have the same uncertainties as Tria.

She glanced at her companions. They had taken up guard positions facing the doorway to the hall. Yes, if attack came, it would come from there.

The channel to Gar remained open, and now Tria heard a babble of terse orders with only a few words intelligible: ". . . team . . . don't let . . . time . . ." Then, quite clearly: "They'll pay for this!"

Who will pay? Tria wondered.

She was beginning to make a new assessment of Jedrik.

Gar came back on: "Are you in immediate danger?"

"I don't know." It was a reluctant admission.

"Stay right where you are. We'll send help. I've notified Broey."

So that was the way Gar saw it. Yes. That was most likely the proper way to handle this new development. Jedrik had eluded them. There was no sense in proceeding alone. It would have to be done Broey's way now.

Tria shuddered as she issued the necessary orders to her companions. They prepared to sell themselves dearly if an attack came, but Tria was beginning to doubt there'd be an immediate attack. This was another message from Jedrik. The trouble came when you tried to interpret the message.

The military mentality is a bandit and raider mentality. Thus, all military represents a form of organized banditry where the conventional mores do not prevail. The military is a way of rationalizing murder, rape, looting, and other forms of theft which are always accepted as part of warfare. When denied an outside target, the military mentality always turns against its own civilian population, using identical rationalizations for bandit behavior.

> —*BuSab Manual, Chapter Five:*
> *"The Warlord Syndrome"*

McKie, awakening from the communications trance, realized how he must've appeared to this strange Gowachin towering over him. Of course a Dosadi Gowachin would think him ill. He'd been shivering and mumbling in the trance, perspiration rolling from him. McKie took a deep breath.

"No, I'm not ill."

"Then it's an addiction?"

Recalling the many substances to which the Dosadi could be addicted, McKie almost used this excuse but thought better of it. This Gowachin might demand some of the addictive substance.

"Not an addiction," McKie said. He lifted himself to his feet, glanced around. The sun had moved perceptibly toward the horizon behind its streaming veil.

And something new had been added to the landscape—that gigantic tracked vehicle, which stood throbbing and puffing smoke from a vertical stack behind the Gowachin intruder. The Gowachin maintained a steady, intense concentration on McKie, disconcerting in its unwavering directness.

McKie had to ask himself: was this some threat, or his Dosadi contact? Aritch's people had said a vehicle would be sent to the contact point, but . . .

"Not ill, not an addiction," the Gowachin said. "Is it some strange condition which only Humans have?

"I *was* ill," McKie said. "But I'm recovered. The condition has passed."

"Do you often have such attacks?"

"I can go years without a recurrence."

"Years? What causes this . . . condition?"

"I don't know."

"I . . . ahhhh." The Gowachin nodded, gestured upward with his chin. "An affliction of the Gods, perhaps."

"Perhaps."

"You were completely vulnerable."

McKie shrugged. Let the Gowachin make of that what he could.

"You were not vulnerable?" Somehow, this amused the Gowachin, who added: "I am Bahrank. Perhaps that's the luckiest thing which has ever happened to you."

Bahrank was the name Aritch's aides had given as McKie's first contact.

"I am McKie."

"You fit the description, McKie, except for your, ahhh, condition. Do you wish to say more?"

McKie wondered what Bahrank expected. This was supposed to be a simple contact handing him on to more important people. Aritch was certain to have knowledgeable observers on Dosadi, but Bahrank was not supposed to be one of them. The warning about this Gowachin had been specific.

"Bahrank doesn't know about us. Be extremely careful what you reveal to him. It'd be very dangerous to you if he were to learn that you came from beyond the God Veil."

The jumpdoor aides had reinforced the warning.

"If the Dosadi penetrate your cover, you'll have to return to your pickup point on your own. We very much doubt that you could make it. Understand that we can give you little help once we've put you on Dosadi."

Bahrank visibly came to a decision, nodding to himself.

"Jedrik expects you."

That was the other name Aritch's people had provided. "Your cell leader. She's been told that you're a new infiltrator from the Rim. Jedrik doesn't know your true origin."

"Who does know?"

"We cannot tell you. If you don't know, then that information cannot be wrested from you. We assure you, though, that Jedrik isn't one of our people."

McKie didn't like the sound of that warning. ". . . wrested from you." As usual, BuSab sent you into the tiger's mouth without a full briefing on the length of the tiger's fangs.

Bahrank gestured toward his tracked vehicle. "Shall we go?"

McKie glanced at the machine. It was an obvious war device, heavily armored with slits in its metal cab, projectile weapons protruding at odd angles. It looked squat and deadly. Aritch's people had mentioned such things.

"We saw to it that they got only primitive armored vehicles, projectile weapons and relatively unimportant explosives, that sort of thing. They've been quite resourceful in their adaptations of such weaponry, however."

Once more, Bahrank gestured toward his vehicle, obviously anxious to leave.

McKie was forced to suppress an abrupt feeling of profound anxiety. What had he gotten himself into? He felt that he had awakened to find himself on a terrifying slide into peril, unable to control the least threat. The sensation passed, but it left him shaken. He delayed while he continued to stare at the vehicle. It was about six meters long with heavy tracks, plus other wheels faintly visible within the shadows behind the tracks. It sported a conventional antenna at the rear for tapping the power transmitter in orbit beneath the barrier veil, but there was a secondary system which burned a stinking fuel. The smoke of that fuel filled the air around them with acridity.

"For what do we wait?" Bahrank demanded. He glared at McKie with obvious fear and suspicion.

"We can go now," McKie said.

Bahrank turned and led the way swiftly, clambering up over the tracks and into a shadowed cab. McKie followed, found the interior a tightly cluttered place full of a bitter, oily smell. There were two hard metal seats with curved backs higher than the head of a seated Human or Gowachin. Bahrank already occupied the seat on the left, working switches and dials. McKie dropped into the other seat. Folding arms locked across his chest and waist to hold him in place; a brace fitted itself to the back of his head. Bahrank threw a switch. The door through which they'd entered closed with a grinding of servomotors and the solid clank of locks.

An ambivalent mood swept over McKie. He had always felt faint agoraphobia in open places such as the area around the rock. But the dim interior of this war machine, with its savage reminders of primitive times, touched an atavistic chord in his psyche and he fought an urge to claw his way outside. This was a trap!

An odd observation helped him overcome the sensation. There was glass over the slits which gave them their view of the outside. Glass. He felt it. Yes, glass. It was common stuff in the ConSentiency—strong yet fragile. He could see that this glass wasn't very thick. The fierce appearance of this machine had to be more show than actuality, then.

Bahrank gave one swift, sweeping glance to their surroundings, moved levers which set the vehicle into lurching motion. It emitted a grinding rumble with an overriding whine.

A track of sorts led from the white rock toward the distant city. It showed the marks of this machine's recent passage, a roadway to follow. Glittering reflections danced from bright rocks along the track. Bahrank appeared very busy with whatever he was doing to guide them toward Chu.

McKie found his own thoughts returning to the briefings he'd received on Tandaloor.

"Once you enter Jedrik's cell you're on your own."

Yes . . . he felt very much alone, his mind a clutter of data which had little relationship to any previous experience. And this planet could die unless he made sense out of that data plus whatever else he might learn here.

Alone, alone . . . If Dosadi died there'd be few sentient watchers. The Caleban's tempokinetic barrier would contain most of that final destructive flare. The Caleban would, in fact, feed upon the released energy. That was one of the things he'd learned from Fannie Mae. One consuming blast, a *meal* for a Caleban, and BuSab would be forced to start anew and without the most important piece of physical evidence — Dosadi.

The machine beneath McKie thundered, rocked, and skidded, but always returned to the track which led toward Chu's distant spires.

McKie studied the driver covertly. Bahrank showed uncharacteristic behavior for a Gowachin: more direct, more Human. That was it! His Gowachin instincts had been contaminated by contact with Humans. Aritch was sure to despise that, fear it. Bahrank drove with a casual expertise, using a complex control system. McKie counted eight different levers and arms which the Gowachin employed. Some were actuated by knees, others by his head. His hands reached out while an elbow deflected a lever. The war machine responded.

Bahrank spoke presently without taking his attention from driving.

"We may come under fire on the second ledge. There was quite a police action down there earlier."

McKie stared at him.

"I thought we had safe passage through."

"You Rimmers are always pressing."

McKie peered out the slits: bushes, barren ground, that lonely track they followed.

Bahrank spoke.

"You're older than any Rimmer I ever saw before."

Aritch's people had warned McKie about this as a basic flaw in his cover, the need to conceal the subtle signs of age.

They'd provided him with some geriatric assistance and an answer to give when challenged. He used that answer now.

"It ages you in a hurry out here."

"It must."

McKie felt that something in Bahrank's response eluded him, but dared not pursue this. It was an unproductive exchange. And there was that reference to a "police action." McKie knew that the Rim Rabble, excluded from Chu, tried periodic raids, most often fruitless. Barbaric!

"What excuse did you use to come out here?" McKie asked.

Bahrank shot a probing glance at him, raised one webbed hand from the controls to indicate a handle in the roof over his head. The handle's purpose was unknown to McKie, and he feared he had already betrayed too much ignorance. But Bahrank was speaking.

"Officially, I'm scouting this area for any hidden surprises the Rimmers may have stored out here. I often do that. Unofficially, everyone thinks I've a secret pond out here full of fertile females."

A pond . . . not a Graluz. Again, it was a relatively fruitless exchange with hidden undertones.

McKie stared silently ahead through a slit. Their dusty track made a slow and wide sweep left, abruptly angled down onto a narrow ledge cut from red rock walls. Bahrank put them through a series of swift changes in speed: slow, fast, slow, fast. The red rock walls raced past. McKie peered out and downward on his side. Far below lay jungle verdure and, in the distance, the smoke and spires of Chu — fluted buildings ranked high over dim background cliffs.

The speed changes appeared purposeless to McKie. And the dizzy drop off the cliff on his side filled him with awe. Their narrow ledge hugged the cliff, turning as the cliff turned — now into shadows and now into light. The machine roared and groaned around him. The smell of oil made his stomach heave. And the faraway city seemed little closer than it had from the cliff top, except that it was taller, more mysterious in its smoky obscurity.

"Don't expect any real trouble until we reach the first ledge," Bahrank said.

McKie glanced at him. First ledge? Yes, that'd be the first elevation outside the city's walls. The gorge within which Chu had been raised came down to river level in broad steps, each one numbered. Chu had been anchored to island hills and flats where the river slowed and split into many arms. And the hills which had resisted the river were almost solid iron ore, as were many of the flanking ledges.

"Glad to get off there," Bahrank said.

Their narrow ledge had turned at right angles away from the cliff onto a broad ramp which descended into grey-green jungle. The growth enclosed them in abrupt green shadows. McKie, looking out to the side, identified hair fronds and broad leaf ficus, giant spikes of barbed red which he had never before seen. Their track, like the jungle floor, was grey mud. McKie looked from side to side; the growth appeared an almost equal mixture of Terran and Tandaloor, interspersed with many strange plants.

Sunlight made him blink as they raced out of the overhanging plants onto a plain of tall grass which had been trampled, blasted, and burned by recent violence. He saw a pile of wrecked vehicles off to the left, twisted shards of metal with, here and there, a section of track or a wheel aimed at the sky. Some of the wrecks looked similar to the machine in which he now rode.

Bahrank skirted a blast hole at an angle which gave McKie a view into the hole's depths. Torn bodies lay there. Bahrank made no comment, seemed hardly to notice.

Abruptly, McKie saw signs of movement in the jungle, the flitting presence of both Humans and Gowachin. Some carried what appeared to be small weapons — the glint of a metal tube, bandoliers of bulbous white objects around their necks. McKie had not tried to memorize all of Dosadi's weaponry; it was, after all, primitive, but he reminded himself now that primitive weapons had created these scenes of destruction.

Their track plunged again into overhanging growth, leaving the battlefield behind. Deep green shadows enclosed the lurching, rumbling machine. McKie, shaken from side to side against the restraints, carried an odor memory with him: deep, bloody musks and the beginnings of rot. Their shaded avenue made a sharp right turn, emerged onto another ledge slashed by a plunging cut into which Bahrank took them, turning onto another cliff-hugging ledge.

McKie stared across Bahrank through the slits. The city was nearer now. Their rocking descent swept his gaze up and down Chu's towers, which lifted like silvery organ pipes out of the Council Hills. The far cliff was a series of misted steps fading into purple grey. Chu's Warrens lay smokey and hazed all around the fluted towers. And he could make out part of the city's enclosing outer wall. Squat forts dotted the wall's top, offset for enfilading fire. The city within the wall seemed so tall. McKie had not expected it to appear so tall— but that spoke of the population pressures in a way that could not be misunderstood.

Their ledge ended at another battlefield plain strewn with bodies of metal and flesh, the death stink an inescapable vapor. Bahrank spun his vehicle left, right, dodged piles of torn equipment, avoided craters where mounds of flesh lay beneath insect blankets. Ferns and other low growth were beginning to spring upright after the monstrous trampling. Grey and yellow flying creatures sported in the ferntops, uncaring of all that death. Aritch's aides had warned McKie that Dosadi's life existed amidst brutal excesses, but the actuality sickened him. He identified both Gowachin and Human forms among the sprawled corpses. The sleek green skin of a young Gowachin female, orange fertility marks prominent along her arms, especially revolted him. McKie turned sharply away, found Bahrank studying him with tawny mockery in the shining Gowachin eyes. Bahrank spoke as he drove.

"There're informers everywhere, of course, and after this . . ." His head nodded left and right. ". . . you'll have to move with more caution than you might've anticipated."

A brittle explosion punctuated his words. Something struck the vehicle's armor on McKie's side. Again they were a target. And again. The clanging of metal against metal came thickly, striking all around them, even on the glass over the view slits.

McKie suppressed his shock. That thin glass did not shatter. He knew about thick shields of tempered glass, but this put a new dimension on what he'd been told about the Dosadi. Quite resourceful, indeed!

Bahrank drove with apparent unconcern.

More explosive attacks came from directly in front of them, flashes of orange in the jungle beyond the plain.

"They're testing," Bahrank said. He pointed to one of the slits. "See? They don't even leave a mark on that new glass."

McKie spoke from the depths of his bitterness.

"Sometimes you wonder what all this proves except that our world runs on distrust."

"Who trusts?"

Bahrank's words had the sound of a catechism.

McKie said:

"I hope our friends know when to stop testing."

"They were told we couldn't take more'n eighty millimeter."

"Didn't they agree to pass us through?"

"Even so, they're expected to try a few shots if just to keep me in good graces with my superiors."

Once more, Bahrank put them through a series of dazzling speed changes and turns for no apparent reason. McKie lurched against the restraints, felt bruising pain as an elbow hit the side of the cab. An explosion directly behind rocked them up onto the left track. As they bounced, Bahrank spun them left, avoided another blast which would've landed directly on them along their previous path. McKie, his ears ringing from the explosions, felt the machine bounce to a stop, reverse as more explosions erupted ahead. Bahrank spun them to the right, then left, once more charged full speed ahead right into an unbroken wall of jungle. With explosions all around, they crashed through greenery, turned to the right along another shadowed muddy track. McKie had lost all sense of direction, but the attack had ceased.

Bahrank slowed them, took a deep breath through his ventricles.

"I knew they'd try that."

He sounded both relieved and amused.

McKie, shaken by the brush with death, couldn't find his voice.

Their shadowy track snaked through the jungle for a space, giving McKie time to recover. By then, he didn't know what to say. He couldn't understand Bahrank's amusement, the lack of enduring concern over such violent threat.

Presently, they emerged onto an untouched, sloping plain as smooth and green as a park lawn. It dipped gently downward into a thin screen of growth through which McKie could see a silver-green tracery of river. What caught and held McKie's attention, however, was a windowless, pock-walled grey fortress which lifted from the plain in the middle distance. It towered over the growth screening the river. Buttressed arms reached toward them to enclose a black metal barrier.

"That's our gate," Bahrank said.

Bahrank turned them left, lined up with the center of the buttressed arms. "Gate Nine and we're home through the tube," he said.

McKie nodded. Walls, tubes, and gates: those were the keys to Chu's defenses. They had "barrier and fortress minds" on Dosadi. This tube would run beneath the river. He tried to place it on the map which Aritch's people had planted in his mind. He was supposed to know the geography of this place, its geology, religions, social patterns, the intimate layout of each island's walled defenses, but he found it hard to locate himself now on that mental map. He leaned forward to the slit, peered upward as the machine began to gather speed, saw the great central spire with its horizontal clock. All the hours of map briefing snicked into place.

"Yes, Gate Nine."

Bahrank, too busy driving, did not reply.

McKie dropped his gaze to the fortress, stifled a gasp.

The rumbling machine was plunging downslope at a frightening pace, aimed directly toward that black metal barrier. At the last instant, when it seemed they would crash into it, the barrier leaped upward. They shot through into a dimly illuminated tube. The gate thundered closed behind them. Their machine made a racketing sound on metal grating beneath the tracks.

Bahrank slowed them, shifted a lever beside him. The machine lifted onto wheels with an abrupt reduction in noise which made McKie feel that he'd been deafened. The feeling was heightened by the realization that Bahrank had said the same thing to him several times.

"Jedrik says you come from beyond the far mountains. Is that true?"

"Jedrik says it." He tried to make it sound wry, but it came out almost questioning.

Bahrank was concentrating on a line of thought, however, as he drove them straight down the grating floor of the dim tube.

"There's a rumor that you Rimmers have started a secret settlement back there, that you're trying to build your own city."

"An interesting rumor."

"Isn't it, though?"

The single line of overhead lights in the tube left the cab's interior darker than it'd been outside, illuminated by only the faint reflections from instruments and dials. But McKie had the odd sensation that Bahrank saw him clearly, was studying every expression. Despite the impossibility of this, the thought persisted. What was behind Bahrank's probing? *Why do I feel that he sees right through me?*

These disquieting conjectures ended as they emerged from the tube onto a Warren street. Bahrank spun them to the right along a narrow alleyway in deep grey shadows.

Although he'd seen many representations of these streets the actuality deepened McKie's feelings of misgiving. So dirty . . . oppressive . . . so many people. They were everywhere!

Bahrank drove slowly now on the silent wheels, the tracks raised off the paving. The big machine eased its way through narrow little streets, some paved with stone, some with great slabs of gleaming black. All the streets were shaded by overhanging upper stories whose height McKie could not judge through the slits. He saw shops barred and guarded. An occasional stairway, also guarded, led up or down into repellent darkness. Only Humans occupied these streets, and no casual, pedestrian expressions on any of them. Jaws were set on grim mouths. Hard, questioning eyes peered at the passing vehicle. Both men and women wore the universal dark, one-piece clothing of the Labor Pool.

Noting McKie's interest, Bahrank spoke.

"This is a Human enclave and you have a Gowachin driver."

"Can they see us in here?"

"They know. And there's trouble coming."

"Trouble?"

"Gowachin against Human."

This appalled McKie, and he wondered if this were the source of those forebodings which Aritch and aides would not explain: destruction of Dosadi from within. But Bahrank continued:

"There's a growing separation between Humans and Gowachin, worse than it's ever been. You may be the last Human to ride with me."

Aritch and company had prepared McKie for Dosadi's violence, hunger, and distrust, but they'd said nothing about species against species . . . only that someone they refused to name could destroy the place from within. What was Bahrank trying to say? McKie dared not expose his ignorance by probing, and this inability dismayed him.

Bahrank, meanwhile, nosed their machine out of a narrow passage onto a wider street which was crowded by carts, each piled with greenery. The carts moved aside slowly as the armored vehicle approached, hatred plain in the eyes of the Humans who moved with the carts. The press of people astonished McKie: for every cart (and he lost count of them within a block) there were at least a hundred people crowding around, lifting arms high, shouting at the ring of people who stood shoulder to shoulder around each cart, their backs to the piled contents and obviously guarding those contents.

McKie, staring at the carts, realized with a shocked sense of recognition that he was staring at carts piled with garbage. The crowds of people were buying garbage.

Again, Bahrank acted the part of tour guide.

"This is called the Street of the Hungry. That's very select garbage, the best."

McKie recalled one of Aritch's aides saying there were restaurants in Chu which specialized in garbage from particular areas of the city, that no poison-free food was wasted.

The passing scene compelled McKie's attention: hard faces, furtive movements, the hate and thinly suppressed violence, all of this immersed in a *normal* commercial operation based on garbage. And the numbers of these people! They were everywhere around: in doorways, guarding and pushing the carts, skipping out of Bahrank's path. New smells assaulted McKie's nostrils, a fetid acridity, a stink such as he had never before experienced. Another thing surprised him: the appearance of antiquity in this Warren. He wondered if all city populations crowded by threats from outside took on this ancient appearance. By ConSentient standards, the population of Chu had lived here only a few generations, but the city looked older than any he'd ever seen.

With an abrupt rocking motion, Bahrank turned their machine down a narrow street, brought them to a stop. McKie, looking out the slit on his right, saw an arched entry in a grimy building, a stairway leading downward into gloom.

"Down there's where you meet Jedrik," Bahrank said. "Down those stairs, second door on your left. It's a restaurant."

"How'll I know her?"

"Didn't they tell you?"

"I . . ." McKie broke off. He'd seen pictures of Jedrik during the Tandaloor briefings, realized now that he was trying to delay leaving Bahrank's armored cocoon.

Bahrank appeared to sense this.

"Have no fear, McKie. Jedrik will know you. And McKie . . "

McKie turned to face the Gowachin.

" . . . go directly to the restaurant, take a seat, wait for Jedrik. You'll not survive long here without her protection. Your skin's dark and some Humans prefer even the green to the dark in this quarter. They remember Pylash Gate here. Fifteen years isn't long enough to erase that from their minds."

Nothing about a Pylash Gate had been included in McKie's briefings and now he dared not ask.

Bahrank moved the switch which opened McKie's door. Immediately, the stink of the street was amplified to almost overpowering proportions. Bahrank seeing him hesitate, spoke sharply.

"Go quickly!"

McKie descended in a kind of olfactory daze, found himself standing on the side of the street, the object of suspicious stares from all around. The sight of Bahrank driving away was the cutting of his last link to the ConSentiency and all the familiar things which might protect him. Never in his long life had McKie felt this much alone

*No legal system can maintain justice unless every partici-
pant—magisters, prosecutors, Legums, defendants, witnesses, all—risks life itself in whatever dispute comes before
the bar. Everything must be risked in the Courtarena. If any
element remains outside the contest and without personal
risk, justice inevitably fails.*

—Gowachin Law

Near sunset there was a fine rain which lasted well into
darkness, then departed on the gorge wind which cleared
Dosadi's skies. It left the air crystalline, cornices dripping
puddles in the streets. Even the omnipresent Warren stink
was diluted and Chu's inhabitants showed a predatory light-
ness as they moved along the streets.

Returning to headquarters in an armored troop carrier
which carried only his most trusted Gowachin, Broey noted
the clear air even while he wondered at the reports which
had brought him racing from the Council Hills. When he entered the conference room, Broey saw that Gar already was
there standing with his back to the dark window which
looked out on the eastern cliffs. Broey wondered how long
Gar had been there. No sign of recognition passed between
Gowachin and Human, but this only emphasized the growing separation of the species. They'd both seen the reports
which contained that most disturbing datum: the killing of a
Human double agent under circumstances which pointed at
Broey himself.

149

Broey crossed to the head of the conference table, flipped the toggle which activated his communicator, addressed the screen which only he could see.

"Assemble the Council and link for conference."

The response came as a distorted buzz filtered through scramblers and suppressed by a privacy cone. Gar, standing across the room, could make no sense out of the noises coming from the communicator.

While he waited for the Council members to come on the conference link, Broey seated himself at the communicator, summoned a Gowachin aide to the screen, and spoke in a low voice masked by the privacy cone.

"Start a security check on all Humans in positions where they might threaten us. Use Plan D."

Broey glanced up at Gar. The Human's mouth worked silently. He was annoyed by the privacy cone and his inability to tell exactly what Broey was doing. Broey continued speaking to his aide.

"I'll want the special force deployed as I told you earlier . . . Yes . . ."

Gar pointedly turned his back on this conversation, stared out at the night.

Broey continued to address his aide in the screen.

"No! We must include even the Humans in this conference. Yes, that's the report Gar made to me. Yes, I also received that information. Other Humans can be expected to riot and drive out their Gowachin neighbors, and there'll be retaliations. Yes, that was my thought when I saw the report."

Broey turned off the privacy cone and scrambler. Tria had just come onto his screen with an override, interrupting the conversation with his security aide. She spoke in a low, hurried voice with only a few words intelligible to Gar across the room. But Broey's suspicions were becoming obvious. He heard Tria out, then:

"Yes . . . it would be logical to suppose that such a killing was made to look like Gowachin work for . . . I see. But the scattered incidents which . . . Indeed? Well, under the circumstances . . ."

He left the thought incomplete, but his words drew a line between Human and Gowachin, even at the highest levels of his Advisory Council.

"Tria, I must make my own decisions on this."

While Broey was speaking, Gar brought up a chair and placed it near the communicator, then sat down. Broey had finished his conversation with Tria and restored the privacy circuits, however, and even though he sat nearby Gar could not penetrate their protective screen. He was close enough now, though, to hear the buzzing of the privacy system and the sound annoyed Gar. He did not try to conceal his annoyance.

Broey saw Gar, but gave no indication that he approved or disapproved Gar's nearness.

"So I understand," Broey said. "Yes . . . I'll issue those orders as soon as I've finished here. No . . . Agreed. That would be best." He closed the circuit. The annoying buzz stopped.

"Jedrik means to set Gowachin against Human, Human against Gowachin," Gar said.

"If so, it's been a long time in secret preparation," Broey said.

His words implied many things: that there was conspiracy in high places, that the situation had achieved dangerous momentum without being detected, that all of the inertial forces could not now be anticipated.

"You expect it to get worse," Gar said.

"Hopefully."

Gar stared at him for a long period, then:

"Yes."

It was clear that Broey wanted a well-defined condition to

develop, one which would provide clear predictions of the major consequences. He was prepared for this. When Broey understood the situation to his own satisfaction, he'd use his own undeniable powers to gain as much as possible during a period of upset.

Gar broke the silence.

"But if we've misunderstood Jedrik's intent—"

"It helps us when the innocent suffer," Broey said, paraphrasing part of an old axiom which every Dosadi knew.

Gar completed the thought for him.

"But who's innocent?"

Before Broey could respond, his screen came alight with the assembled faces of his Council, each face in its own little square. Broey conducted the conference quickly, allowing few interruptions. There were no house arrests, no direct accusations, but his words and manner divided them by species. When he was through, Gar imagined the scrambling which must be going on right then in Chu while the powerful assembled their defenses.

Without knowing how he sensed this, Gar felt that this was exactly what Jedrik had wanted, and that it'd been a mistake for Broey to increase the tensions.

After turning off the communicator, Broey sat back and addressed himself to Gar with great care.

"Tria tells me that Jedrik cannot be found."

"Didn't we expect that?"

"Perhaps." Broey puffed his jowls. "What I don't understand is how a simple Liaitor could elude my people *and* Tria."

"I think we've underestimated this Jedrik. What if she comes from . . ." His chin jerked ceilingward.

Broey considered this. He'd been supervising the interrogation of Bahrank at a secure post deep in the Council Hills when the summons to headquarters had interrupted. The accumulating reports indicated a kind of trouble Chu had known at various times, but never at this magnitude. And Bahrank's information had been disappointing. He'd delivered this Rim infiltrator named McKie to such and such an address. (Security had been unable to check this in time because of the riots.) Bahrank's beliefs were obvious. And perhaps the Rimmers *were* trying to build their own city beyond the mountains. Broey thought this unlikely. His sources in the Rim had proved generally trustworthy and his special source was always trustworthy. Besides, such a venture would require gigantic stocks of food, all of it subject to exposure in the regular accounting. That, after all, was the Liaitor function, why he had . . . No, that was not probable. The Rim subsisted on the lowest of Chu's leavings and whatever could be wrested form Dosadi's poisonous soil. No . . . Bahrank was wrong. This McKie was peculiar, but in quite another way. And Jedrik must've known this before anyone else—except himself. The paramount question remained: who'd helped her?

Broey sighed.

"We have a long association, Gar. A person of your powers who has worked his way from the Rim through the Warrens . . ."

Gar understood. He was being told that Broey looked upon him with active suspicion. There'd never been any real trust between them, but this was something else: nothing openly spoken, nothing direct or specific, but the meaning clear. It was not even sly; it was merely Dosadi.

For a moment, Gar didn't know which way to turn. There'd always been this possibility in his relationship with Broey, but long acceptance had lulled Gar into a dangerous dependency. Tria had been his most valuable counter. He needed her now, but she had other, much more demanding, duties at this juncture.

Gar realized now that he would have to precipitate his own plans, calling in all of the debts and dependencies which were his due. He was distracted by the sound of many people hurrying past in the outer hall. Presumably, things were coming to a head faster than expected.

Gar stood up, stared vaguely out the windows at those dark shadows in the night which were the Rim cliffs. While waiting for Broey, Gar had watched darkness settle there, watched the spots of orange appear which were the Rim's cookfires. Gar knew those cookfires, knew the taste of the food which came from them, knew the flesh-dragging dullness which dominated existence out there. Did Broey expect him to flee back to that? Broey would be astonished at the alternatives open to Gar.

"I will leave you now," Broey said. He arose and waddled from the room. What he meant was: "Don't be here when I return."

Gar continued to stare out the windows. He seemed lost in angry reverie. Why hadn't Tria reported yet? One of Broey's Gowachin aides came in, fussed over papers on a corner table.

It was actually no more than five minutes that Gar remained standing thus. He shook himself presently, turned, and let himself out of the room.

Scarcely had he set foot in the outer passage than a troop of Broey's Gowachin shouldered their way past him into the conference room. They'd been waiting for him to leave.

Angry with himself for what he knew he must do, Gar turned left, strode down the hall to the room where he knew he'd find Broey. Three Gowachin wearing Security brassards followed him, but did not interfere. Two more Gowachin guarded Broey's door, but they hesitated to stop him. Gar's power had been felt here too long. And Broey, not expecting Gar to follow, had failed to issue specific orders. Gar counted on this.

Broey, instructing a group of Gowachin aides, stood over a table cluttered with charts. Yellow light from fixtures directly overhead played shifting shadows on the charts as the aides bent over the table and made notes. Broey broke off at the intrusion, his surprise obvious.

Gar spoke before Broey could order him removed.

"You still need me to keep you from making the worst mistake of your life."

Broey straightened, did not speak, but the invitation for Gar to continue was there.

"Jedrik's playing you like a fine instrument. You're doing precisely what she wants you to do."

Broey's cheeks puffed. The shrug angered Gar.

"When I first came here, Broey, I took certain precautions to insure my continued health should you ever consider violence against me."

Again, Broey gave that maddening Gowachin shrug. This was all so mundane. Why else did this fool Human continue alive and at liberty?

"You've never been able to discover what I did to insure myself against you," Gar said. "I have no addictions. I'm a prudent person and, naturally, have means of dying before your experts on pain could overcome my reason. I've done all of the things you might expect of me . . . and something more, something you now need *desperately* to know."

"I have my own precautions, Gar."

"Of course, and I admit I don't know what they are."

"So what do you propose?"

Gar gave a little laugh, not quite gloating.

"You know my terms."

Broey shook his head from side to side, an exquisitely Human gesture.

"Share the rule? I'm astonished at you, Gar."

"Your astonishment hasn't reached its limits. You don't know what I've really done."

"Which is?"

"Shall we retire to a more private place and discuss it?"

Broey looked around at his aides, waved for them to leave. "We will talk here."

Gar waited until he heard the door close behind him on the last of the departing aides.

"You probably know about the death fanatics we've groomed in the Human enclaves."

"We are prepared to deal with them."

"Properly motivated, fanatics can keep great secrets, Broey."

"No doubt. Are you now going to reveal such a secret?"

"For years now, my fanatics have lived on reduced rations, preserving and exporting their surplus rations to the Rim. We have enough, megatons of food out there. With a whole planet in which to hide it, you'll never find it. City food, every bit of it and we will . . ."

"Another city!"

"More than that. Every weapon the city of Chu has, we have."

Broey's ventricle lips went almost green with anger.

"So you never really left the Rim?"

"The Rim-born cannot forget."

"After all that Chu has done for you . . ."

"I'm glad you didn't mention blasphemy."

"But the Gods of the Veil gave us a mandate!"

"Divide and rule, subdivide and rule even more powerfully, fragment and rule absolutely."

"That's not what I meant." Broey breathed deeply several times to restore his calm. "One city and only one city. That is our mandate."

"But the other city will be built."

"Will it?"

"We've dug in the factories to provide our own weapons and food. If you move against our people inside Chu, we'll come at you from the outside, shatter your walls and . . ."

"What do you propose?"

"Open cooperation for a separation of the species, one city for Gowachin, one for Human. What you do in Chu will be your own business then, but I'll tell you that we of the new city will rid ourselves of the DemoPol and its aristocracy."

"You'd create another aristocracy?"

"Perhaps. But my people will die for the vision of freedom we share. We no longer provide our bodies for Chu!"

"So that's why your fanatics are all Rim-born."

"I see that you don't yet understand, Broey. My people are not merely Rim-born; they are willing, even *eager*, to die for their vision."

Broey considered this. It was a difficult concept for a Gowachin, whose Graluz guilt was always transformed into a profound respect for the survival drive. But he saw where Gar's words must lead, and he built an image in his mind of fleshly Human waves throwing themselves onto all opposition without inhibitions about pain, death, or survival in any respect. They might very well capture Chu. The idea that countless Rim immigrants lived within Chu's walls in readiness for such sacrifice filled him with deep disquiet. It required strong self-control to conceal this reaction. He did not for an instant doubt Gar's story. It was just the kind of thing this dry-fleshed Rimmer would do. But why was Gar revealing this now?

"Did Jedrik order you to prepare me for . . ."

"Jedrik isn't part of our plan. She complicates matters for us, but the kind of upset she's igniting is just the sort of thing we can exploit better than you."

Broey weighed this with what he knew about Gar, found it valid as far as it went, but it still did not answer the basic question.

"Why?"

"I'm not ready to sacrifice my people," Gar said.

That had the ring of partial truth. Gar had shown many times that he could make hard decisions. But numbered among his fanatic hordes there doubtless were certain skills he'd prefer not losing—not yet. Yes, that was the way Gar's mind worked. And Gar would know the profound respect for life which matured in a Gowachin breast after the weeding frenzy. Gowachin, too, could make bloody decisions, but the guilt . . . oh, the guilt . . . Gar counted on the guilt. Perhaps he counted too much.

"Surely, you don't expect me to take an open and active part in your Rim city project?"

"If not open, then passive."

"And you insist on sharing the rule of Chu?"

"For the interim."

"Impossible!"

"In substance if not in name."

"You have been my advisor."

"Will you precipitate violence between us with Jedrik standing there to pick up whatever she can gain from us?"

"Ahhhhhh. . ." Broey nodded.

So that was it! Gar was not part of this Jedrik thing. Gar was afraid of Jedrik, more afraid of her than he was of Broey. This gave Broey cause for caution. Gar was not easily made fearful. What did he know of this Jedrik that Broey did not know? But now there was a sufficient reason for compromise. The unanswered questions could be answered later.

"You will continue as my chief advisor," Broey said.

It was acceptable. Gar signified his consent by a curt nod.

The compromise left an empty feeling in Broey's digestive nodes, though. Gar knew he'd been manipulated to reveal his fear of Jedrik. Gar could be certain that Broey would try to neutralize the Rim city project. But the magnitude of Gar's plotting went far beyond expectations, leaving too many unknowns. One could not make accurate decisions with insufficient data. Gar had given away information without receiving an equal exchange. That was not like Gar. Or was that a correct interpretation of what'd happened here?

Broey knew he had to explore this, risking one piece of accurate information as bait.

"There's been a recent increase of mystical experiences by Gowachin in the Warrens."

"You know better than to try that religious nonsense on me!"

Gar was actually angry.

Broey concealed his amusement. Gar did not know then (or did not accept) that the God of the Veil sometimes created illusions in his flock, that God spoke truly to his anointed and would even answer some questions.

Much had been revealed here, more than Gar suspected. Bahrank had been right. And Jedrik would know about Gar's Rim city. It was possible that Jedrik wanted Broey to know and had maneuvered Gar into revealing the plot. If Gar saw this, that would be enough to make him fearful.

Why didn't the God reveal this to me? Broey wondered. *Am I being tested?*

Yes, that had to be the answer, because there was one thing certain now:

This time, I'll do what the God advises.

People always devise their own justifications. Fixed and immovable Law merely provides a convenient structure within which to hang your justifications and the prejudices behind them. The only universally acceptable law for mortals would be one which fitted every justification. What obvious nonsense. Law must expose prejudice and question justification. Thus, Law must be flexible, must change to fit new demands. Otherwise, it becomes merely the justification of the powerful.

—Gowachin Law
(The BuSab Translation)

It required a moment after Bahrank drove away for McKie to recover his sense of purpose. The buildings rose tall and massive over him, but through a quirk of this Warren's growth, an opening to the west allowed a spike of the silvery afternoon sunlight to slant into the narrow street. The light threw hard shadows on every object, accented the pressure of Human movement. McKie did not like the way people looked at him: as though everyone measured him for some private gain.

Slowly, McKie pressed through the passing throng to the arched entry, observing all he could without seeming to do so. After all those years in BuSab, all of the training and experience which had qualified him for such a delicately powerful agency, he possessed superb knowledge of the ConSentiency's species. He drew on that knowledge now, sensing the powerful secrecy which governed these people. Unfortunately, his experience also was replete with knowledge of what species could do to species, not to mention what a species could do to itself. The Humans around him reminded him of nothing more than a mob about to explode.

Moving with a constant readiness to defend himself, he went down a short flight of stairs into cool shadows where the foot traffic was lighter but the smells of rot and mold were more pronounced.

Second door on the left.

He went to the doorway to which Bahrank had directed him, peered into the opening: another stairway down. Somehow, this dismayed him. The picture of Chu growing in his mind was not at all what Aritch's people had drawn. Had they deliberately misled him? If so, why? Was it possible they really didn't understand their monster? The array of answers to his questions chilled him. What if a few of the observers sent here by Aritch's people had chosen to capitalize on whatever power Dosadi provided?

In all of his career, McKie had never before come across a world so completely cut off from the rest of the universe. This planet was *alone*, without many of the amenities which graced the other ConSentient worlds: no common access to jumpdoors, no concourse of the known species, none of the refined pleasures nor the sophisticated traps which occupied the denizens of other worlds. Dosadi had developed its own ways. And the instructors on Tandaloor had returned time and again to that constant note of warning—that these lonely *primitives* would take over the ConSentiency if released upon the universe.

"Nothing restrains them. Nothing."

That was, perhaps, an overstatement. Some things did restrain the Dosadi physically. But they were not held back by the conventions or mores of the ConSentiency. Anything could be purchased here, any forbidden depravity which the imagination might conceive. This idea haunted McKie. He thought of this and of the countless substances to which many Dosadi were addicted. The power leverage such things gave to the unprincipled few was terrifying.

He dared not pause here wrestling with his indecisions, though. McKie stepped into the stairwell with a boldness which he did not feel, following Bahrank's directions because he had no choice. The bottom landing was a wider space in deep shadows, one dim light on a black door. Two Humans dozed in chairs beside the door while a third squatted beside them with what appeared to be a crude projectile weapon in his hands.

"Jedrik summoned me," McKie said.

The guard with the weapon nodded for him to proceed.

McKie made his way past them, glanced at the weapon: a length of pipe with a metal box at the back and a flat trigger atop the box held by the guard's thumb. McKie almost missed a step. The weapon was a dead-man bomb! Had to be. If that guard's thumb relaxed for any reason, the thing no doubt would explode and kill everyone in the stairwell. McKie glanced at the two sleepers. How could they sleep in such circumstances?

The black door with its one dim light commanded his attention now. A strong smell of highly seasoned cooking dominated the other stinks here. McKie saw that it was a heavy door with a glittering spyeye at face level. The door opened at his approach. He stepped through into a large low room crowded—*jammed!*—with people seated on benches at trestle tables. There was barely room for passage between the benches. And everywhere that McKie looked he saw people spooning food into their mouths from small bowls. Waiters and waitresses hurried through the narrow spaces slapping down bowls and removing empties.

The whole scene was presided over by a fat woman seated at a small desk on a platform at his left. She was positioned in such a way that she commanded the entry door, the entire room, and swinging doors at the side through which the serving people flowed back and forth. She was a monstrous woman and she sat her perch as though she had never been anywhere else. Indeed, it was easy for McKie to imagine that she could not move from her position. Her arms were bloated where they squeezed from the confines of short-sleeved green coveralls. Her ankles hung over her shoe tops in folds.

Take a seat and wait.

Bahrank had been explicit and the warning clear.

McKie looked for an opening on the benches. Before he could move, the fat woman spoke in a squeaky voice.

"Your name?"

McKie's gaze darted toward those beady eyes in their folds of fat.

"McKie."

"Thought so."

She raised a dimpled finger. From somewhere in the crush a young boy came hurrying. He could not have been over nine years old but his eyes were cold with adult wisdom. He looked up to the fat woman for instructions.

"This is the one. Guide him."

The boy turned and, without looking to see if McKie followed, hurried down the narrow pathway where the doors swung back and forth to permit the passage of the servitors. Twice, McKie was almost run down by waiters. His guide was able to anticipate the opening of every door and skipped aside.

At the end of this passage, there was another solid black door with spyeye. The door opened onto a short passage with closed doors on both sides, a blank wall at the end. The blank wall slid aside for them and they descended into a narrow, rock-lined way lighted by widely spaced bulbs overhead. The walls were damp and evil smelling. Occasionally, there were wide places with guards. They passed through several guarded doors, climbed up and went down. McKie lost track of the turns, the doors, and guard posts. After a time, they climbed to another short hallway with doors along its sides. The boy opened the second door on the right, waited for McKie to enter, closed the door. It was all done without words. McKie heard the boy's footsteps recede.

The room was small and dimly lighted by windows high in the wall opposite the door. A trestle table about two meters long with benches down both sides and a chair at each end almost filled the space. The walls were grey stone and unadorned. McKie worked his way around to the chair at the far end, sat down. He remained seated there silently for several minutes, absorbing this place. It was cold in the room: Gowachin temperature. One of the high windows behind him was open a crack and he could hear street noises: a heavy vehicle passing, voices arguing, many feet. The sense of the Warren pressing in upon this room was very strong. Nearer at hand from beyond the single door, he heard crockery banging and an occasional hiss as of steam.

Presently, the door opened and a tall, slender woman entered, slipping through the door at minimal opening. For a moment as she turned, the light from the windows concentrated on her face, then she sat down at the end of the right-hand bench, dropping into shadows.

McKie had never before seen such hard features on a woman. She was brittle rock with ice crystal eyes of palest blue. Her black hair was closely cropped into a stiff bristle. He repressed a shudder. The rigidity of her body amplified the hard expression on her face. It was not the hardness of suffering, not that alone, but something far more determined, something anchored in a kind of agony which might explode at the slightest touch. On a ConSentient world where the geriatric arts were available, she could have been any age between thirty-five and one hundred and thirty-five. The dim light into which she had seated herself complicated his scrutiny, but he suspected she was younger than thirty-five.

"So *you* are McKie."

He nodded.

"You're fortunate Adril's people got my message. Broey's already searching for you. I wasn't warned that you were so dark."

He shrugged.

"Bahrank sent word that you could get us all killed if we're not careful with you. He says you don't have even rudimentary survival training."

This surprised McKie, but he held his silence.

She sighed. "At least you have the good sense not to protest. Well . . . welcome to Dosadi, McKie. Perhaps I'll be able to keep you alive long enough for you to be of some use to us."

Welcome to Dosadi!

"I'm Jedrik as you doubtless already know."

"I recognize you."

This was only partly true. None of the representations he'd seen had conveyed the ruthless brutality which radiated from her.

A hard smile flickered on her lips, was gone.

"You don't respond when I welcome you to our planet."

McKie shook his head. Aritch's people had been specific in their injunction:

"She doesn't know your origin. Under no circumstances may you reveal to her that you come from beyond the God Wall. It could be immediately fatal."

McKie continued to stare silently at her.

A colder look came over Jedrik's features, something in the muscles at the corners of the mouth and eyes.

"We shall see. Now: Bahrank says you carry a wallet of some kind and that you have currency sewn into your clothing. First, hand me the wallet."

My toolkit?

She reached an open hand toward him.

"I'll warn you once, McKie. If I get up and walk out of here you'll not live more than two minutes."

Every muscle quivering protest, he slipped the toolkit from its pocket, extended it.

"And I'll warn you, Jedrik: I'm the only person who can open this without being killed and the contents destroyed."

She accepted the toolkit, turned its flat substance over in her hands.

"Really?"

McKie had begun to interest her in a new way. He was less than she'd expected, yet more. Naive, of course, incredibly naive. But she'd already known that of the people from beyond the God Wall. It was the most suitable explanation. Something was profoundly wrong in the Dosadi situation. The people beyond the Veil would have to send their best here. This McKie was their best? Astonishing.

She arose, went to the door, rapped once.

McKie watched her pass the toolkit to someone outside, heard a low-voiced conversation, neither half of it intelligible. In a flashing moment of indecision, he'd considered trying for some of the toolkit's protective contents. Something in Jedrik's manner and the accumulation of unknowns all around had stopped him.

Jedrik returned to her seat empty-handed. She stared at him a moment, head cocked to one side, then:

"I'll say several things to you. In a way, this is a test. If you fail, I guarantee you'll not survive long on Dosadi. Understood?"

When McKie failed to respond, she pounded a fist on the table.

"Understood?"

"Say what you have to say."

"Very well. It's obvious to me that those who instructed you about Dosadi warned you not to reveal your true origin. Yet, most of those who've talked to you for more than a few seconds suspect you're not one of us—not from Chu, not from the Rim, not from anywhere on Dosadi." Her voice took on a new harshness. "But I know it. Let me tell you, McKie, that there's not even a child among us who's failed to realize that the people imprisoned on Dosadi did not originate here!"

McKie stared at her, shocked.

Imprisoned.

As she spoke, he knew she was telling him the truth. Why hadn't Aritch or the others warned him? Why hadn't he seen this for himself? Since Dosadi was poison to both Human and Gowachin, rejected them, of course they'd know they hadn't originated here.

She gave him time to absorb this before continuing. "There are others among us from your realm, perhaps some we've not identified, better trained. But I was taught to act only on certainty. Of you I'm certain. You do not originate on Dosadi. I've put it to the question and I've the present confirmation of my own senses. You come from beyond the God Wall. Your actions with Bahrank, with Adril, with me . . ." She shook her head sadly.

Aritch set me up for this!

This thought brought back a recurrent question which continued to nag McKie; BuSab's discovery of the Dosadi experiment. Were the Gowachin that clumsy? Would they make such slips? The original plan to conceal this project must have been extensive. Yet, key facts had leaked to BuSab agents. McKie felt overwrought from asking himself the same questions over and over without satisfaction. And now, Jedrik's pressures compounded the burden. The only suitable answer was that Aritch's people had done everything with the intent of putting him in this position. They'd deliberately leaked information about Dosadi. And McKie was their target.

To what purpose?

"Can we be overheard?" he asked.

"Not by my enemies on Dosadi."

He considered this. She'd left open the question of whether anyone from beyond the God Wall might eavesdrop. McKie pursed his lips with indecision. She'd taken his toolkit with such ridiculous ease . . . yet, what choice had he? They wouldn't get anything from the kit and someone out there, one of Jedrik's underlings, would die. That could have a useful effect on Jedrik. He decided to play for time.

"There're many things I could tell you. So many things. I hardly know where to begin."

"Begin by telling me how you came through the God Wall."

Yes, he might be able to confuse her with a loose description of Calebans and jumpdoors. Nothing in her Dosadi experience could've prepared Jedrik for such phenomena. McKie took a deep breath. Before he could speak there was a rap on the door.

Jedrik raised a hand for silence, leaned over, and opened the door. A skinny young man with large eyes beneath a high forehead and thin blond hair slipped through, placed McKie's toolkit on the table in front of Jedrik.

"It wasn't very difficult," he said.

McKie stared at the kit in shock. It lay open with all of its contents displayed in perfect order.

Jedrik gestured the youth to the seat opposite her. She reached for a raygen.

McKie could no longer contain himself.

"Careful! That's dangerous!"

"Be still, McKie. You know nothing of danger."

She removed the raygen, examined it, replaced it neatly, looked at the young man.

"All right, Stiggy. Tell me."

The youth began removing the items from the toolkit one by one, handling each with a knowledgeable correctness, speaking rapidly.

McKie tried hard to follow the conversation, but it was in a code he could not understand. The expressions on their faces were eloquent enough, however. They were elated. Whatever Stiggy was saying about the dangerous toys in McKie's toolkit, his revelations profited both of them.

The uncertainties which had begun during McKie's ride with Bahrank reached a new intensity. The feeling had built up in him like a sickness: disquiet stomach, pains in his chest, and, lastly, an ache across his forehead. He'd wondered for a time if he might be the victim of some new disease native to Dosadi. It could not be the planet's food because he'd eaten nothing yet. The realization came over him as he watched Jedrik and Stiggy that his reactions were his own reasoning system trying to reject something, some assumption or set of assumptions which he'd accepted without question. He tried to empty his mind, not asking any questions in particular. Let come into his awareness what may. It would all have a fresh appraisal.

Dosadi requires you to be coldly brutal in all of your decisions. No exceptions.

Well . . . he'd let go of the toolkit in the belief that someone would die trying to open it. But he'd issued a warning. That warning could've helped them. Probably did.

I must become exactly like them or I cannot survive—let alone succeed.

At last, McKie felt Aritch's fear of Dosadi, understood the Gowachin desperation. What a terrible training ground for the recognition and use of power!

Jedrik and Stiggy finished their conversation over the toolkit. Stiggy closed the kit, arose with it in one hand, speaking at last in words McKie understood.

"Yes, we must lose no time."

Stiggy left with the kit.

Jedrik faced McKie. The toolkit and its contents had helped answer the most obvious question about McKie and his kind. The people beyond the God Wall were the degenerate descendants of those who'd invented such devices. It was the only workable explanation. She felt almost sorry for this poor fool. But that was not a permissable emotion. He must be made to understand that he had no choice but to obey her.

"Now, McKie, you will answer all of my questions."

"Yes."

It was utter submission and she knew it.

"When you've satisfied me in all matters," she said, "then we'll eat and I'll take you to a place where you'll be reasonably safe."

The Family/Clan/Factions of the Rim are still responding to their defeat in the mass attempt on our defenses of last Decamo. They appear severly chastened. Small police actions are all that we need anticipate over the next planning period. Further, our operatives in the Rim find no current difficulties in steering the F/C/F toward a natural and acceptable cultural rejection of economic developments which might lead them to improved food production.

—From a Dosadi Bureau of
Control document

An angry Broey, full out and uninhibited anger, was something to see and quite a number of his Gowachin aides had seen this emotional display during the night. It was now barely dawn. Broey had not slept in two days; but the fourth group of his aides stood before him in the sanctum to receive the full spate of his displeasure. The word had already gone out through their ranks and they, like the others, did not try to hide their fear or their anxious eagerness to restore themselves in Broey's good graces.

Broey stood near the end of the long table where, earlier, he had met with Gar and Tria. The only visible sign of his long sleepless hours was a slight pitting of the fatty nodes between his ventricles. His eyes were as sharp as ever and his voice had lost none if its bite.

"What I'd like explained is how this could happen without a word of warning. And it's not just that we failed to detect this, but that we continued to grind out complacent reports, reports which went exactly contrary to what actually was happening."

171

The aides massed at the other end of the table, all standing, all fidgeting, were not assuaged by Broey's use of "we." They heard him clearly. He was saying: "You! You! You!"

"I will be satisfied by nothing less than an informant," Broey said. "I want a Human informant, either from Chu or from the Rim. I don't care how you get this informant. We must find that store of city food. We must find where they have started their blasphemous Rim city."

One of his aides, a slender young Gowachin in the front rank, ventured a cautious question which had been repeated several times by other chastened aides during the night.

"If we move too strongly against Humans in the Warrens, won't that feed the unrest that . . ."

"We'll have more riots, more turning of Gowachin against Human and Human against Gowachin," Broey agreed. "That's a consequence we are prepared to accept."

This time they understood that Broey used the royal "we." Broey would accept the consequences. Some of his aides, however, were not ready to accept a war between the species within the city's walls. One of the aides farther back in the ranks raised an arm.

"Perhaps we should use only Human troops in the Warrens. If we . . ."

"Who would that fool?" Broey demanded. "We have taken the proper steps to maintain our hold on Chu. You have one task and one task only: find that store of food and those hidden factories. Unless we find them we're finished. Now, get out of here. I don't want to see any of you until you can report success!"

They filed out silently.

Broey stood looking down at the blank screen of his communicator. Alone at last, he allowed his shoulders to slump, breathed heavily through both mouth and ventricles.

What a mess! What a terrible mess.

He knew in his node of nodes that he was behaving pre-

cisely as Jedrik wanted him to behave. She had left him no alternatives. He could only admire her handling of the situation while he waited for the opening which he knew must
come. But what a magnificent intellect operated in that Human head. And a female at that! Gowachin females never developed such qualities. Only on the Rim were Gowachin females used as other than breeders. Human females, on the
other hand, never ceased to amaze him. This Jedrik possessed real leadership qualities. Whether she was the one to
take over the Electorship remained to be seen.

Broey found himself recalling those first moments of terrible awareness in the Graluz. Yes, this was the way of the
world. If one chose the survivors by other than a terrible testing process, all would die. It would be the end of both species. At least, it would be the end of them on Dosadi and only
Dosadi mattered.

He felt bereft, though. He felt betrayed by his God. Why
had God failed to warn him? And when questioned, how
could God respond that only evil could penetrate the mind
of a fanatic? Wasn't God omnipotent? Could any awareness
be closed to God? How could God be *God* them?

I am your God!

He could never forget that voiceless voice reverberating in
his head.

Was that a lie?

The idea that they were puppets of a false god was not a
new one. But if this were the case, then the other uses of
those like Pcharky eluded him. What was the purpose of being a Gowachin in Human form or vice versa if not to elude
the God of the Veil? Quite obviously, Jedrik operated on
such a premise. What other motive could she have than to
prolong her own life? As the City was to the Rim, so was the
power to elude the God (false God or true) to those of the
City. No other assumption fitted a Dosadi justification.

We are plagued by a corrupt polity which promotes unlawful and/or immoral behavior. Public interest has no practical significance in everyday behavior among the ruling factions. The real problems of our world are not being confronted by those in power. In the guise of public service, they use whatever comes to hand for personal gain. They are insane with and for power.

—From a clandestine document circulated on Dosadi

It was dark when a disguised Jedrik and undisguised McKie emerged onto the streets. She led them down narrow passages, her mind full of things McKie had revealed. Jedrik wore a blonde wig and puff-out disguise which made her appear heavy and hunched.

As they passed an open courtyard, McKie heard music. He almost stumbled. The music came from a small orchestra—delicate tympany, soft strings, and a rich chorus of wind instruments. He did not recognize the melody, but it moved him more deeply than any other music of his experience. It was as though the music were played only for him. Aritch and company had said nothing about such magnificent music here.

People still thronged the streets in numbers which astonished him. But now they appeared to pay him little notice.

Jedrik kept part of her attention on McKie, noting the fools with their musical dalliance, noting how few people there were on the streets—little more than her own patrols in this quarter. She'd expected that, but the actuality held an

174

eerie mood in the dim and scattered illumination from lighted corners.

She had debated providing McKie with a crude disguise, but he obviously didn't have the cunning to carry off the double deception she required. She'd begun to sense a real intelligence in him, though. McKie was an enigma. Why had he never encountered the opportunities to sharpen that intelligence? Sensing the sharpness in him, she could not put off the thought that she had missed something vital in his accounts of that social entity which he called the ConSentiency. Whether this failure came from actual concealment by McKie or through his inadequacies, she was not yet willing to judge. The enigma set her on edge. And the mood in the streets did nothing to ease her emotions. She was glad when they crossed the line into the area completely controlled by her own personal cell.

The bait having been trailed through the streets by one who would appear a tame underling, Jedrik allowed herself a slight relaxation. Broey would have learned by this time about the killing of Tria's double agent. He would react to that and to the new bait. It was almost time for phase two of her design for Broey.

McKie followed her without question, acutely aware of every strange glance cast their way. He was emptied of all resistance, knowing he could not survive if he failed to follow Jedrik through the smelly, repellent darkness of her streets.

The food from the restaurant sat heavily in his stomach. It had been tasty: a stew of odd shapes full of shredded greenery, and steaming hot. But he could not shake the realization that his stew had been compounded of someone's garbage.

Jedrik had left him very little. She hadn't learned of the Taprisiot, or the bead in this stomach which probably would not link him to the powers of the ConSentiency if he died. She had not learned of the standard BuSab implantation devices which amplified his senses. And, oddly, she had not explored many of his revelations about BuSab. She'd seemed much more interested in the money hidden about his person and had taken possession of all of it. She'd examined the currency carefully.

"This is real."

He wasn't sure, but he thought she'd been surprised.

"This was given to you *before* you were sent to Dosadi?"

"Yes."

She was a while absorbing the implications, but appeared satisfied. She'd given him a few small currency tokens from her own pockets.

"Nobody'll bother you for these. If you need anything, ask. We may be able to gratify some of your needs."

It was still dark, lighted only by illumination at corners, when they came to the address Jedrik sought. Grey light suffused the street. A young Human male of about ten squatted with his back against the stone wall at the building's corner. As Jedrik and McKie approached, he sprang up, alert. He nodded once to Jedrik.

She did not acknowledge, but by some hidden signal the boy knew she had received his message. He relaxed once more against the wall.

When McKie looked back a few paces beyond where the boy had signaled, he was gone. No sound, no sign—just gone.

Jedrik stopped at a shadowed entryway. It was barred by an openwork metal gate flanked by two armed guards. The guards opened the gate without words. Beyond the gate there was a large, covered courtyard illuminated by glowing tubes on right and left. Three of its sides were piled to the courtyard cover with boxes of various sizes—some taller than a Human and narrow, others short and fat. Set into the stacks as though part of the courtyard's walls was one narrow passage leading to a metal door opposite the gateway.

McKie touched Jedrik's arm.

"What's in the boxes?"

"Weapons." She spoke as though to a cretin.

The metal door was opened from within. Jedrik led McKie into a large room at least two stories tall. The door clanged shut behind them. McKie sensed several Humans along the courtyard wall on both sides of him, but his attention had been captured by something else.

Dominating the room was a gigantic cage suspended from the ceiling. Its bars sparkled and shimmered with hidden energies. A single Gowachin male sat cross-legged in a hammock at the cage's center. McKie had seldom seen a ConSentient Gowachin that aged. His nose crest was fringed by flaking yellow crusts. Heavy wrinkles wormed their way beneath watery eyes beginning to glaze with the degeneration which often blinded Gowachin who lived too long away from water. His body had a slack appearance, with loose muscles and pitted indentations along the nodes between his ventricles. The hammock suspended him off the cage floor and that floor shimmered with volatile energies.

Jedrik paused, divided her attention between McKie and the old Gowachin. She seemed to expect a particular reaction from McKie, but he wasn't certain she found what she sought.

McKie stood a moment in silent examination of the Gowachin. Prisoner? What was the significance of that cage and its shimmering energies? Presently, he glanced around the room, recording the space. Six armed Human males flanked the door through which he and Jedrik had entered. A remarkable assortment of objects crammed the room's walls, some with purpose unknown to him but many recognizable as weapons: spears and swords, flame-throwers, garish armor, bombs, pellet projectors . . .

Jedrik moved a pace closer to the cage. The occupant

stared back at her with faint interest. She cleared her throat.

"Greetings, Pcharky. I have found my key to the God Wall."

The old Gowachin remained silent, but McKie thought he saw a sparkle of interest in the glazed eyes.

Jedrik shook her head slowly from side to side, then: "I have a new datum, Pcharky. The Veil of Heaven was created by creatures called Calebans. They appear to us as suns."

Pcharky's glance flickered to McKie, back to Jedrik. The Gowachin knew the source of her new datum.

McKie renewed his speculations about the old Gowachin. That cage must be a prison, its walls enforced by dangerous energies. Bahrank had spoken of conflict between the species. Humans controlled this room. Why did they imprison a Gowachin? Or . . . was this caged Gowachin, this Pcharky, another agent from Tandaloor? With a tightening of his throat, McKie wondered if his own fate might be to live out his days in such a cage.

Pcharky grunted, then:

"The God Wall is like this cage but more powerful."

His voice was a husky croaking, the words clear Galach with an obvious Tandaloor accent. McKie, his fears reinforced, glanced at Jedrik, found her studying him. She spoke.

"Pcharky has been with us for a long time, very long. There's no telling how many people he has helped to escape from Dosadi. Soon, I may persuade him to be of service to me."

McKie found himself shocked to silence by the possibilities glimpsed through her words. Was Dosadi in fact an investigation of the Caleban mystery? Was that the secret Aritch's people concealed here? McKie stared at the shimmering bars of Pcharky's cage. Like the God Wall? But the God Wall was enforced by a Caleban.

Once more, Jedrik looked at the caged Gowachin.

"A sun confines enormous energies, Pcharky. Are your energies inadequate?"

But Pcharky's attention was on McKie. The old voice croaked.

"Human, tell me: Did you come here willingly?"

"Don't answer him," Jedrik snapped.

Pcharky closed his eyes. Interview ended.

Jedrik, accepting this, whirled and strode to the left around the cage.

"Come along, McKie." She didn't look back, but continued speaking. "Does it interest you that Pcharky designed his own cage?"

"He designed it? Is it a prison?"

"Yes."

"If he designed it . . . how does it hold him?"

"He knew he'd have to serve my purposes if he were to remain alive."

She had come to another door which opened onto a narrow stairway. It climbed to the left around the cage room. They emerged into a long hallway lined with narrow doors dimly lighted by tiny overhead bulbs. Jedrik opened one of these doors and led the way into a carpeted room about four meters wide and six long. Dark wood panels reached from floor to waist level, shelves loaded with books above. McKie peered closely: books . . . actual paper books. He tried to recall where he'd ever before seen such a collection of primitive . . But, of course, these were not primitive. These were one of Dosadi's strange recapitulations.

Jedrik had removed her wig, stopped midway in the room to turn and face McKie.

"This is my room. Toilet there." She pointed to an opening between shelves. "That window . . . " Again, she pointed, this time to an opening opposite the toilet door. " . . . is one-way to admit light, and it's our best. As Dosadi measures such things, this is a relatively secure place."

He swept his gaze around the room.

Her room?

McKie was struck by the amount of living space, a mark of power on Dosadi; the absence of people in the hall. By the standards of this planet, Jedrik's room, this building, represented a citadel of power.

Jedrik spoke, an odd note of nervousness in voice and manner.

"Until recently, I also had other quarters: a prestigious apartment on the slopes of the Council Hills. I was considered a climber with excellent prospects, my own skitter and driver. I had access to all but the highest codes in the master banks, and that's a powerful tool for those who can use it. Now . . ." She gestured. ". . . this is what I have chosen. I must eat swill with the lowest. No males of rank will pay the slightest attention to me. Broey thinks I'm cowering somewhere, a pallet in the Warrens. But I have this . . ." Again, that sweeping gesture. ". . . and this." One finger tapped her head. "I need nothing more to bring those Council Hills crashing down."

She stared into McKie's eyes.

He found himself believing her.

She was not through speaking.

"You're definitely male Human, McKie."

He didn't know what to make of that, but her air of braggadocio fascinated him.

"How did you lose that other . . ."

"I didn't lose it. I threw it away. I no longer needed it. I've made things move faster than our precious Elector, or even your people, can anticipate. Broey thinks to wait for an opening against me?" She shook her head.

Captivated, McKie watched her cross to the window, open a ventilator above it. She kicked a wooden knob below the adjoining bookshelves, pulled out a section of paneling which trailed a double bed. Standing across the bed from McKie, she began to undress. She dropped the wig to the floor, slipped off the coveralls, peeled the bulging inner disguise from her flesh. Her skin was pale cream.

"McKie, I am your teacher."

He remained silent. She was long waisted, slim, and graceful. The creamy skin was marked by two faint scars to the left of the pubic wedge.

"Take off your clothes," she said.

He swallowed.

She shook her head.

"McKie, McKie, to survive here you must become Dosadi. You don't have much time. Get your clothes off."

Not knowing what to expect, McKie obeyed.

She watched him carefully.

"Your skin is lighter than I expected where the sun has not darkened you. We will bleach the skin of your face and hands tomorrow."

McKie looked at his hands, at the sharp line where his cuffs had protected his arms. Dark skin. He recalled Bahrank talking of dark skin and a place called Pylash Gate. To mask the unusual shyness he felt, he looked at Jedrik, asked about Pylash Gate.

"So Bahrank mentioned that? Well, it was a stupid mistake. The Rim sent in shock troops and foolish orders were given for the gate's defenses. Only one troop survived there, all dark-skinned like you. The suspicion of treachery was natural."

"Oh."

He found his attention compelled toward the bed. A dark maroon spread covered it.

Jedrik approached him around the foot of the bed. She stopped less than a hand's width away from him . . . creamy flesh, full breasts. He looked up into her eyes. She stood half a head over him, an expression of cold amusement on her face.

McKie found the musky smell of her erotically stimulating. She looked down, saw this, laughed, and abruptly hurled him onto the bed. She landed with him and her body was all over him, hot and hard and demanding.

It was the strangest sexual experience of McKie's life. Not lovemaking, but violent attack. She groaned, bit at him, clawed. And when he tried to caress her, she became even more violent, frenzied. Through it all, she was oddly careful of his pleasure, watching his reactions, reading him. When it was over, he lay back, spent. Jedrik sat up on the edge of the bed. The blankets were a twisted mess. She grabbed a blanket, threw it across the room, stood up, whirled back to look down at him.

"You are very sly and tricky, McKie."

He drew in a trembling breath, remained silent.

"You tried to catch me with softness," she accused. "Better than you have tried that with me. It will not work."

McKie marshalled the energy to sit up and restore some order to the bed. His shoulder pained him where she'd scratched. He felt the ache of a bite on his neck. He crawled into the bed, pulled the blankets up to his chin. She was a madwoman, absolutely mad. Insane.

Presently, Jedrik stopped looking at him. She recovered the blanket from across the room, spread it on the bed, joined him. He was acutely conscious of her staring at him with an openly puzzled frown.

"Tell me about the relationships between men and women on your worlds."

He recounted a few of the love stories he knew, fighting all the while to stay awake. It was difficult to stifle the gaping yawns. She kept punching his shoulder.

"I don't believe it. You're making this up."

"No . . . no. It's true."

"You have women of your own there?"

"Women of my . . . Well, it's not like that, not ownership . . . ahhh, not possession."

"What about children?"

"What about them?"

"How're they treated, educated?"

He sighed, sketched in some details from his own childhood.

After a while she let him go to sleep. He awakened several times during the night, conscious of the strange room and bed, of Jedrik breathing softly beside him. Once, he thought he felt her shoulders shaking with repressed sobs.

Shortly before dawn, there was a scream in the next block, a terrifying sound of agony loud enough to waken all but the most hardened or the most fatigued. McKie, awake and thinking, felt Jedrik's breathing change. He lay tense and watchful, awaiting a repetition or another sound which might explain that eerie scream. A threatening silence gripped the night. McKie built an image in his mind of what could be happening in the buildings around them: some people starting from sleep not knowing (perhaps not caring) what had awakened them; lighter sleepers grumbling and sinking back into restless slumber.

Finally, McKie sat up, peered into the room's shadows. His disquiet communicated itself to Jedrik. She rolled over, looked up at him in the pale dawn light now creeping into the shadows.

"There are many noises in the Warrens that you learn to ignore," she said.

Coming from her, it was almost conciliatory, almost a gesture of apology, of friendship.

"Someone screamed," he said.

"I knew it must be something like that."

"How can you sleep through such a sound?"

"I didn't."

"But how can you ignore it?"

"The sounds you ignore are those which aren't immediately threatening to you, those which you can do nothing about."

"Someone was hurt."

"Very likely. But you must not burden your soul with things you cannot change."

"Don't you want to change . . . that?"

"I am changing it."

Her tone, her attitude were those of a lecturer in a schoolroom, and now there was no doubt that she was being deliberately helpful. Well, she'd said she was his teacher. And he must become completely Dosadi to survive.

"How're you changing things?"

"You're not capable of understanding yet. I want you to take it one step at a time, one lesson at a time."

He couldn't help asking himself then:

What does she want from me now?

He hoped it was not more sex.

"Today," she said, "I want you to meet the parents of three children who work in our cell."

If you think of yourselves as helpless and ineffectual, it is certain that you will create a despotic government to be your master. The wise despot, therefore, maintains among his subjects a popular sense that they are helpless and ineffectual.

—The Dosadi Lesson:
A Gowachin Assessment

Aritch studied Ceylang carefully in the soft light of his green-walled relaxation room. She had come down immediately after the evening meal, responsive to his summons. They both knew the reason for that summons: to discuss the most recent report concerning McKie's behavior on Dosadi.

The old Gowachin waited for Ceylang to seat herself, observing how she pulled the red robe neatly about her lower extremities. Her features appeared composed, the fighting mandibles relaxed in their folds. She seemed altogether a figure of secure competence, a Wreave of the ruling classes—not that Wreaves recognized such classes. It disturbed Aritch that Wreaves tested for survival only through a complex understanding of sentient behavior, rigid performance standards based on ancient ritual, whose actual origins could only be guessed; there was no written record.

But that's why we chose her.

Aritch grunted, then:

"What can you say about the report?"

"McKie learns rapidly."

185

Her spoken Galach had a faint sibilance.

Aritch nodded.

"I would say rather that he *adapts* rapidly. It's why we chose him."

"I've heard you say he's more Gowachin than the Gowachin."

"I expect him soon to be more Dosadi than the Dosadi."

"If he survives."

"There's that, yes. Do you still hate him?"

"I have never hated him. You do not understand the spectrum of Wreave emotions."

"Enlighten me."

"He has violated my essential pride of self. This requires a specific reaction in kind. Hate would only dull my abilities."

"But *I* was the one who gave you the orders which had to be countermanded."

"My oath of service to the Gowachin contains a specific injunction, that I cannot hold any one of my teachers responsible for either understanding or obeying the Wreave protocols of courtesy. It is the same injunction which frees us to serve McKie's Bureau."

"You do not consider McKie one of your teachers?"

She studied him for a moment, then:

"Not only do I exclude him, but I know him to be one who has learned much about our protocols."

"What if I were to say he is one of your teachers?"

Again, she stared at him.

"I would revise my estimations of him—and of you."

Aritch took a deep breath.

"Yet, you must learn McKie as though you lived in his skin. Otherwise, you will fail us."

"I will not fail you. I know the reasons you chose me. Even McKie will know in time. He dares not spill my blood in the Courtarena, or even subject me to public shame. Were he to do either of these things, half the Wreave universe would go hunting him with death in their mandibles."

Aritch shook his head slowly from side to side.

"Ceylang! Didn't you hear him warn you that you must shed your Wreave skin?"

She was a long time responding and he noted the subtle characteristics which he'd been told were the Wreave adjustments to anger: a twitching of the jowls, tension in the pedal bifurcations . . .

Presently, she said:

"Tell me what that means, Teacher."

"You will be charged with performing under *Gowachin* Law, performing as though you were another McKie. He adapts! Haven't you observed this? He is capable of defeating you—and us—in such a way, *in such a way* that your Wreave universe would shower him with adulation for his victory. That cannot be permitted. Too much is at stake."

Ceylang trembled and showed other signs of distress.

"But I am Wreave!"

"If it comes to the Courtarena, you no longer can be Wreave."

She inhaled several shallow breaths, composed herself.

"If I become too much McKie, aren't you afraid I might hesitate to slay him?"

"McKie would not hesitate."

She considered this.

"Then there's only one reason you chose me for this task."

He waited for her to say it.

"Because we Wreaves are the best in the universe at learning the behavior of others—both overt and covert."

"And you dare not rely on any supposed inhibitions he may or may not have!"

After a long pause, she said:

"You are a better teacher than I'd suspected. Perhaps you're even better than *you* suspected."

"Their law! It is a dangerous foundation for nonauthentic traditions. It is no more than a device to justify false ethics!"

—*Gowachin comment on ConSentient Law*

While they dressed in the dim dawn light coming through the single window, McKie began testing what Jedrik meant by being his teacher.

"Will you answer any question I ask about Dosadi?"

"No."

Then what areas would she withhold from him? He saw it at once: those areas where she gained and held personal power.

"Will anyone resent it that we . . . had sex together?"

"Resent? Why should anyone resent that?"

"I don't . . ."

"Answer my question!"

"Why do I have to answer your every question?"

"To stay alive."

"You already know everything I . . ."

She brushed this aside.

"So the people of your ConSentiency sometimes resent the sexual relationships of others. They are not sure, then, how they use sex to hold power over others."

He blinked. Her quick, slashing analysis was devastating.

She peered at him.

"McKie, what can you do here without me? Don't you know yet that the ones who sent you intended you to die here?"

"Or survive in my own peculiar way."

She considered this. It was another idea about McKie which she had put aside for later evaluation. Indeed, he might well have hidden talents which her questions had not yet exposed. What annoyed her now was the sense that she didn't know enough about the ConSentiency to explore this. Could not take the time right now to explore it. His response disturbed her. It was as though everything she could possibly do had already been decided for her by powers of which she knew next to nothing. They were leading her by the nose, perhaps, just as she led Broey . . . just as those mysterious Gowachin of the ConSentiency obviously had led McKie . . . poor McKie. She cut this short as unprofitable speculation. Obviously, she had to begin at once to search out McKie's talent. Whatever she discovered would reveal a great deal about his ConSentiency.

"McKie, I hold a great deal of power among the Humans and even among some Gowachin in the Warrens—and elsewhere. To do this, I must maintain certain fighting forces, including those who fight with physical weapons."

He nodded. Her tone was that of lecturing to a child, but he accepted this, recognizing the care she took with him.

"We will go first," she said, "to a nearby training area where we maintain the necessary edge on one of my forces."

Turning, she led him out into the hall and down a stairway which avoided the room of the cage. McKie was reminded of Pcharky, though, thinking about that gigantic expenditure of space with its strange occupant.

'Why do you keep Pcharky caged?" he asked, addressing Jedrik's back.

"So I can escape."

She refused to elaborate on this odd answer.

Presently, they emerged into a courtyard nestled into the solid walls of towering buildings. Only a small square of sky was visible directly overhead and far away. Artificial lighting from tubes along the walls provided an adequate illumination. It revealed two squads facing each other in the center of the courtyard. They were Humans, both male and female; all carried weapons: a tube of some sort with a wandlike protrusion from the end near their bodies. Several other Humans stood at observation positions around the two squads. There was a guard station with a desk at the door through which McKie and Jedrik had emerged.

"That's an assault force," Jedrik said, indicating the squads in the courtyard. She turned and consulted with the two young men at the guard station.

McKie made a rough count of the squads: about two hundred. It was obvious that everything had stopped because of Jedrik's presence. He thought the force was composed of striplings barely blooded in Dosadi's cruel necessities. This forced him to a re-evaluation of his own capabilities.

From Jedrik's manner with the two men, McKie guessed she knew them well. They paid close attention to everything she said. They, too, struck him as too young for responsibility.

The training area was another matter. It bore a depressing similarity to other such facilities he'd seen in the backwaters of the ConSentiency. War games were a constant lure among several species, a lure which BuSab had managed thus far to channel into such diversions as weapons fetishes.

Through the omnipresent stink, McKie smelled the faint aroma of cooking. He sniffed.

Turning to him, Jedrik spoke:

"The trainees have just been fed. That's part of their pay."

It was as though she'd read his mind, and now she watched him for some reaction.

McKie glanced around the training area. They'd just been fed here? There wasn't a scrap or crumb on the ground. He thought back to the restaurant, belatedly aware of a fastidious care with food that he'd seen and passed right over.

Again, Jedrik demonstrated the ease with which she read his reactions, his very thoughts.

"Nothing wasted," she said.

She turned away.

McKie looked where her attention went. Four women stood at the far side of the courtyard, weapons in their hands. Abruptly, McKie focused on the woman to the left, a competent-looking female of middle years. She was carrying a . . . it couldn't be, but . . .

Jedrik headed across the courtyard toward the woman. McKie followed, peered closely at the woman's weapon. It was an enlarged version of the pentrate from his kit! Jedrik spoke briefly to the woman.

"Is that the new one?"

"Yes. Stiggy brought it up this morning."

"Useful?"

"We think so. It focusses the explosion with somewhat more concentration than our equipment."

"Good. Carry on."

There were more training cadre near the wall behind the women. One, an older man with one arm, tried to catch Jedrik's attention as she led McKie toward a nearby door.

"Could you tell us when we . . ."

"Not now."

In the passage beyond the door, Jedrik turned and confronted McKie.

"Your impressions of our training? Quick!"

"Not sufficiently versatile."

She'd obviously probed for his most instinctive reaction, demanding the gut response unmonitored by reason. The answer brought a glowering expression to her face, an emotional candor which he was not to appreciate until much later. Presently, she nodded.

"They are a commando. More functions of a commando should be interchangeable. Wait here."

She returned to the training area. McKie, watching through the open door, saw her speak to the woman with the pentrate. When Jedrik returned, she nodded to McKie with an expression of approval.

"Anything else?"

"They're awfully damned young. You should have a few seasoned officers among them to put a rein on dangerous impetuousity."

"Yes, I've already set that in motion. Hereafter, McKie, I want you to come out with me every morning for about an hour. Watch the training, but don't interfere. Report your reactions to me."

He nodded. Clearly, she considered him useful and that was a step in the right direction. But it was an idiotic assignment. These violent infants possessed weapons which could make Dosadi uninhabitable. There was an atavistic excitement in the situation, though. He couldn't deny that. Something in the Human psyche responded to mass violence—really, to violence of any sort. It was related to Human sexuality, an ancient stirring from the most primitive times.

Jedrik was moving on, however.

"Stay close."

They were climbing an inside stairway now and McKie, hurrying to keep up, found his thoughts locked on that pentrate in the hands of one of Jedrik's people. The speed with which they'd copied and enlarged it dazzled him. It was another demonstration of why Aritch feared Dosadi.

At the top of the stairs, Jedrik rapped briefly at a door. A male voice said, "Come in."

The door swung open, and McKie found himself presently in a small, unoccupied room with an open portal at the far wall into what appeared to be a larger, well-lighted area. Voices speaking so softly as to be unintelligible came from there. A low table and five cramped chairs occupied the small room. There were no windows, but a frosted overhead fixture provided shadowless illumination. A large sheet of paper with colored graph lines on it covered the low table.

A swish of fabric brought McKie's attention to the open portal. A short, slender woman in a white smock, grey hair, and the dark, penetrating stare of someone accustomed to command entered, followed by a slightly taller man in the same white. He looked older than the woman, except his hair remained a lustrous black. His eyes, too, held that air of command. The woman spoke.

"Excuse the delay, Jedrik. We've been changing the summation. There's now no point where Broey can anticipate and change the transition from riots to full-scale warfare."

McKie was surprised by the abject deference in her voice. This woman considered herself to be far below Jedrik. The man took the same tone, gesturing to chairs.

"Sit down, please. This chart is our summation."

As the woman turned toward him, McKie caught a strong whiff of something pungent on her breath, a not unfamiliar smell. He'd caught traces of it several times in their passage through the Warrens. She went on speaking as Jedrik and McKie slipped into chairs.

"This is not unexpected." She indicated the design on the paper.

The man intruded.

"We've been telling you for some time now that Tria is ready to come over."

"She's trouble," Jedrik said.

"But Gar . . ."

It was the woman, arguing, but Jedrik cut her off.

"I know: Gar does whatever she tells him to do. The daughter runs the father. He thinks she's the most wonderful thing that ever happened, able to . . ."

"Her abilities are not the issue," the man said.

The woman spoke eagerly.

"Yes, it's her influence on Gar that . . ."

"Neither of them anticipated my moves," Jedrik said, "but I anticipated their moves."

The man leaned across the table, his face close to Jedrik's. He appeared suddenly to McKie like a large, dangerous animal—dangerous because his actions could never be fully predicted. His hands twitched when he spoke.

"We've told you every detail of our findings, every source, every conclusion. Now, are you saying you don't share our assessment of . . ."

"You don't understand," Jedrik said.

The woman had drawn back. Now, she nodded.

Jedrik said:

"It isn't the first time I've had to reassess your conclusions. Hear me: Tria will leave Broey when she's ready, not when he's ready. It's the same for anyone she serves, even Gar."

They spoke in unison:

"Leave Gar?"

"Leave anyone. Tria serves only Tria. Never forget that. Especially don't forget it if she comes over to us."

The man and woman were silent.

McKie thought about what Jedrik had said. Her words were another indication that someone on Dosadi might have other than personal aims. Jedrik's tone was unmistakable: she censured and distrusted Tria because Tria served *only* selfish ambition. Therefore, Jedrik (and this other pair by inference) served some unstated mutual purpose. Was it a form of patriotism they served, species-oriented? BuSab agents were always alert for this dangerous form of tribal madness, not necessarily to suppress it, but to make certain it did not explode into a violence deadly to the ConSentiency.

The white-smocked woman, after mulling her own thoughts, spoke:

"If Tria can't be enlisted for . . . what I mean is, we can use her own self-serving to hold her." She corrected herself. "Unless you believe we cannot convince her we'll overcome Broey." She chewed at her lip, a fearful expression in her eyes.

A shrewd look came over Jedrik's face.

"What is it you suspect?"

The woman pointed to the chart on the table.

"Gar still shares in the major decisions. That shouldn't be, but it is. If he . . ."

The man spoke with subservient eagerness.

"He has some hold on Broey!"

The woman shook her head.

"Or Broey plays a game other than the one we anticipated."

Jedrik looked at the woman, the man, at McKie. She spoke as though to McKie but McKie realized she was addressing the air.

"It's a specific thing. Gar has revealed something to Broey. I know what he's revealed. Nothing else could force Broey to behave this way." She nodded at the chart. "We *have* them!"

The woman ventured a question.

"Have we done well?"

"Better than you know."

The man smiled, then:

"Perhaps this is the time to ask if we could have larger rooms. The damn' children are always moving the furniture. We bump . . ."

"Not now!"

Jedrik arose. McKie followed her example.

"Let me see the children," Jedrik said.

The man turned to the open portal.

"Get out here, you! Jedrik wants you!"

Three children came scurrying from the other room. The woman didn't even look at them. The man favored them with an angry glare. He spoke to Jedrik.

"They've brought no food into this house in almost a week."

McKie studied the children carefully as he saw Jedrik was doing. They stood in a row just inside the room and, from their expressions, it was impossible to tell their reaction to the summons. They were two girls and a boy. The one on the right, a girl, was perhaps nine; on the left, another girl, was five or six. The boy was somewhat older, perhaps twelve or thirteen. He favored McKie with a glance. It was the glance of a predator who recognizes ready prey, but who already has eaten. All three bore more resemblance to the woman than to the man, but the parentage was obvious: the eyes, the set of the ears, nose . . .

Jedrik had completed her study. She gestured to the boy.

"Start sending him to the second training team."

"About time," the woman said. "We'll be glad to get him out of here."

"Come along, McKie."

In the hall, Jedrik said:

"To answer your question, they're pretty typical."

McKie, who had only wondered silently, swallowed in a dry throat. The petty goals of these people: to get a bigger room where they could live without bumping into furniture. He'd sensed no affection for each other in that couple. They were companions of convenience. There had been not the smallest hint of emotion for each other when they spoke. McKie found it diffult to imagine them making love, but apparently they did They had produced three children.

Realization came like an explosion in his head. Of course they showed no emotion! What other protection did they have? On Dosadi, anything cared for was a club to beat you into somebody else's line. And there was another thing.

McKie spoke to Jedrik's back as they went down the stairs. "That couple—they're addicted to something."

Surprisingly, Jedrik stopped, looked back up at him.

"How else do you think I hold such a pair? The substance is called *dis*. It's very rare. It comes from the far mountains, far beyond the . . . far beyond. The Rim sends parties of children as bearers to obtain *dis* for me. In a party of fifty, thirty can except to die on such a trek. Do you get the measure of it, McKie?"

Once more, they headed down the stairs.

McKie, realizing she'd taken the time to teach him another lesson about Dosadi, could only follow, stunned, while she led him into a room where technicians bleached the sun-darkened areas of his skin.

When they emerged, he no longer carried the stigma of Pylash Gate.

When the means of great violence are widespread, nothing is more dangerous to the powerful than that they create outrage and injustice, for outrage and injustice will certainly ignite retaliation in kind.

—BuSab Manual

"It is no longer classifiable as rioting," the aide said.

He was a short Gowachin with pinched features, and he looked across the room to where Broey sat facing a dead communicator. There was a map on the wall behind the aide, its colors made brilliant by harsh morning light coming in the east windows. Below the map, a computer terminal jutted from the wall. Occasionally it clicked.

Gar came into the room from the hall, peered around as though looking for someone, left.

Broey noted the intrusion, glanced at the map.

"Still no sign of where she's gone to ground?"

"Nothing certain."

"The one who paraded McKie through the streets . . ."

"Clearly an expendable underling."

"Where did they go?"

The aide indicated a place on the map, a group of buildings in the Warrens to the northwest.

Broey stared at the blank face of his communications screen. He'd been tricked again. He knew it. That damnable

Human female! Violence in the city teetered on the edge of full-scale war: Gowachin against Human. And still nothing, not even a hint at the location of Gar's Rim stores, the blasphemous factories. It was an unstable condition which could not continue much longer.

His communications screen came alive with a report: violent fighting near Gate Twenty-One. Broey glanced at the map. That made it more than one hundred clearly defined battles between the species along an unresolved perimeter. The report spoke of new weapons and unsuccessful attempts to capture specimens.

Gate Twenty-One?

That wasn't far from the place where McKie had been paraded through . . .

Several things slipped into a new relationship in Broey's mind. He looked at his aide, who stood waiting obediently at the map.

"Where's Gar?"

Aides were summoned, sent running. Gar was not to be found.

"Tria?"

She, too, was unavailable.

Gar's fanatics remained neutral, but more of Jedrik's pattern was emerging. Everything pointed to an exquisite understanding of the weakness implicit in the behavior of Gar and Tria.

And I thought I was the only one who saw that!

Broey hesitated.

Why would the God not speak to him other than to say "I am watched."

Broey felt tricked and betrayed in his innermost being. This had a cleansing effect on his reason. He could only depend on himself. And he began to sense a larger pattern in Jedrik's behavior. Was it possible that Jedrik shared *his* goals? The possibility excited him.

He looked at the aides who'd come running with the negative information about Gar and Tria, began to snap orders.

"Get our people out of all those Warrens, except that corridor to the northeast. Reinforce that area. Everyone else fall back to the secondary walls. Let no Humans inside that perimeter. Block all gates. Get moving!"

This last was shouted as his aides hesitated.

Perhaps it already was too late. He realized now that he'd allowed Jedrik to bait and distract him. It was clear that she'd created in her mind an almost perfect simulation model of Broey. And she'd done it from a Liaitor position! Incredible. He could almost feel sorry for Gar and Tria. They were like puppets dancing to Jedrik's strings.

I was no better.

It came over him that Jedrik's simulation probably encompassed this very moment of realization. Admiration for her permeated him.

Superb!

Quietly, he issued orders for the sequestering of Gowachin females within the inner Graluz bastions which he'd had the foresight to prepare. His people would thank him for that.

Those who survived the next few hours.

The attack by those who want to die—this is the attack against which you cannot prepare a perfect defense.

—Human aphorism

By the third morning, McKie felt that he might have lived all of his life on Dosadi. The place demanded every element of attention he could muster.

He stood alone in Jedrik's room, staring absently at the unmade bed. She expected him to put the place in order before her return. He knew that. She'd told him to wait here and had gone away on urgent business. He could only obey.

Concerns other than an unmade bed distracted him, though. He felt now that he understood the roots of Aritch's fears. The Gowachin of Tandaloor might very well destroy this place, even if they knew that by doing so they blasted open that bloody region where every sentient hid his most secret fears. He could see this clearly now. How the Running Phylum expected him to avoid that monstrous decision was a more elusive matter.

There were secrets here.

McKie sensed Dosadi like a malignant organism beneath his feet, jealously keeping those secrets from him. This place was the enemy of the ConSentiency, but he found himself emotionally siding with Dosadi. It was betrayal of BuSab, of his Legum oath, everything. But he could not prevent that feeling or recognition of it. In the course of only a few generations, Dosadi had become a particular thing. Monstrous? Only if you held to your own precious myths. Dosadi might be the greatest cleansing force the ConSentiency had ever experienced.

The wole prospect of the ConSentiency had begun to sicken him. And Aritch's Gowachin. Gowachin Law? Stuff Gowachin Law!

It was quiet in Jedrik's room. Painfully quiet.

He knew that out on the streets of Chu there was violent warfare between Gowachin and Human. Wounded had been rushed through the training courtyard while he was there with Jedrik. Afterward, she'd taken him to her command post, a room across the hall and above Pcharky's cage. He'd stood nearby, watched her performance as though she were a star on an entertainment circuit and he a member of the audience. It was fascinating. Broey will do this. Broey will give that order. And each time, the reports revealed how precisely she had anticipated her opponent.

Occasionally, she mentioned Gar or Tria. He was able to detect the subtle difference in her treatment of that pair.

On their second night together, Jedrik had aroused his sexual appetites softly, deftly. She had treated him to a murmurous compliance, and afterward had leaned over him on an elbow to smile coldly.

"You see, McKie: I can play your game."

Shockingly, this had opened an area of awareness within him which he'd not even suspected. It was as though she'd held up his entire previous life to devastating observation.

And *he* was the observer!

Other beings formed lasting relationships and operated from a secure emotional base. But he was a product of BuSab, the Gowachin . . . and much that had gone before. It had become increasingly obvious to him why the Gowachin had chosen him to groom for this particular role.

I was damaged and they could rebuild me the way they wanted!

Well, the Gowachin could still be surprised by what they produced. Dosadi was evidence of that. They might not even suspect what they'd actually produced in McKie.

He was bitter with a bitterness he knew must've been fermenting in him for years. The loneliness of his own life with its central dedication to BuSab had been brought to a head by the loneliness of this imprisoned planet. An incredible jumble of emotions had sorted themselves out, and he felt new purpose burning within him.

Power!

Ahhhh . . . that was how it felt to be Dosadi!

He'd turned away from Jedrik's cold smile, pulled the blankets around his shoulder.

Thank you, loving teacher.

Such thoughts roamed through his mind as he stood alone in the room the following day and began to make the bed. After her revelation, Jedrik had resumed her interest in his memories, napping only to awaken him with more questions.

In spite of his sour outlook, he still felt it his duty to examine her behavior in every possible light his imagination could produce. Nothing about Dosadi was too absurd. He had to build a better picture of this society and its driving forces.

Before returning to Jedrik's room, he'd made another tour of the training courtyard with her. There'd been more new weapons adapted from his kit, and he'd realized the courtyard was merely Jedrik's testing ground, that there must be many more training areas for her followers.

McKie had not yet revealed to her that Aritch's people might terminate Dosadi's people with violence. She'd been centering on this at dawn. Even while they shared the tiny toilet cubicle off her room she'd pressed for answers.

For a time, McKie had diverted her with questions about

Pcharky. What were the powers in that cage? At one point, he'd startled her.

"Pcharky knows something valuable he hopes to trade for his freedom."

"How'd you know?"

"It's obvious. I'll tell you something else: he came here of his own free will . . . for whatever purpose."

"You learn quickly, McKie."

She was laughing at him and he glared at her.

"All right! I don't know that purpose, but it may be that you only think you know it."

For the briefest flicker, something dangerous glared from her eyes, then:

"Your *jumpdoors* have brought us many fools, but Pcharky is one of the biggest fools. I know why he came. There've been many like him. Now . . . there is only one. Broey, for all of his power, cannot search out his own Pcharky. And Keila Jedrik is the one who frustrates him."

Too late, she realized that McKie had goaded her into this performance. How had he done that? He'd almost found out too much too soon. It was dangerous to underestimate this naive intruder from beyond the God Wall.

Once more, she'd begun probing for things he had not yet revealed. Time had protected him. Aides had come urging an early inspection of the new weapons. They were needed.

Afterward, they'd gone to the command post and then to breakfast in a Warren dining room. All through breakfast, he'd plied her with questions about the fighting. How extensive was it? Could he see some of the prisoners? Were they using the weapons built from the patterns in his kit? Were they winning?

Sometimes she merely ignored his questions. Most of her answers were short, distracted. Yes. No. No. Yes. McKie realized she was answering in monosyllables to fend him off. He was a distraction. Something important had been communicated to her and he'd missed it. Although this angered him, he tried to mask the emotion, striving to penetrate her wall of concern. Oddly, she responded when he changed his line of questioning to the parents of the three children and the conversation there.

"You started to designate a particular place: 'Beyond the . . .' Beyond what?"

"It's something Gar thinks I don't know. He thinks only his death fanatics have that kind of rapport with the Rim."

He stared at her, caught by a sudden thought. By now, he knew much about Gar and Tria. She answered his questions about them with candor, often using him openly to clarify her own thoughts. But—death fanatics?

"Are these fanatics homosexual?"

She pounced.

"How'd you know?"

"A guess."

"What difference would it make?"

"Are they?"

"Yes."

McKie shuddered.

She was peremptory.

"Explain!"

"When Humans for any reason go terminal where survival of their species is concerned, it's relatively easy to push them the short step further into *wanting* to die."

"You speak from historical evidence?"

"Yes."

"Example."

"With rare exceptions, primitive Humans of the tribal eras reserved their homosexuals as the ultimate shock troops of desperation. They were the troops of last resort, sent into battle as berserkers who expected, who *wanted*, to die."

She had to have the term *berserkers* explained, then showed by her manner that she believed him. She considered this, then:

"What does your ConSentiency do about this susceptibility?"

"We take sophisticated care to guide all natural sexual variants into constructive, survival activities. We protect them from the kinds of pressures which might tip them over into behavior destructive of the species."

Only later had McKie realized she had not answered his question: *beyond what?* She'd rushed him off to a conference room where more than twenty Humans were assembled, including the two parents who'd made the chart about Tria and Gar. McKie realized he didn't even know their names.

It put him at a disadvantage not knowing as many of these people by sight and name as he should. They, of course, had ready memories of everyone important around them and, when they used a name, often did it with such blurred movement into new subjects that he was seldom sure who had been named. He saw the key to it, though. Their memories were anchored in explicit references to relative abilities of those around them, relative dangers. And it wasn't so much that they concealed their emotions as that they *managed* their emotions. Nowhere in their memories could there be any emotive clouding such as thoughts of love or friendship. Such things weakened you. Everything operated on the strict basis of *quid pro quo,* and you'd better have the cash ready—whatever that cash might be. McKie, pressed all around by questions from the people in the conference room, knew he had only one real asset: he was a key they might use to open the God Wall. Very important asset, but unfortunately owned by an idiot.

Now, they wanted his information about death fanatics. They milked him dry, then sent him away like a child who has performed for his elders but is sent to his room when important matters are brought up for discussion.

The more control, the more that requires control. This is the road to chaos.

—*PanSpechi aphorism*

By the fourth morning of the battle for Chu, Tria was in a vile humor. Her forces had established lines holding about one-eighth of the total Warren territory, mostly low buildings, except along Broey's corridor to the Rim. She did not like the idea that Jedrik's people held an unobstructed view down onto most of the death fanatics' territory. And most of those leaders who'd thrown in their lot with Tria were beginning to have second thoughts, especially since they'd come to realize that this enclave had insufficient food production facilities to maintain itself. The population density she'd been forced to accept was frightening: almost triple the Warren norm.

Thus far, neither Broey nor Jedrik had moved in force against her. Tria had finally been brought to the inescapable conclusion that she and Gar were precisely where Jedrik wanted them. They'd been cut out of Broey's control as neatly and cleanly as though by a knife. There was no going back. Broey would never accept Human help under present circumstances. That, too, spoke of the exquisite care with which Jedrik had executed her plan.

Tria had moved her command post during the night to a high building which faced the canyon walls to the north. Only the river, with a single gate under it, separated her from the Rim. She'd slept badly, her mind full of worries. Chief among her worries was the fact that none of the contact parties she'd sent out to the Rim had returned. There'd been no fires on the Rim ledges during the night. No word from *any* of her people out there.

Why?

Once more, she contemplated her position, seeking some advantage, any advantage. One of her lines was anchored on Broey's corridor to the Rim, one line on the river wall with its single gate, and the rest of her perimeter meandered through a series of dangerous salients from the fifth wall to the river.

She could hear sounds of battle along the far side of Broey's corridor. Jedrik's people used weapons which made a great deal of noise. Occasionally, an explosive projectile landed in Tria's enclave. These were rare, but she'd taken casualties and the effect on morale was destructive. That was a major problem with fanatics: they demanded to be used, to be wasted.

Tria stared down at the river, aware of the bodies drifting on its poison currents—both Human and Gowachin bodies, but more Gowachin than Human. Presently, she turned away from the scene, padded into the next room, and roused Gar.

"We must contact Jedrik," she said.

He rubbed sleep from his eyes.

"No! We must wait until we make contact with our people on the Rim. Then we can .   ."

"Faaaaa!"

She'd seldom showed that much disgust with him.

"We're not going to make contact with our people on the Rim. Jedrik and Broey have seen to that. It wouldn't surprise me if they were cooperating to isolate us."

"But we've . . ."

"Shut up, Father!" She held up her hands, stared at them. "I was never really good enough to be one of Broey's chief advisors. I always suspected that. I always pressed too hard. Last night, I reviewed as many of my decisions as I could. Jedrik deliberately made me look good. She did it oh so beautifully!"

"But our forces on the Rim . . ."

"May not be ours! They may be Jedrik's."

"Even the Gowachin?"

"Even the Gowachin."

Gar could hear a ringing in his ears. Contact Jedrik? Throw away all of their power?

"I'm good enough to recognize the weakness of a force such as ours," Tria said. "We can be goaded into spending ourselves uselessly. Even Broey didn't see that, but Jedrik obviously did. Look at the salients along her perimeter!"

"What have salients . . ."

"They can be pinched off and obliterated! Even *you* must see that."

"Then pull back and . . ."

"Reduce our territory?" She stared at him, aghast. "If I even intimate I'm going to do that, our auxiliaries will desert wholesale. Right now they're . . ."

"Then attack!"

"To gain what?"

Gar nodded. Jedrik would fall back across mined areas, blast the fanatics out of existence. She held enough territory that she could afford such destruction. Clearly, she'd planned on it.

"Then we must pinch off Broey's corridor."

"That's what Jedrik wants us to do. It's the only negotiable counter we have left. That's why we must contact Jedrik."

Gar shook his head in despair.

Tria was not finished, though.

"Jedrik might restore us to a share of power in the Rim city if we bargain for it now. Broey would never do that. Do you understand now the mistake you made with Broey?"

"But Broey was going to . . ."

"You failed to follow my orders, Father. You must see now why I always tried to keep you from making independent decisions."

Gar fell into abashed silence. This was his daughter, but he could sense his peril.

Tria spoke.

"I will issue orders presently to all of our commanders. They will be told to hold at all costs. They will be told that you and I will try to contact Jedrik. They will be told why."

"But how can . . ."

"We will permit ourselves to be captured."

QUESTION: *Who governs the governors?*
ANSWER: *Entropy.*

—*Gowachin riddle*

Many things conspired to frustrate McKie. Few people other than Jedrik answered his questions. Most responded as though to a cretin. Jedrik treated him as though he were a child of unknown potential. At times, he knew he amused her. Other times, she punished him with an angry glance, by ignoring him, or just by going away—or worse, sending him away.

It was now late afternoon of the fifth day in the battle for Chu, and Broey's forces still held out in the heart of the city with their slim corridor to the Rim. He knew this from reports he'd overheard. He stood in a small room off Jedrik's command post, a room containing four cots where, apparently she and/or her commanders snatched occasional rest. One tall, narrow window looked out to the south Rim. McKie found it difficult to realize that he'd come across that Rim just six days previously.

Clouds had begun to gather over the Rim's terraced escarpments, a sure sign of a dramatic change in the weather. He knew that much, at least, from his Tandaloor briefings.

Dosadi had no such thing as weather control. Awareness of this left him feeling oddly vulnerable. Nature could be so damnably capricious and dangerous when you had no grip on her vagaries.

McKie blinked, held his breath for a moment.

Vagaries of nature.

The vagaries of sentient nature had moved the Gowachin to set up this experiment. Did they really hope to control that vast, seething conglomerate of motives? Or had they some other reason for Dosadi, a reason which he had not yet penetrated? Was this, after all, a test of Caleban mysteries? He thought not.

He knew the way Aritch and aides *said* they'd set up this experiment. Observations here bore out their explanations. None of that data was consistent with an attempt to understand the Calebans. Only that brief encounter with Pcharky, a thing which Jedrik no longer was willing to discuss.

No matter how he tried, McKie couldn't evade the feeling that something essential lay hidden in the way this planet had been set upon its experimental course; something the Gowachin hadn't revealed, something they perhaps didn't even understand themselves. What'd they done at the beginning? They had this place, Dosadi, the subjects, the Primary . . . yes, the Primary. The inherent inequality of individuals dominated Gowachin minds. And there was that damnable DemoPol. How had they mandated it? Better yet: how did they maintain that mandate?

Aritch's people had hoped to expose the inner workings of sentient social systems. So they said. But McKie was beginning to look at that explanation with Dosadi eyes, with Dosadi scepticism. What had Fannie Mae meant about not being able to leave here in his own body/node? How could he be Jedrik's *key* to the God Wall? McKie knew he needed more information than he could hope to get from Jedrik. Did Broey have this information? McKie wondered if he might in the

end have to climb the heights to the Council Hills for his answers. Was that even possible now?

When he'd asked for it, Jedrik had given him almost the
run of this building, warning:

"Don't interfere."

Interfere with what?

When he'd asked, she'd just stared at him.

She had, however, taken him around to familiarize everyone with his status. He was never quite sure what that status
might be, except that it was somewhere between guest and
prisoner.

Jedrik had required minimal conversation with her people. Often, she'd used only hand waves to convey the necessary signals of passage. The whole traverse was a lesson for
McKie, beginning with the doorguards.

"McKie." Pointing at him.

The guards nodded.

Jedrik had other concerns.

"Team Nine?"

"Back at noon."

"Send word."

Everyone subjected McKie to a hard scrutiny which he felt
certain would let them identify him with minimal interruption.

There were two elevators: one an express from a heavily
guarded street entrance on the side of the building, the other
starting above the fourth level at the ceiling of Pcharky's
cage. They took this one, went up, pausing at each floor for
guards to see him.

When they returned to the cage room, McKie saw that a
desk had been installed just inside the street door. The father of those three wild children sat there watching Pcharky,
making occasional notations in a notebook. McKie had a
name for him now, Ardir.

Jedrik paused at the desk.

"McKie can come and go with the usual precautions."

McKie, addressing himself finally to Jedrik, had said:

"Thanks for taking this time with me."

"No need to be sarcastic, McKie."

He had not intended sarcasm and reminded himself once more that the usual amenities of the ConSentiency suffered a different interpretation here.

Jedrik glanced through Ardir's notes, looked up at Pcharky, back to McKie. Her expression did not change.

"We will meet for dinner."

She left him then.

For his part, McKie had approached Pcharky's cage, noting the tension this brought to the room's guards and observers. The old Gowachin sat in his hammock with an indifferent expression on his face. The bars of the cage emitted an almost indiscernible hissing as they shimmered and glowed.

"What happens if you touch the bars?" McKie asked.

The Gowachin jowls puffed in a faint shrug.

McKie pointed.

"There's energy in those bars. What is that energy? How is it maintained?"

Pcharky responded in a hoarse croaking.

"How is the universe maintained? When you first see a thing, is that when it was created?"

"Is it a Caleban thing?"

Shrug.

McKie walked around the cage, studying it. There were glistening bulbs wherever the bars crossed each other. The rods upon which the hammock was suspended came from the ceiling. They penetrated the cage top without touching it. The hammock itself appeared to be fabric. It was faintly blue. He returned to his position facing Pcharky.

"Do they feed you?"

No answer.

Ardir spoke from behind him.

"His food is lowered from the ceiling. His excreta are hosed into the reclamation lines."

McKie spoke over his shoulder.

"I see no door into the cage. How'd he get in there?"

"It was built around him according to his own instructions."

"What are the bulbs where the bars cross?"

"They came into existence when he activated the cage."

"How'd he do that?"

"We don't know. Do you?"

McKie shook his head from side to side.

"How does Pcharky explain this?"

"He doesn't."

McKie had turned away to face Ardir, probing, moving the focus of questions from Pcharky to the planetary society itself. Ardir's answers, especially on matters of religion and history, were banal.

Later, as he stood in the room off the command post reviewing the experience, McKie found his thoughts touching on a matter which had not even come into question.

Jedrik and her people had known for a long time that Dosadi was a Gowachin creation. They'd known it long before McKie had appeared on the scene. It was apparent in the way they focused on Pcharky, in the way they reacted to Broey. McKie had added one significant datum: that Dosadi was a Gowachin *experiment*. But Jedrik's people were not using him in the ways he might expect. She said he was the key to the God Wall, but how was he that key?

The answer was not to be found in Ardir. That one had not tried to evade McKie's questions, but the answers betrayed a severely limited scope to Ardir's knowledge and imagination.

McKie felt deeply disturbed by this insight. It was not so much what the man said as what he did not say when the reasons for speaking openly in detail were most demanding. Ar-

dir was no dolt. This was a Human who'd risen high in Jedrik's hierarchy. Many speculations would've crossed his
mind. Yet he made no mention of even the more obvious
speculations. He raised no questions about the way Dosadi
history ran to a single cutoff point in the past without any
trace of evolutionary beginnings. He did not appear to be a
religious person and even if he were, Dosadi would not permit the more blatant religious inhibitions. Yet Ardir refused
to explore the most obvious discrepancies in those overt religious attitudes McKie had been told to expect. Ardir played
out the right attitudes, but there was no basis for them un-
derneath. It was all surface.

McKie suddenly despaired of ever getting a deep answer
from any of these people—even from Jedrik.

An increase in the noise level out in the command post
caught McKie's attention. He opened the door, stood in the
doorway to study the other room.

A new map had been posted on the far wall. There was a
position board; transparent and covered with yellow, red,
and blue dots, over the map. Five women and a man—all
wearing earphones—worked the board, moving the colored
markers. Jedrik stood with her back to McKie, talking to several commanders who'd just come in from the streets. They
still carried their weapons and packs. It was their conversation which had attracted McKie. He scanned the room, noted
two communications screens at the left wall, both inactive.
They were new since his last view of the room and he wondered at their purpose.

An aide leaned in from the hallway, called out:

"Gate Twenty-One just reported. Everything has quieted
there. They want to know if they should keep their reserves
on the alert."

"Have them stand down," Jedrik said.

"The two prisoners are being brought here," the aide added.

"I see it," Jedrik said.

She nodded toward the position board.

McKie, following the direction of her gaze, saw two yellow markers being moved with eight blue companions. Without knowing how he understood this, he saw that this must be the prisoners and their escort. There were tensions in the command post which told him this was an important event. Who were those prisoners?

One of Jedrik's commanders spoke.

"I saw the monitor at . . ."

She was not listening to him and he broke off. Two people on the position board exchanged places, trading earphones. The messenger who'd called out the information about the gate and the prisoners had gone. Another messenger came in presently, conferred in a soft voice with people near the door.

In a few moments, eight young Human males entered carrying Gar and Tria securely trussed with what appeared to be shining wire. McKie recognized the pair from Aritch's briefings. The escort carried their prisoners like so much meat, one at each leg and each arm.

"Over here," Jedrik said, indicating two chairs facing her.

McKie found himself suddenly aware, in an extremely Dosadi way, of many of the nuances here. It filled him with elation.

The escort crossed the room, not bothering to steer clear of all the furniture. The messenger from the hallway delayed his departure, reluctant to leave. He'd recognized the prisoners and knew something important was about to happen.

Gar and Tria were dumped into the two chairs.

"Release their bindings," Jedrik said.

The escort obeyed.

Jedrik waited, staring across at the position board. The two yellow and eight blue markers had been removed. She continued to stare at the board, though. Something there was more important than these two prisoners. She pointed to a cluster of red markers in an upper corner.

"See to that."

One of her commanders left the room.

McKie took a deep breath. He'd spotted the flicker of her movement toward the commander who'd obeyed. So that was how she did it! McKie moved farther into the room to put Jedrik in profile to him. She made no response to his movement, but he knew she was aware of him. He stepped closer to what he saw as the limit of her tolerance, noted a faint smile as she turned toward the prisoners.

There was an abrupt silence, one of those uncomfortable moments when people realize there are things they must do, but everyone is reluctant to start. The messenger still stood by the door to the hall, obviously wanting to see what would happen here. The escort who'd brought the prisoners remained standing in a group at one side. They were almost huddled, as though seeking protection in their own numbers.

Jedrik glanced across at the messenger.

"You may go."

She nodded to the escort.

"And you."

McKie held his cautious distance, waiting, but Jedrik took no notice of him. He saw that he not only would be allowed to stay, but that he was expected to use his wits, his off-world knowledge. Jedrik had read things in his presence: a normal distrust, caution, patience. And the fears, of course.

Jedrik took her time with the prisoners. She leaned forward, examined first Tria, then Gar. From the way she looked at them, it was clear to McKie she weighed many possibilities on how to deal with this pair. She was also building the tensions and this had its effect. Gar broke.

"Broey has a way of describing people such as you," Gar said. "He calls you 'rockets,' which is to say you are like a display which shoots up into the sky—and falls back."

Jedrik grinned.

McKie understood. Gar was not managing his emotions very well. It was a weakness.

"Many rockets in this universe must die unseen," Jedrik said.

Gar glared at her. He didn't like this response, glanced at Tria, saw from her expression that he had blundered.

Tria spoke now, smiling faintly.

"You've taken a personal interest in us, Jedrik."

To McKie, it was as though he'd suddenly crossed a threshold into the understanding of another language. Tria's was a Dosadi statement, carrying many messages. She'd said that Jedrik saw an opportunity for personal gain here and that Tria knew this. The faint smile had been the beginning of the statement. McKie felt a new awe at the special genius of the Dosadi awareness. He moved a step closer. There was something else about Tria . . . something odd.

"What is that one to you?"

Tria spoke to Jedrik, but a flicker of the eyes indicated McKie.

"He has a certain utility," Jedrik said.

"Is that the reason you keep him near you?"

"There's no single reason."

"There've been certain rumors . . ."

"One uses what's available," Jedrik said.

"Did you plan to have children by him?"

Jedrik shook with silent mirth. McKie understood that Tria probed for weaknesses, found none.

"The breeding period is so incapacitating for a female," Tria said.

The tone was deliberately goading, and McKie waited for a response.

Jedrik nodded.

"Offspring produce many repercussions down through the generations. Never a casual decision for those of us who understand."

Jedrik looked at Gar, forcing McKie to shift his attention.

Gar's face went suddenly bland, which McKie interpreted as shock and anger. The man had himself under control quickly, however. He stared at McKie, directed a question to Jedrik.

"Would his death profit us?"

Jedrik glanced at McKie.

Shocked by the directness of the question, McKie was at least as intrigued by the assumptions in Gar's question. *"Us!"* Gar assumed that he and Jedrik had common cause. Jedrik was weighing that assumption and McKie, filled with elation, understood. He also recognized something else and realized he could now repay all of Jedrik's patient teaching.

Tria!

Something about Tria's way of holding her head, the inflections in her spoken Galach, struck a chord in McKie's memory. Tria was a Human who'd been trained by a PanSpechi—that way of moving the eyes before the head moved, the peculiar emphasis in her speech mannerisms. But there were no PanSpechi on Dosadi. Or were there?

None of this showed on McKie's face. He continued to radiate distrust, caution, patience. But he began to ask himself if there might be another loose thread in this Dosadi mystery. He saw Jedrik looking at him and, without thinking about it, gave her a purely Dosadi eye signal to follow him, returned to the adjoining room. It was a measure of how she read him that she came without question.

"Yes?"

He told her what he suspected.

"These PanSpechi, they are the ones who can grow a body to simulate that of another species?"

"Except for the eyes. They have faceted eyes. Any PanSpechi who could act freely and simulate another species would be only the surface manifestation. The freely moving one is only one of five bodies; it's the holder of the ego, the identity.

This passes periodically to another of the five. It's a PanSpechi crime to prevent that transfer by surgically fixing the ego in only one of the bodies."

Jedrik glanced out the doorway. "You're sure about her?"

"The pattern's there."

"The faceted eyes, can that be disguised?"

"There are ways: contact lenses or a rather delicate operation. I've been trained to detect such things, however, and I can tell you that the one who trained her is not Gar."

She looked at him.

"Broey?"

"A Graluz would be a great place to conceal a creche but . . ." He shook his head. ". . . I don't think so. From what you tell me about Broey . . ."

"Gowachin," she agreed. "Then who?"

"Someone who influenced her when she was quite young."

"Do you wish to interrogate the prisoners?"

"Yes, but I don't know their potential value."

She stared at him in open wonder. His had been an exquisitely penetrating Dosadi-style statement. It was as though a McKie she thought she knew had been transformed suddenly right in front of her eyes. He was not yet sufficiently Dosadi to trust completely, but she'd never expected him to come this far this quickly. He did deserve a more detailed assessment of the military situation and the relative abilities of Tria and Gar. She delivered this assessment in the Dosadi way: barebones words, swift, clipped to an essential spareness which assumed a necessary broad understanding by the listener.

Absorbing this, McKie sensed where she limited her recital, tailoring it for his abilities. In a way, it was similar to a response by his Daily Schedule back on Central Central. He could see himself in her attitudes, read her assessment of him. She was favoring him with a limited, grudging respect tempered by a certain fondness as by a parent toward a child.

And he knew that once they returned to the other room, the fondness would be locked under a mask of perfect concealment. It was there, though. It was there. And he dared not betray her trust by counting on that fondness, else it would be locked away forever.

"I'm ready," he said.

They returned to the command post, McKie with a clearer picture of how to operate here. There was no such thing as mutual, unquestioning trust. You always questioned. You always managed. A sort of grudging respect was the nearest they'd reveal openly. They worked together to survive, or when it was overwhelmingly plain that there was personal advantage in mutual action. Even when they united, they remained ultimate individualists. They suspected any gift because no one gave away anything freely. The safest relationships were those in which the niches of the hierarchy were clear and solidly held—minimum threat from above and from below. The whole thing reminded McKie of stories told about behavior in Human bureaucracies of the classical period before deep space travel. And many years before he had encountered a multispecies corporation which had behaved similarly until the ministrations of BuSab had shown them the error of their ways. They'd used every dirty trick available: bribing, spying and other forms of covert and overt espionage, fomenting dissent in the opposition, assassination, blackmail, and kidnapping. Few in the ConSentiency had not heard of InterRealm Supply, now defunct.

McKie stopped three paces from the prisoners.

Tria spoke first.

"Have you decided what to do with us?"

"There's useful potential in both of you," McKie said, "but we have other questions."

The "we" did not escape Tria or Gar. They both looked at Jedrik, who stood impassively at McKie's shoulder.

McKie addressed himself to Gar.

"Is Tria really your daughter, your natural child?"

Tria appeared surprised and, with his new understanding, McKie realized she was telling him she didn't care if he saw this reaction, that it suited her for him to see this. Gar, however, had betrayed a flicker of shock. By Dosadi standards, he was dumbfounded. Then Tria was not his natural daughter, but until this moment, Tria had never questioned their relationship.

"Tell us," McKie said.

The Dosadi spareness of the words struck Gar like a blow. He looked at Jedrik. She gave every indication of willingness to wait forever for him to obey, which was to say that she made no response either to McKie's words or Gar's behavior.

Visibly defeated, Gar returned his attention to McKie.

"I went with two females, only the three of us, across the far mountains. We tried to set up our own production of pure food there. Many on the Rim tried that in those days. They seldom came back. Something always happens: the plants die for no reason, the water source runs dry, something steals what you grow. The Gods are jealous. That's what we always said."

He looked at Tria, who studied him without expression.

"One of the two women died the first year. The other was sick by the following harvest season, but survived through the next spring. It was during that harvest . . . we went to the garden . . . ha! The garden! This child was there. We had no idea of where she'd come from. She appeared to be seven or eight years old, but her reactions were those of an infant. That happens often enough on the Rim—the mind retreats from something too terrible to bear. We took her in. Sometimes you can train such a child back to usefulness. When the woman died and the crop failed, I took Tria and we headed back to the Rim. That was a very bad time. When we returned . . . I was sick. Tria helped me then. We've been together ever since."

McKie found himself deeply touched by this recital and hard put to conceal his reaction. He was not positive that he did conceal it. With his new Dosadi awareness, he read an entire saga into that sparse account of events which probably were quite ordinary by Rim standards. He found himself enraged by the other data which could be read into Gar's words.

PanSpechi trained!

That was the key. Aritch's people had wanted to maintain the purity of their experiment: only two species permitted. But it would be informative to examine Pan Spechi applications. Simple .Take a Human female child. Put her exclusively under PanSpechi influence for seven or eight years. Subject that child to selective memory erasure. Hand her over to convenient surrogate parents on Dosadi.

And there was more: Aritch lied when he said he knew little about the Rim, that the Rim was outside the experiment.

As these thoughts went through his head, McKie returned to the small adjoining room. Jedrik followed. She waited while he assembled his thoughts.

Presently, McKie looked at her, laid out his deductions. When he finished, he glanced at the doorway.

"I need to learn as much as I can about the Rim."

"Those two are a good source."

"But don't you require them for your other plans, the attack on Broey's corridor?"

"Two things can go forward simultaneously. You will return to their enclave with them as my lieutenant. That'll confuse them. They won't know what to make of that. They will answer your questions. And in their confusion they'll reveal much that they might otherwise conceal from you."

McKie absorbed this. Yes . . . Jedrik did not hesitate to put him into peril. It was an ultimate message to everyone. McKie would be totally at the mercy of Gar and Tria. Jedrik was saying, "See! You cannot influence me by any threat to

McKie." In a way, this protected him. In an extremely devious Dosadi way, this removed many possible threats to McKie, and it told him much about what her true feelings toward him could be. He spoke to this.

"I detest a cold bed."

Her eyes sparkled briefly, the barest touch of moisture, then, arming him:

"No matter what happens to me, McKie—free us!"

Given the proper leverage at the proper point, any sentient awareness may be exploded into astonishing self-under-standing.

—from an ancient Human mystic

"Unless she makes a mistake, or we find some unexpected advantage, it's only a matter of time until she overruns us," Broey said.

He sat in his aerie command post at the highest point of the dominant building on the Council Hills. The room was an armored oval with a single window about fifteen meters away directly in front of Broey looking out on sunset through the river's canyon walls. A small table with a com-municator stood just to his left. Four of his commanders waited near the table. Maps, position boards, and the other appurtenances of command, with their attendants, occupied most of the room's remaining space.

Broey's intelligence service had just brought him the re-port that Jedrik had taken Gar and Tria captive.

One of his commanders, slender for a Gowachin and with other deprivation marks left from birth on the Rim, glanced at his three companions, cleared his throat.

"Is it time to capitulate?"

Broey shook his head in a Human gesture of negation.

It's time I told them, he thought.

He felt emptied. God refused to speak to him. Nothing in his world obeyed the old mandates.

We've been tricked.

The Powers of the God Wall had tricked him, had tricked his world and all of its inhabitants. They'd . . .

"This McKie," the commander said.

Broey swallowed, then:

"I doubt if McKie has even the faintest understanding of how she uses him."

He glanced at the reports on his communicator table, a stack of reports about McKie. Broey's intelligence service had been active.

"If we captured or killed him . . ." the commander ventured.

"Too late for that," Broey said.

"Is there a chance we won't have to capitulate?"

"There's always that chance."

None of the four commanders liked this answer. Another of them, fat and silky green, spoke up:

"If we have to capitulate, how will we know the . . ."

"We must never capitulate, and we must make certain she knows this," Broey said. "She means to exterminate us."

There! He'd told them.

They were shocked but beginning to understand where his reasoning had led him. He saw the signs of understanding come over their faces.

"The corridor . . ." one of them ventured.

Broey merely stared at him. The fool must know they couldn't get more than a fraction of their forces onto the Rim before Jedrik and Tria closed off that avenue. And even if they could escape to the Rim, what could they do? They hadn't the faintest idea of where the damned factories and food stores were buried.

"If we could rescue Tria," the slim commander said.

Broey snorted. He'd prayed for Tria to contact him, to open negotiations. There'd been not a word, even after she'd fallen back into that impossible enclave. Therefore, Tria had lost control of her people outside the city. All the other evidence supported this conclusion. There was no contact with the Rim. Jedrik's people had taken over out there. Tria would've sent word to him the minute she recognized the impossibility of her position. Any valuable piece of information, any counter in this game would've leaped into Tria's awareness, and she'd have recognized who the highest bidder must be.

Who was the highest bidder? Tria, after all, was Human.

Broey sighed.

And McKie—an idiot savant from beyond the God Wall, a *weapons* expert. Jedrik must've known. But how? Did the Gods talk to her? Broey doubted this. Jedrik gave every evidence of being too clever to be sucked in by trickster Gods.

More clever, more wary, more Dosadi than I.

She deserved the victory.

Broey arose and went to the window. His commanders exchanged worried glances behind him. Could Broey *think* them out of this mess?

A corner of his slim corridor to the Rim was visible to Broey. He could not hear the battle, but explosive orange blossoms told him the fighting continued. He knew the gamble Jedrik took. Those Gowachin beyond the God Wall, the ones who'd created this hellish place, were slow—terrifyingly slow. But eventually they would be unable to misunderstand Jedrik's intentions. Would they step in, those mentally retarded Gowachin out there, and try to stop Jedrik? She obviously thought they would. Everything she did told Broey of the care with which Jedrik had prepared for the stupids from Outside. Broey almost wished her success, but he could not bear the price he and his people would have to pay.

Jedrik had the time-edge on him. She had McKie. She had

played McKie like a superb instrument. And what would McKie do when he realized the final use Jedrik intended to make of him? Yes . . . McKie was a perfect tool for Jedrik. She'd obviously waited for that perfect instrument, had known when it arrived.

Gods! She was superb!

Broey scratched at the nodes between his ventricles. Well, there were still things a trapped people could do. He returned to his commanders.

"Abandon the corridor. Do it quietly, but swiftly. Fall back to the prepared inner walls."

As his commanders started to turn away, Broey stopped them.

"I also want some carefully selected volunteers. The fix we're in must be explained to them in such a way that there's no misunderstanding. They will be asked to sacrifice themselves in a way no Gowachin has ever before contemplated."

"How?"

It was the slender one.

Broey addressed himself to this one. A Gowachin born on the Rim should be the first to understand.

"We must increase the price Jedrik's paying. Hundreds of their people for every *one* of ours."

"Suicide missions," the slender one said.

Broey nodded, continued:

"One more thing. I want Havvy brought up here and I want orders issued to increase the food allotment to those Humans we've held in special reserve."

Two of his commanders spoke in unison:

"They won't sacri . . ."

"I have something else in mind for them."

Broey nodded to himself. Yes indeed. Some of those Humans could still serve his purposes. It wasn't likely they could serve him as McKie served Jedrik, but there was still a chance . . . yes, a chance. Jedrik might not be certain of what Broey could do with his Humans. Havvy, for example. Jedrik had certainly considered and discarded Havvy. In itself, that might be useful. Broey waved for his commanders to leave and execute his orders. They'd seen the new determination in him. They'd pass that along to the ones beneath them. That, too, would serve his purposes. It would delay the moment when his people might suspect that he was making a desperate gamble.

He returned to his communicator, called his search people, urged them to new efforts. They might still achieve what Jedrik obviously had achieved with Pcharky . . . if they could find a Pcharky.

Knowledge is the province of the Legum, just as knowledge is a source of crime.

—*Gowachin Law*

McKie told himself that he might've known an assignment from Jedrik could not be simple. There had to be Dosadi complications.

"There can be no question in their minds that you're really my lieutenant."

"Then I must be your lieutenant."

This pleased her, and she gave him the bare outline of her plan, warning him that the upcoming encounter could not be an act. He must respond as one who was fully aware of this planet's demands.

Night fell over Chu while she prepared him and, when they returned to the command post where Gar and Tria waited, the occasion presented itself as Jedrik had told him it would. It was a sortie by Broey's people against Gate Eighteen. Jedrik snapped the orders at him, sent him running.

"Find the purpose of that!"

McKie paused only to pick up four waiting guards at the command post door, noting the unconcealed surprise in Gar and Tria. They'd formed a particular opinion of McKie's position and now had to seek a new assessment. Tria would be most upset by this, confused by self-doubts. McKie knew Jedrik would immediately amplify those doubts, telling Gar and Tria that McKie would go with them when he returned from Gate Eighteen.

"You must consider his orders as my orders."

Gate Eighteen turned out to be more than a minor problem. Broey had taken the gate itself and two buildings. One of the attackers, diving from an upper window into one of Jedrik's best units, had blown himself up with a nasty lot of casualties.

"More than a hundred dead," a breathless courier told him.

McKie didn't like the implications of a suicide attack, but couldn't pause to assess it. They had to eliminate this threat. He gave orders for two feints while a third force blasted down one of the captured buildings, smothering the gate in rubble. That left the other captive building isolated. The swiftness of this success dazzled Jedrik's forces, and the commanders snapped to obedience when McKie issued orders for them to take captives and bring those captives to him for interrogation.

At McKie's command, one of his original four guards brought a map of the area, tacked it to a wall. Less than an hour had passed since he'd left Jedrik, but McKie felt that he'd entered another world, one even more primitive than that surrounding the incredible woman who'd set all of this in motion. It was the difference between second- and third-hand reports of action and the physical feeling of that action all around him. Explosions and the hissing of flamers down on the streets jarred his awareness.

Staring at the map, McKie said, "This has all the marks of a trap. Get all but a holding force out of the area. Tell Jedrik."

People scurried to obey.

One of the guards and two sub-commanders remained. The guard spoke.

"What about this place?"

McKie glanced around him. It was a square room with brown walls. Two windows looked out on the street away from the battle for the isolated building near the gate. He'd hardly looked at the room when they'd brought him here to set up his command post. Four streets with isolated holdouts cushioned him from the main battle. They could shoot a cable bridge to another building if things became hot here. And it'd help morale if he remained in the danger area.

He spoke to one of the sub-commanders:

"Go down to the entry. Call all the elevators down there and disable all but one. Stand by that one with a holding force and put guards in the stairway. Stand by yourself to bring up captives. Comment?"

"I'll send up two cable teams and make sure the adjoining buildings are secure."

Of course! McKie nodded.

Gods! How these people reacted in emergencies. They were as direct and cutting as knives.

"Do it," McKie said.

He had less than a ten-minute wait before two of Jedrik's special security troops brought up the first captive, a young Gowachin whose eyelids bore curious scars—scroll-like and pale against the green skin.

The two security people stopped just inside the doorway. They held the Gowachin firmly, although he did not appear to be struggling. The sub-commander who'd brought them up closed the door as he left.

One of the captors, an older man with narrow features, nodded as he caught McKie's attention.

"What'll we do with him?"

"Tie him in a chair," McKie instructed.

He studied the Gowachin as they complied.

"Where was he captured?"

"He was trying to escape from that building through a perimeter sewage line."

234 / Frank Herbert

"Alone?"

"I don't know. He's the first of a group of prisoners. The others are waiting outside."

They had finished binding the young Gowachin, now took up position directly behind him.

McKie studied the captive. He wore black coveralls with characteristic deep vee to clear the ventricles. The garment had been cut and torn in several places. He'd obviously been searched with swift and brutal thoroughness. McKie put down a twinge of pity. The scar lines on the prisoner's eyelids precluded anything but the most direct Dosadi necessities.

"They did a poor job removing your Phylum tattoos," McKie said. He'd already recognized the scar lines: Deep Swimmers. It was a relatively unimportant Phylum, small in numbers and sensitive about their status.

The young Gowachin blinked. McKie's opening remark had been so conversational, even-toned, that the shock of his words came after. Shock was obvious now in the set of the captive's mouth.

"What is your name, please?" McKie asked, still in that even, conversational way.

"Grinik."

It was forced out of him.

McKie asked one of the guards for a notebook and stylus, wrote the Gowachin's name in it, adding the Phylum identification.

"Grinik of the Deep Swimmers," he said. "How long have you been on Dosadi?"

The Gowachin took a deep, ventricular breath, remained silent. The security men appeared puzzled. This interrogation wasn't going as they'd expected. McKie himself did not know what to expect. He still felt himself recovering from surprise at recognition of the badly erased Phylum tattoos.

"This is a very small planet," McKie said. "The universe

from which we both come is very big and can be very cruel. I'm sure you didn't come here expecting to die."

If this Grinik didn't know the deadly plans of his superiors, that would emerge shortly. McKie's words could be construed as a personal threat beyond any larger threat to Dosadi as a whole. It remained to see how Grinik reacted.

Still, the young Gowachin hesitated.

When in doubt, remain silent.

"You appear to've been adequately trained for this project," McKie said. "But I doubt if you were told everything you should know. I even doubt if you were told things essential to you in your present position."

"Who are you?" Grinik demanded. "How dare you speak here of matters which . . ." He broke off, glanced at the two guards standing at his shoulders.

"They know all about us," McKie lied.

He could smell the sweet perfume of Gowachin fear now, a floral scent which he'd noted only on a few previous occasions. The two guards also sensed this and showed faint smiles to betray that they knew its import.

"Your masters sent you here to die," McKie said. "They may very well pay heavily for this. You ask who I am? I am Jorj X. McKie, Legum of the Gowachin Bar, Saboteur Extraordinary, senior lieutenant of Jedrik who will shortly rule all of Dosadi. I make formal imposition upon you. Answer my questions for the Law is at stake."

On the Gowachin worlds, that was a most powerful motivator. Grinik was shaken by it.

"What do you wish to know?"

He barely managed the words.

"Your mission on Dosadi. The precise instructions you were given and who gave them to you."

"There are twenty of us. We were sent by Mrreg."

That name! The implications in Gowachin lore stunned McKie. He waited, then:

"Continue."

"Two more of our twenty are out there."

Grinik motioned to the doorway, clearly pleading for his captive associates.

"Your instructions?"

"To get our people out of this terrible place."

"How long?"

"Just . . . sixty hours remain."

McKie exhaled slowly. So Aritch and company had given up on him. They were going to eliminate Dosadi.

"Where are the other members of your party?"

"I don't know."

"You were, of course, a reserve team trained and held in readiness for this mission. Do you realize how poorly you were trained?"

Grinik remained silent.

McKie put down a feeling of despair, glanced at the two guards. He understood that they'd brought him this particular captive because this was one of three who were not Dosadi. Jedrik had instructed them, of course. Many things became clearer to him in this new awareness. Jedrik had put sufficient pressure on the Gowachin beyond the God Wall. She still had not imagined the extremes to which those Gowachin might go in stopping her. It was time Jedrik learned what sort of fuse she'd lighted. And Broey must be told. Especially Broey—before he sent many more suicide missions.

The outer door opened and the sub-commander leaned in to speak.

"You were right about the trap. We mined the area before pulling back. Caught them nicely. The gate's secure now, and we've cleared out that last building."

McKie pursed his lips, then:

"Take the prisoners to Jedrik. Tell her we're coming in."

A flicker of surprise touched the sub-commander's eyes.

"She knows."

Still the man hesitated.

"Yes?"

"There's one Human prisoner out here you should question before leaving."

McKie waited. Jedrik knew he was coming in, knew what had gone on here, knew about the Human prisoner out there. She wanted him to question this person. Yes . . . of course. She left nothing to chance . . . by her standards. Well, her standards were about to change, but she might even know that.

"Name?"

"Havvy. Broey holds him, but he once served Jedrik. She says to tell you Havvy is a reject, that he was contaminated."

"Bring him in."

Havvy surprised him. The surface was that of a bland-faced nonentity, braggadocio clearly evident under a mask of secret knowledge. He wore a green uniform with a driver's brassard. The uniform was wrinkled, but there were no visible rips or cuts. He'd been treated with more care than the Gowachin who was being led out of the room. Havvy replaced the Gowachin in the chair. McKie waved away the bindings.

Unfocused questions created turmoil in McKie's mind. He found it difficult to delay. Sixty hours! But he felt that he could almost touch the solution to the Dosadi mystery, that in only a few minutes he would know names and real motives for the ones who'd created this monster. Havvy? He'd served Jedrik. In what way? Why rejected? Contaminated?

Unfocused questions, yes.

Havvy sat in watchful tension, casting an occasional glance around the room, at the windows. There were no more explosions out there.

As McKie studied him more carefully, certain observations emerged. Havvy was small but solid, one of those Humans of lesser stature who concealed heavy musculature which could surprise you if you suddenly bumped into them. It was difficult to guess his age, but he was not Dosadi. A member of Grinik's team? Doubtful. Clearly not Dosadi, though. He didn't examine those around him with an automatic status assessment. His reactions were slow. Too much that should remain under shutters flowed from within him directly to the surface. Yes, that was the ultimate revelation. It bothered McKie that so much went unseen beneath the surface here, so much for which Aritch and company had not prepared him. It would take a lifetime to learn all the nuances of this place, and he had less than sixty hours remaining to him.

All of this flowed through McKie's mind in an eyeblink. He reached his decision, motioned the guards and others to leave.

One of the security people started to protest, but McKie silenced him with a glance, pulled up a chair, and sat down facing the captive.

The door closed behind the last of the guards.

"You were sent here deliberately to seek me out," McKie said.

It was not the opening Havvy had expected. He stared into McKie's eyes. A door slammed outside. There was the sound of several doors opening and shutting, the shuffling of feet. An amplified voice called out:

"Move these prisoners out!"

Havvy chewed at his upper lip. He didn't protest. A deep sigh shook him, then:

"You're Jorj X. McKie of BuSab?"

McKie blew out through pursed lips. Did Havvy doubt the evidence of his own senses? Surprising. McKie shook his head, continued to study the captive.

"You can't be McKie!" Havvy said.

"Ahhhhhh . . ." It was pressed out of McKie.

Something about Havvy: the body moved, the voice spoke, but the eyes did not agree.

McKie thought about what the Caleban, Fannie Mae, had said. *A light touch.* He was overtaken by an abrupt certainty: someone other than Havvy looked out through the man's eyes. Yessss. Aritch's people controlled the Caleban who maintained the barrier around Dosadi. The Caleban could contact selected people here. She'd have a constant updating on everything such people learned. There must be many such spies on Dosadi, all trained not to betray the Caleban contact—no twitching, no lapses into trance. No telling how many agents Aritch possessed here.

Would all the other people on Dosadi remain unaware of such a thing, though? That was a matter to question.

"But you must be McKie," Havvy said. "Jedrik's still working out of . . ." He broke off.

"You must've provided her with some amusement by your bumbling," McKie said. "I assure you, however, that BuSab is *not* amused."

A gloating look came over Havvy's face.

"No, she hasn't made the transfer yet."

"Transfer?"

"Haven't you figured out yet how Pcharky's supposed to buy his freedom?"

McKie felt off balance at this odd turn.

"Explain."

"He's supposed to transfer your identity into Jedrik's body and her identity into your body. I think she was going to try that with me once, but . . ."

Havvy shrugged.

It was like an explosion in McKie's newly sensitized awareness. Rejected! Contaminated! Body exchange! McKie was accusatory!

"Broey sent you!"

"Of course." Offensive.

McKie contained his anger. The Dosadi complexities no longer baffled him as once they had. It was like peeling back layer upon layer of concealment. With each new layer you expected to find *the* answer. But that was a trap the whole universe set for the unwary. It was the ultimate mystery and he hated mystery. There were those who said this was a necessary ingredient for BuSab agents. You eliminated that which you hated. But everything he'd uncovered about this planet showed him how little he'd known previously about any mystery. Now, he understood something new about Jedrik. There was little doubt that Broey's Human messenger told the truth.

Pcharky had penetrated the intricacies of PanSpechi ego transfer. He'd done it without a PanSpechi as his subject, unless . . . yes . . . that expanded the implications in Tria's history. Their PanSpechi experiment had assumed even more grotesque proportions.

"I will speak directly to your Caleban monitor," McKie said.

"My what?"

It was such obvious dissimulation that McKie only snorted. He leaned forward.

"I will speak directly to Aritch. See that he gets this message without any mistakes."

Havvy's eyes became glassy. He shuddered.

McKie felt the inner tendrils of an attempted Caleban contact in his own awareness, thrust them aside.

"No! I will speak openly through your agent. Pay close attention, Aritch. Those who created this Dosadi horror cannot run far enough, fast enough, or long enough to escape. If you wish to make every Gowachin in the universe a target for violence, you are proceeding correctly. Others, including BuSab, can employ mass violence if you force it upon them. Not a pleasant thought. But unless you adhere to your own Law, to the honored relationship between Legum and Client, your shame will be exposed. Innocent Gowachin as well as you others whose legal status has yet to be determined—all will pay the bloody price."

Havvy's brows drew down in puzzlement.

"Shame?"

"They plan to blast Dosadi out of existence."

Havvy pressed back into the chair, glared at McKie.

"You're lying."

"Even you, Havvy, are capable of recognizing a truth. I'm going to release you, pass you back through the lines to Broey. Tell him what you learned from me."

"It's a lie!" They're not going to . . ."

"Ask Aritch for yourself."

Havvy didn't ask "Aritch who?" He lifted himself from the chair.

"I will."

"Tell Broey we've less than sixty hours. None of us who can resist mind erasure will be permitted to escape."

"Us?"

McKie nodded, thinking: *Yes, I am Dosadi now.* He said:

"Get out of here."

It afforded him a measure of amusement that the door was opened by the sub-commander just as Havvy reached it.

"See to him yourself," McKie said, indicating Havvy. "I'll be ready to go in a moment."

Without any concern about whether the sub-commander understood the nature of the assignment, McKie closed his eyes in thought. There remained the matter of Mrreg, who'd sent twenty Gowachin from Tandaloor to get *his people* off the planet. Mrreg. That was the name of the mythical monster who'd tested the first primitive Gowachin people almost to extinction, setting the pattern of their deepest instincts.

Mrreg?

Was it code, or did some Gowachin actually use that name? Or was it a role that some Gowachin filled?

Does a populace have informed consent when a ruling minority acts in secret to ignite a war, doing this to justify the existence of the minority's military forces? History already has answered that question. Every society in the ConSentiency today reflects the historical judgment that failure to provide full information for informed consent on such an issue represents an ultimate crime.

           —*from* The Trial of Trials

Less than an hour after closing down at Gate Eighteen, McKie and his escort arrived back at Jedrik's headquarters building. He led them to the heavily guarded side entrance with its express elevator, not wanting to pass Pcharky at this moment. Pcharky was an unnecessary distraction. He left the escort in the hallway with instructions to get food and rest, signaled for the elevator. The elevator door was opened by a small Human female of about fifteen years who nodded him into the dim interior.

McKie, his natural distrust of even the young on this planet well masked, nevertheless kept her under observation as he accepted the invitation. She was a gamin child with dirty face and hands, a torn grey single garment cut off at the knees. Her very existence as a Dosadi survivor said she'd undoubtedly sold her body many times for scraps of food. He realized how much Dosadi had influenced him when he found that he couldn't raise even the slightest feeling of censure at this knowledge. You did what the conditions around you demanded when those conditions were overwhelming. It was an ultimate question: this or death? And certainly some of them chose death.

"Jedrik," he said.

She worked her controls and he found himself presently in an unfamiliar hallway. Two familiar guards stood at a doorway down the hall, however. They betrayed not the slightest interest in him as he opened the door between them swiftly and strode through.

It was a tiny anteroom, empty, but another door directly in front of him. He opened this with more confidence than he felt, entered a larger space full of projection-room gloom with shadowed figures seated facing a holographic focus on his left. McKie identified Jedrik by her profile, slipped into a seat beside her.

She kept her attention on the h-focus where a projection of Broey stood looking out at something over their shoulders. McKie recognized the subtle slippage of computer simulation. That was not a flesh-and-blood Broey in the focus.

Someone on the far side of the room stood up and crossed to sit beside another figure in the gloom. McKie recognized Gar as the man moved through one of the projection beams.

McKie whispered to Jedrik, "Why simulation?"

"He's beginning to do things I didn't anticipate."

The suicide missions. McKie looked at the simulation, wondered why there was no sync-sound. Ahhh, yes. They were lip-reading, and it was silent to reduce distractions, to amplify concentration. Yes, Jedrik was reworking the simulation model of Broey which she carried in her head. She would also carry another model, even more accurate than the one of Broey, which would give her a certain lead time on the reactions of one Jorj X. McKie.

"Would you really have done it?" he asked.

"Why do you distract me with such nonsense?"

He considered. Yes, it was a good question. He already knew the answer. She would have done it: traded bodies with him and escaped outside the God Wall as McKie. She might still do it, unless he could anticipate the mechanics of the transfer.

By now, she knew about the sixty-hour limit and would suspect its significance. Less than sixty hours. And the Dosadi could make extremely complex projections from limited data. Witness this Broey simulation.

The figure in the focus was talking to a fat Human female who held a tube which McKie recognized as a communicator for field use.

Jedrik spoke across the room to Gar.

"She still with him?"

"Addicted."

A two-sentence exchange, and it condensed an entire conversation about possible uses of that woman. McKie did not ask addicted to what. There were too many such substances on Dosadi, each with peculiar characteristics, often involving odd monopolies with which everyone seemed familiar. This was a telltale gap in Aritch's briefings: the monopolies and their uses.

As McKie absorbed the action in the focus, the reasons behind this session became more apparent. Broey was refusing to believe the report from Havvy.

And there was Havvy in the focus.

Jedrik favored McKie with one flickering glance as Havvy-simulation appeared. Certainly. She factored McKie into her computations.

McKie compressed his lips. She knew Havvy would contaminate me. They couldn't say "I love you" on this damned planet. Oh, no. They had to create a special Dosadi production number.

"Most of the data for this originated before the breakup," McKie said. "It's useless. Rather than ask the computer to play pretty pictures for us, why don't we examine our own memories? Surely, somewhere in the combined experiences with Broey . . ."

A chuckle somewhere to the left stopped him.

Too late, McKie saw that every seat in the room had an arm keyed to the simulations. They were doing precisely what he'd suggested, but in a more sophisticated way. The figures at the focus were being adjusted to the combined memories. There was such a keyed arm at McKie's right hand. He suddenly realized how tactless and lecturing he still must appear to these people. They didn't waste energy on unnecessary words. Anyone who did must be subnormal, poorly trained or . . . or not from Dosadi.

"Does he always state the obvious?" Gar asked.

McKie wondered if he'd blown his lieutenancy, lost the opportunity to explore the mystery of the Rim, but . . . no, there wasn't time for that now. He'd have to penetrate the Rim another way.

"He's new," Jedrik said. "New is not necessarily naive, as you should know."

"He has you doing it now," Gar said.

"Guess again."

McKie put a hand to the simulation controls under his right hand, tested the keys. He had it in a moment. They were similar to such devices in the ConSentiency, an adaptation from the DemoPol inputs, no doubt. Slowly, he changed the Broey at the focus, heavier, the sagging jowls and node wattles of a breeding male Gowachin. McKie froze the image.

"Tentative?" Gar asked.

Jedrik answered for him.

"It's knowledge he brought here with him." She did something to her controls, stopped the projection, and raised the room lights.

McKie noted that Tria was nowhere in the room.

"The Gowachin have sequestered their females somewhere," McKie said. "That somewhere should not be difficult to locate. Send word to Tria that she must not mount her attack on Broey's corridor just yet."

"Why delay?" Gar demanded.

"Broey will have all but evacuated the corridor by now," McKie said.

Gar was angry and showing it.

"Not a single one of them has gone through that Rim gate."

"Not to the Rim," Jedrik said.

It was clear to her now. McKie had supplied the leverage she needed. It was time now to employ him as she'd always intended. She glanced at McKie.

"We have unfinished business. Are you ready?"

He held his silence. How could he answer such a Dosadi-weighted question? There were so many things left unspoken on this planet, only the native-born could understand them all. McKie felt once more that he was a dull outsider, a child of dubious potential among normal adults.

Jedrik arose, looked across at Gar.

"Send word to Tria to hold herself in readiness for another assignment. Tell Broey. Call him on an open line. We now have an excellent use for your fanatics. If only a few of your people fight through to that Graluz complex, it'll be enough and Broey will know it."

McKie noted that she spoke to Gar with a familiar teaching emphasis. It was the curiously weighted manner she'd once used with McKie, but no longer found necessary. His recognition of this amused her.

"Come along, McKie. We haven't much time."

Does a population have informed consent when that population is not taught the inner workings of its monetary system, and then is drawn, all unknowing, into economic adventures?

—*from* The Trial of Trials

For almost an hour after the morning meal, Aritch observed Ceylang as she worked with the McKie simulator. She was pushing herself hard, believing Wreave honor at stake, and had almost reached the pitch Aritch desired.

Ceylang had set up her own simulator situation: McKie interviewing five of Broey's Gowachin. She had the Gowachin come to McKie in surrender, hands extended, the webbed fingers exposed to show that the talons were withdrawn.

Simulator-McKie merely probed for military advantages.

"Why does Broey attack in this fashion?"

Or he'd turn to some places outside the h-focus of the simulator.

"Send reinforcements into that area."

Nothing about the Rim.

Earlier, Ceylang had tried the issue with a prisoner simulation where the five Gowachin tried to confuse McKie by presenting a scenario in which Broey massed his forces at the corridor. The makings of a breakout to the Rim appeared obvious.

Simulator-McKie asked the prisoners why they lied.

Ceylang cleared the simulator and sat back. She saw Aritch at the observation window, opened a channel to him.

"Something has to be wrong in the simulation. McKie cannot be led into questioning the purposes of the Rim."

"I assure you that simulation is remarkable in its accuracy. Remarkable."

"Then why . . ."

"Perhaps he already knows the answer. Why don't you try him with Jedrik? Here . . ." Aritch operated the controls at the observer station. "This might help. This is a record of McKie in recent action on Dosadi."

The simulator presented a view down a covered passage through a building. Artificial light. Darkness at the far end of the passage. McKie, two blocky guards in tow, approached the viewers.

Ceylang recognized the scene. She'd watched this action at Gate Eighteen from several angles, had seen this passage empty before the battle, acquainting herself with the available views. As she'd watched it then, the passage had filled with Human defenders. There was a minor gate behind the viewer and she knew the viewer itself to be only a bright spot, a fleck of glittering impurity in an otherwise drab brick over the gate's archway.

Now, the long passage seemed strange to Ceylang without its throng of defenders. There were only a few workmen along its length as McKie passed. The workmen repaired service pipes in the ceiling. A cleanup crew washed down patches of blood at the far end of the passage, the high-water mark of the Gowachin attack. An officer leaned against a wall near the viewer, a bored expression on his face which did not mislead Ceylang. He was there to watch McKie. Three soldiers squatted nearby rolling hexi-bones for coins which lay in piles before each man. Every now and then, one of the gamblers would pass a coin to the watching officer. A repair supervisor stood with his back to the viewer, notebook in hand, writing a list of supplies to complete the job. McKie and his guards were forced to step around these people. As they passed, the officer turned, looked directly into the viewer, smiled.

"That officer," Ceylang said. "One of your people?"

"No."

The viewpoint shifted, looking down on the gate itself, McKie in profile. The gatekeeper was a teenager with a scar down his right cheek and a broken nose. McKie showed no signs of recognition, but the youth knew McKie.

"You go through on request."

"When did she call?"

"Ten."

"Let us through."

The gate was opened. McKie and his guards went through, passed beyond the viewer's focus.

The youthful gatekeeper stood up, smashed the viewer. The h-focus went blank.

Aritch looked down from his observation booth for a moment before speaking.

"Who called?"

"Jedrik?" Ceylang spoke without thinking.

"What does that conversation tell you? Quickly!"

"That Jedrik anticipated his movements, was observing him all the time."

"What else?"

"That McKie . . . knows this, knows she can anticipate him."

"She carries a better simulation of him in her head than we have . . . there."

Aritch pointed at the h-focus area.

"But they left so much unspoken!" Ceylang said.

Aritch remained silent.

Ceylang closed her eyes. It was like mind reading. It confused her.

Aritch interrupted her musings.

"What about that officer and the gatekeeper?"

She shook her head.

"You're wise to use living observers there. They all seem to know when they're being watched. And how it's done."

"Even McKie."

"He didn't look at the viewers."

"Because he assumed from the first that we'd have him under almost constant observation. He's not concerned about the mechanical intrusions. He has built a simulation McKie of his own who acts on the surface of the real McKie."

"That's your assumption?"

"We arrived at this from observation of Jedrik in her dealings with McKie. She peels away the simulation layers one at a time, coming closer and closer to the actuality at the core."

Another observation bothered Ceylang.

"Why'd the gatekeeper shut down that viewer just then?"

"Obviously because Jedrik told him to do that."

Ceylang shuddered.

"Sometimes I think those Dosadi play us like a fine instrument."

"But of course! That's why we sent them our McKie."

The music of a civilization has far-reaching consequences on consciousness and, thus, influences the basic nature of a society. Music and its rhythms divert and compel the awareness, describing the limits within which a consciousness, thus fascinated, may operate. Control the music, then, and you own a powerful tool with which to shape the society.

—The Dosadi Analysis, BuSab Documents

It was a half-hour before Jedrik and McKie found themselves in the hallway leading to her quarters. McKie, aware of the effort she was expending to conceal a deep weariness, watched her carefully. She concentrated on presenting a show of vitality, her attention glued on the prospect ahead. There was no way of telling what went on in her mind. McKie did not attempt to break the silence. He had his own worries.

Which was the real Jedrik? How was she going to employ Pcharky? Could he resist her?

He knew he was close to a solution of the Dosadi mystery, but the prospect of the twin gambles he was about to take filled him with doubts.

On coming from the projection room, they'd found themselves in a strange delaying situation, as though it were something planned for their frustration. Everything had been prepared for their movement—guards warned, elevator waiting, doors opened. But every time they thought the way clear, they met interference. Except for the obvious importance of the matters which delayed them, it was easy to imagine a conspiracy.

A party of Gowachin at Gate Seventy wanted to surrender, but they demanded a parley first. One of Jedrik's aides didn't like the situation. Something about the assessment of the offer bothered her, and she wanted to discuss it with Jedrik. She stopped them halfway down the first hall outside the projection room.

The aide was an older woman who reminded McKie vaguely of a Wreave lab worker at BuSab, one who'd always been suspicious of computers, even antagonistic toward them. This Wreave had read every bit of history he could find about the evolution of such instruments and liked to remind his listeners of the misuses of the DemoPol. Human history had provided him with abundant ammunition, what with its periodic revolts against "enslavement by machines." Once, he'd cornered McKie.

"Look here! See this sign: 'Gigo.' That's a very old sign that was hung above one of your ancient computers. It's an acronym: 'Garbage In, Garbage Out.' You see! They knew."

Yes. Jedrik's female aide reminded him of that Wreave.

McKie listened to her worries. She roamed all around a central disquiet, never settling on a particular thing. Aware of Aritch's deadline and Jedrik's fatigue, McKie felt the pressures bearing down upon him. The aide's data was accurate. Others had checked it. Finally, he could hold his impatience no longer.

"Who fed this data into your computer?"

The aide was startled at the interruption, but Jedrik turned to him, waiting.

"I think it was Holjance," the aide said. "Why?"

"Get him in here."

"Her."

"Her, then! Make sure she's actually the one who fed in that data."

Holjance was a pinch-faced woman with deep wrinkles around very bright eyes. Her hair was dark and wiry, skin almost the color of McKie's. Yes, she was the one who'd fed the data into the computer because it had arrived on her shift, and she'd thought it too important to delegate.

"What is it you want?" she demanded.

He saw no rudeness in this. It was Dosadi directness. Important things were happening all around. *Don't waste time.*

"You saw this assessment of the surrender offer?" he asked.

"Yes."

"Are you satisfied with it?"

"The data went in correctly."

"That's not my question."

"Of course I'm satisfied!"

She stood ready to defend herself against any charge that she'd slighted her job.

"Tell me, Holjance," he said, "if you wanted the Gowachin computers to produce inaccurate assessments, what would you do?"

She thought about this a moment, blinked, glanced almost furtively at Jedrik who appeared lost in thought. "Well, sir, we have a regular filtering procedure for preventing . . ."

"That's it," Jedrik said. "If I were a Gowachin, I would not be doing that right now."

Jedrik turned, barked orders to the guards behind her.

"That's another trap! Take care of it."

As they emerged from the elevator on Jedrik's floor, there was another delay, one of the escort who'd been with McKie at Gate Eighteen. His name was Todu Pellas and McKie addressed him by name, noting the faint betrayal of pleasure this elicited. Pellas, too, had doubts about carrying out a particular order.

"We're supposed to back up Tria's move by attacking across the upper parkway, but there are some trees and other growth knocked down up there that haven't been moved for two days."

"Who knocked down those trees?" McKie asked.

"We did."

McKie understood. You feinted. The Gowachin were supposed to believe this would provide cover for an attack, but there'd been no attack for two days.

"They must be under pretty heavy strain," Jedrik said.

McKie nodded. That, too, made sense. The alternative Gowachin assumption was that the Humans were trying to fake them into an attack at that point. But the cover had not been removed by either side for two days.

Jedrik took a deep breath.

"We have superior firepower and when Tria . . . well, you should be able to cut right through there to . . ."

McKie interrupted.

"Call off that attack."

"But . . ."

"Call it off!"

She saw the direction of his reasoning. Broey had learned much from the force which Gar and Tria had trained. And Jedrik herself had provided the final emphasis in the lesson. She saw there was no need to change her orders to Pellas.

Pellas had taken it upon himself to obey McKie, not waiting for Jedrik's response, although she was his commander. He already had a communicator off his belt and was speaking rapidly into it.

"Yes! Dig in for a holding action."

He spoke in an aside to Jedrik.

"I can handle it from here."

In a few steps, Jedrik and McKie found themselves in her room. Jedrik leaned with her back against the door, no longer trying to conceal her fatigue.

"McKie, you're becoming very Dosadi."

He crossed to the concealing panels, pulled out the bed.

"You need rest."

"No time."

Yes, she knew all about the sixty-hour deadline—less than fifty-five hours now. Dosadi's destruction was a reaction she hadn't expected from "X," and she blamed herself.

He turned, studied her, saw that she'd passed some previously defined limit of personal endurance. She possessed no amplifiers of muscles or senses, none of the sophisticated aids McKie could call upon in emergencies. She had nothing but her own magnificent mind and body. And she'd almost run them out. Still, she pressed on. This told him a great deal about her motivation.

McKie found himself deeply touched by the fact that she'd not once berated him for hiding that ultimate threat which Aritch held over Dosadi. She'd accepted it that someone in Aritch's position could erase an entire planet, that McKie had been properly maneuvered into concealing this.

The alternative she offered filled McKie with misgivings.

Exchange bodies?

He understood now that this was Pcharky's function, the price the old Gowachin paid for survival. Jedrik had explained.

"He will perform this service one more time. In exchange, we release him from Dosadi."

"If he's one of the original . . . I mean, why doesn't he just leave?"

"We haven't provided him with a body he can use."

McKie had suppressed a feeling of horror. But the history of Dosadi which Jedrik unfolded made it clear that a deliberate loophole had been left in the Caleban contract which imprisoned this planet. Fannie Mae had even said it. He could leave in another body. That was the basic purpose behind this experiment.

New bodies for old!

Aritch had expected this to be the ultimate enticement,

luring McKie into the Gowachin plot, enlisting McKie's supreme abilities and his powerful position in BuSab.

A new body for his old one.

All he'd have to do would be to cooperate in the destruction of a planet, conceal the real purpose of this project, and help set up another body-trade planet better concealed.

But Aritch had not anticipated what might be created by Jedrik plus McKie. They now shared a particular hate and motivation.

Jedrik still stood at the door waiting for him to decide.

"Tell me what to do," he said.

"You're sure that you're willing to . . ."

"Jedrik!"

He thought he saw the beginning of tears. It wasn't that she hid them, but that they reached a suppression level barely visible and she defied them. She found her voice, pointed.

"That panel beside the bed. Pressure latch."

The panel swung wide to reveal two shimmering rods about two centimeters in diameter. The rods danced with the energies of Pcharky's ~age. They emerged from the floor, bent at right angles about waist height and, as the panel opened, they rotated to extend into the room—two glowing handles about a meter apart.

McKie stared at them. He felt a tightness in his breast. What if he'd misread Jedrik? Could he be sure of any Dosadi? This room felt as familiar to him now as his quarters on CC. It was here that Jedrik had taught him some of the most essential Dosadi lessons. Yet . . . he knew the old pattern of what she proposed. The discarded body with its donor ego had always been killed immediately. Why?

"You'll have your answer to that question when we've done this thing."

A Dosadi response, ambiguous, heavy with alternatives.

He glanced around the room, found it hard to believe that

he'd known this place only these few days. His attention returned to the shimmering rods. Another trap?

He knew he was wasting precious time, that he'd have to go through with this. But what would it be like to find himself in Jedrik's flesh, wearing her body as he now wore his own? PanSpechi transferred an ego from body to body. But something unspeakable which they would not reveal happened to the donor.

McKie took a trembling breath.

It had to be done. He and Jedrik shared a common purpose. She'd had many opportunities to use Pcharky simply to escape or to extend her life . . . the way, he realized now, that Broey had used the Dosadi secret. The fact that she'd waited for a McKie forced him to believe her. Jedrik's followers trusted her—and they were Dosadi. And if he and Jedrik escaped, Aritch would find himself facing a far different McKie from the one who'd come so innocently across the Rim. They might yet stay Aritch's hand.

The enticement had been real, though. No doubting that. Shed an old body, get a new one. And the Rim had been the major source of *raw material*: strong, resilient bodies. Survivors.

"What do I do?" he asked.

He felt a hand on his shoulder, and she spoke from beside him.

"You are very Dosadi, McKie. Astonishing."

He glanced at her, saw what it had cost her to move here from the door. He slipped a hand around her waist, eased her to a sitting position on the bed and within reach of the rods.

"Tell me what to do."

She stared at the rods, and McKie realized it was rage driving her, rage against Aritch, the embodiment of "X," the embodiment of a contrived fate. He understood this. The solution of the Dosadi mystery had left him feeling empty, but on the edges there was such a rage as he'd never before experienced. He was still BuSab, though. He wanted no more bloodshed because of Dosadi, no more Gowachin justifications.

Jedrik's voice interrupted his thoughts and he saw that she also shared some of his misgivings.

"I come from a long line of heretics. None of us doubted that Dosadi was a crime, that somewhere there was a justice to punish the criminals."

McKie almost sighed. Not the old Messiah dream! Not that! He would not fill that role, even for Dosadi.

It was as though Jedrik read his mind. Perhaps, with that simulation model of him she carried in her head, this was exactly what she did.

"We didn't expect a hero to come and save us. We knew that whoever came would suffer from the same deficiencies as the other non-Dosadi we saw here. You were so . . . slow. Tell me, McKie, what drives a Dosadi?"

He almost said, "Power."

She saw his hesitation, waited.

"The power to change your condition," he said.

"You make me very proud, McKie."

"But how did you know I was . . ."

"McKie!"

He swallowed, then: "Yes, I guess that was the easiest part for you."

"It was much more difficult finding your abilities and shaping you into a Dosadi."

"But I might've been . . ."

"Tell me how I did it, McKie."

It was a test. He saw that. How had she known absolutely that he was the one she needed?

"I was sent here in a way that evaded Broey."

"And that's not easy." Her glance flickered ceilingward. "They tried to bait us from time to time. Havvy . . ."

"Compromised, contaminated . . ."

"Useless. Sometimes, a stranger looks out of Havvy's eyes."

"My eyes are my own."

"The first thing Bahrank reported about you."

"But even before that . . ."

"Yes?"

"They used Havvy to tell you I was coming . . . and he told you that you could use my body. He had to be truthful with you up to a point. You could read Havvy! How clever they thought they were being! I had to be vulnerable . . . really vulnerable."

"The first thing . . ."

". . . you found out about me." He nodded. "Suspicions confirmed. All of that money on my person. Bait. I was someone to be eliminated. I was a powerful enemy of your enemies."

"And you were angered by the right things."

"You saw that?"

"McKie, you people are so easy to read. So *easy!*"

"And the weapons I carried. You were supposed to use those to destroy yourselves. The implications . . ."

"I would've seen that if I'd had first-hand experience of Aritch. You *knew* what he intended for us. My mistake was to read your fears as purely personal. In time . . ."

"We're wasting time."

"You fear we'll be too late?"

Once more, he looked at the shimmering rods. What was it Pcharky did? McKie felt events rushing over him, engulfing him. What bargain had Jedrik really driven with Pcharky? She saw the question on his face.

"My people knew all along that Pcharky was just a tool of

the God who held us prisoner. We forced a bargain on that God—that Caleban. Did you think we would not recognize the identity between the powers of that cage and the powers of our God Wall? No more delays, McKie. It's time to test our bargain."

Geriatric or other life extension for the powerful poses a similar threat to a sentient species as that found historically in the dominance of a self-perpetuating bureaucracy. Both assume prerogatives of immortality, collecting more and more power with each passing moment. This is power which draws a theological aura about itself: the unassailable Law, the God-given mandate of the leader, manifest destiny. Power held too long within a narrow framework moves farther and farther away from the adaptive demands of changed conditions. The leadership grows ever more paranoid, suspicious of inventive adaptations to change, fearfully protective of personal power and, in the terrified avoidance of what it sees as risk, blindly leads its people into destruction.

— *BuSab Manual*

"Very well, I'll tell you what bothers me," Ceylang said. "There are too many things about this problem that I fail to understand."

From her seated position, she looked across a small, round room at Aritch, who floated gently in a tiny blue pool. His head at the pool's lip was almost on a level with Ceylang's. Again, they had worked late into the night. She understood the reasons for this, the time pressures were quite apparent, but the peculiar Gowachin flavor of her training kept her in an almost constant state of angry questioning.

This whole thing was so un-Wreave!

Ceylang smoothed the robe over her long body. The robe was blue now, one step away from Legum black. Appropriately, there was blue all around her: the walls, the floor, the ceiling, Aritch's pool.

The High Magister rested his chin on the pool's edge to speak.

"I require specific questions before I can even hope to penetrate your puzzlement."

"Will McKie defend or prosecute? The simulator . . ."

"Damn the simulator! Odds are that he'll make the mistake of prosecuting. Your own reasoning powers should . . ."

"But if he doesn't?"

"Then selection of the judicial panel becomes vital."

Ceylang twisted her body to one side, feeling the chairdog adjust for her comfort. As usual, Aritch's answer only deepened her sense of uncertainty. She voiced that now.

"I continue to have this odd feeling that you intend me to play some role which I'm not supposed to discover until the very last instant."

Aritch breathed noisily through his mouth, splashed water onto his head.

"This all may be moot. By this time day after tomorrow, Dosadi *and* McKie may no longer exist."

"Then I will not advance to Legum?"

"Oh, I'm fairly certain you'll be a Legum."

She studied him, sensing irony, then:

"What a delicate line you walk, High Magister."

"Hardly. My way is wide and clear. You know the things I cannot countenance. I cannot betray the Law or my people."

"I have similar inhibitions. But this Dosadi thing—so tempting."

"So dangerous! Would a Wreave don Human flesh to learn the Human condition? Would you permit a Human to penetrate Wreave society in this . . ."

"There are some who might conspire in this! There are even Gowachin who . . ."

"The opportunities for misuse are countless."

"Yet you say that McKie already is more Gowachin than a Gowachin."

Aritch's webbed hands folded over the pool's edge, the claws extended.

"We risked much in training him for this task."

"More than you risk with me?"

Aritch withdrew his hands, stared at her, unblinking.

"So that's what bothers you."

"Precisely."

"Think, Ceylang, how near the core of Wreavedom you would permit me to come. Thus far and no farther will we permit you."

"And McKie?"

"May already have gone too far for us to permit his continued existence."

"I heed your warning, Aritch. But I remain puzzled as to why the Calebans couldn't prevent . . ."

"They profess not to understand the ego transfer. But who can understand a Caleban, let alone control one in a matter so delicate? Even this one who created the God Wall . . ."

"It's rumored that McKie understands Calebans."

"He denies it."

She rubbed her pocked left jowl with a prehensile mandible, felt the many scars of her passage through the Wreave triads. Family to family to family until it was a single gigantic family. Yet, all were Wreave. This Dosadi thing threatened a monstrous parody of Wreavedom. Still . . .

"So fascinating," she murmured.

"That's its threat."

"We should pray for the death of Dosadi."

"Perhaps."

She was startled.

"What . . ."

"This might not die with Dosadi. Our sacred bond assures that you will leave here with this knowledge. Many Gowachin know of this thing."

"And McKie."

"Infections have a way of spreading," Aritch said. "Remember *that* if this comes to the Courtarena."

*There are some forms of insanity which, driven to an ulti-
mate expression, can become the new models of sanity.*

> — BuSab Manual

"McKie?"

It was the familiar Caleban presence in his awareness, as
though he heard and felt someone (or some*thing*) which he
knew was not there.

The preparation had been deceptively simple. He and Jedrik clasped hands, his right hand and her left, and each
grasped one of the shimmering rods with the other hand.

McKie did not have a ready identity for this Caleban and
wondered at the questioning in her *voice*. He agreed, however, that he was indeed McKie, shaping the thought as sub-
vocalized conversation. As he spoke, McKie was acutely
aware of Jedrik beside him. She was more than just another
person now. He carried a tentative simulation model of her,
sometimes anticipating her responses.

"You make mutual agreement?" the Caleban asked.

McKie sensed Pcharky then: a distant presence, the monitor for this experience. It was as though Pcharky had been
reduced to a schematic which the Caleban followed, a set of
complex rules, many of which could not be translated into

264

words. Some part of McKie responded to this as though a monster awakened within him, a sleeping monster who sat up full of anger at being aroused thus, demanding:

"Who is it that dares awaken me?"

McKie felt his body trembling, felt Jedrik trembling beside him. The Caleban/Taprisiot-trembling, the sweaty response to trance! He saw these phenomena now in a different light. When you walked at the edge of this abyss . . .

While these thoughts passed through his mind, he felt a slight shift, no more than the blurred reflection of something which was not quite movement. Now, while he still felt his own flesh around him, he also felt himself possessed of an inner contact with Jedrik's body and knew she shared this experience.

Such a panic as he had not thought possible threatened to overwhelm him. He felt Jedrik trying to break the contact, to stop this hideous sharing, but they were powerless in the grip of a force which would not be stopped.

No time sense attached itself to this experience, but a fatalistic calm overcame them almost simultaneously. McKie felt awareness of Jedrik/flesh deepen. Curiosity dominated him now.

So this is woman!

This is man?

They shared the thoughts across an indistinct bridge.

Fascination gripped McKie. He probed deeper.

He/She could feel himself/herself breathing. And the differences! It was not the genitalia, the presence or lack of breasts. She felt bereft of breasts. He felt acutely distressed by their presence, self-consciously aware of profound implications. The sense of difference went back beyond gamete McKie/Jedrik.

McKie sensed her thoughts, her reactions.

Jedrik: "You cast your sperm upon the stream of time."

McKie: "You enclose and nurture . . ."

266 / Frank Herbert

"I cast/I nurture."

It was as though they looked at an object from opposite sides, aware belatedly that they both examined the same thing.

"We cast/we nurture."

Obscuring layers folded away, and McKie found himself in Jedrik's mind, she in his. Their thoughts were one entity.

The separate Dosadi and ConSentient experiences melted into a single relationship.

"Aritch . . . ah, yes. You see? And your PanSpechi friend, Bildoon. Note that. You suspected, but now you know . . ."

Each set of experiences fed on the other, expanding, refining . . . condensing, discarding, creating . . .

So that's the training of a Legum.

Loving parents? Ahhh, yes, loving parents.

"I/we will apply pressure there . . . and there . . . They must be maneuvered into choosing that one as a judge. Yes, that will give us the required leverage. Let them break their own code."

And the awakened monster stirred within them. It had no dimension, no place, only existence. They felt its power.

"*I do what I do!*"

The power enveloped them. No other awareness was permitted. They sensed a primal current, unswerving purpose, a force which could override any other thing in their universe. It was not God, not Life, not any particular species. It was something so far beyond such articulations that Jedrik/McKie could not even contemplate it without a sense that the next instant would bring obliteration. They felt a question hurled at their united, fearful awareness. The question was framed squarely in anger, astonishment, cold amusement, and threat.

"For *this* you awaken *me*?"

Now, they understood why the old body and donor-ego

had always been slain immediately. This terrible sharing made a . . . made a noise. It awakened a questioner.

They understood the question without words, knowing they could never grasp the full meaning and emotive thrust, that it would burn them out even to try. Anger . . . astonishment . . . cold amusement . . . threat. The question as their own united mind(s) interpreted it represented a limit. It was all that Jedrik/McKie could accept.

The intrusive questioner receded.

They were never quite sure afterward whether they'd been expelled or whether they'd fled in terror, but the parting words were burned into their combined awareness.

"Let the sleeper sleep."

They walked softly in their minds then. They understood the warning, but knew it could never be translated in its fullest threat for any other sentient being.

Concurrent: McKie/Jedrik felt a projection of terror from the God Wall Caleban, unfocused, unexplained. It was a new experience in the male-female collective memory. Caleban Fannie Mae had not even projected this upon original McKie when she'd thought herself doomed.

Concurrent: McKie/Jedrik felt a burntout fading from Pcharky. Something in that terrible contact had plunged Pcharky into his death spiral. Even as McKie/Jedrik realized this, the old Gowachin died. It was a slammed door. But this came after a blazing realization by McKie/Jedrik that Pcharky had shared the original decision to set up the Dosadi experiment.

McKie found himself clothed in living, breathing flesh which routed its messages through his awareness. He wasn't sure which of their two bodies he possessed, but it was distinct, separate. It wrapped him in Human senses: the taste of salt, the smell of perspiration, and the omnipresent Warren stink. One hand held cold metal, the other clasped the hand of a fellow Human. Perspiration drenched this body, made the clasped hands slippery. He felt that knowing which hand held another hand was of utmost importance, but he wasn't ready to face that knowledge. Awareness of self, this new self, and a whole lifetime of new memories, demanded all of the attention he could muster.

Focus: A Rim city, never outside Jedrik's control because she had fed the signals through to Gar and Tria with exquisite care, and because those who gave the orders on the Rim had shared in the generations of selective breeding which had produced Jedrik. She was a biological weapon whose sole target was the God Wall.

Focus: Loving parents can thrust their child into deadly peril when they know everything possible has been done to prepare that child for survival.

The oddity to McKie was that he felt such things as personal memories.

"I did that."

Jedrik suffered the throes of similar experiences.

Which body?

So that was the training of a BuSab agent. Clever . . . almost adequate. Complex and full of much that she found to be new, but why did it always stop short of a full development?

She reviewed the sessions with Aritch and Ceylang. A matched pair. The choice of Ceylang and the role chosen for her appeared obvious. How innocent! Jedrik felt herself free to pity Ceylang. When allowed to run its course, this was an interesting emotion. She had never before felt pity in uncolored purity.

Focus: McKie actually loved her. She savored this emotion in its ConSentient complexity. The straight flow of selected emotions fascinated her. They did not have to be bridled!

In and out of this creative exchange there wove an intimacy, a pure sexuality without inhibitions.

McKie, savoring the amusement Jedrik had felt when Tria

had suggested a McKie/Jedrik breeding, found himself caught by demanding male eroticism and knew by the sensation that he retained his old body.

Jedrik, understanding McKie's long search for a female to complete him, found her amusement converted to the desire to demonstrate that completion. As she turned toward him, releasing the dull rod which had once shimmered in contact with Pcharky, she found herself in McKie's flesh looking into her own eyes.

McKie gasped in the mirror experience.

Just as abruptly, driven by shock, they shifted back into familiar flesh: McKie male, Jedrik female. Instantly, it became a thing to explore—back—and forth. Eroticism was forgotten in this new game.

"We can be either sex/body at will!"

It was something beyond Taprisiots and Calebans, far more subtle than the crawling progression of a PanSpechi ego through the bodies from its creche.

They knew the source of this odd gift even as they sank back on the bed, content to be familiar male and female for a time.

The sleeping monster.

This was a gift with barbs in it, something *loving parents* might give their child in the knowledge that it was time for this lesson. Yet they felt revitalized, knowing they had for an instant tapped an energy source without limits.

A pounding on the door interrupted this shared reverie.

"Jedrik! Jedrik!"

"What is it?"

"It's Broey. He wishes to talk to McKie."

They were off the bed in an instant.

Jedrik glanced at McKie, knowing she had not one secret from him, that they shared a reasoning base. Out of the mutual understanding in this base, she spoke for both of them.

"Does he say why?"

"Jedrik . . ."

They both recognized the voice of a trusted aide and heard the fear in it.

". . . it's midmorning and there is no sun. God has turned off the sun!"

"Sealed us in . . ."

". . . to conceal the final blast."

Jedrik opened the door, confronted the frightened aide.

"Where is Broey?"

"Here—in your command post. He came alone without escort."

She glanced at McKie. "You will speak for us."

Broey waited near the position board in the command post. Watchful Humans stood within striking distance. He turned as McKie and Jedrik entered. McKie noted that the Gowachin's body was, indeed, heavy with breeding juices as anticipated. Unsettling for a Gowachin.

"What are your terms, McKie?"

Broey's voice was guttural, full of heavy breathing.

McKie's features remained Dosadi-bland, but he thought: *Broey thinks I'm responsible for the darkness. He's terrified.*

McKie glanced at the threatening black of the windows before speaking. He knew this Gowachin from Jedrik's painstaking study. Broey was a sophisticate, a collector of sophistication who surrounded himself with people of the same stripe. He was a professional sophisticate who read everything through that peculiar Dosadi screen. No one could come into his circle who didn't share this pose. All else remained outside and inferior. He was an ultimate Dosadi, a distillation, almost as Human as Gowachin because he'd obviously once worn a Human body. He was Gowachin at his origins, though—no doubt of it.

"You followed my scent," McKie said.

"Excellent!"

Broey brightened. He had not expected a Dosadi exchange, pared to the nonemotional essentials.

"Unfortunately," McKie said, "You have no position from which to negotiate. Certain things will be done. You will comply willingly, your compliance will be forced, or we will act without you."

It was a deliberate goading on McKie's part, a choice of non-Dosadi forms to abbreviate this confrontation. It said more than anything else that McKie came from beyond the God Wall, that the darkness which held back the daylight was the least of his resources.

Broey hesitated, then:

"So?"

The single word fell on the air with countless implications: an entire exchange discarded, hopes dashed, a hint of sadness at lost powers, and still with that sophisticated reserve which was Broey's signature. It was more subtle than a shrug, more powerful in its Dosadi overtones than an entire negotiating session.

"Questions?" McKie asked.

Broey glanced at Jedrik, obviously surprised by this. It was as though he appealed to her: they were both Dosadi, were they not? This outsider came here with his gross manners, his lack of Dosadi understanding. How could one speak to such one? He addressed Jedrik.

"Have I not already stated my submission? I came alone, I . . ."

Jedrik picked up McKie's cue.

"There are certain . . . peculiarities to our situation."

"Peculiarities?"

Broey's nictating membrane blinked once.

Jedrik allowed her manner to convey a slight embarrassment.

"Certain delicacies of the Dosadi condition must be overlooked. We are now, all of us, abject supplicants . . . and we are dealing with people who do not speak as we speak, act as we act . . ."

"Yes." He pointed upward. "The mentally retarded ones. We are in danger then."

It was not a question. Broey peered upward, as though trying to see through the ceiling and intervening floors. He drew in a deep breath.

"Yes."

Again, it was compressed communication. Anyone who could put the God Wall there could crush an entire planet. Therefore, Dosadi and all of its inhabitants had been brought to a common subjection. Only a Dosadi could have accepted it this quickly without more questions, and Broey was an ultimate Dosadi.

McKie turned to Jedrik. When he spoke, she anticipated every word, but she waited him out.

"Tell your people to stop all attacks."

He faced Broey.

"And your people."

Broey looked from Jedrik to McKie, back to Jedrik with a puzzled expression openly on his face, but he obeyed.

"Which communicator?"

Where pain predominates, agony can be a valued teacher.

— *Dosadi aphorism*

McKie and Jedrik had no need to discuss the decision. It was a choice which they shared and knew they shared through a memory-selection process now common to both of them. There was a loophole in the God Wall and even though that wall now blanketed Dosadi in darkness, a Caleban contract was still a Caleban contract. The vital question was whether the Caleban of the God Wall would respond.

Jedrik in McKie's body stood guard outside her own room while a Jedrik-fleshed McKie went alone into the room to make the attempt. Who should he try to contact? Fannie Mae? The absolute darkness which enclosed Dosadi hinted at an absolute withdrawal of the guardian Caleban. And there was so little time.

McKie sat cross-legged on the floor of the room and tried to clear his mind. The constant strange discoveries in the female body he now wore interfered with concentration. The moment of exchange left an aftershock which he doubted would ever diminish. They had but to share the desire for the change now and it occurred. But this different body—

ahh, the multiplicity of differences created its own confusions. These went far beyond the adjustments to different height and weight. The muscles of his/her arms and hips felt wrongly attached. The bodily senses were routed through different unconscious processes. Anatomy created its own patterns, its own instinctual behavior. For one thing, he found it necessary to develop consciously monitored movements which protected his/her breasts. The movements were reminiscent of those male adjustments by which he prevented injury to testes. These were movements which a male learned early and relegated to an automatic behavior pattern. The problem in the female body was that he had to *think* about such behavior. And it went far beyond the breast-testes interlock.

As he tried to clear his mind for the Caleban contact, these webbed clusters of memory intruded. It was maddening. He needed to clear away bodily distractions, but this female body demanded his attention. In desperation, he hyperventilated and burned his awareness into a pineal focus whose dangers he knew only too well. This was the way to permanent identity loss if the experience were prolonged. It produced a sufficient clarity, however, that he could fill his awareness with memories of Fannie Mae.

Silence.

He sensed time's passage as though each heartbeat were a blow.

Fear hovered at the edges of the silence.

It came to him that something had put a terrible fear into the God Wall Caleban.

McKie felt anger.

"Caleban! You owe me!"

"McKie?"

The response was so faint that he wondered whether it might be his hopes playing tricks on him.

"Fannie Mae?"

"Are you McKie?"

That was stronger, and he recognized the familiar Caleban presence in his awareness.

"I am McKie and you owe me a debt."

"If you are truly McKie . . . why are you so . . . strange . . . changed?"

"I wear another body."

McKie was never sure, but he thought he sensed consternation. Fannie Mae responded more strongly then.

"I remove McKie from Dosadi now? Contract permits."

"I will share Dosadi's fate."

"McKie!"

"Don't argue with me, Fannie Mae. I will share Dosadi's fate unless you remove another node/person with me."

He projected Jedrik's patterns then, an easy process since he shared all of her memories.

"She wears McKie's body!"

It was accusatory.

"She wears *another* body," McKie said. He knew the Caleban saw his new relationship with Jedrik. Everything depended now on the interpretation of the Caleban contract.

"Jedrik is Dosadi," the Caleban protested.

"So am I Dosadi . . . now."

"But you are McKie!"

"And Jedrik is also McKie. Contact her if you don't believe me."

He broke the contact with an angry abruptness, found himself sprawled on the floor, still twitching. Perspiration bathed the female body which he still wore. The head ached.

Would Fannie Mae do as he'd told her? He knew Jedrik was as capable of projecting his awareness as he was of projecting hers. How would Fannie Mae interpret the Dosadi contract?

Gods! The ache in this head was a burning thing. He felt alien in Jedrik's body, misused. The pain persisted and he wondered if he'd done irreparable harm to Jedrik's brain through that intense pineal focus.

Slowly, he pushed himself upright, got to his feet. The Jedrik legs felt weak beneath him. He thought of Jedrik outside that door, trembling in the zombielike trance required for this mind-to-mind contact. What was taking so long? Had the Calebans withdrawn?

Have we lost?

He started for the door but before he'd taken the second step, light blazed around him. For a fractional heartbeat he thought it was the final fire to consume Dosadi, but the light held steady. He glanced around, found himself in the open air. It was a place he recognized immediately: the courtyard of the Dry Head compound on Tandaloor. He saw the familiar phylum designs on the surrounding walls: green Gowachin script on yellow bricks. There was the sound of water splashing in the corner pool. A group of Gowachin stood in an arched entry directly ahead of him and he recognized one of his old teachers. Yes—this was a Dry Head sanctus. These people had protected him, trained him, introduced him to their most sacred secrets.

The Gowachin in the shadowed entry were moving excitedly into the courtyard, their attention centered on a figure sprawled near them. The figure stirred, sat up.

McKie recognized his own body there.

Jedrik!

It was an intense mutual need. The body exchange required less than an eyeblink. McKie found himself in his own familar body, seated on cool tiles. The approaching Gowachin bombarded him with questions.

"McKie, what is this?"

"You fell through a jumpdoor!"

"Are you hurt?"

He waved the questions away, crossed his legs, and fell into the long-call trance focused on that bead in his stomach. That bead Bildoon had never expected him to use!

As it was paid to do, the Taprisiot waiting on CC enfolded his awareness. McKie rejected contact with Bildoon, made six calls through the responsive Taprisiot. The calls went to key agents in BuSab, all of them ambitious and resourceful, all of them completely loyal to the agency's mandate. He transmitted his Dosadi information in full bursts, using the technique derived from his exchanges with Jedrik—mind-to-mind.

There were few questions and those easily answered.

"The Caleban who holds Dosadi imprisoned plays God. It's the letter of the contract."

"Do the Calebans approve of this?"

That question came from a particularly astute Wreave agent sensitive to the complications implicit in the fact that the Gowachin were training Ceylang, a Wreave female, as a Legum.

"The concepts of approval or disapproval are not applicable. The role was necessary for that Caleban to carry out the contract."

"It was a game?"

The Wreave agent was outraged.

"Perhaps. There's one thing certain: the Calebans don't understand harmful behavior and ethics as we understand them."

"We've always known that."

"But now we've really learned it."

When he'd made the six calls, McKie sent his Taprisiot questing for Aritch, found the High Magister in the Running Phylum's conference pool.

"Greetings, Client."

McKie projected wry amusement. He sensed the Gowachin's shock.

"There are certain things which your Legum instructs you to do under the holy seal of our relationship," McKie said.

"You will take us into the Courtarena, then?"

The High Magister was perceptive and he was a beneficiary of Dosadi's peculiar gifts, but he was not a Dosadi. McKie found it relatively easy to manipulate Aritch now, enlisting the High Magister's deepest motivations. When Aritch protested against cancelling the God Wall contract, McKie revealed only the first layer of stubborn determination.

"You will not add to your Legum's difficulties."

"But what will keep them on Dosadi?"

"Nothing."

"Then you will defend rather than prosecute?"

"Ask your pet Wreave," McKie said. "Ask Ceylang."

He broke the contact then, knowing Aritch could only obey him. The High Magister had few choices, most of them bad ones. And Gowachin Law prevented him from disregarding his Legum's orders once the pattern of the contest was set.

McKie awoke from the call to find his Dry Head friends clustered around Jedrik. She was explaining their predicament. Yes . . . There were advantages to having two bodies with one purpose. McKie got to his feet. She saw him, spoke.

"My head feels better."

"It was a near thing." And he added:

"It still is. But Dosadi is free."

In the classical times of several species, it was the custom of the powerful to nudge the power-counters (money or other economic tabulators, status points, etc.) into occasional violent perturbations from which the knowledgeable few profited. Human accounts of this experience reveal edifying examples of this behavior (for which, see Appendix G). Only the PanSpechi appear to have avoided this phenomenon, possibly because of creche slavery.

— *Comparative History, The BuSab Text*

McKie made his next series of calls from the room the Dry Heads set aside for him. It was a relatively large room reserved for Human guests and contained well-trained chairdogs and a wide bedog which Jedrik eyed with suspicion despite her McKie memories of such things. She knew the things had only a rudimentary brain, but still they were . . . *alive.*

She stood by the single window which looked out on the courtyard pool, turning when she heard McKie awaken from his Taprisiot calls.

"Suspicions confirmed," he said.

"Will our agent friends leave Bildoon for us?" she asked.

"Yes."

She turned back to the window.

"I keep thinking how the Dosadi sky must look now . . . without a God Wall. As bright as this." She nodded toward the courtyard seen through the window. "And when we get jumpdoors . . ."

279

She broke off. McKie, of course, shared such thoughts. This new intimacy required considerable adjustment.

"I've been thinking about your training as a Legum," she said.

McKie knew where her thoughts had gone.

The Gowachin chosen to train him had all appeared open in their relationship. He had been told that his teachers were a select group, chosen for excellence, the best available for the task: making a Gowachin Legum out of a non-Gowachin.

A silk purse from a sow's ear!

His teachers had appeared to lead conventional Gowachin lives, keeping the usual numbers of fertile females in family tanks, weeding the Graluz tads with necessary Gowachin abandon. On the surface of it, the whole thing had assumed a sense of the ordinary. They had introduced him to intimate aspects of their lives when he'd inquired, answered his questions with disarming frankness.

McKie's Jedrik-amplified awareness saw this in a different light now. The contests between Gowachin phylums stood out sharply. And McKie knew now that he had not asked the right questions, that his teachers had been selected by different rules than those revealed to him at the time, that their private instructions from their Gowachin superiors contained nuances of vital importance which had been hidden from their student.

Poor Ceylang.

These were unsettling reflections. They changed his understanding of Gowachin honor, called into question all of those inadvertent comparisons he'd made between Gowachin forms and the mandate of his own BuSab. His BuSab training came in for the same questioning examination.

Why . . . why . . . why . . . why . . .

Law? Gowachin Law?

The value in having a BuSab agent as a Legum of the Gowachin had gained a new dimension. McKie saw these matters now as Jedrik had once seen through the God Wall. There existed other forces only dimly visible behind the visible screen. An unseen power structure lay out there—people who seldom appeared in public, decision makers whose slightest whim carried terrible import for countless worlds. Many places, many worlds would be held in various degrees of bondage. Dosadi had merely been an extreme case for a special purpose.

New bodies for old. Immortality. And a training ground for people who made terrible decisions.

But none of them would be as completely Dosadi as this Jedrik-amplified McKie.

He wondered where the Dosadi decision had been made. Aritch had not shared in it; that was obvious. There were others behind Aritch—Gowachin and non-Gowachin. A shadowy power group existed. It could have its seat on any world of the ConSentiency. The power merchants would have to meet occasionally, but not necessarily face to face. And never in the public eye. Their first rule was secrecy. They would employ many people who lived at the exposed fringes of their power, people to carry out shadowy commands—people such as Aritch.

And Bildoon.

What had the PanSpechi hoped to gain? A permanent hold on his creche's ego? Of course. That . . . plus new bodies—Human bodies, undoubtedly, and unmarked by the stigmata of his PanSpechi origins.

Bildoon's behavior—and Aritch's—appeared so transparent now. And there'd be a Mrreg nearby creating the currents in which Aritch swam. Puppet leads to Puppet Master.

Mrreg.

That poor fool, Grinik, had revealed more than he thought.

And Bildoon.

"We have two points of entry," McKie said.

282 of Frank Herbert

She agreed.

"Bildoon and Mrreg. The latter is the more dangerous."

A crease beside McKie's nose began to itch. He scratched at it absently, grew conscious that something had changed. He stared around, found himself standing at the window and clothed in a female body.

Damn! It happened so easily.

Jedrik stared up at him with his own eyes. She spoke with his voice, but the overtones were pure Jedrik. They both found this amusing.

"The powers of your BuSab."

He understood.

"Yes, the watchdogs of justice."

"Where were the watchdogs when my ancestors were lured into this Dosadi trap?"

"Watchdogs of justice, very dangerous role," he agreed.

"You know our feelings of outrage," she said.

"And I know what it is to have loving parents."

"Remember that when you talk to Bildoon."

Once more, McKie found himself on the bed, his old familiar body around him.

Presently, he felt the mental tendrils of a Taprisiot call, sensed Bildoon's awareness in contact with him. McKie wasted no time. The shadow forces were taking the bait.

"I have located Dosadi. The issue will come to the Court-arena. No doubt of that. I want you to make the preliminary arrangements. Inform the High Magister Aritch that I make the formal imposition of the Legum. One member of the judicial panel must be a Gowachin from Dosadi. I have a particular Gowachin in mind. His name is Broey."

"Where are you?"

"On Tandaloor."

"Is that possible?"

McKie masked his sadness. *Ahhh, Bildoon, how easily you are read.*

"Dosadi is temporarily out of danger. I have taken certain retaliatory precautions."

McKie broke the contact.

Jedrik spoke in a musing voice.

"Ohh, the perturbations we spread."

McKie had no time for such reflections.

"Broey will need help, a support team, an extremely reliable troop which I want you to select for him."

"Yes, and what of Gar and Tria?"

"Let them run free. Broey will pick them up later."

Communal/managed economics have always been more destructive of their societies than those driven by greed. This is what Dosadi says: Greed sets its own limits, is self-regulating.

—*The Dosadi Analysis/BuSab Text*

McKie looked around the Legum office they'd assigned him. Afternoon smells from Tandaloor's fern jungles came in an open window. A low barrier separated him from the Courtarena with its ranks of seats all around. His office and adjoining quarters were small but fitted with all requisite linkages to libraries and the infrastructure to summon witnesses and experts. It was a green-walled space so deceptively ordinary that its like had beguiled more than one non-Gowachin into believing he knew how to perform here. But these quarters represented a deceptive surface riding on Gowachin currents. No matter that the ConSentient Pact modified what the Gowachin might do here, this was Tandaloor, and the forms of the frog people dominated.

Seating himself at the single table in the office space, McKie felt the chairdog adjust itself beneath him. It was good to have a chairdog again after Dosadi's unrelenting furniture. He flipped a toggle and addressed the Gowachin face which appeared on the screen inset into his table.

"I require testimony from those who made the actual decision to set up the Dosadi experiment. Are you prepared to meet this request?"

"Do you have the names of these people?"

Did this fool think he was going to blurt out: "Mrreg"?

"If you force me to it," McKie warned, "I will bind Aritch to the Law and extract the names from him."

This had no apparent effect on the Gowachin. He addressed McKie by name and title, adding:

"I leave the formalities to you. Any witness I summon must have a name."

McKie suppressed a smile. Suspicions confirmed. This was a fact which the watchful Gowachin in the screen was late recognizing. Someone else had read the interchange correctly, however. Another, older, Gowachin face replaced the first one on the screen.

"What're you doing, McKie?"

"Determining how I will proceed with this case."

"You will proceed as a Legum of the Gowachin Bar."

"Precisely."

McKie waited.

The Gowachin peered narrowly at him from the screen.

"Jedrik?"

"You are speaking to Jorj X. McKie, a Legum of the Gowachin Bar."

Belatedly, the older Gowachin saw something of the way the Dosadi experience had changed McKie.

"Do you wish me to place you in contact with Aritch?"

McKie shook his head. They were so damned obvious, these underlings.

"Aritch didn't make the Dosadi decision. Aritch was chosen to take the blow if it came to that. I will accept nothing less than the one who made that ultimate decision which launched the Dosadi experiment."

The Gowachin stared at him coldly, then:

"One moment. I will see what I can do."

The screen went blank, but the audio remained. McKie heard the voices.

"Hello . . . Yes, I'm sorry to interrupt at this time."

"What is it?"

That was a deep and arrogant Gowachin voice, full of annoyance at the interruption. It was also an accent which a Dosadi could recognize in spite of the carefully overlaid masking tones. Here was one who'd used Dosadi.

The voice of the older Gowachin from McKie's screen continued:

"The Legum bound to Aritch has come up with a sensitive line of questioning. He wishes to speak to you."

"To me? But I am preparing for Laupuk."

McKie had no idea what Laupuk might be, but it opened a new window on the Gowachin for him. Here was a glimpse of the rarified strata which had been concealed from him all of those years. This tiny glimpse confirmed him in the course he'd chosen.

"He is listening to us at this time."

"Listening . . . why?"

The tone carried threats, but the Gowachin who'd intercepted McKie's demands went on, unwavering:

"To save explanations. It's clear that he'll accept nothing less than speaking to you. This caller is McKie, but . . ."

"Yes?"

"You will understand."

"I presume you have interpreted things correctly. Very well. Put him on."

McKie's screen flickered, revealed a wide view of a Gowachin room such as he'd never before seen. A far wall held spears and cutting weapons, streamers of colorful pennants, glistening rocks, ornate carvings in a shiny black substance. All of this was backdrop for a semireclining chairdog occupied by an aged Gowachin who sat spraddle-legged being anointed by two younger Gowachin males. The attendants poured a thick, golden substance onto the aged Gowachin from green crystal flasks. The flasks were of a spiral design. The contents were gently massaged into the Gowachin's skin. The old Gowachin glistened with the stuff and when he blinked—no Phylum tattoos.

"As you can see," he said, "I'm being prepared for . . ."

He broke off, recognizing that he spoke to a non-Gowachin. Certainly, he'd known this. It was a slow reaction for a Dosadi.

"This is a mistake," he said.

"Indeed." McKie nodded pleasantly. "Your name?"

The old Gowachin scowled at this gaucherie, then chuckled.

"I am called Mrreg."

As McKie had suspected. And why would a Tandaloor Gowachin assume the name, no, the *title* of the mythical monster who'd imbued the frog people with a drive toward savage testing? The implications went far beyond this planet, colored Dosadi.

"You made the decision for the Dosadi experiment?"

"Someone had to make it."

That was not a substantive answer, and McKie decided to take it to issue. "You are not doing me any favors! I now know what it means to be a Legum of the Gowachin Bar and I intend to employ my powers to their limits."

It was as though McKie had worked some odd magic which froze the scene on his screen. The two attendants stopped pouring unguent, but did not look toward the pickup viewer which was recording their actions for McKie. As for Mrreg, he sat utterly still, his eyes fixed unblinking upon McKie.

McKie waited.

Presently, Mrreg turned to the attendant on his left.

"Please continue. There is little time."

McKie took this as though spoken to himself.

'You're my client. Why did you send a proxy?"

Mrreg continued to study McKie.

"I see what Ekris meant." Then, more briskly: "Well, McKie, I followed your career with interest. It now appears I did not follow you closely enough. Perhaps if we had not . . ."

He left the thought incomplete.

McKie picked up on this.

"It was inevitable that I escape from Dosadi."

"Perhaps."

The attendants finished their work, departed, taking the oddly shaped crystal flasks with them.

"Answer my question," McKie said.

"I am not required to answer your question."

"Then I withdraw from this case."

Mrreg hunched forward in sudden alarm. "You cannot! Aritch isn't . . ."

"I have no dealings with Aritch. My client is that Gowachin who made the Dosadi decision."

"You are engaging in strange behavior for a Legum. Yes, bring it." This last was addressed to someone offscreen. Another attendant appeared, carrying a white garment shaped somewhat like a long apron with sleeves. The attendant proceeded to put this onto Mrreg, who ignored him, concentrating on McKie.

"Do you have any idea what you're doing, McKie?"

"Preparing to act for my client."

"I see. Who told you about me?"

McKie shook his head.

"Did you really believe me unable to detect your presence or interpret the implications of what my own senses tell me?"

McKie saw that the Gowachin failed to see beneath the surface taunting. Mrreg turned to the attendant who was tying a green ribbon at the back of the apron. The old Gowachin had to lean forward for this. "A little tighter," he said.

The attendant retied the ribbon.

Addressing McKie, Mrreg said, "Please forgive the distraction. This must proceed at its own pace."

McKie absorbed this, assessed it Dosadi fashion. He could see the makings of an important Gowachin ritual here, but it was a new one to him. No matter. That could wait. He continued speaking, probing this Mrreg.

"When you found your own peculiar uses for Dosadi . . ."

"Peculiar? It's a universal motivation, McKie, that one tries to reduce the competition."

"Did you assess the price correctly, the price you might be asked to pay?"

"Oh, yes. I knew what I might have to pay."

There was a clear tone of resignation in the Gowachin's voice, a rare tone for his species. McKie hesitated. The attendant who'd brought the apron left the room, never once glancing in McKie's direction, although there had to be a screen to show whatever Mrreg saw of his caller.

"You wonder why I sent a proxy to hire the Legum?" Mrreg asked.

"Why Aritch?"

"Because he's a candidate for . . . greater responsibilities. You know, McKie, you astonish me. Undoubtedly you know what I could have done to you for this impertinence, yet that doesn't deter you."

This revealed more than Mrreg might have intended, but he remained unaware (or uncaring) of what McKie saw. For his part, McKie maintained a bland exterior, as blank as that of any Dosadi.

"I have a single purpose," McKie said. "Not even my client will sway me from it."

"The function of a Legum," Mrreg said.

The attendant of the white apron returned with an unsheathed blade. McKie glimpsed a jeweled handle and glittering sweep of cutting edge about twenty centimeters long.

290 / Frank Herbert

The blade curved back upon itself in a tight arc at the tip. The attendant, his back to McKie, stood facing Mrreg. The blade no longer was visible.

Mrreg, his left side partly obscured from McKie by the attendant, leaned to the right and peered up at the screen through which he watched McKie.

"You've never been appraised of the ceremony we call Laupuk. It's very important and we've been remiss in leaving this out of your education. Laupuk was essential before such a . . . project as Dosadi could be set in motion. Try to understand this ritual. It will help you prepare your case."

"What was your Phylum?" McKie asked.

"That's no longer important but . . . very well. It was Great Awakening. I was High Magister for two decades before we made the Dosadi decision."

"How many Rim bodies have you used up?"

"My final one. That, too, is no longer important. Tell me, McKie, when did you suspect Aritch was only a proxy?"

"When I realized that not all Gowachin were born Gowachin."

"But Aritch . . ."

"Ahh, yes: Aritch aspires to greater responsibilities."

"Yes . . . of course. I see. The Dosadi decision had to go far beyond a few phylums or a single species. There had to be a . . . I believe you Humans call it a 'High Command.' Yes, that would've become obvious to one as alert as you now appear. Your many marriages deceived us, I think. Was that deliberate?"

Secure behind his Dosadi mask, McKie decided to lie.

"Yes."

"Ahhhhhhhhh."

Mrreg seemed to shrivel into himself, but rallied.

"I see. We were made to believe you some kind of dilettante with perverted emotions. It'd be judged a flaw which we could exploit. Then there's another High Command and we never suspected."

It all came out swiftly, revealing the wheels within wheels which ruled Mrreg's view of the ConSentient universe. McKie marveled at how much more was said than the bare words. This one had been a long time away from Dosadi and had not been born there, but there were pressures on Mrreg now forcing him to the limits of what he'd learned on Dosadi.

McKie did not interrupt.

"We didn't expect you to penetrate Aritch's role, but that was not our intent, as you know. I presume . . ."

Whatever Mrreg presumed, he decided not to say it, musing aloud instead.

"One might almost believe you were born on Dosadi."

McKie remained silent, allowing the fear in that conjecture to fill Mrreg's consciousness.

Presently, Mrreg asked, "Do you blame all Gowachin?"

Still, McKie remained silent.

Mrreg became agitated.

"We are a government of sorts, my High Command. People can be induced not to question a government."

McKie decided to press this nerve.

"Governments always commit their entire populations when the demands grow heavy enough. By their passive acceptance, these populations become accessories to whatever is done in their name."

"You've provided free use of jumpdoors for the Dosadi?"

McKie nodded. "The Calebans are aware of their obligation. Jedrik has been busy instructing her compatriots."

"You think to loose the Dosadi upon the ConSentiency and hunt down my High Command? Have a care, McKie. I warn you not to abandon your duties as a Legum, or to turn your back on Aritch."

McKie continued silent.

"Don't make that error, McKie. Aritch is your client. Through him you represent all Gowachin."

"A Legum requires a responsible client," McKie said. "Not a proxy, but a client whose acts are brought into question by the case being tried."

Mrreg revealed Gowachin signs of deep concern.

"Hear me, McKie. I haven't much time."

In a sudden rush of apprehension, McKie focused on the attendant with the blade who stood there partly obscuring the seated Gowachin. Mrreg spoke in a swift spill of words.

"By our standards, McKie, you are not yet very well educated in Gowachin necessities. That was our error. And now your . . . impetuosity has put you into a position which is about to become untenable."

The attendant shifted slightly, arms moving up. McKie glimpsed the blade tip at the attendant's right shoulder.

"Gowachin don't have families as do Humans or even Wreaves," Mrreg said. "We have graduated advancement into groups which hold more and more responsibility for those beneath them. This was the pattern adopted by our High Command. What you see as a Gowachin family is only a breeding group with its own limited rules. With each step up in responsibility goes a requirement that we pay an increasing price for failure. You ask if I know the price? Ahhh, McKie. The breeding male Gowachin makes sure that only the swiftest, most alert of his tads survive. A Magister upholds the forms of the Law. The High Command answers to a . . . Mrreg. You see? And a Mrreg must make only the best decisions. No failures. Thus . . . Laupuk."

As he spoke the final word, the blade in the attendant's hands flashed out and around in a shimmering arc. It caught the seated Gowachin at the neck. Mrreg's head, neatly severed, was caught in the loop at the blade's tip, lifted high, then lowered onto the white apron which now was splashed with green gore.

The scene blanked out, was replaced by the Gowachin who had connected McKie with Mrreg.

"Aritch wishes to consult his Legum," the Gowachin said.

In a changing universe, only a changing species can hope to be immortal and then only if its eggs are nurtured in widely scattered environments. This predicts a wealth of unique individuals.

> —*Insights (a glimpse of early Human philosophy),*
> *BuSab Text*

Jedrik made contact with McKie while he waited for the arrival of Aritch and Ceylang. He had been staring absently at the ceiling, evaluating in a profoundly Dosadi way how to gain personal advantage from the upcoming encounter, when he felt the touch of her mind on his.

McKie locked himself in his body.

"No transfer."

"Of course not."

It was a tiny thing, a subtle shading in the contact which could have been overlooked by anyone with a less accurate simulation model of Jedrik.

"You're angry with me," McKie said.

He projected irony, knew she'd read this correctly.

When she responded, her anger had been reduced to irritation. The point was not the shading of emotion, it was that she allowed such emotion to reveal itself.

"You remind me of one of my early lovers," she said.

McKie thought of where Jedrik was at this moment: safely rocked in the flower-perfumed air of his floating island on the planetary sea of Tutalsee. How strange such an environment must be for a Dosadi—no threats, fruit which could be picked and eaten without a thought of poisons. The memories she'd taken from him would coat the island with familiarity, but her flesh would continue to find that a strange experience. His memories—yes. The island would remind her of all those wives he'd taken to the honeymoon bowers of that place.

McKie spoke from this awareness.

"No doubt that early lover failed to show sufficient appreciation of your abilities, outside the bedroom, that is. Which one was it . . ."

And he named several accurate possibilities, lifting them from the memories he'd taken from Jedrik.

Now, she laughed. He sensed the untainted response, real humor and unchecked.

McKie was reminded in his turn of one of his early wives, and this made him think of the breeding situation from which Jedrik had come—no confusions between a choice for breeding mate and a lover taken for the available enjoyment of sex. One might even actively dislike the breeding mate.

Lovers . . . wives . . . What was the difference, except for the socially imprinted conventions out of which the roles arose? But Jedrik did remind him of that one particular woman, and he explored this memory, wondering if it might help him now in his relationship with Jedrik. He'd been in his midthirties and assigned to one of his first personal BuSab cases, sent out with no oldtimer to monitor and instruct him. The youngest Human agent in the Bureau's history ever to be released on his own, so it was rumored. The planet had been one of the Ylir group, very much unlike anything in McKie's previous experience: an ingrown place with deep entryways in all of the houses and an oppressive silence all around. No animals, no birds, no insects—just that awesome silence within which a fanatic religion was reported forming.

All conversations were low voiced and full of subtle intonations which suggested an inner communication peculiar to Ylir and somehow making sport with all outsiders not privy to their private code. Very like Dosadi in this.

His wife of the moment, safely ensconced on Tutalsee, had been quite the opposite: gregarious, sportive, noisy.

Something about that Ylir case had sent McKie back to this wife with a sharpened awareness of her needs. The marriage had gone well for a long time, longer than any of the others. And he saw now why Jedrik reminded him of that one: they both protected themselves with a tough armor of femininity, but were extremely vulnerable behind that facade. When the armor collapsed, it collapsed totally. This realization puzzled McKie because he read his own reaction clearly: he was frightened.

In the eyeblink this evaluation took, Jedrik read him:

"We have not left Dosadi. We've taken it with us."

So that was why she'd made this contact, to be certain he mixed this datum into his evaluations. McKie looked out the open window. It would be dusk soon here on Tandaloor. The Gowachin home planet was a place which had defied change for thousands of standard years. In some respects, it was a backwater.

The ConSentiency will never be the same.

The tiny trickle of Dosadi which Aritch's people had hoped to cut off was now a roaring cataract. The people of Dosadi would insinuate themselves into niche after niche of ConSentient civilization. What could resist even the lowliest Dosadi? Laws would change. Relationships would assume profound and subtle differences. Everything from the most casual friendship to the most complex business relationship would take on some Dosadi character.

McKie recalled Aritch's parting question as Aritch had sent McKie to the jumpdoor which would put him on Dosadi.

"Ask yourself if there might be a price too high to pay for the Dosadi lesson."

That had been McKie's first clue to Aritch's actual motives and the word *lesson* had bothered him, but he'd missed the implications. With some embarrassment, McKie recalled his glib answer to Aritch's question:

"It depends on the lesson."

True, but how blind he'd been to things any Dosadi would have seen. How ignorant. Now, he indicated to Jedrik that he understood why she'd called such things to his attention.

"Aritch didn't look much beyond the uses of outrage and injustice . . ."

"And how to turn such things to personal advantage."

She was right, of course. McKie stared out at the gathering dusk. Yes, the species tried to make everything its own. If the species failed, then forces beyond it moved in, and so on, *ad infinitum.*

I do what I do.

He recalled those words of the sleeping monster with a shudder, felt Jedrik recoil. But she was proof even against this.

"What powers your ConSentiency had."

Past tense, right. And not *our* ConSentiency because that already was a thing of the past. Besides . . . she was Dosadi.

"And the illusions of power," she said.

He saw at last what she was emphasizing, and her own shared memories in his mind made the lesson doubly impressive. She'd known precisely what McKie's personal ego-focus might overlook. Yet, this was one of the glues which held the ConSentiency together.

"Who can imagine himself immune from any retaliation?" he quoted.

It was right out of the BuSab Manual.

Jedrik made no response.

McKie needed no more emphasis from her now. The lesson of history was clear. Violence bred violence. If this violence got out of hand, it ran a course depressing in its repetitive pattern. More often than not, that course was deadly to the innocent, the so-called "enlistment phase." The ex-innocents ignited more violence and more violence until either reason prevailed or all were destroyed. There were a sufficient number of cinder blocks which once had been planets to make the lesson clear. Dosadi had come within a hair of joining that uninhabited, uninhabitable list.

Before breaking contact, Jedrik had another point to make.

"You recall that in those final days, Broey increased the rations for his Human auxiliaries, his way of saying to them: 'You'll be turned out onto the Rim soon to fend for yourselves.'"

"A *Dosadi* way of saying that."

"Correct. We always held that thought in reserve: that we should breed in such numbers that some would survive no matter what happened. We would thus begin producing species which could survive there without the city of Chu . . . or any other city designed solely to produce nonpoisonous foods."

"But there's always a bigger force waiting in the wings."

"Make sure Aritch understands that."

*Choose containable violence when violence cannot be avoid-
ed. Better this than epidemic violence.*

—Lessons of Choice, The BuSab Manual

The senior attendant of the Courtarena, a squat and
dignified Gowachin of the Assumptive Phylum, confronted
McKie at the arena door with a confession:

"I have delayed informing you that some of your witnesses
have been excluded by Prosecution challenge."

The attendant, whose name was Darak, gave a Gowachin
shrug, waited.

McKie glanced beyond the attendant at the truncated oval
of the arena entrance which framed a lower section of the
audience seats. The seats were filled. He had expected some
such challenge for this first morning session of the trial, saw
Darak's words as a vital revelation. They were accepting his
gambit. Darak had signaled a risky line of attack by those
who guided Ceylang's performance. They expected McKie
to protest. He glanced back at Aritch, who stood quietly sub-
missive three steps behind his Legum. Aritch gave every appearance of having resigned himself to the arena's conditions.

"*The forms must be obeyed.*"

Beneath that appearance lay the hoary traditions of Gowachin Law—*The guilty are innocent. Governments always do evil. Legalists put their own interests first. Defense and prosecution are brother and sister. Suspect everything.*

Aritch's Legum controlled the initial posture and McKie had chosen defense. It hadn't surprised him to be told that Ceylang would prosecute. McKie had countered by insisting that Broey sit on a judicial panel which would be limited to three members. This had caused a delay during which Bildoon had called McKie, probing for any betrayal. Bildoon's approach had been so obvious that McKie had at first suspected a feint within a feint.

"McKie, the Gowachin fear that you have a Caleban at your command. That's a force which they . . ."

"The more they fear the better."

McKie had stared back at the screen-framed face of Bildoon, observing the signs of strain. Jedrik was right: the non-Dosadi were very easy to read.

"But I'm told you left this Dosadi in spite of a Caleban contract which prohibited . . ."

"Let them worry. Good for them."

McKie watched Bildoon intently without betraying a single emotion. No doubt there were others monitoring this exchange. Let them begin to see what they faced. Puppet Bildoon was not about to uncover what those shadowy forces wanted. They had Bildoon here on Tandaloor, though, and this told McKie an essential fact. The PanSpechi chief of Bu-Sab was being offered as bait. This was precisely the response McKie sought.

Bildoon had ended the call without achieving his purpose. McKie had nibbled only enough to insure that Bildoon would be offered again as bait. And the puppet masters still feared that McKie had a Caleban at his beck and call.

No doubt the puppet masters had tried to question their God Wall Caleban. McKie hid a smile, thinking how that conversation must have gone. The Caleban had only to quote the letter of the contract, and if the questioners became accusatory the Caleban would respond with anger, ending the exchange. And the Caleban's words would be so filled with terms subject to ambiguous translation that the puppet masters would never be certain of what they heard.

As he stared at the patiently waiting Darak, McKie saw that they had a problem, those shadowy figures behind Aritch. Laupuk had removed Mrreg from their councils and his advice would have been valuable now. McKie had deduced that the correct reference was "The Mrreg" and that Aritch headed the list of possible successors. Aritch might be Dosadi-trained but he was not Dosadi-born. There was a lesson in this that the entire ConSentiency would soon learn.

And Broey as a judge in this case remained an unchangeable fact. Broey was Dosadi-born. The Caleban contract had kept Broey on his poison planet, but it had not limited him to a Gowachin body. Broey knew what it was to be both Human and Gowachin. Broey knew about the Pcharkys and their use by those who'd held Dosadi in bondage. And Broey was now Gowachin. The forces opposing McKie dared not name another Gowachin judge. They must choose from the other species. They had an interesting quandary. And without a Caleban assistant, there were no more Pcharkys to be had on Dosadi. The most valuable *coin* the puppet masters had to offer was lost to them. They'd be desperate. Some of the older ones would be very desperate.

Footsteps sounded around the turn of the corridor behind Aritch. McKie glanced back, saw Ceylang come into view with her attendants. McKie counted no less than twenty leading Legums around her. They were out in force. Not only Gowachin pride and integrity, but their sacred view of Law stood at issue. And the desperate ones stood behind them, goading. McKie could almost see those shadowy figures in the shape of this entourage.

Ceylang, he saw, wore the black robes and white-striped hood of Legum Prosecutor, but she'd thrown back the hood to free her mandibles. McKie detected tension in her movements. She gave no sign of recognition, but McKie saw her through Dosadi eyes.

I frighten her. And she's right.

Turning to address the waiting attendant and speaking loudly to make sure that the approaching group heard, McKie said:

"Every law must be tested. I accept that you have given me formal announcement of a limit on my defense."

Darak, expecting outraged protest and a demand for a list of the excluded witnesses, showed obvious confusion.

"Formal announcement?"

Ceylang and entourage came to a stop behind Aritch.

McKie went on in the same loud voice:

"We stand here within the sphere of the Courtarena. All matters concerning a dispute in the arena are formal in this place."

The attendant glanced at Ceylang, seeking help. This response threatened him. Darak, hoping someday to be a High Magister, should now be recognizing his inadequacies. He would never make it in the politics of the Gowachin Phyla, especially not in the coming Dosadi age.

McKie explained as though to a neophyte:

"Information to be verified by my witnesses is known to me in its entirety. I will present the evidence myself."

Ceylang, having stooped to hear a low-voiced comment from one of her Gowachin advisors, showed surprise at this. She raised one of her ropey tendrils, called, "I protest. The Defense Legum cannot give . . ."

"How can you protest?" McKie interrupted. "We stand here before no judicial panel empowered to rule on any protest."

"I make *formal* protest!" Ceylang insisted, ignoring an advisor on her right who was tugging at her sleeve.

McKie permitted himself a cold smile.

"Very well. Then we must call Darak into the arena as witness, he being the only party present who is outside our dispute."

The edges of Aritch's jaws came down in a Gowachin grimace.

"At the end, I warned them not to go with the Wreave," he said. "They cannot say they came here unwarned."

Too late, Ceylang saw what had happened. McKie would be able to question Darak on the challenges to the witnesses. Some of those challenges were certain to be overturned. At the very least, McKie would know who the Prosecution feared. He would know it in time to act upon it. There would be no delays valuable to Prosecution. Tension, fear, and pride had made Ceylang act precipitately. Aritch had been right to warn them, but they counted on McKie's fear of the interlocked Wreave triads. Let them count. Let them blunt their awareness on that and on a useless concern over the excluded witnesses.

McKie motioned Darak through the doorway into the arena, heard him utter an oath. The reason became apparent as McKie pressed through in the crowded surge of the Prosecutor's party. The instruments of Truth-by-Pain had been arrayed on their ancient rack below the judges. Seldom brought out of their wrappings even for display to visiting dignitaries these days, the instruments had not been employed in the arena within the memory of a living witness. McKie had expected this display. It was obvious that Darak and Ceylang had not. It was interesting to note the members of Ceylang's entourage who were watching for McKie's response.

He gave them a grin of satisfaction.

McKie turned his attention to the judicial panel. They had given him Broey. The ConSentiency, acting through BuSab, held the right of one appointment. Their choice delighted McKie. Bait, indeed! Bildoon occupied the seat on Broey's right. The PanSpechi chief of bureau sat there all bland and reserved in his unfamiliar Gowachin robes of water green. Bildoon's faceted eyes glittered in the harsh arena lighting. The third judge had to be the Gowachin choice undoubtedly maneuvered (as Bildoon had been) by the puppet masters. It was a Human and McKie, recognizing him, missed a step, recovered his balance with a visible effort.

What were they doing?

The third judge was named Mordes Parando, a noted challenger of BuSab actions. He wanted BuSab eliminated—either outright or by removing some of the bureau's key powers. He came from the planet Lirat, which provided McKie with no surprises. Lirat was a natural cover for the shadowy forces. It was a place of enormous wealth and great private estates guarded by their own security forces. Parando was a man of somewhat superficial manners which might conceal a genuine sophisticate, knowledgeable and erudite, or a completely ruthless autocrat of Broey's stamp. He was certainly Dosadi-trained. And his features bore the look of the Dosadi Rim.

There was one more fact about Parando which no one outside Lirat was supposed to know. McKie had come upon it quite by chance while investigating a Palenki who'd been an estate guard on Lirat. The turtlelike Palenki were notoriously dull, employed chiefly as muscle. This one had been uncommonly observant.

"Parando makes advice on Gowachin Law."

This had been responsive to a question about Parando's relationship with the estate guard being investigated. McKie, not seeing a connection between question and answer, had not pursued the matter, but had tucked this datum away for future investigation. He had been mildly interested at the time because of the rumored existence of a legalist enclave on Lirat and such enclaves had been known to test the limits of legality.

The people behind Aritch would expect McKie to recognize Parando. Would they expect Parando to be recognized as a legalist? They were certain to know the danger of putting Parando on a Gowachin bench. Professional legalists were absolutely prohibited from Gowachin judicial service.

"Let the people judge."

Why would they need a legalist here? Or were they expecting McKie to recognize the Rim origins of Parando's body? Were they warning McKie not to raise *that* issue here? Body exchange and the implications of immortality represented a box of snakes no one wanted to open. And the possibility of one species spying on another . . . There was fragmentation of the ConSentiency latent in this case. More ways than one.

If I challenge Parando, his replacement may be more dangerous. If I expose him as a legalist after the trial starts . . . Could they expect me to do that? Let us explore it.

Knowing he was watched by countless eyes, McKie swept his gaze around the arena. Above the soft green absorbent oval where he stood were rank on rank of benches, every seat occupied. Muted morning light from the domed translucent ceiling illuminated rows of Humans, Gowachin, Palenki, Sobarips . . . McKie identified a cluster of ferret Wreaves just above the arena, limber thin with a sinuous flexing in every movement. They would bear watching. But every species and faction in the ConSentiency would be represented here. Those who could not come in person would watch these proceedings via the glittering transmitter eyes which looked down from the ceiling's edges.

Now, McKie looked to the right at the witness pen set into the wall beneath the ranked benches. He identified every witness he'd called, even the challenged ones. The forms were being obeyed. While the ConSentient Covenant required certain modifications here, this arena was still dominated by Gowachin Law. To accent that, the blue metal box from the

Running Phylum occupied the honor place on the bench in front of the judicial panel.

Who will taste the knife here?

Protocol demanded that Prosecutor and Defense approach to a point beneath the judges, abase themselves, and call out acceptance of the arena's conditions. The Prosecutor's party, however, was in disarray. Two of Ceylang's advisors were whispering excited advice to her.

The members of the Judicial panel conferred, glancing at the scene below them. They could not act formally until the obeisance.

McKie passed a glance across the panel, absorbed Broey's posture. The Dosadi Gowachin's enlightened greed was like an anchor point. It was like Gowachin Law, changeable only on the surface. And Broey was but the tip of the Dosadi advisory group which Jedrik had approved.

Holding his arms extended to the sides, McKie marched forward, abased himself face down on the floor, stood and called out:

"I accept this arena as my friend. The conditions here are my conditions but Prosecution has defiled the sacred traditions of this place. Does the court give me leave to slay her outright?"

There was an exclamation behind him, the sound of running, the sudden flopping of a body onto the arena's matted floor. Ceylang could not address the court before this obeisance and she knew it. She and the others now also knew something else just as important—that McKie was ready to slay her despite the threat of Wreave vendetta.

In a breathless voice, Ceylang called out her acceptance of the arena's conditions, then:

"I protest this trick by Defense Legum!"

McKie saw the stirring of Gowachin in the audience. A trick? Didn't Ceylang know yet how the Gowachin dearly loved legal tricks?

The members of the judicial panel had been thoroughly briefed on the surface demands of the Gowachin forms, though it was doubtful that Bildoon understood sufficiently what went on beneath those forms. The PanSpechi confirmed this now by leaning forward to speak.

"Why does the senior attendant of this court enter ahead of the Legums?"

McKie detected a fleeting smile on Broey's face, glanced back to see Darak standing apart from the prosecution throng, alone and trembling.

McKie took one step forward.

"Will the court direct Darak to the witness pen? He is here because of a formal demand by the Prosecutor."

"This is the senior attendant of your court," Ceylang argued. "He guards the door to . . ."

"Prosecution made formal protest to a matter which occurred in the presence of this attendant," McKie said. "As an attendant, Darak stands outside the conflicting interests. He is the only reliable witness."

Broey stirred, looked at Ceylang, and McKie realized how strange the Wreave must appear to a Dosadi. This did not deter Broey, however.

"Did you protest?"

It was a direct question from the bench. Ceylang was required to answer. She looked to Bildoon for help but he remained silent. Parando also refused to help her. She glanced at Darak. The terrified attendant could not take his attention from the instruments of pain. Perhaps he knew something specific about their presence in the arena.

Ceylang tried to explain.

"When Defense Legum suggested an illegal . . ."

"Did you protest?"

"But the . . ."

"This court decides on all matters of legality. Did you protest?"

"I did."

It was forced out of her. A fit of trembling passed over the slender Wreave form.

Broey waved Darak to the witness pen, had to add a vocal order when the frightened attendant failed to understand. Darak almost ran to the shelter of the pen.

Silence pervaded the arena. The silence of the audience was an explosive thing. They sat poised in the watching ovals, all of those species and factions with their special fears. By now, they'd heard many stories and rumors. Jumpdoors had spread the Dosadi emigres all across the ConSentiency. Media representatives had been excluded from Dosadi and this court on the Gowachin argument that they were "prey to uninformed subjective reactions," but they would be watching here through the transmitter eyes at the ceiling.

McKie looked around at nothing in particular but taking in every detail. There were more than three judges in this arena and Ceylang certainly must realize that. Gowachin Law turned upon itself, existing "only to be changed." But that watching multitude was quite another matter. Ceylang must be made to understand that she was a sacrifice of the arena. ConSentient opinion stood over her like a heavy sledge ready to smash down.

It was Parando's turn.

"Will opposing Legums make their opening arguments now?"

"We can't proceed while a formal protest is undecided," McKie said.

Parando understood. He glanced at the audience, at the ceiling. His actions were a direct signal: Parando knew which *judges* really decided here. To emphasize it, he ran a hand from the front of his neck down his chest, the unique Rim Raider's salute from Dosadi signifying "Death before surrender." Subtle hints in the movement gave McKie another datum: Parando was a Gowachin in a Human body. They'd dared put two Gowachin on that panel!

With Dosadi insight, McKie saw why they did this. They were prepared to produce the Caleban contract here. They were telling McKie that *they* would expose the body-exchange secret if he forced them to it. All would see that loophole in the Caleban contract which confined the Dosadi-born, but released outsiders in Dosadi flesh.

They think I'm really Jedrik in this flesh!

Parando revealed even more. His people intended to find the Jedrik body and kill it, leaving this *McKie* flesh forever in doubt. He could protest his McKie identity all he wanted. They had but to demand that he prove it. Without the other person . . . What had their God Wall Caleban told them?

"He is McKie, she is McKie. He is Jedrik, she is Jedrik."

His mind in turmoil, McKie wondered if he dared risk an immediate mind contact with Jedrik. Together, they'd already recognized this danger. Jedrik had hidden herself on McKie's hideaway, a floating island on Tutalsee. She was there with a special Taprisiot contract prohibiting unwanted calls which might inadvertently reveal her location.

The judges, led by Parando, were acting, however, moving for an immediate examination of Darak. McKie forced himself to perform as a Legum.

His career in ruins, the attendant answered like an automaton. In the end, McKie restored most of his witnesses. There were two notable exceptions: Grinik (that flawed thread which might have led to The Mrreg) and Stiggy. McKie was not certain why they wanted to exclude the Dosadi weapons genius who'd transformed a BuSab wallet's content's into instruments of victory. Was it that Stiggy had broken an *unbreakable* code? That made sense only if Prosecution intended to play down the inherent Dosadi superiority.

Still uncertain, McKie prepared to retire and seek a way to avoid Parando's gambit, but Ceylang addressed the bench.

"The issue of witnesses having been introduced by Defense," she said, "Prosecution wishes to explore this issue. We note many witnesses from Dosadi called by Defense. There is a noteworthy omission whose name has not yet been introduced here. I refer to a Human by the name of Jedrik. Prosecution wishes to call Keila Jedrik as . . ."

"One moment!"

McKie searched his mind for the forms of an acceptable escape. He knew that his blurted protest had revealed more than he wanted. But they were moving faster than he'd expected. Prosecution did not really want Jedrik as a witness, not in a Gowachin Courtarena where the roles were never quite what they appeared to non-Gowachin. This was a plain message to McKie.

"We're going to find her and kill her."

With Bildoon and Parando concurring, a jumpdoor was summoned and Ceylang played her trump.

"Defense knows the whereabouts of witness Keila Jedrik."

They were forcing the question, aware of the emotional bond between McKie and Jedrik. He had a choice: argue that a personal relationship with the witness excluded her. But Prosecution and all the judges had to concur. They obviously would not do this—not yet. A harsh lock on his emotions, McKie gave the jumpdoor instructions.

Presently, Jedrik stepped onto the arena floor, faced the judges. She'd been into the wardrobe at his bower cottage and wore a yellow and orange sarong which emphasized her height and grace. Open brown sandals protected her feet. There was a flame red blossom at her left ear. She managed to look exotic and fragile.

Broey spoke for the judges.

"Do you have knowledge of the issues at trial here?"

"What issues are at trial?"

She asked it with a childlike innocence which did not even fool Bildoon. They were forced to explain, however, because of those other *judges* to whom every nuance here was vital. She heard them out in silence.

"An alleged experiment on a sentient population confined

to a planet called Dosadi . . . lack of informed consent by subject population charged . . . accusations of conspiracy against certain Gowachin and others not yet named . . ."

Two fingers pressed to his eyes in the guise of intense listening, McKie made contact with Jedrik, suggesting, conferring. They had to find a way out of this trap! When he looked up, he saw the suspicions in Parando's face: *Which body, which ego? McKie? Jedrik?*

In the end, Ceylang hammered home the private message, demanding whether Jedrik had "any personal relationship with Defense Legum?"

Jedrik answered in a decidedly un-Dosadi fashion.

"Why . . . yes. We are lovers."

In itself, this was not enough to exclude her from the arena unless Prosecution and the entire judicial panel agreed. Ceylang proposed the exclusion. Bildoon and Parando were predictable in their agreement. McKie waited for Broey.

"Agreed."

Broey had a private compact with the shadow forces then. Jedrik and McKie had expected this, but had not anticipated the form confirmation would take.

McKie asked for a recess until the following morning.

With the most benign face on it, this was granted. Broey announced the decision, smiling down at Jedrik. It was a measure of McKie's Dosadi conditioning that he could not find it in himself to blame Broey for wanting personal victory over the person who had beaten him on Dosadi.

Back in his quarters, Jedrik put a hand on McKie's chest, spoke with eyes lowered.

"Don't blame yourself, McKie. This was inevitable. Those judges, none of them, would've allowed any protest from you before seeing me in person on that arena floor."

"I know."

She looked up at him, smiling.

"Yes . . . of course. How like one person we are."

For a time after that, they reviewed the assessment of the aides chosen for Broey. Shared memories etched away at minutiae. Could any choice be improved? Not one person was changed—Human or Gowachin. All of those advisors and aides were Dosadi-born. They could be depended upon to be loyal to their origins, to their conditioning, to themselves individually. For the task assigned to them, they were the best available.

McKie brought it to a close.

"I can't leave the immediate area of the arena until the trial's over."

She knew that, but it needed saying.

There was a small cell adjoining his office, a bedog there, communications instruments, Human toilet facilities. They delayed going into the bedroom, turned to a low-key argument over the advisability of a body exchange. It was procrastination on both sides, outcome known in advance. Familiar flesh was familiar flesh, less distracting. It gave each of them an edge which they dared not sacrifice. McKie could play Jedrik and Jedrik could play McKie, but that would be dangerous play now.

When they retired, it was to make love, the most tender experience either had known. There was no submission, only a giving, sharing, an open exchange which tightened McKie's throat with joy and fear, sent Jedrik into a fit of un-Dosadi sobbing.

When she'd recovered, she turned to him on the bed, touched his right cheek with a finger.

"McKie."

"Yes?"

"I've never had to say this to another person, but . . ." She silenced his attempted interruption by punching his shoulder, leaning up on an elbow to look down at him. It reminded McKie of their first night together, and he saw that she had gone back into her Dosadi shell . . . but there was something else, a difference in the eyes.

"What is it?"

"Just that I love you. It's a very interesting feeling, especially when you can admit it openly. How odd."

"Stay here with me."

"We both know I can't. There's no safe place here for either of us, but the one who . . ."

"Then let's . . ."

"We've already decided against an exchange."

"Where will you go?"

"Best you don't know."

"If . . ."

"No! I wouldn't be safe as a witness; I'm not even safe at your side. We both . . ."

"Don't go back to Dosadi."

"Where is Dosadi? It's the only place where I could ever feel at home, but Dosadi no longer exists."

"I meant . . ."

"I know."

She sat up, hugged her knees, revealing the sinewy muscles of her shoulders and back. McKie studied her, trying to fathom what it was she hid in that Dosadi shell. Despite the intimacy of their shared memories, something about her eluded him. It was as though he didn't want to learn this thing. She would flee and hide, of course, but . . . He listened carefully as she began to speak in a faraway voice.

"It'd be interesting to go back to Dosadi someday. The differences . . ."

She looked over her shoulder at him.

"There are those who fear we'll make over the ConSentiency in Dosadi's image. We'll try, but the result won't be Dosadi. We'll take what we judge to be valuable, but that'll change Dosadi more than it changes you. Your masses are less alert, slower, less resourceful, but you're so numerous. In the end, the ConSentiency will win, but it'll no longer be the ConSentiency. I wonder what it'll be when . . ."

She laughed at her own musings, shook her head.

"And there's Broey. They'll have to deal with Broey and the team we've given him. Broey Plus! Your ConSentiency hasn't the faintest grasp of what we've loosed among them."

"The predator in the flock."

"To Broey, your people are like the Rim—a natural resource."

"But he has no Pcharkys."

"Not yet."

"I doubt if the Calebans ever again will participate in . . ."

"There may be other ways. Look how easy it is for us."

"But we were printed upon each other by . . ."

"Exactly! And they continue to suspect that you're in my body and I'm in yours. Their entire experience precludes the free shift back and forth, one body to another . . ."

"Or this other thing . . ."

He caressed her mind.

"Yes! Broey won't suspect until too late what's in store for him. They'll be a long time learning there's no way to sort you from . . . me!"

This last was an exultant shout as she turned and fell upon him. It was a wild replay of their first night together. McKie abandoned himself to it. There was no other choice, no time for the mind to dwell on depressing thoughts.

In the morning, he had to tap his implanted amplifiers to bring his awareness to the required pitch for the arena. The process took a few minutes while he dressed.

Jedrik moved softly with her own preparations, straightened the bedog and caressed its resilient surface. She summoned a jumpdoor then, held him with a lingering kiss. The jumpdoor opened behind her as she pushed away from him.

McKie smelled familiar flowers, glimpsed the bowers of his Tutalsee island before the door blinked out of existence, hiding Jedrik and the island from him. Tutalsee? The moment of shocked understanding delayed him. She'd counted on that! He recovered, sent his mind leaping after her.

I'll force an exchange! By the Gods . . .

His mind met pain, consuming, blinding pain. It was agony such as he'd not even imagined could exist.

Jedrik!

His mind held an unconscious Jedrik whose awareness had fled from pain. The contact was so delicate, like holding a newborn infant. The slightest relaxation and he knew he would lose her to . . . He felt that terrifying monster of the first exchange hovering in the background, but love and concern armed him against fear.

Frantic, McKie held that tenuous contact while he called a jumpdoor. There was a small delay and when the door opened, he saw through the portal the black, twisted wreckage which had been his bower island. A hot sun beat down on steaming cinders. And in the background, a warped metal object which might have been one of Tutalsee's little four-place flitters rolled over, gurgled, and sank. The visible wreckage said the destructive force had been something like a pentrate, swift and all-consuming. The water around the island still bubbled with it. Even while he watched, the island began breaking up, its cinders drifting apart on the long, low waves. A breeze flattened the steaming smoke. Soon, there'd be nothing to show that beauty had floated here. With a pentrate, there would be nothing to recover . . . not even bodies to . . .

He hesitated, still holding his fragile grasp on Jedrik's unconscious presence. The pain was only a memory now. Was it really Jedrik in his awareness, or only his remembered imprint of her? He tried to awaken the sleeping presence, failed. But small threads of memory emerged, and he saw that the destruction had been Jedrik's doing, response to attack. The attackers had wanted a live hostage. They hadn't anticipated that violent, unmistakable message.

"You won't hold *me* over McKie's head!"

But if there were no bodies . . .

Again, he tried to awaken that unconscious presence. Her memories were there, but she remained dormant. The effort strengthened his grip upon her presence, though. And he told himself it had to be Jedrik, or he wouldn't know what had happened on the bower island.

Once more, he searched the empty water. Nothing. A pentrate would've torn and battered everything around it. Shards of metal, flesh reduced to scattered cinders . . .

She's dead. She has to be dead. A pentrate . . .

But that familiar presence lay slumbering in his mind.

The door clacker interrupted his reverie. McKie released the jumpdoor, turned to look through the bedside viewer at the scene outside his Legum quarters. The expected deputation had arrived. Confident, the puppet masters were moving even before confirmation of their Tutalsee gambit. They could not possibly know yet what McKie knew. There could be no jumpdoor or any other thread permitted to connect this group to Tutalsee.

McKie studied them carefully, keeping a bridle on his rage. There were eight of them, so contained, so well schooled in Dosadi self-control. So transparent to a Jedrik-amplified McKie. They were four Humans and four Gowachin. Overconfident. Jedrik had seen to that by leaving no survivors.

Again, McKie tried to awaken that unconscious presence. She would not respond.

Have I only built her out of my memories?

There was no time for such speculation. Jedrik had made her choice on Tutalsee. He had other choices to make here and now—for both of them. That ghostly presence locked in his mind would have to wait.

McKie punched the communicator which linked him to Broey, gave the agreed-upon signal.

"It's time."

He composed himself then, went to the door.

They'd sent no underlings. He gave them that. But they addressed him as Jedrik, made the anticipated demands, gloated over the hold they had upon him. It was only then that McKie saw fully how well Jedrik had measured these people; and how she had played upon her McKie in those last hours together like an exquisitely tuned instrument. Now, he understood why she'd made that violent choice.

As anticipated, the members of the delegation were extremely surprised when Broey's people fell upon them without warning.

For the Gowachin, to stand alone against all adversity is the most sacred moment of existence.

—*The Gowachin, a BuSab analysis*

The eight prisoners were dumped on the arena floor, bound and shackled. McKie stopped near them, waiting for Ceylang to arrive. It was not yet dawn. The ceiling above the arena remained dark. A few of the transmitter eyes around the upper perimeter glittered to reveal that they were activated. More were coming alive by the moment. Only a few of the witness seats were occupied, but people were streaming in as word was passed. The judicial bench remained empty.

The outer areaway was a din of Courtarena security forces coming and going, people shouting orders, the clank of weapons, a sense of complete confusion there which gradually resolved itself as Broey led his fellow judges up onto their bench. The witness pen was also filling, people punching sleep from their eyes, great gaping yawns from the Gowachin.

McKie looked to Broey's people, the ones who'd brought in the prisoners. He nodded for the captors to leave, giving them a Dosadi hand signal to remain available. They left.

318

Ceylang passed them as she entered, still fastening her robe. She hurried to McKie's side, waited for the judges to be seated before speaking.

"What is the meaning of this? My attendants . . ."

Broey signaled McKie.

McKie stepped forward to address the bench, pointed to the eight bound figures who were beginning to stir and push themselves upright.

"Here you see my client."

Parando started to speak, but Broey silenced him with a sharp word which McKie did not catch. It sounded like "frenzy."

Bildoon sat in fearful fascination, unable to wrest his attention from the bound figures, all of whom remained silent. Yes, Bildoon would recognize those eight prisoners. In his limited, ConSentient fashion, Bildoon was sharp enough to recognize that he was in personal danger. Parando, of course, knew this immediately and watched Broey with great care.

Again, Broey nodded to McKie.

"A fraud has been perpetrated upon this court," McKie said. "It is a fraud which was perpetrated against those great and gallant people, the Gowachin. Both Prosecution and Defense are its victims. The Law is its ultimate victim."

It had grown much quieter in the arena. The observer seats were jammed, all the transmitter eyes alive. The faintest of dawn glow touched the translucent ceiling. McKie wondered what time it was. He had forgotten to put on any timepiece.

There was a stir behind McKie. He glanced back, saw attendants belatedly bringing Aritch into the arena. Oh, yes—they would have risked any delay to confer with Aritch. Aritch was supposed to be the other McKie expert. Too bad that this Human who looked like McKie was no longer the McKie they thought they knew.

Ceylang could not hold her silence. She raised a tendril for attention.

"This Tribunal . . ."

McKie interrupted.

". . . is composed of three people. Only three."

He allowed them a moment to digest this reminder that Gowachin trial formalities still dominated this arena, and were like no other such formalities in the ConSentiency. It could've been fifty judges up there on that bench. McKie had witnessed Gowachin trials where people were picked at random off the streets to sit in judgment. Such jurists took their duties seriously, but their overt behavior could lead another sentient species to question this. The Gowachin chattered back and forth, arranged parties, exchanged jokes, asked each other rude questions. It was an ancient pattern. The jurists were required to become "a single organism." Gowachin had their own ways of rushing that process.

But this Tribunal was composed of just three judges, only one of them visibly Gowachin. They were separate entities, their actions heavy with mannerisms foreign to the Gowachin. Even Broey, tainted by Dosadi, would be unfamiliar to the Gowachin observers. No "single organism" here holding to the immutable forms beneath Gowachin Law. That had to be deeply disturbing to the Legums who advised Ceylang.

Broey leaned forward, addressed the arena.

"We'll dispense with the usual arguments while this new development is explored."

Again, Parando tried to interrupt. Broey silenced him with a glance.

"I call Aritch of the Running Phylum," McKie said.

He turned.

Ceylang stood in mute indecision. Her advisors remained at the back of the arena conferring among themselves. There seemed to be a difference of opinion among them.

Aritch shuffled to the death-focus of the arena, the place

where every witness was required to stand. He glanced at the instruments of pain arrayed beneath the judicial bench, cast a wary look at McKie. The old High Magister appeared harried and undignified. That hurried conference to explore this development must've been a sore trial to the old Gowachin.

McKie crossed to the formal position beside Aritch, addressed the judges.

"Here we have Aritch, High Magister of the Running Phylum. We were told that if guilt were to be found in this arena, Aritch bore that guilt. He, so we were led to believe, was the one who made the decision to imprison Dosadi. But how can that be so? Aritch is old, but he isn't as old as Dosadi. Then perhaps his alleged guilt is to be found in concealing the imprisonment of Dosadi. But Aritch summoned an agent of BuSab and sent that agent openly to Dosadi."

A disturbance among the eight shackled prisoners interrupted McKie. Several of the prisoners were trying to get to their feet, but the links of the shackles were too short.

On the judicial bench, Parando started to lean forward, but Broey hauled him back.

Yes, Parando and others were recalling the verities of a Gowachin Courtarena, the constant reversals of concepts common throughout the rest of the ConSentiency.

To be guilty is to be innocent. Thus, to be innocent is to be guilty.

At a sharp command from Broey, the prisoners grew quiet.

McKie continued.

"Aritch, conscious of the sacred responsibilities which he carried upon his back as a mother carries her tads, was deliberately named to receive the punishment blow lest that punishment be directed at all Gowachin everywhere. Who chose this innocent High Magister to suffer for all Gowachin?"

McKie pointed to the eight shackled prisoners.

"Who are these people?" Parando demanded.

McKie allowed the question to hang there for a long count. Parando knew who these eight were. Did he think he could divert the present course of events by such a blatant ploy?

Presently, McKie spoke.

"I will enlighten the court in due course. My duty, however, comes first. My client's *innocence* comes first."

"One moment."

Broey held up a webbed hand.

One of Ceylang's advisors hurried past McKie, asked and received permission to confer with Ceylang. A thwarted Parando sat like a condemned man watching this conversation as though he hoped to find reprieve there. Bildoon had hunched forward, head buried in his arms. Broey obviously controlled the Tribunal.

The advisor Legum was known to McKie, one Lagag of a middling reputation, an officer out of breeding. His words to Ceylang were low and intense, demanding.

The conference ended, Lagag hurried back to his companions. They now understood the tenor of McKie's *defense*. Aritch must have known all along that he could be sacrificed here. The ConSentient Covenant no longer permitted the ancient custom where the Gowachin audience had poured into the arena to kill with bare hands and claws the *innocent* defendant. But let Aritch walk from here with the brand of innocence upon him; he would not take ten paces outside the arena's precincts before being torn to pieces.

There'd been worried admiration in the glance Lagag had given McKie in passing. Yes . . . now they understood why McKie had maneuvered for a small and vulnerable judicial panel.

The eight prisoners began a new disturbance which Broey silenced with a shout. He signaled for McKie to continue.

"Aritch's design was that I expose Dosadi, return and defend him against the charge that he had permitted illegal psychological experiments upon an unsuspecting populace. He was prepared to sacrifice himself for others."

McKie sent a wry glance at Aritch. Let the High Magister try to fight in half-truths in that defense!

"Unfortunately, the Dosadi populace was *not* unsuspecting. In fact, forces under the command of Keila Jedrik had moved to take control of Dosadi. Judge Broey will affirm that she had succeeded in this."

Again, McKie pointed to the shackled prisoners.

"But these conspirators, these people who designed and profited from the Dosadi Experiment, ordered the death of Keila Jedrik! She was murdered this morning on Tutalsee to prevent my using her at the proper moment to prove Aritch's *innocence.* Judge Broey is witness to the truth of what I say. Keila Jedrik was brought into this arena yesterday only that she might be traced and killed!"

McKie raised both arms in an eloquent gesture of completion, lowered his arms.

Aritch looked stricken. He saw it. If the eight prisoners denied the charges, they faced Aritch's fate. And they must know by now that Broey wanted them *Gowachin-guilty*. They could bring in the Caleban contract and expose the bodyexchange plot, but that risked having McKie defend or prosecute them because he'd already locked them to his actual *client*, Aritch. Broey would affirm this, too. They were at Broey's mercy. If they were *Gowachin-guilty*, they walked free only here on Tandaloor. *Innocent*, they died here.

As though they were one organism, the eight turned their heads and looked at Aritch. Indeed! What would Aritch do? If he agreed to sacrifice himself, the eight might live. Ceylang, too, focused on Aritch.

Around the entire arena there was a sense of collective held breath.

McKie watched Ceylang. How candid had Aritch's people

been with their Wreave? Did she know the full Dosadi story?

She broke the silence, exposing her knowledge. She chose to aim her attack at McKie on the well-known dictum that, when all else failed, you tried to discredit the opposing Legum.

"McKie, is this how you defend these eight people whom only *you* name as client?" Ceylang demanded.

Now, it was delicate. Would Broey go along?

McKie countered her probe with a question of his own.

"Are you suggesting that you'd prosecute these people?"

"I didn't charge them! You did."

"To prove Aritch's innocence."

"But you call them client. Will you defend them?"

A collective gasp arose from the cluster of advisors behind her near the arena doorway. They'd seen the trap. If McKie accepted the challenge, the judges had no choice but to bring the eight into the arena under Gowachin forms. Ceylang had trapped herself into the posture of prosecutor against the eight. She'd said, in effect, that she affirmed their guilt. Doing so, she lost her case against Aritch and her life was immediately forfeit. She was caught.

Her eyes glittered with the unspoken question.

What would McKie do?

Not yet, McKie thought. *Not yet, my precious Wreave dupe.*

He turned his attention to Parando. Would they dare introduce the Caleban contract? The eight prisoners were only the exposed tip of the shadowy forces, a vulnerable tip. They could be sacrificed. It was clear that they saw this and didn't like it. No Gowachin Mrregs here with that iron submission to responsibility! They loved life and its power, especially the ones who wore Human flesh. How precious life must be for those who'd lived many lives! *Very* desperate, indeed.

To McKie's Dosadi-conditioned eyes, it was as though he read the prisoners' thoughts. They were safest if they remained silent. Trust Parando. Rely on Broey's enlightened greed. At the worst, they could live out what life was left to them here on Tandaloor, hoping for new bodies before the flesh they now wore ran out of vitality. As long as they still lived they could hope and scheme. Perhaps another Caleban could be hired, more Pcharkys found . . .

Aritch broke, unwilling to lose what had almost been his.

The High Magister's Tandaloor accent was hoarse with protest.

"But I did supervise the tests on Dosadi's population!"

"To what tests do you refer?"

"The Dosadi . . ."

Aritch fell silent, seeing the trap. More than a million Dosadi Gowachin already had left their planet. Would Aritch make targets of them? Anything he said could open the door to proof that the Dosadis were superior to non-Dosadis. Any Gowachin (or Human, for that matter) could well become a target in the next few minutes. One had only to denounce a selected Human or Gowachin as Dosadi. ConSentient fears would do the rest. And any of his arguments could be directed into exposure of Dosadi's real purpose. He obviously saw the peril in that, had seen it from the first.

The High Magister confirmed this analysis by glancing at the Ferret Wreaves in the audience. What consternation it would create among the secretive Wreaves to learn that another species could masquerade successfully as one of their own!

McKie could not leave matters where they stood, though. He threw a question at Aritch.

"Were the original transportees to Dosadi apprised of the nature of the project?"

"Only *they* could testify to that."

"And their memories were erased. We don't even have historical testimony on this matter."

Aritch remained silent. Eight of the original designers of the Dosadi project sat near him on the arena floor. Would he

326 / Frank Herbert

denounce them to save himself? McKie thought not. A person deemed capable of performing as The Mrreg could not possess such a flaw. Could he? Here was the real point of no return.

The High Magister confirmed McKie's judgment by turning his back on the Tribunal, the ages-old Gowachin gesture of submission. What a shock Aritch's performance must have been for those who'd seen him as a possible Mrreg. A poor choice except at the end, and that'd been as much recognition of total failure as anything else.

McKie waited, knowing what had to happen now. Here was Ceylang's moment of truth.

Broey addressed her.

"You have suggested that you would prosecute these eight prisoners. The matter is in the hands of Defense Legum."

Broey shifted his gaze.

"How say you, Legum McKie?"

The moment to test Broey had come. McKie countered with a question.

"Can this Courtarena suggest another disposition for these eight prisoners?"

Ceylang held her breath.

Broey was pleased. He had triumphed in the end over Jedrik. Broey was certain in his mind that Jedrik did not occupy this Legum body on the arena floor. Now, he could show the puppet masters what a Dosadi-born could do. And McKie saw that Broey intended to move fast, much faster than anyone had expected.

Anyone except Jedrik, and she was only a silent (memory?) in McKie's awareness.

Having given the appearance of deliberation, Broey spoke.

"I can order these eight bound over to ConSentient jurisdiction if McKie agrees."

The eight stirred, subsided.

"I agree," McKie said. He glanced at Ceylang. She made no protest, seeing the futility. Her only hope now lay in the possible deterrent presence of the Ferret Wreaves.

"Then I so order it," Broey said. He spared a triumphant glance for Parando. "Let a ConSentient jurisdiction decide if these eight are guilty of murder and other conspiracy."

He was well within the bounds of the Covenant between the ConSentiency and Gowachin, but the Gowachin members of his audience didn't like it. Their Law was best! Angry whistlings could be heard all around the arena.

Broey rose half-out of his seat, pointed at the instruments of pain arrayed beneath him. Gowachin in the audience fell silent. They, better than anyone, knew that no person here, not even a member of the audience, was outside the Tribunal's power. And many understood clearly now why those bloody tools had been displayed here. Thoughtful people had anticipated the problem of keeping order in this arena.

Responding to the silent acceptance of his authority, Broey sank back into his seat.

Parando was staring at Broey as though having just discovered the presence of a monster in this Gowachin form. Many people would be reassessing Broey now.

Aritch held his attitude of complete submission.

Ceylang's thoughts almost hummed in the air around her. Every way she turned, she saw only a tangle of unmanageable tendrils and a blocked passage.

McKie saw that it was time to bring matters to a head. He crossed to the foot of the judicial bench, lifted a short spear from the instruments there. He brandished the barbed, razor-edged weapon.

"Who sits on this Tribunal?"

Once, Aritch had issued such a challenge. McKie, repeating it, pointed with the spear, answered his own question.

"A Gowachin of my choice, one supposedly wronged by the Dosadi project. Were you wronged, Broey?"

"No."

McKie faced Parando.

"And here we have a Human from Lirat. Is that not the case, Parando?"

"I am from Lirat, yes."

McKie nodded.

"I am prepared to bring a parade of witnesses into this arena to testify as to your occupation on Lirat. Would you care to state that occupation?"

"How dare you question this Tribunal?"

Parando glared down at McKie, face flushed.

"Answer his question."

It was Broey.

Parando looked at Bildoon, who still sat with face concealed in his arms, face down on the bench. Something about the PanSpechi repelled Parando, but he knew he had to have Bildoon's vote to overrule Broey. Parando nudged the PanSpechi. Inert flesh rolled away from Parando's hand.

McKie understood.

Facing doom, Bildoon had retreated into the creche. Somewhere, an unprepared PanSpechi body was being rushed into acceptance of that crushed identity. The emergence of a new Bildoon would require considerable time. They did not have that time. When the creche finally brought forth a functioning persona, it would not be heir to Bildoon's old powers in BuSab.

Parando was alone, exposed. He stared at the spear in McKie's hand.

McKie favored the arena with a sweeping glance before speaking once more to Parando.

"I quote that renowned expert on Gowachin Law, High Magister Aritch: 'ConSentient Law always makes aristocrats of its practitioners. Gowachin Law stands beneath that pretension. Gowachin Law asks: Who knows the people? Only such a one is fit to judge in the Courtarena.' That is Gowachin Law according to High Magister Aritch. That is the law in this place."

Again, McKie gave Parando a chance to speak, received only silence.

"Perhaps you are truly fit to judge here," McKie suggested. "Are you an artisan? A philosopher? Perhaps you're a humorist? An artist? Ahhh, maybe you are that lowliest of workmen, he who tends an automatic machine?"

Parando remained silent, gaze locked on the spear.

"None of these?" McKie asked. "Then I shall supply the answer. You are a professional legalist, one who gives legal advice, even to advice on Gowachin Law. You, a Human, not even a Legum, dare to speak of Gowachin Law!"

Without any muscular warning signal, McKie leaped forward, hurled the spear at Parando, saw it strike deeply into the man's chest.

One for Jedrik!

With bubbling gasp, Parando sagged out of sight behind the bench.

Broey, seeing the flash of anger in McKie's effort, touched the blue box in front of him.

Have no fear, Broey. Not yet. I still need you.

But now, more than Broey knew it was really McKie in this flesh. Not Jedrik. Those members of the shadow force watching this scene and able to plot would make the expected deduction because they did not know how freely and completely Jedrik and McKie had shared. To the shadow force, McKie would've known Parando's background. They'd trace out that mistake in short order. So this was McKie in the arena. But he'd left Dosadi. There could be only one conclusion in the plotters' minds.

McKie had Caleban help!

They had Calebans to fear.

And McKie thought: *You have only McKie to fear.*

He grew aware that grunts of Gowachin approval were

sounding all around the arena. They accepted him as a Legum, thus they accepted his argument. Such a judge deserved killing.

Aritch set the precedent. McKie improved on it.

Both had found an approved way to kill a flawed judge, but McKie's act had etched a Gowachin precedent into the ConSentient legal framework. The compromise which had brought Gowachin and ConSentient Law into the Convenant of shared responsibility for the case in this arena would be seen by the Gowachin as a first long step toward making their Law supreme over all other law.

Aritch had half-turned, looking toward the bench, a glittering appraisal in his eyes which said the Gowachin had salvaged something here after all.

McKie strode back to confront Ceylang. He faced her as the forms required while he called for judgment.

"Bildoon?"

Silence.

"Parando?"

Silence.

"Broey?"

"Judgment for Defense."

The Dosadi accent rang across the arena. The Gowachin Federation, only member of the ConSentiency which dared permit a victim to judge those accused of victimizing him, had received a wound to its pride. But they'd also received something they would consider of inestimable value—a foothold for their Law in the ConSentiency, plus a memorable court performance which was about to end in the drama they loved best.

McKie stepped to within striking distance of Ceylang, extended his right hand straight out to the side, palm up.

"The knife."

Attendants scurried. There came the sound of the blue box being opened. Presently, the knife handle was slapped firmly into McKie's palm. He closed his fingers around it, thinking as he did so of all those countless others who had faced this moment in a Gowachin Courtarena.

"Ceylang?"

"I submit to the ruling of this court."

McKie saw the Ferret Wreaves rise from their seats as one person. They stood ready to leap down into the arena and avenge Ceylang no matter the consequences. They could do nothing else but carry out the role which the Gowachin had designed for them. Few in the arena had misunderstood their presence here. No matter the measurement of the wound, the Gowachin did not suffer such things gladly.

An odd look of camaraderie passed between Ceylang and McKie then. Here they stood, the only two non-Gowachin in the ConSentient universe who had passed through that peculiar alchemy which transformed a person into a Legum. One of them was supposed to die immediately, and the other would not long survive that death. Yet, they understood each other the way siblings understand each other. Each had shed a particular *skin* to become something else.

Slowly, deliberately, McKie extended the tip of his blade toward Ceylang's left jowl, noting the myriad pocks of her triad exchanges there. She trembled but remained firm. Deftly, with the swiftest of flicking motions, McKie added another pock to those on her left jowl.

The Ferret Wreaves were the first to understand. They sank back into their seats.

Ceylang gasped, touched a tendril to the wound. Many times she had been set free by such a wound, moving on to new alliances which did not completely sunder the old.

For a moment, McKie thought she might not accept, but the increasing sounds of approval all around the arena overcame her doubts. The noise of that approval climbed to a near deafening crescendo before subsiding. Even the Gowachin joined this. How dearly they loved such legal nuances!

Pitching his voice for Ceylang alone, McKie spoke.

"You should apply for a position in BuSab. The new director would look with favor upon your application."

"You?"

"Make a Wreave bet on it."

She favored him with the grimace which passed for a smile among Wreaves, spoke the traditional words of triad farewell.

"We were well and truly wed."

So she, too, had seen the truth in their unique closeness.

McKie betrayed the extent of his esoteric knowledge by producing the correct response.

"By my mark I know you."

She showed no surprise. A good brain there, not up to Dosadi standards, but good.

Well and truly wed.

Keeping a firm lock on his emotions (the Dosadi in him helped), McKie crossed to confront Aritch.

"Client Aritch, you are innocent."

McKie displayed the fleck of Wreave blood on the knife tip.

"The forms have been obeyed and you are completely exonerated. I rejoice with all of those who love justice."

At this point in the old days, the jubilant audience would've fallen on the hapless client, would've fought for bloody scraps with which to parade through the city. No doubt Aritch would've preferred that. He was a traditionalist. He confirmed that now.

"I am glad to quit these times, McKie."

McKie mused aloud.

"Who will be The Mrreg now that you're . . . disqualified? Whoever it is, I doubt he'll be as good as the one he replaces. It will profit that next Mrreg to reflect upon the fragile and fugitive value to be gained from the manipulation of others."

Glowering, Aritch turned and shambled toward the doorway out of the arena.

Some of the Gowachin from the audience already were leaving, no doubt hoping to greet Aritch outside. McKie had no desire to witness that remnant of an ancient ritual. He had other concerns.

Well and truly wed.

Something burned in his eyes. And still he felt that soft and sleeping presence in his awareness.

Jedrik?

No response.

He glanced at Broey who, true to his duty as a judge, would be the last to leave the arena. Broey sat blandly contemplating this place where he'd displayed the first designs of his campaign for supremacy in the ConSentiency. He would accept nothing less short of his own death. Those shadowy puppet masters would be the first to feel his rule.

That fitted the plan McKie and Jedrik had forged between them. In a way, it was still the plan of those who'd bred and conditioned Jedrik for the tasks she'd performed so exquisitely.

It was McKie's thought that those nameless, faceless Dosadis who stood in ghostly ranks behind Jedrik had made a brave choice. Faced with the evidence of body exchange all around, they'd judged that to be a deadly choice—the conservatism of extinction. Instead, they'd trusted sperm and ova, always seeking the new and better, the changed, the adapted. And they'd launched their simultaneous campaign to eliminate the Pcharkys of their world, reserving only that one for their final gamble.

It was well that this explosive secret had been kept here. McKie felt grateful to Ceylang. She'd known, but even when it might've helped her, she'd remained silent. BuSab would now have time to forge ways of dealing with this problem. Ceylang would be valuable there. And perhaps more would be learned about PanSpechi, Calebans, and Taprisiots. If only Jedrik . . .

He felt a fumbling in his memories.

"If only Jedrik what?"

She spoke laughingly in his mind as she'd always spoken there.

McKie suppressed a fit of trembling, almost fell.

"Careful with our body," she said. "It's the only one we have now."

"Whose body?"

She caressed his mind.

"Ours, love."

Was it hallucination? He ached with longing to hold her in his arms, to feel her arms around him, her body pressed to him.

"That's lost to us forever, love, but see what we have in exchange."

When he didn't respond, she said:

"One can always be watching while the other acts . . . or sleeps."

"But where are you?"

"Where I've always been when we exchanged. See?"

He felt her parallel to him in the shared flesh and, as he voluntarily drew back, he came to rest in contact with her mutual memories, still looking from his own eyes but aware that someone else peered out there, too, that someone else turned this body to face Broey.

Fearful that he might be trapped here, McKie almost panicked, but Jedrik gave him back the control on their flesh.

"Do you doubt me, love?"

He felt shame. There was nothing she could hide from him. He knew how she felt, what she'd been willing to sacrifice for him.

"You'd have made their perfect Mrreg."

"Don't even suggest it."

She went pouring through his arena memories then and her joy delighted him.

"Oh, marvelous, McKie. Beautiful! I couldn't have done it better. And Broey still doesn't suspect."

Attendants were taking the eight prisoners out of the arena now, all of them still shackled. The audience benches were almost empty.

A sense of joy began filtering through McKie.

I lost something but I gained something.

"You didn't lose as much as Aritch."

"And I gained more."

McKie permitted himself to stare up at Broey then, studying the Gowachin judge with Dosadi eyes and two sets of awareness. Aritch and the eight accused of murder were things of the past. They and many others like them would be dead or powerless before another ten-day. Broey already had shown the speed with which he intended to act. Supported by his troop of Jedrik-chosen aides, Broey would occupy the seats of power, consolidating lines of control in that shadow government, eliminating every potential source of opposition he could touch. He believed Jedrik dead and, while McKie was clever, McKie and BuSab were not a primary concern. One struck at the real seats of power. Being Dosadi, Broey could not act otherwise. And he'd been almost the best his planet had ever produced. Almost.

Jedrik-within chuckled.

Yes, with juggernaut certainty, Broey would create a single target for BuSab. And Jedrik had refined the simulation pattern by which Broey could be anticipated. Broey would find McKie waiting for him at the proper moment.

Behind McKie would be a new BuSab, an agency directed by a person whose memories and abilities were amplified by the one person superior to Broey that Dosadi had ever produced.

Standing there in the now silent arena, McKie wondered:

When will Broey realize he does our work for us?

"When we show him that he failed to kill *me* !"

In the purest obedience to Gowachin forms, without any sign of the paired thoughts twining through his mind, McKie bowed toward the surviving jurist, turned, and left. And all the time, Jedrik-within was planning . . . plotting . . . planning . . .